MONSTROUS

BOOK ONE OF
COTERIE OF MAGES

THOMAS K. CARPENTER

Monstrous
Book One of Coterie of Mages

Hardcover Version

by Thomas K. Carpenter

Published by Black Moon Books

Cover design by
G&S Cover Designs

Chapter Heading by HelenaKrivoruchko

Discover other titles by this author on:
www.thomaskcarpenter.com

ISBN-13: 978-1-958498-28-6

MONSTROUS

The Hundred Halls Universe

<u>Season One</u>

THE HUNDRED HALLS
Trials of Magic
Web of Lies
Alchemy of Souls
Gathering of Shadows
City of Sorcery

THE RELUCTANT ASSASSIN
The Reluctant Assassin
The Sorcerous Spy
The Veiled Diplomat
Agent Unraveled
The Webs That Bind

GAMEMAKERS ONLINE
The Warped Forest
Gladiators of Warsong
Citadel of Broken Dreams
Enter the Daemonpits
Plane of Twilight

ANIMALIANS HALL
Wild Magic
Bane of the Hunter
Mark of the Phoenix
Arcane Mutations
Untamed Destiny

STONE SINGERS HALL
Song of Siren and Blood
House of Snake and Tome
Storm of Dragon and Stone
Sonata of Shadow and Thorn
Well of Demon and Bone

THE ORDER OF MERLIN
The Order of Merlin
Infernal Alliances
Tower of Horn and Blood

The Hundred Halls Universe

Season Two

THE CRYSTAL HALLS
Shadows in Amber
The Emerald Eclipse
The Sapphire Strategem
Chains of Obsidian
The Bloodstone Rebellion

AURA HEALERS HALL
Half-Pint Hex
Full Moon Demon
Blood Witch Curse
Twilight Horn
Deathless King

COTERIE OF MAGES
Monstrous
Ruthless
Vicious
Merciless
Bloodlust

Other Works

ALEXANDRIAN SAGA
Fires of Alexandria
Heirs of Alexandria
Legacy of Alexandria
Warmachines of Alexandria
Empire of Alexandria
Voyage of Alexandria
Goddess of Alexandria

OTHER SERIES
The Dashkova Memoirs
Kingmakers Saga
Gamers
Mirror Shards

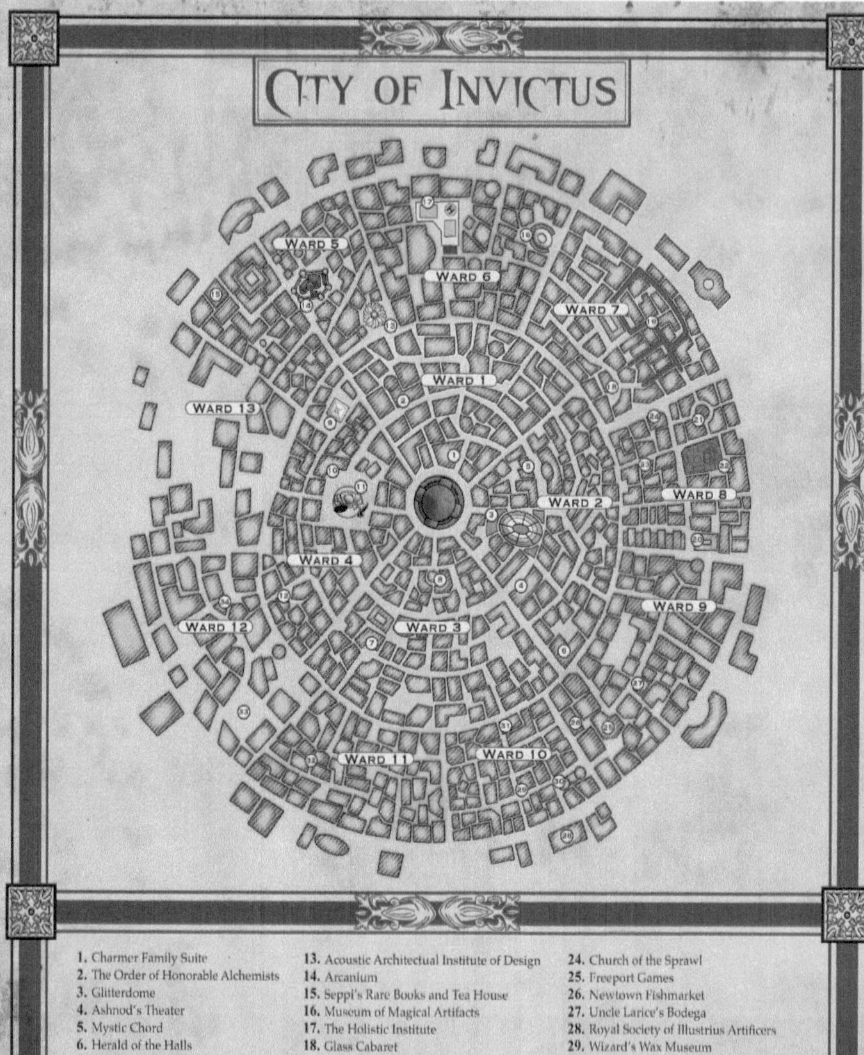

1. Charmer Family Suite
2. The Order of Honorable Alchemists
3. Glitterdome
4. Ashnod's Theater
5. Mystic Chord
6. Herald of the Halls
7. Left Tower Books
8. Protectors
9. Coterie of Mages
10. City Library
11. Statue of Invictus
12. Amber & Smoke
13. Acoustic Architectual Institute of Design
14. Arcanium
15. Seppi's Rare Books and Tea House
16. Museum of Magical Artifacts
17. The Holistic Institute
18. Glass Cabaret
19. The Canal District
20. Oestomancium
21. Animalians
22. Invictus Menagerie and Cryptozoo
23. Goblin's Romp
24. Church of the Sprawl
25. Freeport Games
26. Newtown Fishmarket
27. Uncle Larice's Bodega
28. Royal Society of Illustrius Artificers
29. Wizard's Wax Museum
30. Metallium Nocturn
31. Howling Madwoman's Fortunes and Spells
32. Enoichian District
33. Oba's Autumnal Garden
34. Gamemakers Hall

Obelisk MAP

Third Level
PYRAMID
Second Level
OASIS
First Level
Level Five - Telchine's Star, Kill Rooms, Classrooms
Level Four - Telchine's Circle, Classrooms, Testing Rooms
Level Three - Professor Living Quarters
Level Two - Student Living Quarters
Level One - Dining Hall, Meeting Rooms, Grand Hall

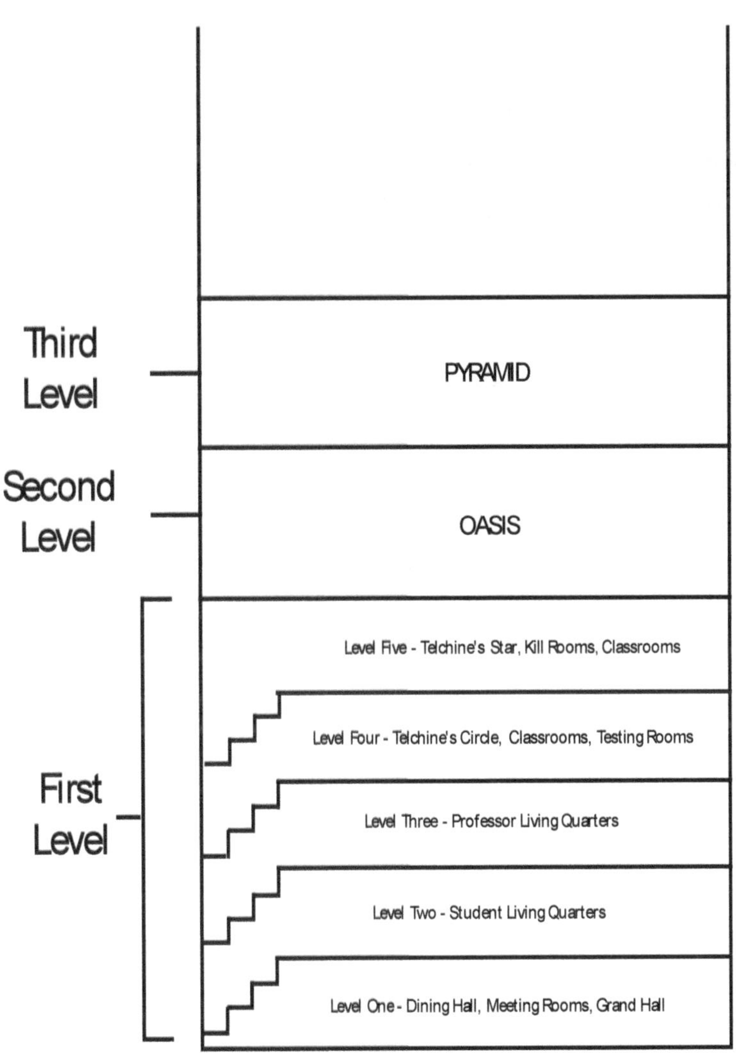

Arcanium loves books
Coterie adores power
Assassins will kill you
Stone Singers has a stone flower

Animalians is a zoo
Alchemists, you'll devour
Tinkers loves gadgets
Protectors makes you cower

Aura Healers wants to fix you
Blue Flame has a tower
Dramatics loves the spectacle
Oculus has grown sour

One Hundred Halls
Each with their own magic
The Patrons protect
Because faez madness is tragic

In the city of sorcery
Invictus is the Head
His students are many
But the foolish end up dead

- A Children's Rhyme

ONE

Iona braced for thunder as she ran recklessly towards the silver Greyhound bus, praying that it wouldn't leave before she arrived. The sky crackled as the onslaught of unforgiving winds shook the nearby elms, throwing wet leaves in her face.

She shoved the large envelope under her shirt while rain pelted her like a thousand tiny arrows from the sky. The roar of the diesel engine and crunch of gravel provided fuel for the final sprint. Iona screamed into the storm, willing the driver to hear her. The bus accelerated away, widening the gulf between the life she had and the one she wanted.

Iona skidded to a stop, out of breath and coated with rain and disappointment.

The spell would have to be quick. The gestures felt stiff after clutching the documents for over three miles. Never mind the blisters on her feet from the ill-fitting work boots, or the burning in her thighs. Or the fear. Unrepentant fear drove her forward: thoughtless and never looking back. Never. That would be the death of her.

She made the gestures as she'd observed but rarely practiced except in darkness. She felt the icy chill at the base of her skull where faez—the raw stuff of magic—originated. Crimson sparks flew from her fingertips like cheap fireworks. The display was feeble in the face of the symphony above as bruise-black clouds were briefly illuminated by pounding flashes.

The bus continued to accelerate.

Iona felt that doorway closing before she could reach it. Her chance lost to fate and the cruelty of others' addictions and ambitions. Then. Miraculously. The wet glare of red lights exploded on the back end of the silver bus. Brake lights. Iona made the last sprint, slipping past the soaked Missouri elms that grabbed at her shirt, trying to keep her from escaping, as she reached the open accordion doors.

"Iona?"

The bus driver looked like a wizened raisin behind the massive wheel.

She nodded.

Too tired to speak, Iona fished the crumpled ticket out of her pocket. The waterlogged paper looked barely passable. The driver stared at it suspiciously.

"No bags?"

Iona shook her head, which slapped dripping blonde hair against her neck. The driver shrugged and nodded into the back, where tired riders had briefly stirred to see the reason for their delay. Nothing more than a soaking wet girl left them returning to their gopher holes.

She took a spot halfway to the back and out of direct line of the AC unit, shivering already. An old woman with a knitting bag sat directly across. Iona rubbed her ankles as if that would end the ache of blisters that had formed during her long run.

"Do you need a towel?" asked the old woman, reaching into a carpet-bag.

"I'm fine."

The small towel was tossed into her lap. It looked like it'd been cut from a larger version and smelled like cheap perfume. Iona smiled at the woman's frugality.

"You'll catch the death of cold if you don't dry off."

"Thanks," said Iona.

She quickly wiped the rain from her arms and face, then tried to dry her hair, but the small piece of terry cloth was already soaked, so she draped it over the back of the seat next to her.

Iona settled into the spot, rubbing her arms for warmth. Once she had stopped shivering she checked the envelope, thanking her paper-thin luck that the university administrators had chosen a sturdy envelope in which to send her scholarship documents. Wrinkly fingers touched her arm, making Iona jump.

"Is that blood?"

Iona recoiled.

"Paint. I was painting."

She wiped away the fresh scab near her wrist and hid her hands so the woman wouldn't see the recent scars from when she'd failed to prepare the ritual correctly, though it hadn't been her fault that Fenris had purchased cheap silvered salt.

The old woman frowned.

"Are you sure you're okay?" asked the old woman.

The repeated question brought roiling thoughts as if the seas were preparing to boil. She resisted the urge to look backwards. The faster they got to Invictus, the City of Sorcery, the better.

Iona sensed the old woman wouldn't take a simple answer, so she wiped the wet hair from her face and offered a reassuring smile.

"I had to run the last three miles to get here. I thought I was late and going to miss the bus. It's my only chance."

"Only chance?"

Iona glanced to the front, suddenly worried that she'd gotten on the wrong bus.

"We're going to Invictus, right?"

"Why yes."

"Oh, good. I was worried."

The old woman pulled her arms close to her stomach. She looked like she was having a moment of indigestion.

"Are you a Hall student?"

Iona searched the woman's face for clues to her state of mind. Outside of the major cities, distrust of magic ran fierce. Or at least that's what she'd been told. She had no experience of her own to confirm. Maybe those had been lies, expressly given to make it harder for her to escape.

"I'm going to the Trials of Magic. I won a scholarship. I want to be a mage."

Iona had never spoken her desires out loud. Until today, she'd kept her thoughts as hidden as possible, not even daring to think about escaping for fear that she'd be found out. The relief of hearing her own voice speaking what she'd so long desired made the knot in her chest uncoil.

The woman's overly plucked eyebrows rose, making her look like she'd let a grandchild draw lines on her forehead.

"That place is a death trap for children."

"I know," said Iona, nodding tightly.

"Aren't you afraid of what magic will do to you?" The old woman leaned forward conspiratorially. "Some mages go mad with power, or just plain mad."

"I won't go mad."

"Of course you won't, sweetie. You look like a fine young woman," she said, patting her leg.

Iona wasn't sure how the old woman could come to that conclusion. She was wearing cutoff jeans with frayed edges, mud-stained work boots, and a long-sleeve shirt with a bucking bronco on the front that was the logo for the big, fancy truck stop off Hwy-72 that Fenris had taken her to twice for good behavior.

A gentleman behind them with a hat over his face shushed them and pointed to his watch. The old woman lifted both shoulders and leaned back into her seat, freeing Iona from further interaction.

Sliding to the window seat, Iona stared out the rain-streaked window as blurry lights occasionally passed. The big oaks and elms looked the same as home, yet she could feel the difference in her chest. Or maybe she just wanted it to be that way. Was she crazy for doing this? She imagined that Fenris had figured out she was missing and had rampaged through the old house with malice on the mind.

The memories of his anger brought a quiver to her lip, but she fought to control it, punching her leg until she was no longer shaking.

She rubbed her wrists. It was strange not to have the bracelets anymore.

"I'm fine. I'll be fine."

Iona dug into her front pocket, producing the only other things of value she'd dared to take. The stolen seed was as big as a walnut and bound with charms. She rolled the nut around in her palm, feeling the way the contained magic trembled to get out.

Then she checked the hard oblong object the size of her thumb. A petrified butterfly chrysalis. Unlike the seed, it contained no magic. It was exactly what it looked like: a rock formed from the body of a long dead pupa who'd never made the transition to butterfly. Iona rubbed her thumb along the bumpy edges before she shoved both items back in her front pocket.

Last, she checked the tattoos on the inside of her forearms to make sure they weren't awake. The words were written in a long-dead language. There were other tattoos as well, but she only needed to check these to confirm that he hadn't figured out where she'd gone yet. Iona wondered if he'd ever learned that she could tell when he was in the house by the tattoos.

Probably not, or he might not have taken such a long trip.

Iona leaned her forehead against the cool window and let the relief flood in. She'd gotten away. He didn't know where she was yet. But he would soon.

Don't attract attention.

Stick to the lesser tome.

Never use the tattoos.

These were rules she'd devised for herself. To keep her safe. Hidden. If she stuck to them in the City of Sorcery, maybe she'd be able to learn enough to defend herself. With the panic of the last few hours starting to recede, Iona settled against the wall.

The old woman turned suddenly and made a show of focusing on her knitting, but Iona knew when someone had been watching. Not that it mattered. She was safe and on a bus heading east, away from Fenris and towards the City of Sorcery. A little old woman with her knitting couldn't hurt her.

§

Iona couldn't figure out why she was awake. The bus was no longer moving and it was still dark. A different kind of dark. The kind that lived in cities. A nimbus of light was on the wrong side of the bus. Premorning. A time of renewal and rebirth. That's what she hoped for anyway.

She made her way off the empty bus to find the rest of the passengers huddled in a knot while the driver and two others had their heads in the engine compartment. The old woman unexpectedly gave her a nasty look as Iona stretched her neck and turned around. The sight made her stumble because she hadn't been expecting it.

The Spire.

The enormous skyscraper touched the clouds. The impossibly lofty tower, twice as tall and nearly three times wider than the next largest, had caught the morning sun and was lit up like a candle at the very tip. Biggest damn candle in all the realms. The seat of the Hundred Halls, the only magical university in the entire world.

Iona inhaled, expecting woody oaks and petrichor, but it looked like the rain had been left far behind in the night. Instead, she caught the scent of discarded oil and old trash.

The surrounding area was dilapidated buildings and crumbling factories covered in graffiti and orangish-red rust. Iona guessed by the position of the sun and their location in relation to the Spire that they were either slightly west of the city, or right on the edge of the twelfth ward.

Iona smacked her lips, wishing she had something to drink. She had to use the bathroom too, but it didn't look like there was anything nearby.

She approached the old woman. The other bus riders scowled at her approach, which confused Iona since she'd been asleep for nearly the entire ride.

"What time is it?" she asked.

The old woman clutched the ugly carpet bag with knitting needles sticking out the top to her chest.

"Why does it matter?"

"I have to get to the Spire by 9 am."

The old woman leaned forward, her grandmotherly expression twisted with anger until she looked like one of Fenris's drawings.

"You did this. You ruined our trip with your sorcery."

"What? Why would I do that? I need to get to the city the same as you all."

"I saw those hex focusers in your pocket, and the tattoos. You're not on the way to the Trials, you're a beast who tricked their way onto the bus to ruin us."

She made warding signs and spat on the ground.

"I didn't do anything," said Iona, anger rising in her gut until she imagined wrapping her hands around the woman's neck.

She unconsciously took a step forward but a taller man in a trucker hat stepped in her way.

"You're not welcome here. Even if they get the bus fixed, we ain't letting you on. You get that?"

A knot formed in her throat. She couldn't believe this was happening.

"I don't understand."

The first rock came from the back of the group. It hit her right in the shoulder bone, which sent a sharp pain through her chest.

"Ow, that hurt!"

Before she could think to defend herself, more rocks came. Blinding rage filled her vision until she wanted to burn them to ashes, but she couldn't allow that to happen, so she did the only thing she could think to do.

She ran.

Iona raced down the roadside in her muddy work boots. The blisters she'd gotten from her late-night run exploded, the tortured flesh ripping free and exposing the wounds beneath, turning into little hot spots of pain. But stopping wasn't an option. The rocks would hurt if they struck her, but that wasn't her real fear. If she didn't reach the Spire by nine, the Trials of Magic would begin without her.

TWO

The second floor at Amber & Smoke had been cleared out and replaced with round tables for the traditional pre-Trials breakfast for St. Jude's alumni. A host of waiters moved through space, bringing the finest champagnes, caviar, and gold-dusted hellbender eggs. A string quartet played enchanting tunes for the small, but elite crowd.

Zuri hadn't wanted to attend, but she knew not showing up would make her look weak. She couldn't afford that.

"Sorry, Mum and Dad couldn't make it," said Nandi as she sipped at the golden liquid while silvery bangles collected around her wrist. "You know how it is. There's only a few months to enjoy the alpine sports in Ice Hold."

Her sister's rich black skin glowed against her crimson top as she covertly reviewed the rest of the assembled. Probably to check if there was anyone more famous than her in attendance. The only one Zuri thought was remotely close was Justice Thornlock, but his shine had worn off decades ago.

Zuri sipped her water and ignored the caviar on her plate. Her stomach wasn't quite up to eating, given she'd be entering the Trials in a few hours.

"I wasn't expecting them, but I am glad you showed up. I know you're busy and all."

Nandi gave an exaggerated eye roll.

"Busy? Hardly. The Foundation pays me an exorbitant amount of money despite my expertise being practically null and void at this point. I thought a specialization in demonology would have set me up for life. Pity I didn't let them overrun the city for my career's sake."

"You're not serious, are you?"

"Don't be daft, sister. Of course not. There'd be no careers period if they'd won."

A waiter opened one of the sliding doors for the private booths. Zuri spotted Blake sitting next to a gorgeous redhead as he laughed at some joke. She tried to look away, but he caught her staring and lifted his drink in her direction.

"What's wrong?" asked Nandi.

"Don't look. Dammit."

Nandi turned back with a shrug as the sliding door closed.

"Is that…?"

"Yes. That was Blake."

"I see why you two were a thing at St. Jude's. He's quite the looker."

"He's a sociopath."

"I know, sister," said Nandi, reaching out and cupping her hand. "If there was justice in the world, he'd be in prison right now."

"I hope he fails the Trials," Zuri growled under her breath.

"You know that's not happening. The pass rate for St. Jude's students is, what, eighty or ninety percent? And the ones that failed shouldn't have been there in the first place, trading on Mummy and Daddy's name and money. Though I still don't know why you specialized as you did. You know the saying, a good offense..."

"That works great if you have a preset team already, but I had to go heavy ward. No one will even talk to me anymore. They think I sold them out when I testified against Blake."

Nandi neatly shoved a caviar-covered cracker in her mouth and squealed with excitement.

"You know, I almost wish I could do it again."

"What? The Trials?"

"The Trials, the Obelisk, everything. Despite, oh, nearly getting killed dozens of times, it was quite invigorating. Now I just speak at conferences and sign my name on papers I barely know anything about. It's rather *boring*, if you ask me."

The knot in Zuri's chest that had been there for a week leading up to the Trials had a lot to say about her sister's comment. It felt like someone had shoved a boulder in her stomach and was expecting her to carry it around.

"Oh, Zuri, don't make that face." She leaned forward in a whisper. "And if you have to, you know, clear some room in the stomach, just make sure no one sees you do it, for Merlin's sake."

"I wouldn't dare," said Zuri, then forced herself to take a drink of water.

She couldn't wait for the Trials to start. She'd spent her entire life preparing for this moment and now it was almost upon her.

"I have to get in first time."

Nandi raised an eyebrow.

"Maybe it would be good to fail. Then you wouldn't be in the same class as Blake."

"It wouldn't matter. He'd still come after me, even if I was in the next class."

"True."

"Any advice for when I'm in the Obelisk?"

"You know I'm forbidden to say anything. Those charms are pretty powerful."

"Then about the professors," said Zuri as she pushed her food around the plate, watching the little black eggs falling off the pristine cracker.

Nandi raised an eyebrow.

"I don't see why...oh, that's what it is. You need some distraction, sister."

"Nandi, please—"

Nandi sighed and took a long drink from her champagne flute.

"Let's see. There's Ilsa Kingsley, enchantments and wards, you'll love her. Everyone does, really. She's a doll. Then there's Professor Phillip Sinclair, who was my mentor. My understanding is that he's acting patron since Malden is taking a long, well-earned vacation. I personally would have never put him in that position, he's rather milquetoast, but since his specialty is rather underwhelming now, he had to have *some* job.

"I don't know anything about Horace Green, he joined after I left. Must have been a friend of Malden's from the early days because I'm not aware that he was ever actually in Coterie. Then there's Annette Cornwallis. I hate to bitch shame, but when a girl has it, you don't get in her way. Faezology is her specialty. Don't get on her bad side. They say when she was a student, she personally killed nearly a fifth of her class. A record as far as I'm aware. Professor Tatiana Petrov can be a little rough around the edges, and takes no bullshit, but her charms and hexes are superb. Last, but definitely not least, is Professor Gideon Ravenscroft. Gideon is everyone's favorite, not least because he teaches Kemetic magics, which had I known what was going to happen after I graduated, I would have gone that route instead of demonology."

Zuri was going to ask a follow-up question, when she felt a presence to her right. She looked up into the smiling faces of Blake Lockwood and Scarlett Calloway. They both looked like they were on their way to a photo shoot for The Elitist.

"Talking professors? Shouldn't you be giving her advice on where to hide in the Obelisk so her nasty classmates don't kill her the first week?" asked a smug Blake.

Scarlett was clinging to his arm. Zuri remembered what it was like to be in a relationship with him. He'd made her feel like a queen, until everything went sideways.

"How's life in the fast lane, Blake?" asked Zuri.

He screwed up his face.

"What?"

She pounded her fist on the table hard enough to rattle silverware and spill champagne on the linen. The other tables looked worriedly at their little conversation.

"Oh, too slow. You just got run over. Roadkill again. Shame that didn't happen during your court-appointed community service," she said loud enough for the entire room.

"I paid someone to do it for me."

"Probably a good thing. I wouldn't want to be picked up by you either if I was trash. Got to have standards."

Blake leaned into her face.

"I've already got a killer team ready for the Obelisk. You won't last a week."

"And you never lasted more than two shakes," said Zuri, holding her cupped hand in the air and shuffling it back and forth. "And I never got that biker fetish. Does he ask you to wear a smelly leather jacket and spank him with the latest issue of *Truck Stop Hobo*, Scarlett?"

"Grow up, Zuri."

Heat rose to her face. She wanted to scream. She wanted to flip the table over and start a fistfight with the both of them. She wanted them to go away.

"Grow up? Gemma never got to, so I don't see why I should either."

"It was an accident," said Scarlett as her soft curls bounced around her cheeks. "Blake shouldn't have that following him around for the rest of his life. He's going to do great things."

"Accident? Keep believing that, Red. You're gonna be the next one when he gets bored of your vapid comments about the latest nail polish."

"Come on, we shouldn't have bothered talking to the trash," said Blake as he pulled Scarlett after him.

Zuri grabbed the champagne and downed the glass in one draw. She squeezed her hand into a fist to hide the shaking.

"Why didn't you defend me?"

Nandi frowned.

"I'm not going to be there to protect you. You have to figure this out on your own, but I'm not sure taunting your biggest enemy was a good idea."

"Probably not, but it felt good."

"Did it?"

Nandi glanced past her to where Blake and Scarlett had disappeared down the ornate wooden stairs.

"You know, I really thought you two would get into the Halls together, get married, and be a powerful mage couple."

"I did too until he killed my friend."

Zuri waved down the waiter with the champagne.

"They said it was an accident."

"It wasn't. I know it wasn't, even if I never had the proof. Gemma saw him for what he was, when I couldn't. She paid the price for my blindness. Never again."

"You can't fight the system, Zuri."

"Better than being complicit."

"Zuri."

The stern tone made her look into her sister's eyes. It was the one she used when they were both at home and she was about to get into trouble. Real trouble. Zuri wished that Nandi had been around when she'd been at St. Jude's. Then maybe the world wouldn't have crashed onto her shoulders.

"I need you to stop with this self-destructive behavior. Stop trying to get back at Blake and focus on surviving at Coterie. You need allies and you need them fast. See if you can't find them at the Trials. And kick ass. Everyone loves a winner. If you're top of the lists, then some of those other assholes will see past Blake's threats and team up with you."

Zuri checked the time as she noticed other aspirants getting ready to leave.

"I should go."

Nandi walked her to the street where a black SUV was waiting to take her to the Spire. Before she could say anything, Nandi pulled her into her arms and held her tight, which made the tension in her chest relax a hair.

"Focus on the Trials. It's your best shot to get ahead of whatever Blake has planned for you."

"I will."

Nandi kissed her on the cheek.

"And if that doesn't work, then you have to take someone down. Show the rest of your class you mean business."

"Nandi..."

"I'm serious. I can't tell you much about the Obelisk, but I can tell you that it's a cutthroat business once you get in there. People turn into monsters in the Obelisk."

"Did you?"

Nandi looked her straight in the eyes.

"I did what I had to do. I'm not proud of it, but I survived. That's all that matters. And because of it, I was ready to face the real demons of this world."

"I don't want to be a monster."

"We're all monsters in the dark."

Zuri climbed into the back of the black SUV. The driver pressed a button, closing the door behind her, and surged into traffic, heading towards the towering Spire at the center of the City of Sorcery.

THREE

The city was so *big.* Iona felt like she'd been running for hours and she was no closer to anything resembling civilization. She was still in the twelfth ward, passing run-down buildings and graffiti-covered factories that looked like they hadn't been in service for a hundred years.

The Spire was everything in her vision, but it grew no closer. She slowed to a stop and leaned on her knees, heaving with breath. She'd probably run more in the past two days than she had in her entire life. Thighs and lungs burned, but that wasn't the worst part. Her feet were on fire. But if she couldn't reach the Spire in time, she'd be a sitting duck whenever Fenris found her.

"I'll walk a few minutes and then run again," she told herself when the agony grew to be too much.

But she knew that was a lie. Every step felt like walking over hot coals. Iona couldn't imagine how many blisters she had on her feet.

A rumble in her belly reminded her that she hadn't eaten since yesterday. She smacked her lips. Water would be good. Just a sip, even.

Iona was so focused on her thirst, she didn't see the men on the corner until she was almost upon them. A pea-green Chevy Faez Rocket was parked on the sidewalk, still running with the radio on, while four guys covered in tattoos were smoking and watching her approach.

"Hey, sugar tits, did you get lost on your way to the hillbilly halfway house?"

The smile was filled with gold-plated teeth. Iona felt like Little Red Riding Hood staring into the Big Bad Wolf's toothy grin.

Heart in her throat, she kept walking, hoping against hope that they would let her pass, but then they surged towards her like a pack of hyenas, cutting her off.

"What are you supposed to be?" asked Gold Teeth as he blocked her path.

A part of her wanted to throw herself on their mercy, but she knew that would only encourage them. She reminded herself they were predators like Fenris.

"On my way to the Trials," she said with lifted chin.

The immediate laughter nearly broke her. Gold Teeth took a long drag from his cigarette as he turned towards the Spire, which showed off the tattoo of a black widow on his neck.

"The Trials? You're going all the way there? I think that sounds like a load of bullshit."

Someone grabbed her, so she spun around with a fist, but by the time she'd turned, another one of Gold Teeth's gang squeezed her ass. Heat rose to her cheeks. She wanted to scream. She hadn't worked this hard to escape Fenris only to get unlucky with her bus breaking down and then getting caught by a bunch of street thugs. Iona wished she knew better spells and had been able to practice them. She'd be more likely to injure herself than hurt them.

"Don't make me—"

"Don't make you, what?" replied Gold Teeth menacingly as he flicked his cigarette into the street.

He looked at her the way Fenris did when he was giving her instructions for a ritual. That long, hard stare that said if you mess with me, or screw anything up, I will make you pay, now and forever. But she didn't have time to be meek and wait for a chance to escape. That time was now. She had to get to the Spire.

"What's under her shirt?"

A hand grabbed for the bottom hem. At first she thought they were just trying to take her clothes off until she remembered the manila envelope. Iona slapped the hand away.

"Don't you dare."

"Oh, baby, I dare, I dare," said Gold Teeth. "Now if you don't mind, I think you're either going to hand over everything you have that has any value, or you're going to come with us and we'll take it anyway."

"Why are you even giving her the option?" asked another thug.

"Shut up," said Gold Teeth with his teeth bared.

Four of them. One of her. She wasn't going to get away without losing something. Iona eyed the rumbling car. Then she reached into her front pocket, digging out the seed.

"This is all I have worth anything to you."

"A walnut? You *are* batshit?" asked one of the thugs.

"It's got weird writing on it," said another.

Gold Teeth leaned in close, examining the seed.

"I don't get it."

Iona held her palm flat, letting him get a closer look.

"You will soon."

She slammed the seed onto the ground as she shouted the command word. The explosion of smoke and light had the thugs throwing their arms up. Iona tried to break free of their circle, but someone grabbed her arm. She clawed at his face.

"What in the—" asked Gold Teeth.

Emerging from the smoke was a lanky creature with deep, inset eyes and too-long arms that ended in talons. Iona was a little stunned herself. She hadn't known what was in the seed, only that it potentially could help her against Fenris should it come to that.

A sharp hook went right into the guy holding her arm. He screamed and she ran straight to the car. Gold Teeth was pulling out a handgun as she threw herself into the front seat, sliding across until she was behind the wheel.

Bang. Bang. Bang.

Iona ignored the screams as she frantically searched for the gear shifter. She'd never driven a car before. Everything she knew about them came from a handful of videos she'd watched out of curiosity.

A glance over was horrifying—and a little exciting—as she saw Gold Teeth being lifted up by a talon in his chest. He'd dropped the gun and the other thugs were fleeing. The lanky, nightmare creature looked directly at Iona. It felt like it could see into her soul, but she stared right back at it. After all, it'd become her unexpected ally. She should thank it for saving her.

She found the shifter and threw it forward, pounding her foot on the gas. The acceleration was startling. The car fishtailed into a streetlamp, before she managed to get control of the wheel and slide into the road.

Iona checked the rearview mirror to see Gold Teeth getting thrown onto the sidewalk and the creature from the seed loping after the others. The thrill at seeing their demise lasted until she realized what had happened and she pushed those thoughts down. Deep. That wasn't her. Couldn't be her.

Then she saw the time.

It was well after eight o'clock. She had less than an hour to reach the Spire and get into the Trials.

Despite her fear, Iona punched the gas pedal, accelerating down the street at frightening speeds. The buildings and other cars flew past, but she held onto the wheel, over-steering at times, but managing to correct before catastrophe.

"If I die, at least he wouldn't be able to get me," she told herself as she gunned it through a red light, narrowly avoiding a car crossing the intersection. But she didn't want to die. She wanted more out of life than the shit deal she'd gotten so far. No family. Trapped in the middle of nowhere with a murderous warlock. Nothing about her life had been normal, or easy.

She wanted more.

Adrenaline fueled her race to the Spire. The enormous tower grew closer at an excruciating pace.

"You can do this. You can do this."

The refrain felt like a spell. She kept repeating it even as she passed other cars at high speeds, feeling both out of control and alive for the first time in a long time.

The traffic light flashed red long before she'd reached the intersection. Iona gunned it as she saw the crossing vehicles. A squeal slipped out of her lips as she narrowly avoided getting T-boned, followed by laughter and tears in her eyes. She'd never felt so alive.

Iona turned onto a cross street, thankful she'd bothered to memorize the directions before she'd left Missouri. She spotted the glass gondola long before she saw the station. A glass box filled with people floated through the air on invisible wires. It didn't seem real. Nothing about the city did.

She was so busy watching the glass gondola float through the sky, she didn't see the turn until it was too late. Iona spun the wheel hard as she hit the brakes. The pea-green Chevy Faez Rocket spun out, careening down the road until it slammed into the side of an apartment building, clipping at least two other cars on the way.

The impact rattled her teeth, but she was relatively fine. A few pedestrians were approaching the car. She couldn't get bogged down with the police. Iona darted out, stumbling as her legs were jolted with adrenaline, but quickly found her form and sprinted through the parking lot towards the gondola station.

The line was long, so she barged through the people, apologizing along the way that she was going to be late. She received a lot of angry comments and glares, but it appeared there were no more applicants in line, which meant she was cutting it close.

The gondola attendant held the door open, fitting her into the last spot. When it shifted away from the station, her heart leapt into her throat.

With nothing to do but wait until they arrived, Iona stared out the glass at the city below. She'd never seen so many big buildings. The scale of everything seemed like a dream. It was hard to imagine that people could live here. The pictures on the Internet didn't do the City of Sorcery justice. As they rose above the streets, she watched a vendor use a novelty wand to create a miniature illusionary dragon that curled around him and spit harmless flames over a family of four.

As the gondola approached the Spire, the lack of food and overreliance on adrenaline to keep going caught up. A wave of dizziness had her leaning against the glass until it passed.

They approached the landing area and Iona pressed her face against the glass trying to see the top of the Spire, but they were too close and the clouds were covering the tip. Once the door opened, she sprinted into the building, encouraged by Hall attendants that yelled directions.

Iona found a maze of velvet ropes completely empty while the staff was packing up. An older lady with a reticulated snake on her shoulders waved Iona down. The snake flared its wings upon reaching her.

"Application documents?"

Iona handed over the manila envelope. The woman pulled out the papers, squinted briefly, and nodded towards the hallway.

"We'll take care of this for you. Make sure you stop by the Tome of Record before you enter."

Despite the pain of each step, she felt like she was floating over the carpet.

The woman at the Tome of Record frowned.

"Quickly, write your preferred Halls in the Tome, or just write all or any if you don't have a preference."

Iona grabbed the fancy quill pen and quickly scrawled Coterie of Mages, which brought raised eyebrows. The woman seemed incredulous at her choice, but if there was one place that Iona knew would help her against Fenris, it would be Coterie.

"Hurry!"

The final sprint felt like a lifetime. She reached the open doors, wishing she had a moment to examine their exquisite carved exteriors. She entered the auditorium to thousands of curious gazes as the doors silently closed behind her. She'd made it into the Trials of Magic.

FOUR

Zuri found a spot in the auditorium on the opposite side from where Blake was holding court with the other St. Jude alumni. Now that she was inside the Trials, her heart wouldn't stop thumping against her chest.

She knew logically there was little chance of her failing, or not getting into Coterie, especially with her famous sister, but logic no longer applied when matters of the heart were in question.

Assessing the other applicants for their chances of making it through the Trials became a game for Zuri. The nervous kid in the Hundred Halls T-shirt who looked like he was going to either throw up, pass out, or both was almost certain to fail on the first Trial, while the three girls in formfitting tracksuits that were practicing their five element spells looked like they had a solid shot.

The room was filled with thousands of potentials. At least five thousand, maybe more. Despite the horrific events of the last decade, enrollment had increased. Some equated it to the charismatic and very young Head Patron, while others said it was fear of the unknown. Zuri thought that no matter what the reason, there were far too many of them. The ability to wield magic shouldn't be given out to anyone with the aptitude. Far too many magical accidents could be attributed to inexperience or a lack of respect for magic.

As Zuri strolled through the crowd, she spotted the thick, muscular form of Orion Dreadmarsh. He looked like the kind of guy that spent his days at the gym, but she knew for a fact he'd never stepped foot in one, which gave oxygen to the rumors that he had infernal lineage. She didn't remember him at the St. Jude's alumni breakfast, but it didn't surprise her that he'd skipped it. If there was one person that could survive Coterie as a lone wolf, it was Orion. The Dreadmarsh name alone inspired fear, and Orion's reputation only added to the mystique.

"Zuri!"

She turned to find the mousy Justine Thornlock waiting with her hands clasped in front. After an awkward hug, Zuri nodded nonchalantly at the crowd.

"I was nervous until I saw the competition. A lot of people here aren't going to make it past the first Trial."

"You? Nervous? And really, do you think?" asked Justine with her eyes darting.

At that moment, they heard a group of people making noises of disgust and backing away from a girl who had just vomited on the hardwood floor.

"They're being far too lenient with who they let in anymore."

Justine swallowed hard. Her smile wasn't very convincing.

"Yeah, I guess."

"You'll do great, Justine."

"I hope so," said Justine as she twirled her thin black hair around a finger.

Zuri found it hard to believe that Justice Thornlock was her father. He'd been one of the more brutal students to ever graduate from Coterie, a famous thunderball player in his day, and had been an early explorer of the Montanhas realm.

"I never saw you with the St. Jude tutors. I assume you were working with a private mage. If you don't mind me prying a little bit, what were you working on?" asked Zuri.

The lack of eye contact and ever-moving hands made Justine look like she was working the strings of an invisible puppet.

"I probably shouldn't say..."

"Justine. I'm not your enemy. In fact, I'd love to work with you once we get into the Obelisk," said Zuri in her sweetest tone and offering the most welcoming smile she could muster.

Justine wasn't Zuri's first choice. She wouldn't be her tenth choice either, but Blake had poisoned the waters and she needed to find allies where she could. It sucked that it'd come down to this, but survival in Coterie was paramount.

"I'm sorry..."

The rejection felt like a dagger to the chest, but Zuri kept her face neutral as if she'd only heard that they didn't have the lobster *and* prime rib that she had her heart set on.

"Right. Of course. You already have a group. Very smart to lock one down as soon as possible."

Justine shook her hands out as if they were going numb.

"I would have loved to have grouped with you, but the things that are being said..."

"I know. Blake Lockwood has been saying a lot of things about me."

"It's not just that. He says that he'll personally kill anyone that teams up with you. I don't think I can handle that kind of stress. I'm nervous enough about Coterie."

"You shouldn't be, Justine. You're the daughter of Justice Thornlock."

"I don't feel like it most days."

"You'll find your courage in the Obelisk. My sister said that she slept in her closet covered in a blanket of protective runes the first month until she realized everyone was as nervous as her. And I bet with all the training your father gave you that you're more than ready."

Justine looked like she was going to be sick.

"He trained you, right?" asked Zuri.

"Not exactly. It's not that he didn't want to, but our sessions were always a disaster. One time we were working in the backyard and I flubbed a hex, which blew the back wall off the servant's cottage. It didn't matter how much he worked with me. I just couldn't do what he wanted me to do."

"Then what did you train? I'm not trying to get an advantage over you. I specialized in wards. If that makes you feel better."

Justine shoved her fidgeting hands into the pockets of her stylish blazer with a St. Jude's crest on the front.

"I probably shouldn't say."

"Justine. I know we haven't been close friends, but we've been friends. I'm going into Coterie to survive. I'm not like those other assholes, and you know it."

A flash of pain crossed Justine's soft blue eyes.

"I know, Zuri. You stood up for Gemma when no one else did. I wanted—"

The girl's head snapped around as if she'd been spotted by a predator.

"I should go. I shouldn't have stopped to talk to you."

Zuri had forgotten that Gemma and Justine had been best friends when they were in grade school, but had a falling out over something her father had said. Gemma had never been one to keep her mouth shut when it came to things she disagreed with. The night she died, she and Blake had been screaming at each other.

Across the auditorium, she spied Blake with a circle of adoring sycophants laughing at his every word. They didn't love him. They were afraid of him. She didn't know why she never saw that before. Gemma had tried to warn her that he was a sociopath, but she didn't see it until it was too late. Until Gemma was dead.

Snatches of that night flickered through her mind, making her turn away as not to relive it again. Zuri squeezed her hands into fists.

"I'm sorry, Gemma. I should have listened."

A trickle of laughter started at the entrance side of the auditorium and quickly gained speed until the entire auditorium of applicants was chuckling or, at the very least, smiling with disdain. Zuri turned to find a curious sight standing right inside the doors as they closed.

At first, Zuri couldn't believe what she was seeing. The pale-blonde girl was wearing cutoff jeans, a truck stop T-shirt, and muddy oversized work boots. She looked like she'd stepped out of a stereotype.

"I think we know who'll be the first to get knocked out," said a guy from somewhere behind, eliciting more laughter.

Zuri studied the blonde newcomer. There was something odd and contradictory about her, and it wasn't just the tattoos peeking from her sleeves.

"That poor girl isn't going to last a minute."

She had no more time to consider the newcomer when the crowd started whooping and hollering at the appearance of the professor who would be leading their Trials. The gentleman in rune-lined robes wasn't visible until he stepped onto the dais and then Zuri immediately recognized him. Gideon Ravenscroft. He was as handsome as Nandi had described, with thick, dark hair and a mischievous twinkle to his brown eyes.

The cheering trickled to silence when he raised his hand from the center of the dais.

"Congratulations! You made it! I'm Professor Gideon Ravenscroft from Coterie of Mages, and it is my great honor to be here with you on this auspicious day, the first day of the Trials of Magic!"

The crowd applauded his enthusiasm. Zuri added her own as she let a smile rest on her lips. She knew he was charismatic, but seeing him in action was a revelation.

"I know many of you are nervous. It's natural. I won't lie to you, the Trials are difficult. Deadly even. But being a mage is much worse. That's why we put you through such challenging events. To test your resolve and cunning when it comes to the world of magic. But I don't want to stand up here and scare you. I want to applaud you. Celebrate you, even!"

Professor Ravenscroft clapped his hands at the crowd as he spun in a slow circle. The crowd joined him until it was thunderous.

"To *even* be here this day is a triumph. Know that there are tens of thousands of other potentials who never dare to join the Trials. You are an elite few. Be proud of that. And for those of you that are here for the first time, know that most do not pass, but the experience will give you the knowledge you need to come back next year and be successful in your Trials.

"As for the Trials themselves, I'm sure you all know what to expect. And if you don't, then I think I'll be seeing you again next year," he said, adding a playful wink.

The crowd laughed at his easygoing banter.

"Three Trials." He held three fingers aloft. "The first is a solo Trial, pitting your fledgling magic and creativity against a challenging environment. The second is the partner round against an upperclassman. The third, well, this is where it all comes down. The group round. Anything can and will happen. If you manage to pass all three, and your score is high enough, you will be invited to an individual Hall depending on what you put in the Tome of Record and the opinion of the selection committee.

"But let's not get ahead of ourselves. First I must offer you my protection so you can safely use magic during the Trials. Open your minds to your magic, close your eyes if it helps, and let it collect in your fist. Afterwards, raise your hand. When you feel a tingling climb up your arm, pull the faez back into your mind, completing the connection. It'll feel uncomfortable, but when it's over, you can lower your hand."

Thousands of fists thrust into the air. Zuri added hers to the throng. When she was younger, Nandi had performed this trick with her, releasing the connection soon after, so the experience wasn't as unfamiliar as it was for the other aspirants. Yet, the sensation at the base of her skull was colder than she remembered and she could taste hot sand on her tongue at the moment of connection with Professor Gideon.

"Last, I must tell you that if you feel the Trials are not for you at any time when you are in this auditorium, you may put your hands on the runed doors and repeat, 'I am defeated,' three times. But I don't think that will be necessary. I can see this is a strong group.

"Finally, when your name flashes on the tapestries, report to the red door on the opposite side of the auditorium for your first Trial. May Merlin's luck be with you all today!"

Gideon's leaving had less excitement than when he'd arrived because everyone had turned towards the tapestries as they flickered with thousands of names until twenty of them remained at the top of the list.

Zuri pumped her fist at her side when she saw her name. Better to get it over with than stand around and let her imagination get the best of her. She pushed through the crowd towards the red door, nerves melting away as she prepared to enter the first Trial.

FIVE

The longer the day went on and her name wasn't called, the more Iona's imagination got the best of her. Especially as she watched the other applicants practicing their five elements spells with grace and alacrity.

Iona felt like an imposter. One that would be exposed in the first Trial.

As the auditorium emptied of students, she studied the tapestry for clues to the difficulty of the challenge. At least a third of the students received a DNF, or "Did Not Finish," which meant their time at the Trials was over. Another third received ridiculously low scores that would be difficult to overcome.

Iona worried that would be her. She wasn't going to give up, but she feared she lacked the knowledge to complete the Trials. Listening to the other applicants discussing the intricacies of magic made her feel like she'd been studying the wrong language for a test. Fenris had inadvertently taught her a lot, but none of it seemed to be useful in this situation.

The way the others looked at her didn't help her confidence either. It'd been bad enough having the entire auditorium laugh when she stumbled in through the door at the last minute. She'd never been in a crowd that big, let alone one that clearly didn't think she should be there.

It'd been a relief when the professor arrived and took the spotlight off her. Not that the knowing glances and smirks went away. Once the Trials had begun, she frequently saw other applicants covertly pointing and laughing in her direction. They thought she was a joke. Iona wasn't sure they were wrong.

A tap on her shoulder had her spinning around. A handsome guy wearing eyeliner and his hair in a ponytail was grinning at her.

"My friends and I were curious how many cows you know?"

"What?"

"You look like you were born in a barn, so we figured you had a lot of cows for friends."

He laughed in her face and returned to his friends, who high-fived him.

"That didn't even make any sense," muttered Iona to herself.

When it was down to the last couple of hundred applicants, Iona's name finally appeared on the tapestry. She felt relief and a surge of adrenaline as she approached the red door. Her feet ached from the blisters, but she'd learn to shunt away the pain from years of assisting Fenris with his rituals. Better to endure brutal cold or searing heat than spend time in the punishment cage.

The girl beyond the door tried not to smirk when Iona came through.

"Iona Storm?"

"That's me."

As soon as she said it, Iona could hear the Missouri accent in her own voice. The girl did too. The mirth in her eyes was barely contained.

"You know the deal? Three items to help you through the first Trial."

The girl gestured towards a table where a fancy scroll, a gnarled staff, and a small vial of light blue liquid waited, but Iona could hardly pay attention because she was staring at the swirling mist beneath the archway on the opposite side.

"The scroll is a spell of Winter's Respite, the staff has three charges of Ice Shard, and the vial is a healing balm, but be careful, it's sticky as all get-out. Might as well be paste."

"I just go through the archway?"

"Once you do, the timer starts. If you can't reach the end, or you want out at any time, just repeat 'I am defeated' three times and you'll be brought out of the Trial."

"I won't do that."

"I'm sure you won't, but I have to tell everyone."

After collecting the three items, Iona closed her eyes and centered herself. Once she stepped through the archway, her life would be on the line. She opened her eyes and moved towards the entrance to the Trial.

"Hey..."

Iona paused.

"Is that all real?"

"Is what real?"

"You know, everything. The cutoffs, the boots. Are you messing with everyone?"

"I don't understand," said Iona.

The girl's face broke with sympathy.

"Right. Sorry I bothered you."

As Iona approached the archway, she realized it wasn't just magic that she knew nothing about. Fashion, social expectations, common lingo, everything. She might as well have been born yesterday, because that's what it felt like. And if she managed against all odds to pass the Trials, she would enter Coterie of Mages, which would leave her in even less familiar territory.

"You don't have to do it if you don't want to," said the girl. "There's no shame in giving up."

Iona gripped the staff in her fist and stared back at the attendant with the intensity of a firestorm.

"I don't have a choice. I have nowhere else to go."

Before the girl could say anything, Iona stepped through the swirling mist.

The sudden vertigo felt like she'd been thrown off a mountain. Her stomach hit her throat and the meager contents of her stomach threatened to come up.

The cold hit her before she realized where she was.

Iona was kneeling in thick snow at least a foot deep while heavy winds whipped around her. She was at the base of a mountain covered in thick pines. Already she was shivering from the chill and wrapped her arms around her midsection for warmth.

"Maybe this was a mistake..."

Iona unrolled the parchment only to find a spell with instructions she didn't understand.

"Figures."

The tomes Fenris had were ancient, with languages and instructions that made little sense compared to modern conventions. But it was all she knew. The spell was clearly meant to protect her from the weather, but she'd never be able to cast it.

A path headed out of the snowy clearing. Iona followed it until she came to a wide area with paths leading in three different directions. An icy blue humanoid in a black formal jacket and a top hat was waiting for her.

"Jokul Bore at your service," said the figure as he tipped his hat.

"What are you?" asked Iona as her lower lip quivered.

"Your guide to the first Trial. As you can see, there are three paths to the summit, which is your goal. To the left you'll find challenges befitting a scholar, to the right is best if you're clever with your spells, while the center is a good scrap."

Iona tipped her head back to examine the summit. It was a long way up. The peak was lit up by the sun even as she was in the middle of a brisk winter storm.

"What are those wires?" she asked, pointing to the twin parallel lines that went from a location straight ahead to nearly the top of the mountain.

"You'll have to see for yourself, but each path provides a faster way to ascend if you can survive the challenge."

"Thanks," said Iona, trudging through the snow.

Not far past Jokul Bore was a gondola station, not much different than the one she'd ridden to the Spire. Gathered near the entrance were a dozen silvery constructs holding dull iron truncheons. They looked like mobsters made out of shiny metal.

It appeared there was only one way into the building. The sides were covered in snowdrifts and there were no windows.

Iona thought about trying one of the other paths, but she knew she wouldn't survive the climb up the mountain. Not without better protection against the cold.

On the other hand, she had no reliable way to defeat the mobster constructs. The staff only had three charges and there were a dozen of them. Iona searched her mind for a helpful spell, but the kinds of arcana she knew were based on ancient languages meant for obscure rituals.

But she did have one trick they probably hadn't anticipated.

Iona peeked under her T-shirt to the intricate tattoos that covered her shoulders and upper back. Fenris had given them to her less than six months ago and she'd only gotten to use them a few times under his supervision.

Much like the connection ceremony with Professor Ravenscroft, she closed her eyes and reached for the magic at the base of her skull. But instead of directing it into her fist, she diverted it into the tattoos, letting the faez charge up like a human battery.

Don't use the tattoos.

It was a pact she'd made with herself when she escaped from Fenris, but she saw no other way to get past the Trial. If she couldn't get into the Halls, then what was the point of holding back?

Fenris had never explained what they were for, only that they were important. The collection of faez warmed her shoulders even as the potential magic made her twitchy. Iona kept pulling faez into the tattoos beyond the limits that Fenris had imposed. She wasn't sure if it was dangerous to take in that much, but she also didn't know if her plan was going to work.

With unspent magic making her entire body quiver, Iona marched back to the entrance where the ice man Jokul Bore was waiting.

"The paths are the other way," he told her.

"I know."

Jokul's eyes widened as he stepped back.

"I'll have you know that the spell on the scroll will not harm me and I'm nearly impervious to all but the most potent magic. Turn around before I make you regret this!"

Iona tried to keep her expression as calm and neutral as possible so she could get close to Jokul.

"Would you lend me your jacket?" she asked sweetly.

The ice man's face wrinkled with consternation.

"Don't come any—"

When she reached the final distance, Iona lunged forward, and as her fingers touched the little catch at the base of his neck, she unleashed the pent-up magic in her tattoos.

The blast threw her backwards to land in a snowdrift. After a moment of dizziness, Iona returned to the spot where Jokul Bore had once been. She found a mostly intact jacket and a top hat with the lid popped, but nothing else. The strange satisfaction at his total annihilation was mixed with the worry that it was a trap she couldn't afford to step into, so she pushed those feelings away and focused on survival.

Before she could grab the warm clothing, she felt an ominous pang deep in her flesh beneath the tattoos. Almost like a homing signal, or a flare. If Fenris hadn't known where she was before, he would likely know now.

Iona slipped on the jacket, feeling an unexpected warmth, which she didn't understand until she noticed the runes on the interior. She didn't have any use for the top hat, but brought it in case she might need it later.

When she returned to the gondola station, Iona circled wide through the trees until she reached the side. Using the heavy drifts, she managed to scramble on top of the building. She'd intended to slip inside if she could and use the gondola, but saw that there were more constructs inside and the control station was covered in unfamiliar runes.

Iona checked between the interior and the parallel wires leading to the summit before she settled on an idea. She went to the back of the building where the wires started their ascent and set the staff across them, using the top hat as a makeshift seat.

Her first attempt at pulling herself upward ended quickly when her hands tried to freeze against the wire. She thought about ripping up the jacket, but didn't want to damage the warming runes.

The parchment from the scroll was easy to rip in half. Using each piece and some of the sticky healing balm, Iona made two "gloves" that allowed her to grab the wire. She experimented with sitting and then kneeling on the staff, finding the latter worked better, and shortly after, she was pulling herself up the twin wires.

Progress was slow but it was better than dealing with the multitude of challenges that she had little experience to pass. It might take her a while to reach the summit, but at least she would do so safely.

Iona was about a hundred meters from the station when her hands wouldn't unclench. The makeshift gloves were protecting her hands from freezing to the wire, but they didn't help with the cold. After checking how far she had to go to reach the summit, she realized she'd never get there before frostbite would set in, and a mage without their hands wasn't a mage at all.

Dropping from the wires didn't seem like a good idea. She was at least fifty feet in the air and the snow didn't look deep enough to cushion her fall. Iona almost set her head against the wire, but remembered at the last second that it would freeze to her forehead.

Remembering how she felt when she shunted faez into her tattoos, Iona closed her eyes and repeated the process. She put far less than she had before, but it was enough to provide inner warmth as her body vibrated with unspent energy.

Iona managed to climb another fifty meters before the migraine set in. She'd never held faez in the tattoos for that long and it was causing spots in her vision.

"Frostbite or migraine. What a choice."

The magic was easy to release. She sent it out through her hands to give her a little more time before she'd have to repeat the process. The return of the cold was immediate.

Then she felt the wires vibrate.

She searched for the source of the shaking only to find that the gondola at the station had begun its ascent. She'd somehow woken the machine with the magic she'd loosed.

The gondola was ascending fast.

The thought of jumping from the wires was ludicrous even as she contemplated it. She looked for a tree she could land in, but the space beneath the wires had been cleared for the passage of the gondola.

Iona prepared herself for impact, bending her knees slightly, balancing on the staff, and keeping her body loose.

The gondola hit the bottom of her boots like a slow moving car. The impact threw her up the wire only to be hit again as the gondola caught up. After a few unstable bounces in which she nearly toppled from the wires, Iona managed to get her feet against the car, which propelled her upward at a good speed.

As she flew up the slope, she saw other obstacles that she would have had to pass had she climbed the mountain on foot. Strange creatures made of thick fur with long arms claimed one area, while pale wasps that shot ice from their stingers patrolled another.

When the gondola neared the final station, Iona realized that if she didn't get down the car would crush her. With no other way to get off, Iona pulled the staff off the wires—bouncing off the front of the gondola—and careened through the air to land in a thick snowdrift.

Snow went everywhere.

In her boots, under her cutoff jeans, in her mouth. She climbed out of the drift without the staff or the vial, clutching her arms around her chest for warmth as her lower lip shook.

Iona made her way around the upper gondola station only to find more of the silvery constructs waiting for whoever was supposed to get off. She went wide, sneaking through the trees as she was only a short climb to the final summit.

With her head on a swivel, expecting more obstacles, Iona was surprised when she climbed past a huge boulder to find a swirling archway that matched the one she'd entered waiting for her. Iona did a quick check to make sure there wasn't anything lurking nearby before she made the final sprint through the portal.

SIX

The morning of the second day was a little blurry for Zuri. It'd been a horror to have to sleep with so many others in the same place. An absolute insult. If she were to become a famous alumnus like her sister, she would suggest to the administration that they needed better lodging. Or at least the option to pay more for personalized space.

And the bunk beds might as well have been torture devices for the amount of sleep she'd gotten. She barely paid attention to Professor Ravenscroft's speech since there was little he had to say that she didn't already know.

Instead, she was studying the rankings after the first day. Zuri had been pleased with her first Trial. The snow devils had given her a little trouble, but then she'd yoked the infernal moose with a submission chain and ridden the beast nearly to the top. Her performance had earned her fifth place, which was a good thirty places above Blake and a few more than that for Scarlett.

In general, St. Jude's alumni were all over the top one hundred places, which was to be expected. Even Justine managed a spot in the top two hundred, which had to be a confidence boost.

But it wasn't the other potential Coterie students that confused her.

The talk of the morning was the second position, which had been earned by Iona Storm. At first, everyone had thought that was one of the students that had come from an overseas training academy like St. Jude's. They didn't know who she was until Blake had sent one of his minions to ask the blonde girl—who was still in her cutoffs, truck stop T-shirt, and work boots—what her name was.

Iona Storm.

Zuri still couldn't believe it. That wide-eyed girl who probably smelled like a pig farm had somehow been the second best of the entire applicant class? Either she'd chosen that outfit to throw everyone off, or there was something in her past that had made her uniquely suited to the Trials. Zuri didn't buy it. She'd probably gotten lucky. Or one of the administrators running the Trials had screwed up. There was no way an untrained girl like that could have done so well.

Either way, it wouldn't matter because even if she managed to pass the final two Trials, she'd never be in Coterie, which meant she'd be a mystery that would never matter to Zuri.

For the second Trial, Zuri had to wait a few hours for her turn. When she went through the red door, she found a familiar fiery redhead tapping her foot.

Scarlett Calloway.

"Of course, it's you," said Scarlett with the practiced disdain of an empress.

"I've always wondered if you really have that color of hair, or you thought you needed it to be that color because of your name."

"Do you know what he told me about you?"

"That my tits could cause world peace and my farts smell like an angel's breath?"

"Oh grow up, he told me you were like a dead fish in bed."

"Yeah, it wasn't my first choice of roleplay, but you gotta stand by your man when he has a fetish. Though in retrospect, rubbing the old fish guts all over my naked body was a little weird."

The attendant with their second Trial items, who had been watching them silently, cleared her throat.

"If you don't go into the second Trial soon, you'll be penalized."

Zuri snatched the gold signet ring from the table and gestured towards the inner door.

"After you, Princess."

"What does the ring do?" Scarlett asked the attendant.

"Puts up a deflection shield when you trigger it with faez."

Scarlett glared at the piece of jewelry.

"That's it? That's what our Coterie item is supposed to be? What a joke."

"Fits your red hair, clown," said Zuri.

"Piss off."

Zuri smirked.

"Did Blake ask you to do that too? You look like the kind of girl that would enjoy that."

"Excuse me," said the attendant. "You have ten seconds before you get docked points."

Scarlett barged through the door before Zuri could beat her. The interior of the second Trial was an enormous sphere with platforms and ladders climbing all the way to the top, where a figure in all black waved at them.

"I guess we have to get up there," said Scarlett with her neck craned.

"You think? Did you come up with that all by yourself? It's wonderful that Blake gave you permission to use your brain."

Scarlett turned on Zuri.

"At least I was smart enough not to testify against him. You really screwed up when you claimed he killed Gemma. You're lucky he didn't sue you for libel."

White-hot rage filled Zuri's vision. She was swinging before she even thought about it. The blow connected with Scarlett's jaw, snapping her head to the side.

"You—"

The force blast was unexpectedly quick, throwing Zuri across the platform. She landed beyond the starting line, which triggered the clock to start.

Before Scarlett could hit her with a second blast, Zuri threw up a reflecting ward. The rebound nearly threw the redhead off the opening area.

They both reached their feet at the same time, throwing spells with reckless abandon. Sparks, crackles of lightning, and pulsing white force darts filled the air between them. Their impromptu battle lasted for half a minute before they each retreated to platforms inside the dome. Zuri hid behind a concrete wall as she assessed her next move.

"Hey," said a male voice from above. "You're supposed to be fighting me. Don't you want to pass?"

"Stay out of our way, or I'll track you down after the Trials and show you why you don't mess with Coterie," yelled Scarlett.

"I hate to say it, but she's right. You'd better not interfere."

"Merlin's tits, you bitches are crazy."

Zuri thought for a moment that their upperclassman opponent might stand down, but then glowing red missiles whistled down at them in curling trajectories. One blew up near her side, sending bright pain through her body and making her stiffen. The exploding spells caused numbness.

A direct hit would immobilize her.

Scarlett used the opportunity to advance across the thin platform, but got caught when a missile disabled her leg and made her fall onto her back.

The redhead crawled behind the barrier as she punched her leg to wake it back up.

"Deal with this asshole first?"

"Agreed."

Zuri didn't trust Scarlett but she knew they couldn't battle each other with their opponent raining magic down upon their heads.

"You take that side and I'll take this one. He can't fire at both of us," said Zuri.

Scarlett looked annoyed, but another missile exploded near her head. "Fine. You go first."

Using the golden signet ring, Zuri made a force barrier that hovered a few feet from her hand. She burst out from behind her hiding spot, rushing towards the ramp that led to the next level while missiles bounced off her shield.

When she reached the next level, Zuri hid behind a short wall and sent covering fire at the upperclassman while Scarlett ascended. It was too far for an ice-bind hex, but Zuri managed to explode earth shards over his head, forcing him to duck.

The two of them methodically worked their way up the levels until they reached the final third, but the advantage switched to their assailant as they were near enough that he could send crimson missiles at both of them without repercussion.

"What do we do?" asked Scarlett as she ducked behind her ring shield.

"Do you know the light blind spell?"

Scarlett shook her head.

"What about a Brutalist ritual? He'd be easy to take out then."

Zuri sighed.

"We've never get the ritual off, and we wasted too much time below."

"And you wonder why no one wants to work with you," said Scarlett.

For the first time, the quip stung. While Blake had poisoned the waters with potential allies for Coterie, it wasn't lost on her that except for Gemma, she'd struggled to find friends. It was why she'd refused to let what Blake did to her pass unchallenged, because Gemma had been the one person who'd seen who she really was beneath the reputation.

Being in an elite prep school hadn't been the party she'd thought it would be as she listened to Nandi's stories growing up. Instead it'd been a constant battle of social expectations with whispers and rumors foreshadowing the magic that they'd later use to undermine each other.

When she'd first started dating Blake, it'd been a masterstroke of social status. Even her parents had applauded her choice. But she hadn't realized she'd bound herself to a sociopath until it was too late.

"One of us needs to make the first move so the other can flank him and take him down."

"Whoever does that is getting immobilized for sure. We're too close to avoid his shots now, so it isn't going to be me," said Scarlett.

Zuri peered across the gap to see Scarlett's left leg sticking beyond the barrier. An ice-bind hex would freeze her in place, but that wouldn't help her pass the second Trial. If this was going to work, they both needed to get through, and that meant dealing with the black-clad upperclassman only a dozen yards away.

"I'll do it," she said quietly, hoping only Scarlett could hear. "But you be ready to take him out."

"This isn't a trick, is it?"

"I wish it was. Just be ready, okay? I want to be done with this so I don't have to hear your stupid voice anymore."

"I've been told I have a perfectly pleasing voice—"

"Shut up, Scarlett." Zuri huffed. "On a visual count of three."

Holding one hand behind the barrier so Scarlett could see and using the other for the ring shield, Zuri prepared herself for the final move.

One.

Two.

Three.

Zuri burst out from behind the barrier expecting to catch a blast from the upperclassman but he was throwing crimson missiles in Scarlett's direction, which meant he'd probably heard them and after all their bickering had decided that what they'd said had been a deception.

He realized his mistake too late.

As he turned to retarget her with his wand, Zuri caught him with the ice-bind hex. A sheath of pale ice encased him like a cocoon, freezing him into place.

"That was—"

The last word never left her lips as crackling black energy overtook her. She hadn't even heard Scarlett speak the spell, but that was little solace as she tipped over like a stiff board, landing flat on her side. The impact rattled her teeth and sent bright pain through her shoulder.

The tip of a shoe pushed her over until she was looking directly into the face of Scarlett Calloway. The snarl made her ugly.

"Remember this the next time you open your stupid mouth."

Scarlett leaned over, made a fist, and punched Zuri in the face three times.

Then she strode towards the exit door at the back of the platform.

Zuri lay immobilized for what seemed like forever. As the spell wore off, she fought to move and escape the second Trial, feeling her points drain away the longer she was on the ground.

When she was finally free, Zuri found her feet only to be looking at the upperclassman, who was shaking the ice free from his limbs. He had the drop on her, so she didn't bother with a spell.

"Shadows below, what was that?"

"We went to prep school together. Her boyfriend killed my best friend."

The black-clad upperclassman shook his head.

"You Coterie kids are crazy. Get out of here before I change my mind."

As Zuri left the second Trial, she realized that Scarlett could have immobilized her with a spell that would have kept her locked down for much longer than a few minutes. The choice became apparent the moment she saw her score, which placed her near the bottom half of the pack. Scarlett wanted to hurt her position in the Trials, and her social status, but not so much that she didn't pass and make it to Coterie. That way Scarlett and Blake could take care of her permanently in the shadows of the Coterie Obelisk.

SEVEN

No one laughed at Iona anymore, but she could sense their confusion in the questioning stares. They couldn't understand how she'd made it to the third and final Trial. The group round. Half the comments she overheard wondered if her outfit was a joke, while the others were certain that she was the stupid yokel that they represented. Iona just wished she could leave the Spire to retrieve different clothes, not that she had any money.

The second Trial hadn't gone as well as the first, even after she'd had a chance to eat, rest, and get her painful blisters fixed by the medical staff. She'd been a hindrance to her partner during the Trial without mastery of a long-ranged spell, but together they'd managed to make it through, mostly because Iona used herself as a distraction and she'd been adept at fighting through the immobilization.

Now everyone was teaming up for the group round. No one knew how the game would be played, but having allies was important. She'd been wandering around the cafeteria all morning looking for people that didn't look at her with obvious disdain.

"Hey Barry," she said when she found her second Trial partner with a group in a side room. She hated the way she could hear her accent, and the way they reacted with not very covert smirks.

"Iona, hey."

The flat tone made her stomach do backflips.

"I was wondering if..."

"I'm sorry, Iona. Our group is full. We don't want to make it too big in case there are limitations. You never know what to expect."

"Right, yeah. That makes sense. Sorry to bother you."

As Iona walked away she could hear Barry's voice catch up to her.

"...couldn't even make a simple force blast, or wind dart..."

Iona continued making the rounds, peeking into side rooms and corners, looking for allies, but she was continually turned down. Some didn't even let her speak. They would just point the opposite direction, or shake their heads.

She found an empty spot near the pastry table and picked at a chocolate croissant. At another time, she would have devoured it whole and gone back for more. She'd never had anything that tasted so divine. Breakfast in Missouri had usually been cheap greasy sausage and gritty dehydrated scrambled eggs with a heaping of hot sauce to hide the taste. Fenris could afford better, but he didn't like spending money on anything that didn't have to do with his arcane projects.

"Are you Iona?"

She hadn't been paying attention. She'd been picking flecks of crust from the pastry and crumbling them into dust on the table.

Iona looked up to see a pimple-faced guy with an oversized Halls hoodie on. Beneath the roomy fabric he had to be only skin and bones. He glanced to her bare legs.

"That's me."

He gestured to a group of six on the far side of the cafeteria. A mix of girls and guys. A few of them waved.

"Do you want to join us for the final Trial?"

"Me? Really?"

"Yeah, totally. We saw your score after the first round. We'd love to have you in our group."

"I would love to be had." Iona screwed up her face. "Sorry. I would love to join your group."

"I'm Simon."

She shook his hand. It was clammy. He held onto hers longer than was comfortable, but eventually let go.

Iona followed him across the cafeteria. Simon introduced her to the rest of the group. They reminded her of the kids she saw when she was running errands in town for Fenris. Full of pimples. Too big or too small. Spent most of their time on the farm doing work for the family and were as naïve as she was about the world. The perfect group.

For the next hour they traded information about themselves. Most of them were from the Midwest, or rural areas on the East Coast. They were all aiming for the lesser Halls, except for Simon who wanted to be in Arcanium. She lied and told them she'd put "Any" in the Tome of Record, because she knew they'd never believe she had a place in Coterie should she pass. It would also make her different, and she'd had enough of that already, and she rather liked them, even if she had nothing in common since she'd spent her days as Fenris' assistant. In another life, she could imagine herself sitting in the dorm of a normal college laughing at their inside jokes and ordering pizza.

Shortly before they needed to enter the auditorium, Simon asked to talk to her privately.

"Yeah, Iona, I was thinking," he said, eyes darting as he kept swallowing visibly.

"What are you thinking?"

"After the Trials, when we both get in, I wanted to know if we could go on a date. Proper nice and all. A real restaurant. They have a lot of them in the city."

Her insides revolted but she didn't want to make a scene or embarrass him, especially when she'd been the last addition to the group.

"Oh, Simon, that's sweet of you. I really can't think about that right now. I'm just trying to get through the final Trial."

"But you would go on a date with me? You just don't want to say it now? Or are you waiting to turn me down?"

"Simon...we should get back to the others."

He stayed behind while she returned to the group. When he came back, he couldn't meet her gaze.

The group decided it was time to enter the auditorium, which relieved the tension she feared.

Professor Gideon Ravenscroft was waiting upon their arrival as they were one of the last groups. The number of people in the audience was much smaller than the first day. The crowd clustered around the dais.

"Congratulations. You've made it to the final day. One last Trial and you can join the Hundred Halls."

The professor did the thing where he slowly turned, clapping for them, while the crowd matched him. The response wasn't as enthusiastic as the first day. Everyone was tired. Nervous. Afraid to blow their chance before the end. Even the rich kids that had preened their cockiness like bright feathers seemed more subdued.

"As you know, this last Trial is the group round. Sometimes, it's a free-for-all with the challenges clearly black and white, while other times it requires a tight-knit group to survive a trap-filled board. The environment could be a stately castle with a malevolent queen, or it could be a nighttime adventure that requires careful sacrifice. You won't know until you enter the Trial. But know this, the best way to survive is to use your Merlin-given wits to divine the overall strategy and make sure you're not the one without a move to make."

Professor Gideon bent forward in a flourishing bow. When he returned to an upright position, a playful grin was hitched to his lips. Iona wasn't great at reading people, but she knew when someone was feeling quite clever about something they'd done. She'd seen it in Fenris' face whenever he talked about his projects. While she rarely understood what he was getting at, she could see the excitement in his black eyes and knew that whatever it was, it was probably not good for her in the long run.

"Good luck, and we'll see you on the other side!"

The professor raised his hand into a fist, which put off a strange black light. The inverse glow spread out from his location, speeding up as it expanded until the rushing wave of shadows passed over Iona.

She heard gasps and cries all around, but couldn't see anything. The darkness was absolute.

Gut-rumbling vertigo passed through her and then the lights flashed back on, but she wasn't standing in the auditorium. Nor was she with her group.

Iona stood in the middle of a tall forest. The canopy was high above with streaks of sunlight passing through the leaves. No one was directly around her, but she could see others at a distance of fifty feet. Some of them were staring into the sky while others were craning their necks in all directions. It was like they'd all been picked up and placed in a new location, but spread out.

"Simon? Gina?" she called out.

No one nearby looked like her group. Further out she saw the sparks of magic. Shouts. The arcane displays had everyone within range looking at each other like potential enemies.

The good feeling she'd had coming into the third Trial evaporated in the face of uncertainty. No explanation had been given. No rules or guidelines. Iona felt like they'd been left in the dark on purpose.

"Hey," she said to the girl that was closest.

She was short with black hair and a button nose. Eyes darted in all directions at her approach.

"Do you want—"

The words were half out her mouth when the girl started making complex gestures and mumbling under her breath. Iona knew when it was time to flee. She ran the other way, throwing herself around a tree trunk the moment the spell completed. A swirling black-and-green mist slammed into the tree, turning the bark to dust.

Iona turned around in time to see a guy with lustrous black skin wearing a cutoff camo shirt preparing to fire a spell at her defenseless back. She threw herself to the side as condensed white slices of air spun through the air, sending leaves from the undergrowth in all directions.

Before either of her assailants could close the distance, she sprinted perpendicularly, racing forward with her head down. A swirl of black-and-green energy slammed into a trunk to her right, but then her pursuers quickly turned on each other.

"What is going on? Did I miss something?"

Iona crept from trunk to trunk, keeping an eye out for others. A squeak slipped out her lips when she came around a cluster of dense trees to find a small group talking amongst themselves.

"Simon! Hey. Thank Merlin I found you all."

The group of six that she'd just spent the last hour before the Trial with, laughing about the challenges so far and making vague plans for the third one, stared back as if they'd never invited her into the group.

"I'm sorry, Iona. You never really gelled with the team," said Simon.

"If this is about the date..."

She ran before she finished her sentence. The hardening glares were proof enough she was no longer welcome. The crunch of leaves confirmed their pursuit as elemental magics exploded around her head, but she kept using the frequent trees to confuse and block their spells.

Within the first one hundred feet, she knew it was only a matter of time before they tracked her down and eliminated her from the game. At least half of them were faster than she was, and the heavy work boots were only slowing her down. Iona regretted that she knew such little magic that she couldn't take one of them with her.

Iona was so focused on escape and dodging their spells, she didn't realize where she was going until she burst into a clearing filled with high grass where another group was quietly discussing their plans near a small lily-covered pond.

Their surprise quickly turned to gestures and incantations. She was dead in their sights until the rest of her former group burst into the open area, which turned the hunt into open combat.

As magic rained around her head—exploding rocks, swirling winds, and bursts of flame followed by screams—Iona threw herself into the high grass, crawling furiously to escape the mayhem.

Iona kept crawling until the sounds of battle were distant. She found a wide trunk and placed her back against it, relishing the moment to catch her breath, examining her scratched-up and dirty palms as her limbs trembled from the hurried flight.

Eventually the sound of her own breathing wasn't the only thing she could hear. The forest sounded like a battleground, or a fireworks display. Then a heavy rumble shook the earth and Iona feared she was going to be swallowed whole. She peered into the distance, towards the epicenter of the noise, but the forest was too thick. Eventually the rumbling stopped, but she had the impression that something bad had happened.

Without a clear idea of what to do next, she thought back to Professor Gideon's speech. He'd said the best way to survive was to understand the overall strategy. Right now, the only thing she understood was that everyone had gone mad. She cursed herself for ever trusting Simon. He'd probably convinced the rest of the group to invite her because he wanted to ask her out. That was all he saw her as. A pretty face without friends. Prey. She should have known the moment he had sought her out that he didn't have the best of intentions. But she'd been so happy to have a group that she didn't question it.

"Never again."

The best way not to get used was to make sure you were the one doing the asking. If it wasn't on her terms, she had no interest. It was the best way to survive. She should have known that from Fenris. He hadn't taken her as an assistant out of the goodness of his heart. He had a plan for her, one that wasn't going to end well. That much she was certain.

"Screw Fenris. Screw Simon. And screw everyone else."

Anger-fueled thoughts filled her mind with rage. Iona imagined a meteor slamming into the field, causing widespread destruction amongst her fellow aspirants, flame turning them into gray ash.

Part of her wanted to stay against the tree trunk, but she knew that eventually, someone would stumble upon her. She needed to figure out what was going on.

Iona saw a nearby tree that had branches low enough to climb. She hurried over, checking the near distance for others.

When she reached it, she realized that the branch was much higher than she first thought. But this was okay. She knew few normal spells, but when she'd been younger and Fenris had been more kind, he'd taught her an incantation to help with climbing because he'd seen her unsuccessfully try to ascend a tree on his property.

It'd been years since she'd used it, but the gestures and words came back easily. She recalled the first time she'd successfully completed the spell. Fenris had cheered her like a proud father and told her that she was gifted. She'd never forgotten that moment, even if she no longer trusted him. Feared him. But for a short time, she'd thought he'd raise her like the parent she'd never had.

The spell made her palms sticky and her hands strong enough to pull herself into the tree. She moved from limb to limb, ascending the tree carefully and confidently until she reached the higher part of the canopy. When she finally stopped and looked down, she was at least a hundred feet above the forest floor.

Looking out across the game area, she saw a shimmering dome encasing the space, which had to be at least a half mile long and wide. As she studied the shape, she realized it was perfectly square. Strange. It seemed deliberate.

Then she realized the clearing not far from her section of forest was also square. The pattern became clear from her lofty vantage point. There were alternating sections of forest and high grass that spread out like a checkerboard.

As soon as she saw it, Professor Gideon's words came back to her in full.

"It's a chessboard. Everything he said was about chess. Challenges clearly black and white. Trap-filled board. A malevolent queen. Careful sacrifice. Make sure you're not the one without a move to make. Damn."

If she weren't in the middle of it with her life on the line should she not make it past the third Trial, she might have thought it was cool.

A high-pitched shrieking had Iona looking for the source of the noise. She had to circle around to the opposite side of the tree to see a square section of forest two positions away, shaking as if it were in the middle of a hurricane. Leaves were ascending into the sky in a cyclone and then it stopped.

Iona thought back to the rumbling in the earth. This had been different, but felt like the same scale. It definitely hadn't been caused by a single student. No one, no matter how well trained at prep school, could pull off a spell of that magnitude. Which meant it was part of the game. Part of the chessboard.

She rotated around the trunk until she could see the clearing right next to her section of forest. At the center of the high grass was a set of stones jutting up from the earth. They were spaced evenly, almost clock-like, with ethereal colors shifting between them.

A group of aspirants milled about the stones. Probably trying to figure out what they were. Iona couldn't imagine that they wouldn't have an impact on the game. Maybe that's why the other sections had turned into earthquake or hurricane zones.

"What are they for?"

It was a chessboard, that much she'd figured out. But what was it beyond that?

"I have to see the strategy. But how?"

Iona watched the group interacting with the stones. The colors were changing, shifting across them like a game of Simon Says. She could tell they were starting to figure out the puzzle.

Their progress bothered Iona. What if solving the puzzle would create some sort of apocalyptic outcome in a neighboring section much like the previous earthquake or hurricane?

The more she thought about it, the more she knew she was right. If it were a chessboard then maybe solving a puzzle was like moving a piece. But where were the pieces? From her position, it looked like she was in the third row on the black side, if the forest squares were black.

"Merlin-given wits. Merlin-given wits," she muttered. "There has to be a magical way to see the pieces."

The only thing she thought might help her see was the faez detection spell that Fenris had taught her when he was having her use the tattoo batteries. He had to make sure there wasn't excess faez floating around which could affect his rituals.

The spell was one of the easier ones she'd learned. The first time she cast it she saw nothing but a few golden sparkles around her head that dissipated quickly. The spell needed more range.

Iona spent a minute filling the tattoos. The entire time she was watching the group at the colored stones. The patterns were getting longer and longer, which meant they were getting close to the end. Iona worried she wasn't going to be fast enough.

When she cast the faez detection spell a second time, using the tattoo batteries to extend the range, she nearly fell out of the tree in surprise. To her left was an enormous shadowy pawn piece that hovered over the entire forest section. She was on a pawn square.

And forward and to the right, which was a diagonal from her square, where the other group was working through the puzzle, the ghostly image of a bishop piece floated over the field. If they managed to complete the challenge, the bishop would likely take her pawn.

"Oh no."

The scramble down the tree was made worse because her climbing spell had worn off. She nearly slipped when she landed on a heavy branch and then broke another from jumping too far. Iona kept wanting to see where the other group was, but knew that it didn't matter. She needed to focus on the descent.

When she reached the final twenty feet, she heard the hollers of excitement from the nearby field. The wind picked up, whipping through her hair and shaking the leaves.

Iona leapt from the branch. She landed hard and rolled into a thorn bush, which pierced her flesh in multiple spots. Pulling herself free was like trying to climb through a tractor combine. The howling winds were quickly reaching max speeds. From somewhere deeper in the forest square, she heard the painful cries of a girl probably getting speared by flying debris.

She ran towards the field as twigs and leaves pelted her back. A branch the size of a fence post broke across her back, sending her to her knees. Debris slammed into her legs. Iona couldn't see much further because of the dust and leaves and upturned undergrowth. The wind howled around her, sucking the air from her lungs until she was sure she was going to die. Then she put her head down and crawled the last dozen paces until she reached the field, which was as calm as a summer day, collapsing on her back in relief.

The hurricane continued its assault of the forest square for another minute while Iona listened to the sound of her own breathing.

Bloody and battered, she stayed in the high grass. If that group had solved the puzzle, then it was likely that she'd be safe in this square.

But as the winds died down to a low roar, voices rose higher. The group that had been at the stones was moving in her direction. She was running out of time.

With legs aching from the impact and the climbing, Iona pulled herself into a low crouch. She eyed the swirling leaves in the forest square and decided that it was better to get cut up again than to get caught by another group.

Iona sprinted into the trees right around the time the group spotted her. She heard the nonsense words of multiple spells as she ducked beneath a falling tree.

I'm not going back, she told herself. *I'm not going back.*

EIGHT

The moment the Obelisk came into view from her SUV window, Zuri pressed her face against the glass. The home of Coterie was the most iconic in all the Halls, only topped by the Spire, which was the central building of the entire city, and maybe the world.

As tall as a skyscraper, it was made from pure obsidian, which everyone knew was what portals were made of. But no one knew how Malden Anterist had built the Obelisk. The mysteries surrounding it were as deep as the ones about the origins of the former Head Patron Invictus.

The glossy black surface of the structure reflected the sun and sky, but none of the surrounding buildings. It was as if it existed in a different place. Zuri felt the smile break across her lips until her cheeks hurt.

The feeling lasted until they pulled into the receiving area and she saw Blake Lockwood talking with a couple of upperclassmen. He was wearing a stylish black-and-tan suit that made him look like a professional athlete before a big game. His chummy interaction with the upperclassmen only reminded Zuri that she was alone.

Utterly alone.

Zuri was going to hide in her SUV until Blake had gone in, but then he sneered at her vehicle and waved as if he knew she was inside.

She straightened the black-and-gold pantsuit that she'd chosen for elegance with a touch of royalty and climbed from the interior as if she were entering a red carpet. Her driver started unloading luggage onto gold-plated roller carts. Attendants waited to bring her things inside. They had hazy eyes from the enchantments that would keep them from remembering anything inside. Nandi had told her that the kitchen staff had to accept powerful, long-lasting charms that kept them from remembering anything but their job, but they were compensated quite well for their significant loss of memory.

"A lot of stuff for a girl who isn't going to be in Coterie long," said Blake as he strolled up like a prince at court.

"Don't you have a drink to spike somewhere around here?"

Blake scoffed.

"Women throw themselves at me."

"It's called fear. Not love."

"Fear is better than love. Love can turn sour."

"Don't trot your mommy issues out for me. Save it for fire crotch."

Zuri was painfully aware that the other Coterie first years were staring at her and Blake, which wasn't going to help her find any allies.

She was about to tell Blake to find someone else to bother when his jaw dropped.

"I can't even..."

"What?"

She thought he was messing with her at first until she heard the noises of surprise from across the receiving area. Zuri turned to find a dented yellow taxi pulling up with a pale-blonde girl in the back seat pressing her face against the window as she gawked at the Obelisk.

"Is she lost?" asked Zuri.

"I don't think so," said Blake. "Jake told me there was a surprise in our group."

"Why is she still wearing those awful clothes?"

The girl stepped out of the taxi in the same outfit she'd been wearing during the Trials. The driver yelled at her for payment. The two went back and forth while the entire unloading area stared in horror. What had the university inflicted on them?

Thoroughly annoyed, Zuri marched over to the taxi, pulled out a hundred-dollar bill, and handed it to the driver.

"Thanks," said Iona as the taxi pulled away.

"You were making a scene." Zuri scowled. "Are you sure you're in the right place?"

Iona clutched hands before her like a schoolgirl at the principal's office. Yet there was also unexpected fire in her gaze that made Zuri hesitate.

"I got into Coterie."

The words didn't make sense.

"How?"

Further conversation was cut short when the Acting Patron, Professor Sinclair, appeared.

"Iona Storm! Wonderful, wonderful. So glad you could make it. This is quite the surprise. But the Head Patron assures me you're up to the challenge. Where is your luggage, young lady?"

"I don't have any."

"Interesting. Anyway, come with me. I'll personally show you how to check in."

Professor Sinclair led the newcomer towards the Obelisk while the entire receiving area stared as if she were a goat in a dress being led into a fancy restaurant. Zuri couldn't believe it either. How had this farm girl gotten into Coterie, the most exclusive Hall in the world?

The mystery was outweighed by her own problems. If she couldn't find a group within the first few weeks, her time at Coterie would be as short as Iona's.

Zuri caught up with her driver and attendants who had loaded her luggage onto two carts. She'd planned on bringing more, but Nandi had cautioned her that too many things could be a hindrance when it came to defensive wards, so she cut out her formal dresses, knowing she could send for them when an occasion arose.

As she followed the carts towards the Obelisk, Justine gave her a covert wave from her SUV. The mousy girl was bursting with excitement. Zuri waved back.

The sign-in process was relatively quick. Her sister was her formal sponsor. Normally, family sponsors were frowned upon, but given Nandi's reputation, it was allowed. Mostly because her parents' friends hadn't wanted to stick their noses out after Blake's trial. Zuri wondered if that's why they'd made sure they were out of the realm for her big day. It's not like they'd been supportive of her decision, advising her many times to drop the accusation. *Gemma's dead. Why make things worse for everyone? Even if Blake caused it, it was likely an accident. No reason to ruin another life.*

Zuri could hear her parents' arguments over a fancy sushi dinner in the first ward as if she were right there.

"A hit of wasabi would be nice right now."

"Excuse me, ma'am?"

She turned to find her cart attendant staring.

"Nothing."

At the next check-in table, she found Charlotte Bellamy in a blue blazer with the Coterie badge on the lapel. The black and blonde stripes along the side of her hair made her appear much older than when she'd seen her last.

"Blimey. If it isn't that backstabbing prat that's always goin' on about this and that," said Charlotte with her mouth cocked to the side. "Finally put it right in the clown's mouth, didja?"

"I heard clown's mouth is what your boyfriend calls your lady parts, you bloody minger."

"Minger? Well, if it isn't the queen of sass, learning a new insult that a baby could spit. Gonna call me daft next? Or maybe a gormless prat? So you can be as cool as those East Enders?"

"I didn't want to twist your simple mind. You know, it's a wonder that you Brits were able to colonize half the world. If you ask me, I think it was because you were too stupid to know it was a bad idea."

Charlotte broke into a broad grin as she checked to make sure no one was nearby.

"Good to see you, Zuri. Doing well?"

"I've been better."

"Yeah, read all about it. Sorry I didn't message you, but I was in this shithole trying to keep the Brannigan twins from killing me."

"Didn't you date them? At the same time?"

"Yeah, they're a little bitter about how it ended. I may or may not have slept with their auntie when I was staying at their house." Charlotte rolled her eyes. "Anyway, love the fit. You look buttered and ready to eat."

Zuri rolled back the hem at her wrist, revealing runes.

"Reinforced with reflectors."

Charlotte's expression turned serious.

"You're gonna need it from what I hear. Shame about Gemma. She was a real bitch and I loved her for it."

Zuri ground her teeth.

"I miss her every day."

Charlotte leaned forward.

"You ready for this? 'Cause I hear Blake's coming after you and he's been talking to a lot of people. He wants to make an example of you. Burnish his reputation for being tough, if you know what I mean."

"He's informed me personally of his intent."

"What a bloody mess. I'm sorry, Zuri."

"Me too, but I'm not going to sulk about it. I've got shit to do. I'm not letting him take me down. Not without giving it back to him triple."

"That's the spirit, luv." Charlotte checked to the side. "What's this I hear about the Pig Girl?"

"The Pig Girl?"

"Some blonde freak from nowhereland who somehow got into Coterie? I swear we should stage a revolt against the Head Patron for sticking us with a bloody commoner."

Zuri chuckled under her breath. It'd been a while since she'd talked to Charlotte. She'd forgotten that she was distantly related to the royal family. Nothing remotely close to the crown, but she liked to act like she was offended at everything that might insult it.

"I don't think she was a pig farmer and she's not going to last long. She didn't even have luggage, or a way to pay the taxi."

"Do you think she knows, like, spells for better farming? How to make the pig slop not smell? But you're right, she won't be a problem for long. She should have picked an easier Hall. I bet Arcanium would love a pig farmer."

Zuri tapped her fingernail on the table.

"What's the deal with rooms?"

"Oh yeah," said Charlotte, clapping her hands. "They didn't just put me here because of my good looks."

"A London ten for sure."

"You bitch," said Charlotte, laughing.

She opened up her book and ran her finger down the lists.

"Have a preference?"

"The book hasn't been tampered with? I don't want to get a room and find out it's been trapped in advance for me."

"I wouldn't let those wankers have a go at ya like that. Not on my watch," said Charlotte with a crisp British army salute.

"Thanks, Charlotte. Is the Dreadmarsh suite available?"

"No, sorry. Reserved for Orion. Part of the deal should any of that clan decide to bother with Coterie."

"What about the Hawthorne?"

Charlotte ran her fingernail down the list.

"Looks open, but I thought you wanted one that was defensible?"

"I have my reasons. Besides, Blake and his friends are all planning to bunk in the Leo Wing, which gives me some space, and they won't expect me to pick that one, which means it hasn't been tampered with in advance."

"That's a good thought," said Charlotte with a wink as she handed over the key and the password for the defensive wards. "The Hawthorne it is. Good luck, and I'll see you around."

Zuri had the attendants wheel her luggage to the Hawthorne suite on the second floor of the first level. The description of the lower section had been confusing at first until she understood that the floors were connected by stairs while the levels differentiated the spaces that had to be traveled to by portal.

She passed a few busts of famous alumni on the way, but they were of an older style that went better in a dusty old museum than the most famous Hall in the world. As she examined the Egyptian scrollwork and stone archways, she found the place wanting. The interior of the Obelisk wasn't as exclusive as she'd thought it'd be, but maybe she'd heard too many stories from her sister.

"Outside my room will be fine," she told the hazy-eyed attendants.

They made a pile of her luggage. Zuri ran her fingertips over the carved wyrmwood. The fresco was of Patron Malden Anterist battling demons on a featureless plain.

"You can go back now," she said when she realized the attendants were still standing nearby, staring at the wall. It appeared the know-nothing enchantments had been layered too heavily.

Once the attendants were gone, she disabled the defensive wards. Zuri didn't trust that Blake hadn't somehow tampered with them. Before the end of the day, she would change the passwords and all the wards, but for now, they would keep her safe until she finished her protections. While it was customary that the interstudent battles didn't commence until they'd been linked to the Patron, Zuri didn't put it past Blake to try something early.

While he couldn't have known which room she was going to pick and Charlotte wouldn't sell her out, that didn't mean she shouldn't be cautious. Sometimes old wards left by former students could cause problems. Nandi had told her to treat every new space in the Obelisk like a death tomb.

The Hawthorne suite had four rooms. A luxurious lounging area with a painting of The Scream in a protective enchanted case, a kitchen with the latest D'Agastine appliances, a gorgeous bathroom with a whirlpool big enough for an orgy, and a bedroom that looked like it could have been in the Palace of Versailles.

Zuri searched the rooms for enchantments and wards, finding a few minor spells that were easy to unravel. Then she grabbed a small hard case from her luggage, producing twelve black cubes that seemed to absorb the light. She activated them one by one, placing three to a room, which would detect any malevolent magics out to harm her. The warding cubes had been a personal project for the last three years and she felt she'd perfected them.

Once she'd finished setting the cubes, she placed another group of enchantments and wards around the suite. Some were defensive, while others were meant to make her life in Coterie more enjoyable.

The Patronage ceremony wasn't for a few more hours. Zuri thought about taking a bath, but decided that another round of detection spells was in order. She scoured the suite, opening every door, peeking into every nook and cranny, and checking every fixture for secret hexes.

When she was finished, Zuri allowed herself to relax. A safe place to call home. For a little while at least. If she were as successful as she expected to be, she could move into the upper levels and get away from Blake and his cronies.

With thoughts of hidden traps no longer plaguing her mind, Zuri examined The Scream. It was the real deal. The Munch painting had been stolen decades ago and sold to an alumnus of Coterie, who had a facsimile made that fooled the art dealers. After its widely publicized theft, the price had skyrocketed. She wondered what they would think if they knew the real one was in the Obelisk.

The existence of this painting was one of the reasons she'd chosen the Hawthorne suite. At the center of the painting was an androgynous figure holding the sides of their head in a silent scream. She felt a kinship to the figure after the last few years. Everything about her life had gone sideways. Every assumption she'd had about how her life was going to go had been upended. She was still mired in an existential crisis of her own making.

"Blake's doing," she said aloud. "It wasn't my fault."

Zuri turned away, but thought she caught a glimmer of magic, so she checked back to the painting. She searched it with her eyes, then followed up with an elemental faez detector. Everything seemed on the up and up, but...the twisted feeling in her gut had returned.

"I'm safe. I'm fine. I thoroughly checked the suite. It's just Blake in my head. I can't get rid of him."

Zuri headed towards the kitchen for a glass of water. She wanted a drink, but knew that was a bad idea this early in the semester.

Halfway across the living area, she felt prickles on her shoulder blades. The enchanted cuffs of her pantsuit were warning of danger.

Zuri spun around to find a figure crawling out of The Scream. It looked like the person in the painting, except it reeked of sorcery and Veil-magic.

The first hex she threw at it bounced off as if it were made of rubber, smashing a priceless vase on a side table. Black tentacles exploded from the Scream's amorphous body, whipping after her as she backed into the kitchen, throwing spell after spell ineffectively.

A black tentacle caught her arm. The touch burned away flesh, causing eye-watering pain. She knew she was in trouble. Blake had found a way to trap the room without her knowledge. He'd hid it in the protective enchantments of the painting.

A second tentacle nearly took her head off. She threw herself against the silvery refrigerator, which turned on the ice and spilled it across the marble floor.

"Nothing's working!" she screamed in frustration at her spells' ineffectiveness.

The Scream approached in silent apathy, black tentacles undulating as they cut off any chance of escape.

Then she realized why her wards and protections weren't working. Blake knew her inside and out. They'd dated almost the entirety of St. Jude's, which meant he knew exactly what spells she would use in a pinch.

"Inthalus D're!"

The dead language didn't roll off her tongue as easily as the spells she knew by heart, but it was a form of Kemetic magic she'd been studying in the last year, which meant Blake wouldn't have warded for it.

The Scream flinched with indecision. Zuri used the ancient hex again, which kept the tentacles from advancing. It was stopping it, but it wasn't potent enough to destroy the Veil magic.

The spell was one she'd only begun working on, but she knew it was best suited for the task. The phrasing was an awful tongue twister, but it was based on old Kemetic spells, which were known for their difficult elocution.

The Scream sensed its imminent demise and surged forward to finish the job. Tentacles ripped through cabinets and split marble countertops as it raced to end her before the spell's completion.

The Scream was about to pounce when Zuri gathered the potent energies and blasted them forward. The impact sent the apparition flying through the living room, tentacles destroying everything along the way.

It exploded when it hit.

Zuri was only saved by the distance and the open door of the expensive refrigerator that had been reinforced for elixir explosions. Flames licked through the suite. She put out the fire with a dampener spell, but the smoke whipped around as the vents tried to clear out the pollution.

When it was over, Zuri slumped against the destroyed kitchen. The living room was worse. The painting had been crisped by the explosion, with only the top half of the head visible within the char.

The wounds on her arm burned with eye-watering pain, so she pulled out her medic kit and applied a potent salve.

Rage filled her chest.

Not at Blake.

Her hatred for him had become a low simmer because she feared it would consume her, but she was mad at herself for not guessing that he would leave a cunning trap. He'd known she was going to pick the Hawthorne suite exactly because of The Scream. The only thing she didn't understand was how he'd gotten the passwords. Or maybe she was afraid of what it meant that he had.

With half the suite destroyed, Zuri changed out of her mangled, smoke-stained clothes. The Patronage ceremony was in less than an hour. She wanted to look her best when Blake saw that she was still alive.

NINE

The whispers started the moment Iona stepped out of the taxi. Some didn't bother to keep their voices low. She could hear them speculating about her origins, calling her Pig Girl, or other names she didn't have the context to understand.

On the surface everyone was polite when she interacted with them. But she could see their silent smirks, feel the laughter behind their eyes. It hadn't helped that she was wearing the same clothes that she'd arrived in. Thankfully, one of the medics had taught her a simple cleaning spell, which kept the worst of the stink away, otherwise she wasn't sure she would have been able to get out of the taxi.

Entering the Obelisk felt like getting whisked away to a foreign land. The City of Sorcery was imposing enough with the constant noise and bustle. Iona had spent the entirety of her life in an expansive farmhouse in mid-Missouri. It'd just been her and Fenris most days. She only saw other people when she went into town—for groceries or to pick up his packages at the post office.

There was a whole thing with a British girl and room selection. It felt important even though she couldn't understand why. Iona let her pick, content that she even had a room. Did it really matter if it had a whirlpool tub or a six-person shower?

Directions to her room were confusing. The first level was made up of five floors on which the second was her lodging. At least it didn't require a portal to move between the floors. She hadn't gotten used to the way the instantaneous movement upset her stomach.

Getting to her room took forever, only because she stopped every few feet to look at the next priceless work of art that was casually displayed on the walls or in little alcoves. A steel gauntleted fist with runes around the wrist was in a glass case at the top of the stairs. The plaque read: Rodrigo Diaz de Vivar. Then around the corner she found a painting of an old man in medieval garb in a battle of colorful magic with a woman with flaming red hair and covered in snake tattoos. The painting was called *An Inconvenient Breakup*.

Every few feet was a new marvel. It took her longer than she expected to find her room. The Patronage ceremony was in a few hours. She figured she had time to find her room and take a quick nap, because she'd slept like crap during the Trials. The dormitories had been so noisy.

The entrance to the Titan Suite overlooked a rock garden with a koi pond. Iona sensed someone on the other side, but when she looked up, she didn't see them. A trick of imagination, she hoped. The dark corridors and labyrinth passages were spooky enough.

Iona couldn't believe her eyes when she entered the suite. It looked like it belonged to a Roman emperor, with crimson curtains and flashes of gold. A fountain consisting of three mermaids took up the center of the main room.

The kitchen was stocked with fresh fruit and other delicacies like caviar and cured mystdrakon meat. Iona grabbed a handful of cherries and spit the seeds into her hand as she checked out the rest of the suite. When she got to the master bathroom, she nearly fell over. The tiled shower had eight separate heads, including two on the ceiling, for a three-hundred-and-sixty-degree experience.

"Am I hallucinating?"

Iona stripped naked, kicking her clothes into the bedroom. A single button turned all eight showerheads on. The water was the perfect temperature without even having to adjust the dials. She stepped into the center, letting the gently pounding water soothe away the trials of the last few days.

Eyes closed with her head hung, it was like she was suspended in time. Lines of dirty water snaked towards the drains. It was heaven, if such a thing existed.

She was so lost to the experience she wasn't sure what she heard was real or her imagination until she heard it a second time.

"Hello?"

Iona cursed herself the moment she spoke. No one should be in her suite, which meant that if she'd heard something, they weren't supposed to be here. That much she understood from the British girl's little speech. She'd also said something about changing the wards and individualizing the passwords, but Iona had gotten distracted.

She kept the shower running, but stepped to the edge, peering around the corner. A thump made her certain that someone or something was in the suite. Iona reached into her mind and filled her tattoos with faez. Once she'd filled her batteries with enough to give someone a good shock, she crept towards the master bedroom.

As she passed the expansive mirrors, she noticed her tattoos for the first time in a long time. She'd forgotten about the ones on her back and shoulders that looked like thick falcon heads surrounded by a dead language.

After confirming the bedroom was empty, she moved towards the main room, where the fountain made it harder to hear if anyone was lurking inside.

"If anyone is in here, I swear to the seven hells I will blast your ass back to the Stone Age."

A heavy snort from the kitchen had her turning around. Standing in the doorway was the biggest pig she'd ever seen. It had burning, crimson eyes and a thick hairy snout.

"Mercy..."

The enormous pig snorted and pawed the tiled floor as if it were about to charge. The idea of blasting the pig with her charged-up magic went right out of her head. The creature would smash her flat before she ever had a chance to injure it.

"There's food in the kitchen. You can have a feast, all on me."

The pig snorted as it pawed the tiles for a third time.

"Please, don't—"

Before she finished speaking, the pig charged. Iona did the only thing she could think of. She threw herself out the front, slamming the door behind her. As she spun around, the wetness on her foot made her slip and she landed hard on her side, which sent bright pain through her entire body.

Iona groaned. Her bones had been rattled by the impact and her teeth had clacked together so hard she worried she'd chipped a tooth. Lying naked outside her room while collecting her thoughts was the only thing she could do.

She didn't notice the figure in the rock garden until she climbed to her feet.

Big, menacing guy, built like a farmhand, but without the thread-worn clothes she normally associated with farming. He ate well. Bloody steaks. Rich desserts. Fine whiskeys. Iona was reminded of the prized bull at a nearby pasture. The look alone was all the warning she needed.

"Orion?"

She remembered his name from the sign-in table. He'd been two spots ahead of her.

A thump from inside her suite had Iona glancing back. It was only for a blink, but when she checked on Orion, he was no longer standing across the rock garden.

He moved quiet for a big man. Iona swallowed. Even she had sensed the apprehension of her fellow first years around Orion. They treated him like a live bomb.

It wasn't until after he was gone that she remembered she was naked. Heat rushed into her cheeks as she belatedly covered her private parts with her hands.

Was he watching from the shadows? No. He was probably gone. He hadn't reacted to her nakedness, which she didn't know how to interpret. Was he used to naked women? Or not find her attractive? Or maybe wasn't interested in women at all?

But her lack of clothing wasn't the biggest problem. That was the demon in her suite.

Iona peeked through the door to find no sign of the enormous pig. The only thing she saw was a trail of wet footsteps leading to her location.

"Here, piggy, piggy!"

After a moment she checked behind her, hoping no one had heard her say that or she'd never hear the end of it.

She repeated it again.

Nothing.

Iona crept into the suite and examined the floor. There was no sign of the demon pig. No scratches, or pig shit. The room smelled like expensive fresheners.

After a thorough examination of the suite, she found she was alone. The pig had been a trick. An illusion, or something. She hated that she didn't know enough normal magic to know what was possible. The only things she knew how to do...well, she didn't even half know what they did.

Iona cleaned her clothes with a spell and returned to the front area. The keypad for entrance was easy to change, but she had no idea how to add additional wards or protections to her room. If they'd gotten in once, they could do it again.

She headed back down to the first floor for the Patronage ceremony. Everyone was there in their finest clothes, while she was still in cutoff jeans, a truck stop T-shirt, and work boots. Battling the illusionary demon pig wasn't as bad as seeing their smirks.

An older student directed them into two lines. She counted fifty-seven in their first-year group. As she settled in her position, she heard a snort, which made her spin around expecting the demon pig only to hear laughter.

The quiet murmuring fell silent the moment an unassuming man with dusty brown hair arrived. He wore black runed robes over a cardigan sweater that she would expect on a high school geometry teacher. His eyes traveled over the entire group, creasing slightly when they reached her.

I don't belong here.

The thought lasted for a moment before she reminded herself she had nowhere else to go. If she couldn't make this work, then Fenris would find her, drag her back to Missouri, and finish whatever awful plan he intended.

"As you all know, I'm Professor Phillip Sinclair, acting Patron until Malden returns from his long-deserved vacation. I teach Demonology, which I know has fallen out of favor these last few years, but I can assure you that my specialty still has much to teach."

He smiled as if he expected a reaction, but when none was given, he cleared his throat behind a fist and continued.

"Now for the presentation of the Coterie pins and then the Patronage ceremony. Charlotte. Daniel. Would you be so kind."

Professor Sinclair, bracketed by the two students, approached the end of the first line.

"Melanie Westwood, sponsored by Marcus Kensington."

A pin was placed on her chest and then the professor shook her hand before continuing to the next girl, who looked like she had indigestion.

"Justine Thornlock, sponsored by Leonidas Dreadmarsh."

A few soft whistles followed the name, which meant nothing to Iona, but clearly did to the rest of the group. The ceremony continued with solemn deliberateness. A few names stuck out to Iona. The first was Orion Dreadmarsh—there was that name again—who had the same dead expression she'd seen across the rock garden. Had he been the one to put the demon pig in her room?

The next was Zuri Musa, the girl who'd paid her taxi bill before storming away. She had rich black skin that glowed from within and her elegant pantsuit made Iona feel like Zuri had descended from royalty.

Everyone was impressive. Beautiful. Stylish. Extremely put together. Even the mousy Justine would have been a superstar in her hometown. Which made Iona dread the approach of Professor Sinclair even more.

When he reached her, Iona sensed the resignation. Before he could open his mouth, someone made a pig snort from the back row.

"Pig Girl!"

The name was repeated two more times from different people before the professor could call for calm.

"This is unacceptable. Must I remind you that I am Acting Patron and I will have order. This isn't St. Jude's Prep. I can and will punish you severely for anything I deem necessary."

His gaze cast over the two lines.

"Very well. Iona Storm, sponsored by Pythia Silverthorne."

The boos were immediate and shocking after the tirade by the professor, but he tolerated them as he reached for the pin and placed it on her T-shirt. She was repellant. A creature not meant to be in the Obelisk. Iona had always thought she was cute at the very least. The way the boys at the grocery store followed her around had been proof of that, but now she felt like she had warts and facial disfigurements.

When all the pins had been given, Professor Sinclair returned to the front of the group.

"Now you must swear your allegiance to your patron, through me. Just as you did during the Trials, raise your right hand and let the faez flow into it."

Fifty-seven hands rose.

"Today you promise yourself to Coterie of Mages." He paused. "A promise is a pact, a binding between two parties. A contract. As Acting Patron, I promise that you will learn to wield magics that can, and will, make the world tremble. You will learn things within these walls that others fear to even consider. Magic is a tool, a weapon to be wielded. But if you cannot master yourself, the magic will master you.

"For your part of the bargain, you promise yourself to me, and through me, this hall, the Coterie of Mages. You promise to protect its secrets, your fellow students, and the hall itself. But most importantly, you promise yourself to your patron. Who gives you the strength to wield your magics without fear of madness. I am your shield, your protector. And you must do as I say, now and forever."

His voice rose to a crescendo, and he shouted, "I bind you to me!"

The sensation had been difficult, almost painful, during the Trials. This time it was like she'd stuck her tongue in an electrical socket. The world exploded in pain. Bright lights flashed across her eyes and she was certain she was having a stroke.

When she came to, she was kneeling on the hardwood floor. No one had moved to help. In fact, they were looking at her as if she'd grown a second head.

A quiet refrain of Pig Girl was repeated in the back row until Professor Sinclair glared in their direction.

"Are you well enough to continue, Iona?"

"I am."

The way her voice came out weak and uneven made her want to scream inside. Iona climbed to her feet even as flashes of white light appeared in her vision and her stomach roiled like the shifting seas. The connection ceremony had made her feel like she'd been split in two, which made her wonder what Fenris had done to her.

"Congratulations! You are now officially members of the Coterie of Mages! We'll have a celebratory meal in your honor. Please, head to the eating hall."

The grand hall looked big enough to hold a thousand people easily. Long tables were covered in white napkins, fancy plates, and other eating accoutrements that Iona had never seen before.

She tried to take a spot near the others, but everyone shook their heads or told her flat out the spot was taken. Iona had to sit at a table by herself.

As soon as they were all seated, bleary-eyed waitstaff appeared with trays of delicious food. The aromas made her swoon with hunger.

Her table was served last, but she didn't care because it meant it was all for her. Iona didn't recognize the savory meat in a thick, dark purple sauce, but she was ready to tear into it the moment it was on her plate.

Iona loaded her dish with samples from every tray, even the foods that didn't look appetizing at first, as she was determined not to look like she was afraid. The entire time she was aware that others kept staring at her, and there were occasional calls of Pig Girl, but she'd already come to the decision that being made fun of was better than being sacrificed by a mad warlock in mid-Missouri.

As she cut the steaming white meat in dark sauce, Iona felt an itching between her shoulder blades. She turned, only to see the demonic pig standing right behind her. The surprise had her jumping backwards, knocking over the chair and taking her plate of food with her.

The saucy meat splashed over her chest as her head hit the hardwood floor, sending stars through her vision. She was covered in food.

Iona rolled over to find the pig no longer there and the rest of the first years in hysterical gut-busting laughter. The climb to her feet felt like it lasted years.

The idea of sitting alone covered in food made her want to scream. Visions of raining an apocalypse on their heads as fire and destruction turned their bones to ash filled her head. She imagined a hundred of those lanky taloned creatures that had decimated the street thugs descending on the rest of them, yanking entrails out like silly string. She imagined worse and worse, and in every vision, she was the one who was making them pay.

As the other first years laughed and called her Pig Girl, Iona turned and strode out of the cafeteria.

When she reached the Titan Suite, she didn't even care if the demon pig was waiting for her. Iona marched into her kitchen and grabbed a bowl of fresh cherries, before plopping down on the floor next to the mermaid fountain, where she spit seeds into the water and let tears stream down her cheeks.

After she'd eaten her fill of the sweet fruits, Iona cleaned her clothes with the laundry spell, then pushed a cabinet in front of the front door and balanced glassware on the edge so it would fall and break should anyone try to get in.

Then she yanked the sheets from the canopy bed and piled them in the master bedroom closet—which was bigger than her room in Missouri—and tried desperately to keep at bay the images of mass murder.

TEN

The seats that everyone chose in the auditorium for their meeting with the Master of Initiates gave Zuri a good idea of the alliances that had been formed already. Blake and Scarlett formed the largest and most dangerous group at the front, mostly from the powerful old magic families. Three other groups, based on the larger new magic contingent, including the siren sisters, spread out on the higher rows. The rest of the first years were in groups of two or three, including Justine, but those numbers and alliances would probably shift during the year.

Then there were the loners, which she was unfortunately a part of. The only others in this category were Orion Dreadmarsh and the girl who had no place in Coterie, Iona Storm.

Zuri was surprised that Iona had shown up after the welcome dinner two days ago. The girl had been humiliated. Zuri wasn't sure who had created the illusionary pig, but it'd clearly frightened Iona and ensured that she'd be known as Pig Girl for the rest of her short time in Coterie. But there she sat in the back right section by herself in the same clothes she'd stumbled into the first Trial wearing and without an ounce of the shame that had been gouged into her face during dinner.

If Zuri didn't have bigger problems, she might have informed the girl that if she was going to pretend to be a member of Coterie, she should at least look the part. What an awful situation. Zuri hoped that it didn't reflect poorly on the rest of the first years, though given she was unlikely to be the only one with such thoughts, the farm girl wouldn't last long in the cutthroat halls of Coterie.

Zuri was contemplating which of the new magic folks might be willing to join forces when Professor Gideon Ravenscroft arrived.

The professor entered to applause, but he waved them off and sat on the front edge of the desk as if they were having an intimate conversation.

"Good morning, Coterie. I hope you've settled into your quarters. I know the Obelisk isn't the Grand Royal, but we are a university after all. We mustn't begrudge ourselves a little hardship. As you all know, I'm your Master of Initiates, a title that is a little overstated for my actual role, which is more of a helpful guide than a *master*."

He paused and made air quotes over the final word, which brought chuckles from the class.

"First, a little about me. I am a Coterie alum, of course. Graduated first in my class and then after a successful career in the speculative artifact market, I came back to teach Kemetic magic, which in my not-so-humble opinion is the most powerful magic that you can learn in Coterie and perhaps in the Halls themselves.

"But it is not the *only* magic. And that's what makes us special compared to the other Halls. Technically, we have no specific curriculum. We have many subjects that we teach, but what the professors can help you with is only the floor of what you can learn. The ceiling, of course, is limitless."

Professor Gideon rose from the desk and strolled to the front row of students.

"Blake Lockwood. What is it that you want out of Coterie?"

Her former boyfriend cocked a smile at the rest of the class while stretching his arm across the back of Scarlett's seat. Zuri hated the way she missed that feeling of being with him. She'd felt invulnerable.

Blake cocked a smile. "Power. Isn't that why we're all here?"

Professor Gideon nodded enthusiastically and gestured towards the rest of the class.

"That's one answer, but do you know how to achieve that goal?"

"I'm ambitious. I'll figure it out. I always do," said Blake with a wink.

"Ambition is important," said Professor Gideon with a smirk. "But ambition without knowledge is like a flame without fuel, destined to burn out quickly."

The chuckles that passed through the new magic students was like a drug to Zuri and made her realize why Professor Gideon was everyone's favorite. But more importantly, she saw how the other first years despised Blake. An opening for sure, one she'd have to exploit if she wanted allies.

"I have fuel," said Blake quietly, crossing his arms.

Professor Gideon continued strolling in front of the class. He stopped and spun around, extending his arm towards the back.

"Orion Dreadmarsh. Your family is maybe the most famous in the world for being associated with magic. What is it that you want out of Coterie? Are you like Blake and you want power? Or are you here for something different?"

The deadpan stare from the hulking Orion made Zuri uncomfortable and she wasn't even the subject of his glare. It lasted for a good ten seconds, until Orion rose out of his seat, and to gasps and head turns, walked right out of the auditorium.

Professor Gideon appeared perplexed, but he shrugged his shoulders and said, "I guess when you're a Dreadmarsh, the normal rules don't apply. But I still wish him well. The Dreadmarsh name is an important one in the world of magic. I'm certain Orion will make his name proud."

Zuri couldn't imagine that any other student could get away with that kind of behavior, especially to a professor, but such was the power of the Dreadmarsh name—one that if the rumors were true, Orion lived up to in spades.

"Justine Thornlock. What's your opinion?" asked the professor.

"Knowledge. I want to explore the possibilities of magic," said Justine.

Professor Gideon winked.

"Ms. Thornlock was listening it seems. Knowledge is also a good answer. But without heat and pressure can be like weak iron, brittle and too soft to become a worthy blade."

The mousy girl blushed and ducked her head like a turtle returning to her shell. Her hands worked the empty air as if she were knitting.

Professor Gideon faced the class with his hands clasped in front.

"Would anyone else like to tell us why they're here?"

The urge to stay silent and unnoticed was strong. It took two tries before Zuri could get her hand up, but when she did, she raised it tall.

"Ms. Musa? I have to admit, I'm quite interested to hear your opinion."

A warmth rose up from her belly. That little comment from the professor would go a long way to finding allies, assuming she stuck the landing.

"To do what all peoples have done for the entirety of civilization. To protect themselves, their family, and their friends. We didn't coax fire from the elements because it was pretty, or because we were only curious. We needed it to see in the dark, to cook our food, and to use as a weapon. It was the same with magic. The early users had to learn new techniques, not because they were interested in the idea of it, but because those that were afraid of it would hang them in a tree, or burn them alive. I'm here to learn because I want a better life for myself and my friends, and I'm willing to do anything to achieve that goal."

The head nods and smiles from the majority of the class had her beaming inside. Even Professor Gideon seemed impressed, though he only gestured towards her like a game show host acknowledging a correct answer.

"As you can see," he said, "there are many reasons to be in Coterie. But for all the differences in your answers, all the hopes you have about what you're going to learn here, the truth is usually quite different from the expectations.

"Know this. The Obelisk is not a place of traditional scholarship. Nor is it a hallowed hall of knowledge with tome-filled libraries ready to fill your hungry minds with arcane expertise. We're not Arcanium, after all."

The entire class broke into laughter. Nothing brought Coterie together more than their hatred of Arcanium Hall.

"Coterie of Mages, and particularly the Obelisk, your home for the next five years, is a crucible. It is heat and pressure. It is a forge upon which you will be hammered into a deadly blade. The Coterie motto is Limitless for a reason. But no one pushes the limits because they are a little curious. No one delves into forbidden magics because they're wondering what might be on the other side of that knowledge."

The professor pantomimed a student lackadaisically strolling through a doorway providing another round of good-natured laughter.

"No."

He turned on the class, pointing directly at Blake.

"You will push the limits because you'll have no other choice. You'll face your fears because to ignore them will leave you open to retribution.

The other Halls produce such weak mages because they are afraid to hurt them. Afraid that if they lose a few students that no one else will join their Hall. But in Coterie, we're not losing a few students—we're losing the chaff. We're getting rid of the weak metal so we can forge the remaining into strong, healthy weapons.

"Many of you might think you know how Coterie works, and you might be right, but I'm here to tell you how it actually is."

Professor Gideon gestured to the air around them.

"The Obelisk is a place of secrets. While you can attend lectures with the professors of your choice, the real battles will be occurring far above us in places that few outside of Coterie would dare to tread."

Everyone stared at the ceiling as if they could see those secrets.

"In Coterie, we do not give tests, or grades, or any of that ivory tower crap. Your continued existence in Coterie of Mages will depend on one thing and one thing only: can you climb higher in the Obelisk? I won't tell you how many levels there are in the Obelisk because the truth is no one but Patron Malden knows. But know this, if you want to be here for your second year, you'd better find your way to the next level, and the one after that, and the one after that. Because if you haven't, then at the end of the year, you will no longer be a part of Coterie of Mages with all the benefits this Hall provides. Ask yourself if you know anyone that failed out of Coterie."

The professor let the news sink in. Zuri had an inkling of how things worked from the stories Nandi had told her, though her older sister was never specific about the details.

"The first thing you might ask is, how do you get to the next level? Well, that's something you're going to have to figure out. The Obelisk is filled with secrets. More secrets than you could discover in a dozen lifetimes. And know that it's not only your fellow students you have to worry about. The Obelisk is a living, breathing structure. You might find things different than you left them last. Or you might accidentally stumble upon a hidden place that on the surface may seem like an oasis. Be warned. The Obelisk is not a place for the unwary. Does anyone have any questions?"

Half the class raised their hands, which had the professor grinning from ear to ear.

"You should *all* have questions. That's the start, really. Good luck."

For the second time, the entire class was shocked by a sudden departure when Professor Gideon gave them a short incline of his head and walked out, leaving them in silence. Everyone looked around at each other in hopes they might know what had happened.

After a minute had passed, the entire class was still in the room. At St. Jude's, where a good portion of the first years had come from, leaving early or disobeying a teacher was grounds for serious punishment, including corporal.

The rattle of an auditorium chair had everyone looking around to see who'd dared to leave first.

The pale-blonde farm girl strode down the stairs and went straight out the door that the professor had left out of. Zuri was appalled at the lack of respect for the professor. Iona clearly didn't know or care about the rules. Even the unwritten ones.

A few others started to rise until Blake turned and glared at them. Zuri had been prepared to wait until he'd shown his displeasure.

"Screw this. I'm out," said Zuri loudly.

Then half the class, which comprised of the new magic and her, rose and grabbed their personal things.

Zuri cut across the row when she saw where the siren sisters were headed. She caught them in the side hall.

"Coral. Candi."

The two ladies turned simultaneously. Stringy brown hair and kelp thin. Zuri avoided looking directly at them. There was no danger presently, but their dead expressions were like looking into the eyes of a shark.

"Zuri."

The name was spoken in unison and without the vocal tremor that would put hooks in her mind. The siren sisters were some of the few new magic that had gotten into St. Jude's, mostly due to their supernatural background. They weren't full-blooded siren, but enough that their voices could twist minds, especially if either party was in water.

"I'll get straight to the point. You know what an asset I could be in your team. There's no one better at wards, I was president of the Arcana Club, the Elemental Savants, and the Puzzlers. And my Merlin scores were tops in the class."

The sisters glanced at each other before Coral or Candi—Zuri couldn't tell—responded singularly.

"Under normal circumstances, you would make an excellent addition to our team. We'd be lucky to have you. I was in the Puzzlers. I know how your mind works. But Blake has made it very clear that whoever takes you in will be in his crosshairs."

"Coral. He's a blowhard. I know him. Too well. He talks a big game but he doesn't follow through. You saw him firsthand in St. Jude's. He's an average mage at best. As you said, you were in Puzzlers. You know what I can do and what he can't."

"True. But the rest of his group, including his new girlfriend, Scarlett, are formidable. The Obelisk is going to be hard enough without adding another challenge."

"If we don't stick together, assholes like that will take us out one by one. He's a sociopath. Better we work together and take him out right away, and then the rest of our time in the Obelisk will be much simpler."

The siren sisters shared another glance and Zuri knew it wouldn't be good for her.

"Zuri." This time Candi spoke. "If it were just the two of us, we'd team up with you. But the others in our group have concerns."

"Concerns?"

"About confidential matters."

Heat rose to Zuri's chest.

"You mean the trial."

"Yes. You testified against Blake."

"He killed my best friend!"

"An accusation that was unproven. Had you won the case, then things might be different, but for right now, you're seen as the jealous ex-girlfriend who couldn't keep her man."

"Couldn't keep her man?"

Zuri made fists at her side. She wanted to scream. To rage. To blow a hole through the ceiling.

She pointed at herself.

"He was the one that courted me. I thought he was an asshole, but then he showed me his softer side, and I thought that's who he really was. It turned out, it was just an act. He'll do anything to get what he wants."

"You're not exactly making a good case," said Coral.

"He's a sociopath..."

"All the more reason to avoid conflict with him," said Candi.

"Please..."

Coral whispered something in her ear. The words were lost to magic. When Zuri came to, she was alone and angry.

"He's a sociopath," she repeated to herself. "A monster."

If she were truly going to survive, Zuri knew the best way was to take down some of her fellow students. Make them fear her like they did Blake and then some would flock to her side for protection. Especially as they knew she was the better mage.

But these were the kids she'd grown up with. She couldn't be a monster. Not like Blake.

But she desperately needed teammates. Without others to watch her back, she would be easy to take down. It would only be a matter of time.

She'd already talked to most of her class, which meant she was almost out of options. Almost. There was one left, but it hurt her brain to even consider it. Grouping with the farm girl would tarnish her name, but what would it matter if she were dead? The only other option was to do what she didn't want to do.

Then she remembered her sister's last words to her before she got into the SUV for the Trials.

"We're all monsters in the dark."

ELEVEN

Iona was rubbing her eyes when she left the suite, nearly tripping over a lumpy bag outside her door. She checked both ways before kicking it with her boot, which shifted the opening and revealed a pile of clothes.

A quick faez detection spell revealed the clothes were mundane. No enchantments. No lingering spells. Iona carried them into her room and dumped them onto the floor. A half dozen sets of clothing, including a pair of stylish sneakers, had been in the bag.

She picked out a pair of turquoise slacks and a cream shirt with bunched sleeves before heading out to the lecture, taking a new route to reach the cluttered classroom. The clothes didn't fit exactly—the pants were a hair too long—but it was better than wearing the same outfit she'd been in for the last three weeks.

There'd been no more incursions in her suite since she'd changed the passwords and applied a few simple wards that she'd learned in Professor

Kingsley's class. Iona was certain the wards were too simple to keep a determined intruder out, which was why she was still sleeping in the master bedroom closet, a space that was bigger than her room in Missouri.

The classroom was only a quarter full. The least of any of the lectures she'd attended. Professor Horace Green was one of the less popular teachers.

Heads popped up the moment she walked in. There were a few smirks and eye-rolls at her new clothing. Iona hoped to figure out who'd given her the bag, but no one was acting like they already knew, which meant the gift had come from someone else.

Iona took a spot in back, away from any of the other students. Early attempts to introduce herself had only resulted in more alienation, or outright animosity. While she waited for the professor to arrive, she examined the strange artifacts that were scattered amongst the shelves and tables lining the outer perimeter. A black skull with glowing eyes to her right sometimes let smoke out of its mouth, while a glass case filled with sickly green liquid had a living worm inside that liked to attack the barrier whenever anyone came near. The entire classroom was filled with such oddities, but the strangest was a heavy tome on the desk that looked like it was made with human skin and teeth.

"Good morning," said Professor Horace Green upon entry.

He was on the shorter side. Brown skin, thick black hair, and an intense gaze that made it hard to look at him. His clothing choices were a mystery to Iona, who thought they might be Middle Eastern or African, though he gave no indication he was from either region.

"I know last week's lecture was rather dry. The rules of elocution for the Greek-Coptic language primarily used by the Coptic Orthodox Church isn't exactly stimulating, which is why the class is half the size as last week."

The professor looked over the crowd expecting a chuckle, but when none came, he lifted his shoulders.

"Today we're going to discuss a topic that will be more stimulating. Applicable even. Does anyone know what this tome is?"

A long uncomfortable pause.

"No one? Anyone? Not even a guess."

Professor Green sighed.

"This is a version of the *Coffin Text*, or *Book of the Dead* if you prefer. Particularly one assembled by Karl Lepsius, a Prussian researcher who was also thought to be a member of the eighteenth-century Kushtic cult. As hopefully you all know, there is no single version of the *Book of the Dead.* But this one is particularly interesting because of how it was made and the slant of translations which make it one of the more useful versions of the book."

The professor rapped his knuckles on the edge of the ancient tome.

"This one is made from human skin, bone, and teeth using a harvesting technique that is lost to time, but the materials have given the tome an additional layer of protection and if you know the right methods, you'll find hidden spells within the text. Would anyone like to try one of the incantations?"

The sleekly dressed Zuri raised her hand immediately, which wasn't a surprise to anyone in the classroom. Professor Green chuckled.

"There are no grades in the Obelisk, Zuri. You don't need to impress me. Why don't we give someone else a shot at the book." He scanned the room. "Iona. Care to give it a try?"

The entire class turned to look at her. She already felt like an outsider.

"I guess."

A few pig calls were made under their breath on the way up to the front. Professor Green ushered her to the tome.

"Pick one of the spells in the first third. Anything you feel comfortable casting, but without faez—we don't need to summon any death scarabs. And careful with the outer edge. Those teeth do bite."

The outer edge of the tome was covered in human teeth. Iona flinched when she lifted the front cover, which brought heat to her cheeks. Dark-blue ink scrawled across the thick paper in a language that was unfamiliar. A few sections had sketches of the finger gestures or mental images that would need to be rotated in the mind during the incantation. None of them seemed difficult, but she couldn't read the words.

"Take all day, we don't mind," said Professor Green.

The class laughed this time, which only made her feel like a bug in a glass. She could hardly pay attention to words on the page, because she felt the heat of their gazes. A thought formed in the back of her skull which she quickly ignored: *wouldn't it be better if they were all dead?*

"I don't know these."

Professor Green hunched his forehead.

"These are basic-level spells, Miss Storm."

A sharp pain made her yank her hand away from the edge. Blood was beading up on her palm. She sucked it away as she tried to ignore the sea of eyes.

"I warned you the book bites. But if you can't demonstrate any spells, then maybe you should return to your seat."

The disappointment and embarrassment made her dizzy. But she didn't want to leave. A few calls of Pig Girl made it to her.

"Miss Storm? Did you hear me?"

Iona closed her eyes and bit back her fear.

"I did."

He gestured towards the class.

"Then take your seat."

Iona hurriedly flipped the pages, searching for something she recognized. Fenris had versions of the *Coffin Text* and *Pyramid Texts*, but they were in a different language.

"Miss Storm. Take your seat. Now."

A hand grabbed her arm. It was much stronger than she expected. As the professor pulled her away, she found a section that she knew and started repeating it without faez.

The hard grip around her upper arm faded away as the first phrase flowed from her lips. The words came awkwardly, but she grew more confident the longer she spoke. When she finished the incantation, which was a spell to prepare a soul to be captured in a phylactery upon death, the table trembled and the lights flickered.

"How did you know that?" came the accusation.

"It was one of the things I studied before the Halls."

Professor Green seemed perplexed. He looked like he had more to say, but was still working through his thoughts.

"That was...unusual, Miss Storm. You can return to your seat."

The walk to the back of the class felt different this time. The other first years were staring at her with a little apprehension, maybe even fear—that felt far too good to be normal—a feeling that gave her a kernel of hope that she could survive Coterie.

As she settled into her spot, she heard Melanie Westwood ask one of the siren sisters what language it was that she'd used. Iona didn't hear the answer because the professor continued his lecture, which mostly went over her head because it had more to do with the first third of the book.

After class was over, Iona caught Deadra Billington at her desk while everyone else was leaving. She was tall, gorgeous, and looked like she'd been an athlete in prep school.

"Hey."

Deadra returned a blank stare.

"I was wondering if you had any room in your team?"

The attractive first year continued stuffing her notebooks into her backpack without answering. Deadra shoulder-bumped Iona on the way out, knocking her back into the seat.

"I wouldn't talk to her."

Iona didn't realize anyone was speaking to her until she saw the beautiful, lustrous black woman who had paid her taxi tab standing two rows below. The name Zuri popped in her head.

"Why?"

"She's old magic. They barely give the new magic kids the time of day, so they certainly aren't going to entertain a dead magic newcomer."

"Dead magic?"

Zuri gestured.

"That's you."

"I didn't know she was old magic. I don't know much, really."

"Dreadmarsh, Lockwood, Calloway, Kingsley. All old magic. Best to avoid them if you want to survive."

"What are you?"

"A rude question."

"I'm sorry. I mean, are you old or new magic?"

"Old magic."

"Then why are you talking to me?" asked Iona, suddenly suspicious.

Zuri glanced over her shoulder and let out a heavy sigh. The room was empty except for the two of them. Iona wasn't great with reading people, but it wasn't hard to sense the disgust that Zuri wore like a rancid cloak.

"You're looking for a group."

"And?"

The other girl looked like she was working her way up to speaking, chewing her words before managing to spit it out.

"We should team up. You seem to know more than you're letting on, and I'm better than anyone else here."

Iona felt like it was a trap. She couldn't help but think about Simon in the third Trial. He'd lured her into his group for reasons other than he'd first explained. The fact that Zuri was old magic *and* willing to talk to her made Iona suspicious. While she'd gathered there was some friction between her and some of the other old magics, Iona didn't understand the details and didn't think it was enough to clear her motivations.

"I'm sorry. I'm probably better off working alone."

"What? Seriously? *You're* turning me down?"

"I should go. I have a lot of reading to catch up on."

Iona hurried out of the room, leaving Zuri alone. She looked like she'd been smacked in the face with a dead possum. Before Iona disappeared down the hallway, she checked back to see Zuri mumbling to herself and shaking her head.

TWELVE

The darkness had eyes. Zuri was sure of it. But none of her wards were picking anything up. She grumbled under her breath. Nothing was going right these days. Zuri was still fuming about being turned down by the farm girl.

"Focus, Zuri," she reminded herself.

The smooth round stone covered in runes on her palm was dead. Not a flicker of light. Under normal circumstances it was a good sign, but she was certain someone had been lurking near the jackal-headed statue before she arrived.

"Hello?"

She had yet to find the portal that would lead to the second level, but she thought it was near the statue. Too many of her fellow first years had been seen headed in this direction and she'd already explored most of the other areas.

It'd been difficult to explore the Obelisk as a loner. She feared running into Blake and his group, so she'd kept to the times when she knew they were in lecture, or away in the city for an all-night rave. With the biggest and most experienced group, they could afford time off. Zuri didn't feel that way. It was the beginning of October and she hadn't even found the portal to the second level.

Zuri stopped at the base of the jackal-headed statue.

"Hello, Anubis. Will you tell me your secrets? It has to be around here. You're the god of death."

An empty metallic bowl lay at the base of Anubis' feet. Zuri ran her finger around the inside of the bowl and sniffed it. Nothing. A faez detection spell revealed transformative magics across the entire statue and bowl, but the auras were vague enough not to give a clue.

Zuri crossed her arms and stared at the ancient god. She wondered if there'd been an actual Anubis. Not a god, but a powerful mage that could have been mistaken for one by superstitious peoples.

"Anubis is the god of death and death is a metaphor for change. What lesson are you trying to teach me?"

The answer came quickly. Zuri reached into her pack and pulled out a folding knife. The tip pricked the meat of her palm, producing a few beads of dark red blood. She let them drip into the bowl.

As soon as the crimson liquid hit the interior, a slight rumbling echoed through the balls of her feet. The statue shifted to the side, revealing a gap big enough for her to fit.

Before heading through, she peeked back into the bowl to see the blood had evaporated or been absorbed by the material.

Beyond the statue was a hallway covered in ancient Egyptian hieroglyphs. Zuri summoned a mage light to float beside her head.

Once she was in the hallway, the statue shifted back to its previous position. On the backside of the wall written in Latin was a simple spell that she recognized as a way to open the statue without the use of her blood.

The writings on the wall were stories about the Egyptian empire, though the details deviated enough from the normal myths that it made her wonder if these stories were closer to the truth of what happened in those times. She read about Osiris being murdered by his brother Set and then Isis giving birth to Horus so he could seek revenge. The god Ra and his sky boat. The berserker Sekhmet, and how she was tricked into drinking a lake of beer thinking it was blood, to stop her rage-filled slaughter. There was even a story about how Bastet learned to shape-shift into a cat.

She didn't linger long but made mental notes for later. On the other side of the hallway was a grand space with a ceiling that went beyond the reach of her light. At the opposite wall, she spotted magical illumination and a lone figure.

"It's me, Melanie," said Zuri upon approach.

The fellow first year had her hands up as if she had a spell ready. They dropped as soon as Zuri stepped into the light.

"Can't be too careful."

Melanie had attended the Arcanis Academy of Prestige, which was the new magic version of St. Jude's. The two prep schools held a dance together every year. Melanie had her kinky black hair braided into a crown around her head.

"Are you the only one here? Or is another of your group hiding in the shadows?"

"If it were anyone else, I'd lie and tell you that Marcus is back there somewhere, but I'm not going to do that to you. Not after everything that happened last year." She gestured towards the archway. "I figured with Blake and his crew out of the Obelisk preparing for the party it was safe to do a little research."

Zuri checked the archway on the wall. The black stone looked like it was made out of obsidian. Complex and unknown runes covered the outer section.

"This is the portal to level two?"

"As far as anyone can tell, but no one has gotten through it yet. Some are close."

"Blake?"

"Yeah. I've heard they have four of the six figured out."

"Can I?" asked Zuri, gesturing towards the archway.

"Be my guest."

Zuri stepped closer, leaving her back to Melanie. There were six separate collections of runes. Each one a completely different style.

"I see. Faez, Infernal, Veil, Kemetic, Warding, Hexes. The six major topics of study in Coterie."

Melanie shook her head.

"Of course you'd see that right away. How many years in a row did you kick our ass in the Arcanix competition?"

"Three of the four years. I would have won my first year, but our team leader didn't want to listen to me because I was a freshman and a girl."

A buzz on her wrist had Zuri sighing.

"Time to go?"

"Probably best. I'm sure Blake is headed back to the Obelisk to get ready for the party tonight."

"Are you going?" asked Melanie.

"Wouldn't miss it for the world."

Melanie shook her head.

"I don't know how you do it. I would have skipped Coterie. Become a normal. Better than dealing with Blake Lockwood."

"He's a bully and a sociopath, but he's not that smart."

"Not like you," said Melanie with the corner of her generous lips curled upward.

"Is it still just Marcus and you?"

"Yeah."

"Want a third? And yes, I know what Blake has told everyone. But he's all bluster."

"What about Gemma?"

Zuri's stomach tightened.

"He got lucky. I never thought he'd do that, but now that I know, he's easy to avoid."

Melanie appeared pained by the decision.

"I want to. I really do." She checked back to the runed archway. "Did you figure any of them out already?"

Zuri let a grin spread across her face.

"I'm pretty sure I know the Ward one."

"Damn. That's one of the harder ones. Let me talk to Marcus. I'll let you know tonight at the party. We really could use you."

"Great," said Zuri. "See you at the party."

"What are you coming dressed as?" asked Melanie as she gathered her notebooks and shoved them into a backpack.

"Don't want to give away the surprise."

§

The pleated skirt barely fit through the door of the SUV as the driver held it open. Zuri appeared on the sidewalk of the tenth ward, wrinkling her nose at the burning metallics in the air.

"Are you sure this is the right spot, Miss Musa?" asked the driver as he kneaded his hands together.

"I'll be alright, Gentry. Don't worry. The Obelisk is more dangerous than the outer wards." She smiled. "Take the night off. I'll get a ride with one of the others back to Coterie."

Gentry returned to the driver seat, but didn't pull away. She knew he was sitting in the front, waiting to see which way she went. That was the problem with having a driver paid for by her parents. He wasn't really in her employ.

She checked the invitation to the party. The Tyrants' Masquerade on Louis street. The name was a little cliché. Not at all a surprise given that Blake and Scarlett were in charge of the party. That would have been her had events gone differently.

The location of the party was supposed to be the spot she was standing, but she didn't see anything that suggested a large group of Coterie were getting together. Which meant that it would be a treasure hunt to find the final location. It'd been the latest fashion for throwing a party, one that Zuri had found trite and exhausting after the first half dozen.

But she wasn't about to let a little game keep her from showing her face. It was important that no one saw her as afraid. If she could show that Blake was all bluster and big talk, she'd eventually convince some of the other first years to join her side. If she could get Melanie and Marcus to team up with her, then she bet she could pull in at least two or three more. That would give them the size and experience to fend off the larger and meaner group that Blake had assembled.

A group of college students passed Zuri, giggling and laughing behind cupped hands. She snapped a silk fan into existence, waving it furiously to pass cool air across her face while she examined her surroundings.

Zuri spotted the painted fist on the corner of a brick building. Using the tip of her closed fan, she cast a spell that revealed an illusionary CoM floating before the fist.

"Louis Street. Probably a sixteen around here somewhere."

She wondered if Blake had known what costume she was going to wear. Probably not. A coincidence. Nothing to worry about. The painted fist tilted to the right, so Zuri walked down the sidewalk, ignoring the comments from passersby.

Next to a laundromat called The Gilded Cloth she found an outline of a pile of gold on the corner, following it down the alleyway past a rusted blue dumpster smelling of trash.

When the passage went two separate ways, Zuri examined her surroundings until she found the painted outline of a TV screen. Propaganda. The faded lettering on a door said: Cornell Media Studies.

Zuri knew she was near when she heard twinned voices arguing with a bouncer. She hurried ahead to find the Siren Sisters in silvery dresses that looked like they were made from scales.

"I'm sorry," said the bouncer, eyes shifting between the sisters. "I can't let you in unless you're in costume."

"But we are in costume, you thick-necked twit," said one of the twins. "This is exactly what Madam Seriphus wore before she slaughtered our great-grandparents. If anyone's a tyrant it was her."

The bouncer looked to Zuri for help. She shrugged.

"Do you really think it's a good idea to piss off the heirs of an international shipping empire?" asked Zuri.

The bouncer opened and closed his mouth before pulling back the velvet rope.

"Thanks, Zuri," said the twins.

"I'd almost think that Blake did that on purpose."

One of the twins frowned.

"You're better than that."

"Clearly I'm not."

At the end of a long hallway two attendants were standing before big red double doors. They pulled them open, revealing a huge space filled with dance music and a couple hundred Coterie students in costume.

The Siren Sisters darted to the left upon entry, probably not wanting to be seen entering with her. Zuri took in the sights, spotting at least three different Emperor Neros, four Bloody Marys, a couple of Hector the Hexers, and a variety of other historical figures known for being tyrants.

The center of the space was a big knot of dancing students with colored smoke rising above the floor that was part visual and part mild aphrodisiac. Before she'd left Coterie, Zuri had taken an elixir that would keep all but the most potent drugs or alcohol from affecting her. The last thing she needed was to have her senses dulled.

At one of the many bars around the outside of the pop-up venue, Zuri ordered a fizzy water. She was checking out a group of fourth years she remembered from St. Jude's when she heard her name.

"Zuri! I almost didn't recognize you."

She turned to find a tipsy Justine in a gorgeous silk green dress covered in ancient runes and a purple shawl wrapped around her shoulders. A carryall at her side was stuffed with something lumpy.

"Morgan le Fay?"

"The very one. I was going to do Bloody Mary, but thank Merlin I decided not to. I've counted at least six of them." Justine's eyes rounded. "Oh, my. I love it. Marie Antoinette?"

"The very one."

Justine rocked on her feet as she stared into a glass of bright blue liquid.

"This is stronger than I expected."

Zuri reached out and took the drink from Justine.

"You've probably had enough already. Remember, they aren't your friends."

"But they're not supposed to do anything outside of the Obelisk."

"A rule that no one will remember if you're dead."

Justine sighed heavily.

"Being in Coterie is exhausting. I should have skipped the party like Pig Girl."

"She isn't here?"

Justine shook her head tightly as her eyes went unfocused.

"I saw her before we left. She asked where everyone was going."

"I guess that makes sense. Blake not giving her an invitation." Zuri put a hand on Justine's arm to stabilize her. "You really need to head to the bathroom and do a cleansing spell."

Justine screwed up her face and stuck her tongue out as if she were getting sick.

"I hate that spell. It's almost worse than a hangover."

"Better than being dead."

"Thanks, Mom."

To her relief, Justine headed to the bathroom. Zuri was a little surprised at the girl's naivety. Maybe having Justice as her father had insulated her from the rougher parts of magical prep school, but now she didn't have her father to protect her.

Zuri worked the edges of the party, stopping to talk to anyone that made eye contact, but as soon as she tried to interact, they turned their back, or told her point-blank they weren't interested.

"I should have known you'd pick her."

The comment was made with thick derision. Zuri turned to find a matching Marie Antoinette in a red silk dress with a miniature obelisk built into the towering pouf hairstyle.

"It was either Marie or Queen Ravanalona, but I doubted that most people here would have gotten the latter. But I do like your hair, Scarlett. It's not the first time you've had a giant dick in it."

"How's getting to the second level going? We'll be the first group to pass. Probably in a few weeks. I wouldn't be surprised if we're in the third level while you're still stuck in the kiddie zone."

"I guess a million monkeys *can* write the works of Shakespeare. Did you recruit like half the class for your little group? I've never seen such a display of weakness."

"Yes, you're quite clever," said Scarlett. "But you're stupid about the things that really matter. You could have had everything, but you chose that mouthy bitch over your boyfriend. Your loss was my gain."

The urge to blast Scarlett with force magic was strong. Her rival's hand was twitching, readied for a ward. Zuri had to remind herself that doing that would be a mistake. So she let her hands relax and gave Scarlett a deep curtsey.

"Enjoy your party."

"Eat a dick, Zuri."

She hated not standing up for Gemma. Especially with that bitch, but she knew she wasn't going to make gains with her fellow first years by picking a fight.

Zuri went in search of Melanie. She found her in the back of the party on a section of couches with Marcus sitting with his legs in her lap. He was dressed in a silk robe, covered in jewels with his hair in the Roman style, while Melanie was dressed in an ancient dress with bronze jewelry that wasn't easily recognized.

"Emperor Caligula," she said to Marcus, bowing her head.

"Your Marie is stunning. Best one here," said Melanie.

Marcus punched her in the arm.

"Hey, shut up. You know there's only one other."

"I confess I don't know your costume," said Zuri.

Melanie extended an arm into the air with a flourish.

"The Witch of Endor."

"Not much of a tyrant."

Zuri checked to make sure no one else was around.

"Have you two spoken about our earlier conversation?"

Marcus shifted his feet off her lap and immediately rose to his feet.

"I need a new drink. Don't be too long," he said with a glare.

Zuri knew the answer as soon as she saw Melanie's face.

"I'm sorry, Zuri. I really am. We'd make a great team, but Marcus is scared shitless of Blake and his friends. Don't attract attention is his motto. He wasn't even sure he wanted to come tonight."

"What if you ditched Marcus? You know he's average at best."

"Zuri. He's my boyfriend. And the attention you attract is much worse than any of his inadequacies."

"Hopefully those don't extend to the bed."

"Zuri..."

"Sorry. I ran into Scarlett earlier. My mouth is still cocked for battle."

Melanie hunched her shoulders.

"You should go, Zuri. It's not good if I'm seen talking to you."

For the next half-hour, Zuri lurked at the edges of the party. She'd never felt so alone while surrounded by so many people. Until Gemma had been murdered, she'd always been the center of attention. Blake's good looks and connections. Her wit and intelligence. They'd made a great pair. Now her gifts amounted to nothing.

Realizing that she was wearing herself out for no reason, Zuri left. Gentry was waiting for her on the street outside the Gilded Cloth, which didn't surprise her. He didn't say a word as he opened the door so she could climb inside.

"To the Obelisk."

Zuri stared at the passing lights wondering how she was going to survive Coterie as a lone student and with Blake sabotaging her at every turn.

"I have to take him out. Somehow. Or no one will ever touch me."

The idea that she could kill her former boyfriend made her stomach churn. While she'd been raised in a cutthroat world, she'd always thought the battles would be metaphorical, rather than literal.

But that was the choice that faced her. Become a monster, or be killed by one.

THIRTEEN

The city stunk of sorcery and exhaust fumes. Fenris couldn't remember the last time he'd visited. He spat on the sidewalk, trying to get the stench of modern life out of his mouth, receiving a nasty look from an older woman with an armful of shopping bags.

Past the little Korean grocery store with warding symbols on the front window, he craned his neck at the enormous statue of Invictus. *What a preening self-important man.* Fenris had never met the former Head Patron of the Hundred Halls, but he could tell he wouldn't like him. Magic had been better when it had stayed in the shadows. This gross, uncouth display of the arcane made his stomach churn.

"City of Sorcery."

Fenris spat on the concrete again. The air itched with power. He could sense it everywhere.

Except it was being used on trivial things: a kid with a novelty wand, a paper bird flying around the square, or a bright blue bottle of Mage Blast in the hand of a young girl with headphones.

Idiots.

"Hey, watch where you're going."

A middle-aged businessman with a phone to his ear gestured angrily. He'd been in the middle of a heated conversation, but now that he was focused on Fenris, the anger drained from his face until he was as pale as parchment.

Fenris raised a hooked finger and the businessman hurried away, no longer talking on his phone.

"That's better."

On the eastern side of the statue of Invictus, Fenris had a good view of the Spire. It was one of the few things about the city that impressed him. Fenris saw it for what it was: a locus of power. The biggest one the world had ever seen.

But that's not why he'd come. Not why he'd dragged himself across the country, away from his studies and his tomes. No. He'd come because of that disloyal Iona. The girl that he'd raised up from a miserable life. The girl that had been his assistant, sat quietly for the painful tattoos, and kept up his household while he was deep in research.

The girl who was—

The girl who ran.

Fenris checked the address on the crumpled note in his fist. Deborah Grimes. Room 478. The latest keeper of the Tome of Record. He continued northward. The apartment building had a doorman. Fenris pulled out a desiccated claw and spit in the palm as he rubbed the ancient talons. A multicolored hue of spell residue appeared in the air.

He cursed under his breath.

The way was warded and the doorman was covered in protective spells. Not that he couldn't overcome them, but he didn't want to make a scene.

Fenris circled the apartment building, finding no easy ingress. He wracked his brain for a spell that could get him in, but he lacked resources so far from home.

Eventually he settled on a plan. Fenris entered the multi-leveled department store next to the apartment. The perfumes on the first level were worse than the stench of the city. He recoiled away from the ladies with their sprayers, not only because of the overbearing scent, but the layers of magic contained within.

A hunger in his chest woke at the scent. He couldn't tell if it was the defenseless women, or the faez in the air, but he could hear the rumble of awakening, the gnashing of teeth, the frenzied splash of a death spin. Fenris leaned against a glass case until the feeling passed. He couldn't lose his composure here. It would unravel everything.

But without Iona's help, he couldn't keep up with the rituals that would keep the visitor at bay. He stared at the tattoos on his arm that writhed as if they were alive.

To distract himself, Fenris picked up a jar of ointment on the glass case. The Luxe Life. Fenris wanted to smash it on the ground. How sacrilegious it was to use that power for cleaner, smoother skin. The name on the jar read D'Agastine Industries. Fenris remembered a D'Agastine from centuries ago and wondered if it were the same. He applied a spell to the jar that would make the user's skin wither like an old person.

With the hunger passing, Fenris returned to his search. When he couldn't find stairs, he climbed onto the escalators.

The upper floor of the department store was filled with sporting equipment. He found an employee entrance and pushed his way in after disabling the scanner with a spell. The back rooms were offices and storage, where he found a set of stairs that went up to the roof.

The wind whipped his hair around his face. Fenris explored the rooftop until he found which side would lead to the apartment building. The gap was twenty feet. Nothing for a mage like him.

Fenris conjured elemental winds which swirled around his feet like angry clouds. He leapt to the next building, seeing the tiny cars far beneath his boots as he soared over.

The door was locked.

A vial of acid melted away the mechanism, allowing him access to the interior. He found a set of stairs that led to the fourth floor.

The carpet was a grey and black checkerboard pattern which he hated instantly. Room 478 was at the end. He listened to the door to hear the television and a woman talking in a baby voice.

Fenris frowned.

He reached into an inner pocket to produce a piece of carved bone. It'd come from the femur of Catherine the Great. The enchantments layered within made it a formidable focuser.

"Can I help you?"

A voice from down the hall had Fenris shoving the carved bone back into its hiding place and pulling a curved knife instead, keeping it behind him. An older black man with steel gray hair was walking towards him using a cane, his head tilted.

"I'm an old friend of Deborah's."

"Where's your visitor pass?"

Fenris growled inside at his bad luck. He really didn't want to kill another person today. Too many bodies could lead to complications.

"They must have forgotten to give it to me."

The older black man wrinkled his forehead. Fenris sensed his apprehension. A call to the building administrators would greatly complicate his plans.

"If you'd like," said Fenris, using his neutral voice, "I can return downstairs with you to fetch the pass. It won't bother me."

Brown eyes scanned Fenris in a way that was disrespectful. He hated that he couldn't show the man that it was so. It was much easier in the hills of Missouri, where the occasional unexplained death was chalked up to drug use, or suicide.

"No, man. Just grab one on your way out, if you plan on coming back that is."

"Thank you, sir."

The older man limped back the other way, entering a room on the far side of the hallway. The final glance told Fenris that it wouldn't be the last time they'd be seeing each other.

But first Deborah.

The door opened to a subtle spell, bypassing the simple ward. The television was on a rowdy talk show, but Fenris could no longer hear the woman. He crept forward with the focuser in his fist, moving until he was behind the wall next to the living room

The ward on the back of his neck shocked him into action. Fenris threw himself to the right as a slender shape snapped at the place where his head had just been.

A reticulated flying snake.

Fenris splashed elemental magics across the hallway, smashing the airborne serpent against the wall. It crumpled to the ground with its gossamer wings looking like discarded tissue paper. He reached out with his toe to poke the creature, right as the ward on his neck warned him again.

"Zephyr!"

He spun around to find a heavyset woman in a knitted sweater angrily casting a spell. A wave of rolling flame overtook Fenris. The heat singed his eyebrows and the ends of his hair, but his protections let him shrug away the worst of the damage.

A twitch of his wrist stiffened the woman's legs. Deborah careened off the wall, hitting the ground awkwardly.

"My Zephyr," she whined.

The door burst open. The older black gentleman had a handgun in his fist. Before he could get off a shot, Fenris blinded him. The blast went wide, putting a hole through the window.

The older man tried to fire again but Fenris knocked the weapon away with one hand, and with the other, sliced across his neck with the curved dagger. The spurt of blood was followed by a pained gurgle. He fell to his knees and then onto his side with his hands desperately trying to hold back the tide of blood.

Fenris stepped over the dying man and closed the door after checking the hallway was empty. He hoped the daytime visit meant most of the residents were at their jobs, but he would have to be quick in case someone called the police.

"Deborah Grimes. You and I need to have a conversation."

"Why are you doing this? Why did you kill my Zephyr?" she asked as she pulled herself backwards without the use of her legs.

"I need to know a name and Hall from the Tome of Record."

"What? I don't have it with me. The Tome is kept in the Spire behind locked doors, warded and hexed."

She kept glancing to the end table as she scooted on her rear. As she reached out, Fenris kicked her hand away and pulled open the drawer to find a runed-covered blade. He pulled it out and examined the arcane symbols.

"You think this was going to hurt me?"

He placed the sharp edge against his skin and drew the knife across it. A faint white line appeared, but the blade didn't cut.

"Now that we've established who's in charge, you need to tell me a name and Hall from the Tome of Record."

Tears pooled up in Deborah's eyes as she shook her head.

"There are over five thousand names every year. I don't remember the names or the Halls. That's impossible."

"Nothing is impossible."

"I can't. I really can't."

Fenris reached into an inner pocket to grasp something small, hard, and wriggling.

"I can help you, Deborah," he said in a measured voice.

No reason to scare her now. She'd given up. He'd shown her the extent of his power.

A trickle of concern gave him pause.

Iona had once been cowed, too. He'd thought her the good little assistant, doing whatever he asked, even if it meant pain or tedium. She'd been quick too. A diamond in a coal mine.

She wasn't his first assistant. Nor would she be the last. But Iona had shown herself more clever and resilient than he'd given her credit for. Maybe he should have known that with that much potential, she would eventually try to slip her bonds. A lesson for next time. Either he needed new ways of hobbling, or he needed to ensure that his next assistant had none of Iona's rebellious qualities.

"I don't want it," said Deborah, shaking her head emphatically. "Please. Whatever you're going to do, I don't want it."

Fenris put his boot on the woman's chest, pinning her to the floor. The spell had weakened her. She was like a babe.

He unfolded his hand, revealing a glistening black scarab. The legs twitched with excitement.

"No, please, no."

Fenris set the scarab on her belly. The insect scampered up her chest and at the onset of a scream, climbed into her mouth. Her eyes bulged as the scarab entered her brain.

When the thrashing calmed, Fenris took his boot off her chest.

"Tell me, Deborah. Tell me the Hall that Iona Storm joined."

A voice that sounded like it came from a distance responded.

"Coterie of Mages."

Fenris clenched his fist at the name. Any Hall but that one. How she'd managed an invite to the most exclusive Hall in the university was a mystery, but he should have known she would try to join that one given the books he'd acquired over the years. He'd practically dangled the answer before her eyes. A mistake he wouldn't make a second time.

The Obelisk wasn't easy to enter. Nor safe. But he was a patient man. He would find a way to her eventually, or wait outside Coterie for her to emerge like a butterfly out of a chrysalis.

He knelt beside the older man with his throat cut. The metallic scent of his blood had awoken the hunger, but that had been his intent. Without Iona, he couldn't keep it away for long. He would need to feed, and besides, he had a body to dispose of.

Fenris unhinged his jaw.

FOURTEEN

The city felt different the second time. Iona had been in a panicked hurry before, driving the stolen car through the busy streets on the way to the Trials. Now that she had time to enjoy the sights, she was overwhelmed by the busy streets and sidewalks, the shiny buildings and smells of hotdogs, cheap magic, and exhaust fumes.

Coterie was bad enough. Claustrophobic. But the City of Sorcery was overwhelming. Like the first time Fenris had etched a tattoo into her flesh. The heat and pain had been unbearable. The magic of the tattoo had cooked her from inside, making her feel like a lobster in a boiling pot.

Iona checked the directions she'd written on a piece of paper that she'd gotten from the City Library. The pawnshop was one of the few things that felt familiar to her. The grocery store in Licking had been across from one. Ozark Treasures Pawn. She'd watched so many defeated people enter that place.

But what did that make her?

Not defeated.

Biding time.

Preparing. Mystic Exchange looked nothing like the shop in Missouri. The owner wore a tailored suit and had a well-trimmed mustache. The glass cases looked like those in a regular shop, with magical trinkets and other valuable oddities resting in velvet catches.

"Good afternoon, how may I help you?"

Iona had worn the best of her donated clothing and made sure the Coterie pin was prominently displayed on her shirt. She wanted to make a good impression.

"I have something I want to sell."

She hated the sound of her deep Missouri accent, but knew she could never get away with trying to talk like the other students in Coterie.

"May I see it?" he asked as he slipped on thin blue gloves.

Iona handed over the small sculpture of an amorphous head with bulging eyes.

"It was a gift, but I don't really like the style."

She'd stolen it from the Obelisk. It'd been in a little cubby away from the residential areas. She wasn't sure that anyone had seen it in some time, which meant they wouldn't miss it either.

The owner turned the object and examined the bottom before sighing heavily.

"Ma'am. You should really take this to an art auction. This is outside of my usual budget."

"I'm afraid I'm in a bit of a pinch. Are you sure you can't offer me a respectable number? In cash, of course. My sister contracted an awful sewer rot and my parents lost their trinket business because D'Agastine Industries forced them out. I hate to say it, but we're desperate."

Iona feared her story wouldn't hold up. She tried to mimic the sad stories she'd heard in Missouri, but gave it a Coterie twist. Then she saw the greed in the owner's eyes and knew that she'd be okay.

"I'm sure we could work something out."

He wrote a number on a piece of paper and shoved it across the glass.

"Would this do?"

Iona frowned.

"My sister, she's in a bad way. The bills are astronomical. Sir, I know you're going to make a killing. Surely you can do better than this?"

The owner closed his eyes for a moment then smiled big.

"Of course."

He adjusted the number and Iona nodded. A few minutes later, she was walking out of Mystic Exchange with a thick wad of bills in her pocket.

Iona's first stop was Enchanté Couture. She'd heard the other first years talking about the shop and thought it'd be a good place to upgrade her wardrobe. The donated clothes had helped take the worst of the shame away, but she wanted to wear outfits that actually fit.

The sales rep practically fell over herself to help once she saw the Coterie pin. Iona didn't catch her name. She had a strange accent she'd never heard before but the woman was delighted and kept bringing new clothes for her to try on. The price tags were eye-bulging, and would take a chunk out of her wad, but she knew she had to do better to fit in.

The changing room had two mirrors, a chaise lounge, and a tea machine. Iona was stripping down to change into the next outfit when a sharp pain bent her over. The tattoos on her shoulders and back screamed in pain as if they'd been lit on fire. Iona collapsed to her knees and bit the soft fabric of the chair to keep from screaming.

When it was over, she was covered in a patina of sweat and exhausted as if she'd just run a dozen blocks. Iona probed her flesh with her fingers, trying to determine the reason for the sudden pain. Fenris had called them circuits. Had one of them malfunctioned?

A voice from inside the store had her turning her head. Scarlett Calloway. Iona should have known she might show up. She climbed onto the couch in fear that someone might notice that she was in the changing room.

"...she'll be dead before Thanksgiving. Mark my words."

Laughter followed with more conversation that Iona could only partially hear.

"What about Pig Girl?" asked a woman's voice.

More laughter.

"I don't know," said Scarlett. "Have you seen those tattoos? They're kind of badass. Remind me of Kemetic runes in a sexier way. If that poor girl had been born into money, she might actually know how gorgeous she was."

Iona nearly fell off the couch. She probed her face and pulled on her hair while looking into the mirror. She'd always thought her lips were too big, her cheekbones too sharp. Gorgeous wasn't a word that she'd ever thought applied to her, especially how she felt inside, like a gooey blob of feelings that never knew what they were supposed to be.

"It doesn't matter how hot she is, she definitely won't survive the year," said another girl.

"I wouldn't bet on it," said Scarlett. "I got a copy of her scholarship video. It was impressive. Like really impressive. You'd have thought she'd gone to St. Jude's or Arcanis. And then she smoked the first Trial. If she could find a mentor, an upperclassman or one of the professors, she might be able to make a go of it."

"You really think?"

"Weirder things have happened. You were a freckled-faced twig when we were in high school, Ambrosia, and now you look like you had enchantments, but in a good way."

The clothing attendant interrupted their conversation and for the next twenty minutes, Iona sat on her couch and listened to Scarlett and her friends talk clothes. Eventually they got bored and left to have mimosas for brunch.

Iona hauled the things she wanted to buy to the front desk.

"I thought you might have fallen asleep in there," said the woman as her gaze flickered to the Coterie pin. "But then I remembered which Hall Scarlett was from."

"Thanks for not outing me."

The woman leaned forward.

"Is it really as bad as the rumors? If you can tell me. I don't mean to pry."

Iona couldn't help but smile. She had no idea what kind of rumors she was talking about, but it felt good that she thought she should know.

"Worse. Much worse."

"Oh my." She checked back to the front. "I can see why you stayed hidden then."

Iona paid for the outfits she'd picked out. The number didn't feel real. The attendant gave her a hug afterwards and her card, which all felt weird, but Iona supposed that rich people led a different life than normals. Especially those with magic.

When she was on the sidewalk with bags in her hand, Iona remembered the tattoo pain that she'd suffered in the changing room. She felt exposed. She checked over her shoulder, but saw no one familiar on the crowded sidewalk.

But she couldn't shake the feeling that she shouldn't be there. That Fenris had found his way to the city and was trying to find her.

She wouldn't put it past him to have etched a way to track her down in the tattoos, which made her vulnerable in public. She'd planned on making a few more purchases, but now she just wanted to get back to the Obelisk.

Iona looked for a taxi, but there were none in view.

The train station was a block away. Iona hurried with the bags in her hand, pushing past people who cursed her on the way. But she didn't care.

The feeling of doom followed her to the station. Iona stood on the platform, willing the train to arrive. She kept checking over her shoulder.

"Come on. Come on."

A trickle of relief crawled in the moment she saw the approaching train. Once she was on it, she was certain she could get back to the Obelisk safely. Fenris couldn't get her there.

As she readied herself, a tap on the shoulder had her freezing in place. Iona turned slowly, the pit in her stomach growing cavernous.

"You dropped this."

A kid a few years her junior was holding out a crumpled piece of paper.

"Oh, thanks."

She shoved it back in her pocket as the train arrived. Iona took a spot in the corner where she could see everyone around her. No sign of Fenris, but she feared he was near. The tattoos hummed with ache.

The trip to Coterie wasn't long since she was still in the fourth ward. As soon as she stepped off the platform, she ran the rest of the way to the Obelisk. She knew how strange it looked for a young woman dressed in finer clothes to be running down the sidewalk with couture bags in hand, but she didn't care. Better to look foolish than to be dead.

The last hundred meters, Iona felt a trickle in her back tattoos. Like a ghostly hand brushing against her flesh. Iona kept running, hurriedly giving the password before throwing herself through the front doors.

FIFTEEN

A sign on the gym door read No Magic. Zuri frowned at the suggestion as she reached into her workout bag and toggled a button on her phone, before pushing through the doors in her sleek formfitting attire. If the professors thought that sign would keep the students from trying to kill each other in the Hall gym, they were sorely mistaken.

It was a little after four am and there was only one other person in attendance. Blake was on the bench press pushing a healthy amount of weight.

The bar clanked on the catches and he sat up, using a towel to wipe his face. The hint of a smile formed on the corner of his lips when he saw her. She hated how charming it was, and how she couldn't help but smile back. A reminder of old times.

"If you think you're going to catch me by surprise, I knew you were coming long before you entered the gym."

Zuri threw her workout bag on the mat.

"I'm not here for you. I need to get a good sweat in."

"Ballsy of you to show up. How do you know I don't have an ambush planned?"

Zuri shook out her legs and stood in a forward stretching position.

"We don't need to do this."

He wrinkled his forehead.

"Do what?"

"Fight."

"You can't back down now. You were the one that testified against me. You broke my trust. You broke everybody's trust. They won't forget it. And neither will I."

"What did you expect? You killed my best friend."

"I did no such thing. She was a reckless fool, attempting a ritual like that. Gemma let her mouth outrun her ability. It was what she always did. Fuck things up."

Zuri took a step off the mat as heat rose to her cheeks. He was baiting her, but so was she. Zuri just needed him to admit that he'd killed Gemma, which would be caught on the phone in her bag. Not for the trial, that was long over, but to give her a chance to find allies. As long as they thought he was untouchable, he had the advantage. She needed to take him down in the best way she thought possible.

"You sabotaged the ritual. I saw you messing with the salt. You goaded her into it. You two were always bickering."

"If she couldn't handle summoning a post-invasion infernal imp, she had no business thinking she'd be in Coterie. Face it, Zuri, your friend was a screwup. She was jealous because I had turned her down when we were in middle school and she never forgot it."

"You'd like to think you had that much influence."

He cocked a grin as he rose and sauntered to her location. She mentally readied a spell, but didn't move, because she didn't want to give away how nervous she was. Blake leaned against the squat machine.

"You know I do, babe."

"Don't call me babe."

"You used to like it when I did."

"I used to like a lot of things until I learned you were a psychopath."

Blake stretched his arm across the machine.

"You know you can't beat me. I have every advantage. If you leave Coterie today, I'll forgive you. But if you stay, all bets are off."

"I'm not leaving."

"One way or another you are. I know you think you're hot shit, but you're never going to find a single ally and you're never going to get to the second level. It'd be a blessing if you died in Coterie."

Zuri hated the way he could get under her skin. She wanted to scream. To rage. To throw a barbell at him. The way he leaned against the machine, smug and so sure of himself, it was infuriating.

As Blake turned, Zuri saw her chance slipping away. She couldn't kill him outright. She wasn't a monster. Not like him. But she needed to kill him in the best way she knew, destroying his reputation.

"I know you tried to kiss Gemma."

The hitch in his gait told her she had a chance.

"And not in middle school. Junior year. Three months before she died. She never said anything, but I knew. I knew something had changed. You tried because you thought she would be honored by your attentions, not disgusted like I should have been. You couldn't take that someone wouldn't want you. That she saw you as you truly were, a monster."

Blake slowly turned around.

"We're all monsters in the dark. It's just some of us aren't trying to deny the truth."

"Then you did kill her."

His lips curled with anger.

"She killed herself by not seeing how the game was played. If she would have complied, I might have been more attentive that day. I might have seen that she had a bad batch of summoning salt, that the ritual was flawed and that she was doomed to die. Instead, she was a real bitch about everything. Always correcting me. Always wanting to prove that I was wrong. She'd always been mouthy, but after that she really couldn't hold back."

"I would see you burn in hell if there was one."

He scoffed.

"Don't you know, babe? We *are* in hell. You just don't know it yet."

"I hate you."

"That's not true at all. You still love me. I can see it in your eyes. What you're mad about is that you no longer have the life you wanted. That's what you're mad about. Not Gemma. Not the trial. Not any of that bullshit. You're as shallow as the rest of us, battling for your little slice of the good life. You want to believe you're a good person. That you stood up for Gemma because it was the right thing to do. But I know you. I know you did that because you thought it would put me in my place, that you'd be revered as the Girl Who Spoke Up. The one who defended her best friend from the evil boy who killed her by ruining her summoning salt. But what you didn't realize is nobody cares. That's the thing I learned long ago. They all want their piece of the pie. They'll do anything to get it, even if it means killing a rival. Or a friend. Or a former girlfriend.

"When you testified against me, you were really testifying against them. You told everyone you no longer had their backs. That's the thing. You can knife them. You can lie, cheat, and steal. You can even kill them. But you can never expose them. You can never rock the system that keeps them in power. Once you did that, you made yourself expendable. Face it, babe, I'm not going to kill you because I want to. I'm going to do it because they expect me to. For the same reason I killed Gemma when I switched out her salt. She was making me look bad. And if I hadn't, everyone would have seen me as weak. Face it, babe. It's either you or me. And I have no intention of dying in this place."

A single tear formed and broke free from her cheek. Zuri hated how it made her look. She thumbed the tear away as she ground her teeth.

"I hate you. You're a monster."

"You don't hate me. You hate that the only way you can survive is if you become like me. The person you know you are deep down inside. That's why you're so mad. You knew something was wrong between me and Gemma. You could have broken it off. Saved her from me. But you wanted it all. You wanted to be the center of attention *and* feel like a good person. Face it, Zuri. You're at fault as much as I am."

Blake turned to leave, but slowed and spoke over his shoulder as he gestured towards her gym bag.

"And I know you're recording me. I know you want to expose me as Gemma's killer. Feel free to if you want, but it's not going to work out the way you think it will. That recording will only prove to people that you don't have the guts to take me down yourself. That you expect them to do it for you, but that's never going to happen. Especially not in the Obelisk. You might as well cut your own throat if you play that."

Before she knew it, Blake was gone, leaving her stewing in her own regrets. What she hated most was that he was right. She'd thought that if she could prove he'd killed Gemma that his teammates would turn their backs on him. But it would only pull them closer to him, because not only had he killed her, but he'd gotten away with it.

Zuri marched over to her gym bag, pulled out the phone, and erased the recording. Blake was right about one thing. She couldn't expect anyone else to do her dirty work for her. If she was going to survive—no, not survive, but thrive—then she needed to embrace the darkness.

SIXTEEN

The doorway to Professor Cornwallis' office might as well have been a wall as far as Iona was concerned. She raised her hand twice before letting it fall by her side.

Iona checked her surroundings. This was as safe as she'd ever be. It's not that the administration area was off-limits, but catching a professor in crossfire was akin to suicide. But that didn't help with her distrust of doors. Twice this year she'd found the entrance to her suite trapped with a voidbound tangler. The first time she had no idea how to disable it and slept in the library until she found a solution.

This is a mistake.

As she turned her heel, a crisp voice from the other side called out.

"Whoever you are outside my door, you'd either better leave or come in, otherwise I'm going to put a very painful curse on your bones."

Iona pushed through the door.

"I'm sorry, Professor Cornwallis, I was gathering my thoughts."

She'd never been in the professor's office before and couldn't help but gawk at the pictures and other displays on the wall. A huge map of the world marked with the countries that had once been a part of the English Empire took up the central space while another section showed the professor with various members of the royal family.

"Why are you here?" asked Professor Cornwallis, sitting back in her chair, inexplicably with a riding crop in her hand.

Iona had a good idea that question wasn't about the visit to her office.

"I enjoy studying magic."

"I enjoy my rose garden, but if I were in charge they would likely wither and die. That job is more suited for my gardener. They've spent their entire life clipping leaves and digging in the dirt. The same is true the other way around. I would never ask their opinion on a matter of magic. They might have read a few books about the subject, but they would be a fool to open their mouth and call themselves a mage."

"I've spent my entire life studying magic."

The professor smoothed her hand across her immaculate desk while her smile reeked of condescension.

"My dear, I'm sure you think you've expended a lot of effort on this matter, but the problem is you didn't have the right upbringing. The right teachers. You're standing well behind the starting line while the others are already halfway to the goal. This is cruelty allowing you to be here. It's only going to end in tragedy."

Iona stepped forward, which received an eyebrow raise.

"That's why I need a mentor. A guiding hand. To teach me the things that I don't understand. I know I can do serious magic. Advanced Kemetic magic, even. Ask Professor Green or Ravenscroft. I cast spells for both of them no one else in my class could manage. I just need the gaps filled in. I swear to you, you won't regret it. I know I can be a valuable member of Coterie and you're the best professor to help me do it."

Professor Cornwallis leaned back in her chair with a slight smile. Amusement. Iona could feel the hook in her gut even before the woman spoke.

"You're right about one thing. I *am* the only professor who would have a chance to turn you into a passable mage. The kind that would do quite well at Arcanium, or one of the other Halls."

She slapped the riding crop into her other hand.

"But this is Coterie of Mages. We have a legacy, a tradition to uphold. Our students have already had many years of preparatory school to ready them for the unique challenges our Hall presents. You might as well be asking me to teach a monkey to tap dance."

"Professor Cornwallis. If you would just talk to Professors Green or Ravenscroft then you would understand that I know a lot of magic, that I—"

"Know a lot of magic? Is that how you speak? As for Professors Green and Ravenscroft, they're hardly the paragons of arcane scholarship. Gideon is far too enamored of what you students think of him to provide the proper leadership this Hall needs, while Horace… I don't even know where to begin. It's like he just showed up one day. I know he's a friend of our Head Patron, but had Malden consulted me, I would have strongly advised him not to allow Horace to teach in this Hall."

The air chilled between them. Iona averted her eyes.

"I'm sorry, Professor, for wasting your time. I will try to find another professor to be my mentor."

A fist banging on the table startled Iona. It surprised and angered her, even in the face of the professor's disdain.

"My dear, you're not wasting my time. You're wasting this Hall's time. Under no circumstances should you be seeking a mentor from the professors of this great Hall. What you should be doing is taking whatever weird clothes you wore here and marching right out the front of the Obelisk. While I cannot make you leave, I can certainly advise some of your fellow first years in ways that may prove detrimental to your continued health should you decide to seek mentorship within the rest of the Coterie staff. Do I make myself clear?"

Iona imagined holding a knife that was buried in the professor's chest, ready to split her guts open, much as she did to the rabbits caught in her snares.

"Yes."

"Yes, what?" asked Professor Cornwallis as she sat tall and glared across the desk with the heat of a thousand suns.

"Yes, Professor Cornwallis."

"Good. It seems a monkey, or a pig in this case, can be taught. Now remove yourself from my sight before I take your life personally in my hands."

Iona hurried from the room, cringing when she shut the door too hard, then ran directly down the hallway to get as far away from Professor Cornwallis' office—and her own thoughts—as possible.

Once she was out of the administrative area, Iona leaned against one of the many alumni statues that graced the Obelisk. Rubert Tallywag, or some pretentious asshole that had graced the halls of Coterie decades ago.

"Are you okay?"

The appearance of another student startled Iona. She raised her hands defensively until she saw who it was.

"Hey, Justine. Yeah, I'm fine. Stretching my legs. Don't get a lot of exercise sitting in class or studying tomes."

Justine had a lumpy backpack on. She wasn't carrying books, that much was for sure. Iona checked her potential escape routes without giving away her distrust.

"Did you live on a big farm back in...Iowa, was it?"

"Missouri. And no, we didn't have pigs. That's not pig country."

"Oh, I'm sorry. I didn't mean to imply that," said Justine as she smoothed away a strand of brown hair that had fallen into her face.

If Iona didn't know better, she would have thought that Justine's expression was sympathetic. A rare sight in the Obelisk.

"Are you getting along well? Here in Coterie that is," said Justine.

"I, well, it's been a bit of a culture shock. Everyone already knows each other and you talk about stuff I don't have a lick of understanding, but the magical scholarship, I've been enjoying that."

"I think it's terrific that we have new blood in Coterie. The old guard can be rather stuffy."

Iona glanced in the direction of the administration area.

"You ain't kidding about that."

"Why would I be?" asked Justine earnestly.

"I'm sorry to bother you, Justine. I should get back to my room."

"Have you found the test yet?"

"The test?" asked Iona, turning back.

"To get to the second level."

Iona forced a grin.

"It's kinda hard to without a group. Not that I haven't looked, but you know, it's not safe."

Justine checked over her shoulder before speaking in a low voice.

"You should seek death. Only in death can we understand change."

Their parting left Iona with the feeling she understood less about her Hall than she did before. Had Justine been trying to help her? Was that a clue to the location of the level two test? Or was that a veiled threat? Iona didn't think so. It left her with the feeling that despite the dressing down from Professor Cornwallis and the pranks thrown her way, maybe there was a place for her in Coterie. She just needed to keep her eyes open for allies.

SEVENTEEN

Professor Ilsa Kingsley was Zuri's favorite by a large margin and it wasn't just because she taught wards, which was her best skill, nor was it because it appeared that the professor was the only one of the staff who actually cared about her students. Those were all well and good, but the biggest reason Zuri loved Kingsley's classes was because the professor made magic sexy and fun.

"As you can see, if I combine powdered devil's snare with a bit of amethyst dust, applying liberal amounts of raw faez during the mixing process, and then add dried manticore blood right before phase change, you'll see an exothermic reaction."

The professor stepped back the moment she dumped the contents of the beaker into the reinforced bin. An explosion of light and heat rose into the air with a miniature mushroom cloud which quickly dissipated into a bluish-green mist.

Professor Kingsley beamed at the class from behind the alchemy desk. The dark, salacious curls that framed her cherubic face made her look barely older than the students even though everyone knew she'd been teaching at Coterie for nearly thirty years. She was, by and far, the professor that the students lusted after most. Nandi had told her about a student in her class that had gotten drunk on harem elixir and glued himself naked to her office door, which had resulted in a lot of missing skin when they'd finally peeled him off. It didn't help that she dressed in librarian chic with stylish black eye frames and a formfitting skirt that showed off her curves.

Professor Kingsley grabbed a steel glove and picked up the pan, tilting it for the class to see, while everyone leaned forward at their alchemy stations.

"There you have it. A superior runic ward ink, which will increase the potency of your protective spells by at least fifteen to twenty percent. That amount could be increased to thirty percent with powdered mystdrakon bone, but given the scarcity of that reagent, you're best to stick with the manticore blood."

The class applauded. Professor Kingsley bent her knees slightly before winking.

"That's it for today's class. I hope you enjoyed it. Next week's topic will be about various techniques to help you reduce the maintenance of your wards and enchantments. One of the biggest failures of defensive magic is that they're a heavy tax on the caster. Squeezing out even a bit more efficiency from your wards can often be the difference between life and death."

Her ruby-red lips bunched into a smile.

"If you're planning on attending, I recommend bringing a myxion matrix to help with the ward knitting. They can be expensive, but there's no point in saving money if you're dead. Class dismissed."

Zuri had been sitting in the front of class, but somehow the Siren

Sisters managed to beat her to Kingsley's desk. They asked the professor about an easily researched question, which signaled to Zuri that they were merely setting the stage for a bigger ask later on. While there were no grades to manage, getting close with a professor was a good way to squeeze extra advantages out of Coterie.

Behind her, the students that hadn't left were chatting about the upcoming Halloween party. The theme was the Infernal Invasion. Zuri had already planned to go as her sister since she'd had a major role in the defense of the city. She knew some would criticize her choice, but she wanted to remind people she came from noble blood.

"Miss Musa, how can I help you?" asked the professor as she grinned and shook her head. "I should just call you by your first name, Zuri. I can't help but think of your sister when I say it the other way. She was one of my favorite students."

"And you were her favorite professor."

The professor raised an eyebrow, barely containing a smirk.

"Then why did she choose demonology with Professor Sinclair as her focus of study?"

"We have very pushy parents. At the time, demonology was the hot subject. Our parents are very proud of Nandi."

"We all are. We owe a debt to your sister."

"Not that," laughed Zuri. "They're proud of the foundation she got in. To them, a killer salary with perks is much better than being an unpaid hero. They still gripe about how many family resources she blew in defense of the city."

"That must be difficult following in her footsteps," said Professor Kingsley.

"If that were my only concern, I'd be a lucky girl."

The professor's eyes creased.

"Yes, of course. I almost forgot. Was there something I could help you with?"

"There's a passage in *The Ward Weaver's Grimoire* that talks about how protection magics are mathematically inferior to offensive magic. That no matter how hard you try to defend yourself, you're at the mercy of the infinite possibilities of attack. But then you state through proper overlapping and other techniques that you can close that gap."

"Is there a question, Zuri?"

"I'm sorry. I'm getting to it. So I was doing the math on le Fay's paradox using your theory, and no matter how I massage the numbers, I can't get them to equal out. Not even close."

Professor Kingsley chuckled.

"You are aware that the Grimoire was my graduation thesis?"

"Of course, Professor. I'm not suggesting that it's incorrect, but I can't figure out what I'm doing wrong."

"You know, you're the first student to ever try to confirm the math."

"I am?"

"Wards have never been an exciting subject of study. As you just stated, the best defense can't beat a good offense, but not for the reasons you think. They're opposite sides of the same coin."

"Does that have to do with le Fay's paradox?"

Professor Kingsley tilted her head.

"Sometimes too much theory is a bad thing and the answer is right before our eyes. Now I must excuse myself, Miss Musa, I mean Zuri. I have a dinner date tonight and it's going to take me *hours* to get ready."

Zuri chuckled to herself after the professor left. If she'd shown up as is, she'd cause ninety-nine percent of the human population to lose their minds.

Leaving the alchemy laboratory, Zuri took a roundabout way back to the student quarters so no one could ambush her, but the way was unfamiliar as it seemed the route had changed. They'd been warned that the Obelisk could shift or rework itself to open up old passages, or create entirely new ones.

Once Zuri realized this, she took a more cautious approach to the exploration. An older section might contain leftover magics, or creatures that had gotten trapped when the Obelisk shifted. But this was an opportunity too.

In a lighted alcove that would have looked appropriate in a museum, Zuri found a painting titled *Drum Death Darkness.* The imagery was disturbing and the painter was unknown as far as she remembered from her studies. It showed a grim battlefield full of the aftereffects of potent sorcery. Bodies had been blown to pieces, with bloody rib cages and severed arms lying in the mud. Others had been turned to slime or char. She'd only seen the painting in a book, and that had been disturbing enough. The author had suggested that it'd been painted as a warning to the effects of magic on war, but now that she'd seen it in person, she wasn't so sure about that because at the back left of the painting, standing on a hill, was a figure in bloody gray robes preparing another volley of ball lightning at an enemy that was suggested to be off the frame. The mage was triumphant in their gestures and the litter of bodies around them appeared more as a warning about the potency of mages rather than the horrors of war. Zuri could only think of Professor Kingsley's words about a good offense.

Further into the unexplored area, Zuri found a symbol etched into the wall with what appeared to be gold. She checked behind her, because it was similar to the topic that she'd just discussed with Professor Kingsley. Had the Obelisk been listening? Was that even possible?

She knew from her sister's stories that the home of Coterie could be capricious and cruel, but also provide unexpected gifts. Zuri didn't think the Obelisk was alive as some of her fellow students suggested, but advanced magics operated in ways that were unfathomable to the uninitiated.

As she studied the symbol, Zuri realized it was incomplete. Like an almost-finished Sudoku puzzle, it was waiting for the last pieces to be filled in.

She dug through her carryall to find a fresh purple paint marker, but hesitated to use it in case the material was as important as the design. Using three different analytical spells—two were in Sumerian while the third was in a language that had been made up by monks in the fifth century—Zuri managed to decipher the purpose of the gold.

The transmutation of ordinary objects into valuable metals was impossible, but a rough approximation was often enough to satisfy the spell's requirements. Zuri applied a calcifier to the tip of her marker, which transformed the paint before she filled in the rest of the symbol, completing the hidden circuit in the design.

A rumbling in the floor had Zuri jumping back, expecting a trap or the release of a dangerous critter. Deadra had nearly lost her arm when a crystalline spider had jumped out of an old rubbish bin she'd found in a new area. The spiders were only as big as her hand, but were hardened against magic and took blunt force to destroy. The story was that a student many years ago had smuggled one in as a way to take down an enemy, not realizing it was covered in egg sacks. He kept the spider in a cage, but then the hatchlings escaped while he was asleep and he woke in a cocoon of crystalline silk while the babies sucked the magic from his mind until he was a brainless husk.

Nothing came from the darkness exposed by the shifting wall. A passage led deeper into the unexplored section, which filled Zuri with nervous excitement. If she found an old lab or power nexus, she might be able to convince Melanie or one of the other new magics that the find was worth the attention from Blake.

Zuri sent a floating mage light into the space, scanning for potential dangers at the same time as her mind raced with possibilities. If the rumors were true, she'd heard that the Siren Sisters had found an old alchemy lab that had been left with numerous half-finished projects. No one could figure if it'd been left by former students or was a creation of the Obelisk, but the find had convinced Tristan Hollow to switch to their group.

After she revealed there were no lingering magics, Zuri cautiously stepped into the space. Two steps past the entrance, the door slammed shut behind her.

Zuri banged on the door as her heart bounced around her chest. She feared she was trapped until she noticed the round button on the inner frame. Using the meat of her palm, she depressed it. The hidden door slid open.

Content that she could leave when she wanted, Zuri triggered the door to close and continued her exploration. The floating mage light suggested that the passage was a dead end about three meters from her location.

The walls were cold stone and covered in sloppy writing that she recognized as an older form of Kemetic that she could only half translate.

"What is this?"

Zuri ran her fingers across the words as she deciphered their meaning. Kemetic was not her strongest language. Not only was it notoriously difficult to master, but there were numerous offshoots which were different enough to almost make them their own language.

The words didn't feel magical either. Zuri couldn't quite figure out what they were intending until she saw the sketch at the lower right-hand corner. The protruding member was unmistakable and gave her the context to complete the message. The entire thing reminded her of wandering off the main subway lines in London and finding gang tags spray-painted on old concrete barriers set up for construction.

"It's graffiti," she said, shaking her head. "The Siren Sisters get an old lab filled with half-finished magics, and I find a place that someone thought was good for casual sex."

Zuri finished her examination of the space, but could find no other messages or designs that suggested it was anything other than old graffiti—ancient graffiti if her linguistics analysis was correct.

Which didn't make sense to Zuri. It felt the same as the gang tags in the London subway, but the Obelisk had been built a century ago, not millennia like the writings suggested. But the Obelisk was filled with mysteries. As Professor Ravenscroft had said, it would take many lifetimes to uncover all of the mysteries that existed in the Obelisk.

Disappointed that she'd found nothing useful, Zuri closed up the hidden chamber and continued through the passages until she found herself back in familiar territory.

EIGHTEEN

The library was the least popular area in the Obelisk. Coterie's hatred of Arcanium Hall had made it anathema for the students. It wasn't that they didn't like books, or magical tomes—every student had their own private collection brought from home—but the idea of putting them together in a common, public area turned them into communism or something like it for Coterie students.

This made the library a good place to hide out for Iona since it was rarely frequented by the other students. She was sick of having to check her door for traps, or dangerous critters. The week before, a gloomrend had been left in the rock garden outside her room. She hadn't noticed the puffy ball of shadow with glinting claws that was floating across the white rocks until Orion had called out from across the garden. The warning had given her enough time to destroy the gloomrend with a simple force bolt. Orion left before she had a chance to thank him.

Nestled into a comfy couch—which she was sure had to have been brought in by a student because everything in the Obelisk was made for stiff backs—Iona was reading a tome on the Veil. *The Imprints of Our Lives.* It'd been a suggestion from Professor Green when she'd admitted to him after class that she wasn't very knowledgeable about the land between the living and the dead.

The book was dry. A lot of theory about how the Veil wasn't really dead people, but the faded imprints of their lives, captured by the Queen of the Dead for whatever nefarious purposes she intended. Ghosts, apparitions, and the like could still be dangerous as they tried to complete some missing piece of themselves in the real world, but they were not alive.

Iona was deep into a passage about cursed items related to the Veil when she heard the soft scuff of footsteps. She looked up to see a shock of red hair coming around the stacks.

"Oh," said Scarlett.

She was wearing a sleek black–and-crimson outfit that Iona assumed was trendy. It looked like something she'd wear out to a private club, complete with three-inch heels. "I wasn't expecting to find you here."

The urge to flee took hold. Iona closed her book and started reaching for her backpack when Scarlett held out her hand.

"You don't have to leave on my account. I was just looking for a specific title that I swore I had brought, but I guess I left it at home in our private library."

"Private library?"

Scarlett screwed up her face.

"Don't you have one?"

Iona started to say no, but then she remembered Fenris' collection of tomes, which wasn't huge, but after a few months in Coterie, she gathered it was filled with rare and very difficult to find arcana.

"I guess I did."

Iona squeezed the tome to her chest like a shield. Scarlett was looking at her in a way that reminded her of an old woman picking out good fruit at the grocery store.

"You know, I've been wondering," began Scarlett, "where did you get those fabulous tattoos?"

Iona held out her forearms, revealing the two lines of ancient text that Fenris had etched into her skin. She'd never been able to find a translation for them. They were a language she'd never encountered, though sometimes she thought they might be some strange deviation of Kemetic.

"My teacher gave them to me."

"So they *are* magical."

Iona tried to hide her grimace. She hated that she'd given a piece of information away.

"He never told me what they were for."

"What does your teacher think of you joining the Halls?"

Iona wanted to leave, but Scarlett was blocking the little cubby.

"He doesn't know."

"How is that even possible? Oh wait, he's not a Hall mage, is he?"

Iona hated how quickly Scarlett deduced that fact.

"It's okay, Iona," continued Scarlett. "When you travel in the circles we travel in, you'll find a lot of people that found their patronage outside the Hall system. Look at the Dreadmarshes. They were mages for centuries before Invictus came along. Rumors of comingling with infernal beings has followed them for as long as the family has been around. "

"They have?"

Scarlett let her tongue rest on the top of her red lips.

"You know, sometimes I think you're like a long-lost relative to one of the old magic families."

"I really doubt that."

She shrugged.

"Maybe, but you never know. I've seen the kinds of magic you can do. And those tattoos. That's not new magic shit. That's the kind of hard arcana that was practiced in secret."

"Really?" asked Iona, letting the tome fall from her chest into her lap. She was suspicious of Scarlett, but also intrigued.

"Really."

Feeling like she needed to return a compliment, Iona blurted out, "I really like your outfit."

Scarlett chewed on her lower lip.

"This old thing? You never know when things will go sideways here, so I try not to wear too many fresh outfits. I definitely brought too many clothes with me. I've been desperate to get rid of the excess."

A realization hit Iona like a board to the forehead. Scarlett reacted by checking behind her.

"What? Is there something creeping up on me?"

"No, I just realized we're the same size."

"We are."

"You gave me those clothes, didn't you?"

Scarlett blinked before a smile widened on her lips.

"I did, didn't I?"

"Thank you. I've been able to find some of my own since, but wearing the clothes that I came to Coterie in wasn't exactly making me a favorite around here."

Scarlett leaned against the shelves as if they were old friends.

"You shouldn't worry too much about all that Pig Girl stuff. They're just testing you. Finding out what you're made of. It's a cutthroat business being in Coterie. You have to develop thick skin and even thicker wards."

"It has gotten better these last few weeks."

Scarlett reached out with the toe of her high heels and nudged her leg.

"You have good fashion sense. I like what you've done, since you know, I helped you out."

"Thanks. I'll admit that mostly I listened to what the attendant said at Enchanté Couture."

"You have got to be kidding me. That's my favorite store! I got this outfit there. No wonder I like your fit."

"My fit?"

"Your style. Wow, you really are out of things. What did you do in Montana?"

"Missouri. I really didn't have much free time. I was always cleaning the equipment in the alchemy lab, or preparing for a new ritual. If I had free time, I usually studied the tomes."

"That's right. You know some wicked spells. I heard what you did in Professor Green's class. No wonder you aced the first Trial. What was your specialty?"

"My specialty?"

"Yeah, you know, were you wards, curses, hexes, demonology, faezology, whatever?"

"My teacher had very esoteric tastes. Which is why I've struggled at times. I have a lot of gaps in my magical knowledge." She caught Scarlett frowning. "But if I had to say, it would be advanced Kemetic magics."

Iona told herself to shut up, that Scarlett was the enemy and she was giving her free information, but she hadn't realized how desperate she was for human interaction. And Scarlett didn't seem as bad as she first thought. While she was part of Blake's old magic group, she didn't seem like the rest of them. It helped that Iona had overheard Scarlett in Enchanté Couture, which confirmed that she was being honest in her communication.

"Advanced Kemetic. That's the hardest subject in Coterie by far. You should try to get Professor Ravenscroft for a mentor. I'm sure he'd love to have a student already versed in the more difficult aspects."

The warning from Professor Cornwallis about not seeking other mentors rung in her ears.

"I'm not exactly any professor's favorite."

Scarlett clucked her tongue and looked away for a moment. She was either making a show of thinking, or had just thought of something important.

"Have you found the second level test yet?"

"Not yet."

"Blake would kill me for talking about this, but part of the test has to do with Kemetic magic. We have, like, no one in our group that has that background. Not that we're not trying to learn, but it's really frustrating. The syntax doesn't make any sense."

"Are you asking me to look at it for your group?"

Scarlett plopped down on the chair next to Iona and bumped into her gently.

"No, silly. I'm asking if you want to *join* our group. You'd fill in the missing piece for us. We'd be unstoppable."

Iona swallowed as she felt a little dizzy. And then a little angry.

"There's no way they'd accept me."

Scarlett sighed heavily.

"You're partially right. There will be some pushback. But I think this is the right move. And I know this sounds a little crazy, but I like you. I get it. You don't have the same upbringing as any of us, but you're brave and talented. You know who the last person was to get into Coterie without the kind of schooling and family the rest of us have?"

"No."

"Head Patron Pythia Silverthorne."

"Really? I just assumed she was new magic or something."

"Nope. An orphan, if you can believe that."

"I'm an orphan."

"See," said Scarlett, poking her playfully. "Maybe you're the next

Head Patron."

"Come on," said Iona.

"Okay, that one is a bit far-fetched, but I really think you could be great for our group."

A kernel of hope blossomed in Iona's chest. She didn't want it to be there, but Scarlett's beaming smile was like oxygen to the flame. It burned and brightened until Iona was matching the other girl's grin.

"We'll have to convince Blake though. He can be a bit of a stuffy asshole at times, but he'll come around. Especially when you show them what you can do."

"I guess."

Scarlett shook her mane of gorgeous red hair.

"Not a guess. I know people. That's what I'm good at. And I know you're going to kick ass."

"How?"

Scarlett reached out and grabbed Iona's hands. Her first instinct was to flinch away, but she didn't want to insult her, so Iona kept calm.

"There's this secret place we found that we think might help with the level two problem. It has to do with advanced Kemetic magics. If you could solve it for us, then they'd have no choice but to let you into the group."

"I'm not sure..."

"Please," said Scarlett, squeezing her hands like they were old friends. "I want us to be friends. I think this will be good for all of us. You're a diamond in the rough. You just need a little polish."

Every fiber of her being was screaming no, but logically, Iona knew that she'd never reach the second level on her own. She lacked too much knowledge and it was never safe enough for her to explore the Obelisk on her own. She stuck to a few locations she'd learned, and nothing else.

"Okay."

Scarlett squealed and threw her arms around Iona's shoulders.

"You won't regret this. I can't wait."

"What do I do?"

"Do you know where the pool with the Cthulhu jellies is? Past the statue of Grendel Blunderbuss."

"I think so," lied Iona.

"Meet us there at midnight."

"Do I need to bring anything?"

"Whatever you think is prudent," said Scarlett as she rose. "I can't wait for you to show them what you can do. This is gonna be great. Oh, and wear a top that shows off your tattoos."

"Yeah. Great..."

Scarlett checked her watch.

"I have to go. Meeting Deadra for brunch in the city." She winked. "See you tonight!"

After Scarlett was gone, Iona slumped on the chair filled with regrets. How was she going to solve this mysterious Kemetic problem? Sure, she knew some advanced Kemetic magics, but none of it seemed relevant to the challenges the first years faced. It felt like she knew calculus while the class was working on algebra.

But if she could solve the problem for them then she'd be in with the best group in the Obelisk. It would fix everything that had gone wrong since she'd gotten to Coterie and set her up for continued success.

Iona slammed the book shut. Veil magic was all well and good, but she needed to brush up on anything related to Kemetic magics before midnight.

NINETEEN

Iona felt naked without sleeves. The top had a weird tiger on the front and had been something she'd picked out to wear in the privacy of her suite. She reviewed herself in the mirror, turning back and forth to examine the tattoos. The ones on her shoulders looked like falcon heads with more of the dead language written along the edges. Maybe one of Scarlett's group could tell her what they meant.

Leaving her suite took more will than she thought it should. On one hand, she didn't quite trust the old magic group to give her an honest chance at joining them, but on the other, she desperately needed to find allies or she'd never get to stay in the Obelisk. And if she couldn't stay, then she'd be an easy target for Fenris.

Finding the fountain took longer than expected and when she arrived, the group of old magic students were talking about her.

"—she's not going to show up. Why'd you think this was a good idea,

Scarlett?"

Iona scuffed her foot. They spun on her. Seven sets of eyes bored into her like daggers until Scarlett broke free, throwing her arms around Iona.

"I'm so glad you came!"

"I got lost on the way here."

Scarlett hooked her arm.

"Everyone, this is Iona Storm. Iona, this is everyone."

Iona raised her hand to wave but it never made it past her waist.

"Hi."

"Do you need introductions?"

"I know who everyone is."

Blake didn't seem pleased about her presence. He was staring as if he was deciding how he might kill her, which made Iona want to shrink into herself, but she kept her chin up, refusing to let them intimidate her. She'd survived worse with Fenris. Surely this wouldn't be as bad.

"Whoa. Those tattoos are killer," said Jakob in a thick German accent.

Suddenly, she was surrounded as everyone examined her tattoos, making noises of amazement.

"What do they do?" asked the drop-dead gorgeous Deadra.

"They're like a battery."

"That's so fade," said Deadra.

"What's on your back?" asked Jakob.

At first the attention and touching had made her want to squirm away, but then she couldn't help but enjoy it. It'd been so long since anyone had treated her with anything other than contempt. She lifted up her shirt in the back.

"Seven hells," said Jakob. "That is wicked."

Iona had forgotten about the tattoo that straddled her spine. She'd only seen it through the mirror. It didn't really look like anything she'd been able to categorize. Maybe the outline of a crocodile, maybe a heart—with all the spaces filled in with ancient indecipherable text.

"I don't know what it does. As far as I know, it might not be finished," she said.

After a few minutes of examination, the group peeled away, giving Iona room to breathe again.

"Maybe we'll have to call you Tattoo Girl now instead," said Jakob, receiving a glare from Blake.

"What's the challenge?" asked Iona, wanting to get to the part where she showed them how awesome she could be. The first part of the introduction had gone as well as it could have, but she knew that none of it would matter if she couldn't help them.

"You know how there are secret places all over the Obelisk?" asked Scarlett. "And how some of them have hidden treasures? We think we found another one."

The redhead strode forward to a stretch of blank marble wall and released twin mage lights into the air that brightened enough to illuminate the entire area. Iona had been so focused on her fellow first years she hadn't really paid attention to her surroundings. The fountain lay on one side of the room while the other was remarkably empty.

"I don't see anything."

Scarlett pumped her eyebrows.

"Exactly."

She made a gesture that looked like a triangle made with her fingers and pushed forward as she spoke a six-word phrase in Coptic. The air crackled with golden sparkles, which collected on the wall in lines and symbols until the outline of a runed doorway was revealed.

"Sand and stone," she muttered.

"Wicked, eh?" asked Scarlett.

Iona stepped forward until she was inches away from the "door." The writing was an older form of Kemetic. Not quite as unintelligible as her tattoos. The wording was unusual, with slightly different syntax than she was used to.

"I know this."

"See," said Scarlett to her friends. "I told you she could help."

"These words that almost look like wavy lines have to do with the Nile while this other part is the harvest. It's a riddle."

Iona reached out and touched three symbols along the outside. The moment her fingertips brushed the stone, the symbols lit up in copper-patina green. After the third, the outline of the door shifted forward until an actual entrance existed. The display of ancient magic had her grinning.

Everyone clapped. Everyone but Blake, who stared at her with flat lips.

"Nice trick," said Jakob with a wink.

"It doesn't mean anything until we confirm what's inside," said Blake. "Who wants to go?"

No one made eye contact with Blake.

"Why not the whole group? Wouldn't that be safer?" asked Iona.

"Bad idea, new girl," said Blake. "Better one of us goes alone to confirm that it's not dangerous. Some of these spaces are trap-filled. Hate to have the entire group wiped out because one person touched what was clearly an obvious lever."

"It looked like a phallic symbol," said Jakob, holding out his hands palms up. "The Munich Arcana Museum has many. I was intrigued."

"See." Blake checked to the group. "Who's going?"

"I'll go," said Iona.

Blake frowned.

"Are you sure? You don't have to. You got us through the door, which is the part we didn't understand. It might be dangerous," said Scarlett.

Iona checked back to Blake, who had seemed unimpressed by the display. If she was going to win him over, she needed him to believe she would be an asset.

"I'm sure."

The ambivalent shrug from Blake was answer enough.

"Give me a moment to charge the tattoos."

Iona closed her eyes and opened the conduit for her faez. The trickle felt icy at first but warmed as she let more into the tattoos. She could have filled them faster, but was nervous enough she didn't want to overdo it. When she was finished, her body felt tingly and her hands fidgety.

"I'm ready now."

When she opened her eyes, Blake was staring at her strangely, with apprehension maybe.

"You got this, Tattoo Girl," said Jakob, grinning.

Scarlett gave her a nod. Iona pressed a symbol on the edge which made the door swing open.

Walking through the opening made her hands shake. Iona clenched her jaw as she examined the interior space. It looked like a storage room filled with old junk. An antique armoire. A gas lamp from the 1800s. The pile of carpets in back looked like a lumpy monster.

Iona turned to tell them it probably wasn't dangerous when the door slammed shut. It hit with the finality of a bomb. She rushed to the opening, finding nothing on the inside that would force it open.

"Hey! I'm stuck!" she yelled as she banged on the interior.

Scarlett's voice came through faintly. Something about the symbols not working and that she'd have to figure it out.

"Great."

The room wasn't large. About the same as the front space in her suite with the fountain, except it was covered in junk. Iona cautiously examined the materials, being careful not to touch the piles.

A stack of boards near the corner proved to be old plaques that looked like they'd once been displayed on the walls. She examined the one on top.

"Byron Willington. Valedictorian. 1961. Angel Dreadmarsh. Salutatorian. 1964."

The rest of the plaques were similar. Displays for the top students in every year, but they ended in 1983. Did something happen then? Or had Malden changed how he ran the school? And why hide this crap behind a secret door covered in Kemetic runes? Nothing made sense, but then again, nothing about Coterie made any sense to her. She might as well have been dropped into the midst of a remote tribe for all she understood about her fellow first years.

A tarnished golden goblet stuck between the layers of carpet caught her eye. She reached out to pluck it free before yanking her hand back.

"Don't be an idiot, Iona."

The spell came easily as she'd had to practice it frequently, checking her door or other parts of her suite for lingering magics. Pinky out, twist of the wrist, a few words of Old English that sounded like she was saying *pudding patrol*, but it wasn't that at all.

The goblet remained tarnished. No sign of magic. But she caught sight of an object glowing behind the armoire that had been caught by her spell.

Iona yanked the heavy furniture away from the wall, revealing an oblong mirror about three feet high and two feet wide. The frame was made from coppery metal with solar discs and lion heads pressed into the surface.

Mirrors were interesting objects to imbue with magical effects, because they reflected the person standing in front, which could create all kinds of strange and interesting problems. Dangerous too.

The symbols in the frame were suggestive of the door outside. The junk in the room seemed like it'd been left here rather than hauled outside of the Obelisk, while the mirror and some of the fixtures on the wall seemed original. Was the mirror the key to opening the door?

Reading the symbols along the frame left her the impression that if she spoke them aloud, she would activate the mirror. Before going down that path, she checked the rest of the room, looking for other items that might be linked to her escape. When she'd exhausted all other options, Iona returned to the mirror.

The ancient tongue might have been difficult to speak, except that Fenris had drilled her in its diction for his rituals. He hadn't allowed her to help until she could speak them without a single stumble. Iona practiced a half dozen times without sound before reaching for her faez and completing the phrase.

Nothing happened at first. She was staring at herself in the mirror. Sleeveless tiger shirt. Pale blonde hair pulled back in a functional ponytail. A touch of eyeliner which made her appear older. She almost didn't recognize herself compared to the person she was in Missouri.

Then the mirror shifted. Wavered. She was no longer present in the reflection. Nor was the junk or anything else. It looked like the room as it was before it'd become a dumping ground. Except there was a faint figure in back. She leaned forward to examine the creature that was shuffling forward, covered in rune-covered bandages. A mummy. And it wasn't just in the mirror, she realized.

Iona spun around to find a mummy lumbering after her. The ancient dead were not alive by any means, but the embalming process often left a connection to the soul, allowing a conduit back to use the body as its vessel of revenge. That was what the book she'd been reading earlier that day had explained. But it also said that sometimes mummies were created purposely.

What she knew for sure was that she didn't want the mummy to touch her. Rot. Disease. Heart attack. Any of these things could happen. The mix of death and magic was potent, especially if it'd been allowed to linger.

But there was no room to run. The room was so small. She threw herself against the door, hoping that something had changed.

A blast of force magic staggered the mummy. It groaned beneath the bandages, but continued forward. Iona dove when he reached for her, scrambling to her feet to escape the creature while slamming her shoulder into the armoire.

This was going to be her death. Why had she volunteered? The Obelisk had too many dangerous secrets. Too many magics she didn't understand. Professor Cornwallis had been right. She lacked the knowledge the others had, making this place even more dangerous than it had any right to be.

Iona hit the mummy two more times with force magic before realizing that it was only a temporary solution. She got behind the armoire and pushed it over, blocking the mummy from reaching her. As it went around one way, she went the other. Stalemate. But she knew she couldn't keep escaping forever.

The book she'd been reading earlier that day, *The Imprints of Our Lives*, had been filled with spells that could deal with the inhabited bodies of the dead, but she'd barely skimmed over them, promising herself that she would memorize them later. But there was one she had actually read enough that she could remember. It was short and sweet and was supposed to stun any creature with links to the Veil. The spell was two gestures, two words, and the inversion of a pyramid shape in her head.

When the spell completed, she thrust out her arms, expecting the mummy to be knocked backwards like with the force bolts. Nothing happened. The mummy kept coming.

But then the air grew cold and mist formed on the ceiling.

"Oh no. What did I do?"

Iona continued her circular escape from the mummy as a strange darkness condensed above her.

When the first drop hit her arm, she thought she'd mistakenly summoned a rainstorm in the small room. She was too busy to check the wetness on her flesh as she kept moving.

As more drops fell, she sensed something was wrong. Her suspicions were confirmed when a drop hit her on the lips and she tasted a coppery metallic.

Her arms were covered in crimson droplets. It was raining blood. She knew for certain that wasn't the intent of the spell, which meant either the presence of the mummy had interfered, or she'd triggered another deadly aspect to the hidden room.

What had started as a gentle patter turned to a heavy downpour. In the span of ten seconds, she was suddenly struggling through a deluge of blood. The liquid quickly filled the room. Iona splashed through the blood, which was already around her ankles. She could hardly breathe or see past her nose as the falling liquid was so thick. It was like being in the middle of a hot jungle during a downpour.

Iona barely kept ahead of the mummy. A chase that she knew was going to end in one way unless she could figure out the door, or the mummy, or something.

Or the mirror!

She knew little about cursed mirrors, but the little she knew suggested that she needed to focus on the reflective surface rather than the mummy. But she needed time, time she didn't have under constant duress.

The blood had gotten high enough that the armoire was almost floating. When the mummy circled around, opposite the mirror, Iona slammed the armoire into it, pinning it against the wall. Then she grabbed an old metal lamp and used it to fix the heavy furniture in place. It wouldn't last long with the rising blood, but it would give her a chance to focus on the mirror.

The solar discs and lion heads suggested a particular Egyptian god, but Iona couldn't remember which one. Nor did she think it would matter.

The first thing she tried was blasting the mirror with force magic, but the ancient artifact was impervious. Then Iona tried ripping it from the wall to see if there were passphrases on the back—something to dismiss the mummy—but it wouldn't budge.

The mummy was almost free of the armoire. Covered in blood, the wrappings looked pink. She was going to die by a pink mummy in a trapped room that she volunteered for.

Iona grabbed a heavy pewter mug and smashed it into the face of the mirror with no effect. It was protected from regular blows.

The blood was up to her knees. Once the mummy was free, she wouldn't be able to stay ahead of it for long. She was already tired from the chase. And even if she did, the blood would fill the room and she would drown in the sticky liquid. An ignoble end.

In a fit of desperation, Iona grabbed the edges of the mirror with both hands, then she channeled the faez she'd stored in her tattoos into the frame in one big burst. Pushing that much raw magic through her body was like trying to swallow a cantaloupe. The agony of pressure as she slammed the mirror with magic, hoping to overload the artifact, nearly made her pass out.

As she screamed with pain and hope, the mummy broke free. The floating armoire shifted out of the way and the undead creature reached out to grab her—right as the mirror exploded in her fists.

The waist-deep blood rushed out of the room as the warded door flew open. Iona was carried out, slamming against the armoire, her hands screaming in pain from the explosion.

She came to by the fountain, lying in a puddle of blood, dizzy and disoriented. Iona checked her hands to find the skin on her palms mauled, and before she could consider what was happening, she rolled onto her knees and vomited out a stomachful of crimson liquid.

It took her a while of panting and moaning to realize that she wasn't the only one in the space. Iona raised her weary head to see Blake Lockwood sitting on the far edge of the empty fountain in clothes that would have looked appropriate on a yacht, peering at her with his head tilted.

Iona struggled to her knees and raised her hands defensively. The smirk. The finely coifed hair. The air of supreme arrogance. They all sent warning signs through her head. That and the absence of the others.

"Where'd they go?"

"You thought they would wait to see if you could get out? Are you really that dense? They all assumed you were too stupid to escape. I wasn't so sure. There's something about you that reminds me of...it doesn't matter. You should have died in there, but you didn't."

A heavy fist clung to her heart.

"You were never going to let me into your group."

"I can't believe you even thought it was possible. You. Pig Girl. You're nothing. You're a joke. Worse than white trash, because you actually believe you matter. I would rather fail Coterie than help a nothing like you climb even one rung. Scarlett thought it'd be a fun little game to see how far you could go, but I didn't like it. Not one bit. The idea that you would even *think* that you could join us made me sick, but I have to say, watching you get washed out of the room in a river of blood was quite the experience."

He hopped off the edge of the fountain, staying clear of the blood.

"But now I think our little game is at an end. No more playtime for Pig Girl."

Blake began muttering and making arcane gestures. He was going to kill her. She'd survived the mummy only to be murdered in a pool of blood that wasn't her own.

"Try me," she said, climbing to her feet. "I'm still charged up with magic and ready to go."

The words she spoke were nonsense. Old poems written in Kemetic that she'd memorized because they'd been interesting, and there was little else to do in Fenris' place.

Blake's eyes went white. He stumbled backwards as he left his spell unfinished. He ran into the darkness, letting the shadows hide his escape. Iona kept up her muttering until she was certain he was gone.

"Coward."

The absence of distractions intensified the pain in her hands. It looked like she'd tried to pick up handfuls of broken glass. The rips in her flesh were deep. She was still covered in blood, so couldn't tell how bad the wounds were.

Iona yanked her soaking wet shirt off and ripped it into pieces, wrapping her hands to stop the bleeding until she could get back to her room and apply real healing magics.

When she was finished with her hands, Iona spotted a smooth black stone the size of her thumb. It was either an enormous onyx or a leftover piece of the mummy. Or both. Using the remainder of her shirt, Iona wrapped it up for examination later, then trudged back through the Obelisk, taking back passages to avoid any chance of running into Blake or his friends.

Back in her suite, after laboriously reinforcing the wards, Iona went straight to the shower and let warm water run over her naked body until she was certain not a single drop of blood remained. Then she pulled out the healer kit that she'd assembled from her classes and repaired the worst of the damage to her palms, though she assumed she'd have permanent scarring. Once her hands were fixed, Iona opened the hidden catch she'd found in the closet and placed the onyx inside.

The urge to examine it magically was strong, but her hunger and exhaustion from the ordeal was worse. She would worry about the onyx later, but for now she needed sustenance, and sleep.

"And a new set of brains, Iona. What were you thinking, believing that they would let you in their group?"

TWENTY

The city was wrapped in tinsel and magic, in preparation for the holiday season now that Thanksgiving was over. Zuri pushed through the busy streets in the first ward, annoyed by the oblivious tourists and pushy businessmen who thought they were the only important people in the world.

She checked the address again when she reached the center of the ward, surrounded by skyscrapers that looked childlike next to the enormous Spire that was wrapped in a halo of thin clouds.

"There's no way it can be here."

Zuri had messaged her sister about a bookstore she'd overheard a couple of third years talking about at dinner the other night. Grimoire & Gold. She'd found no listings online, or other information that might lead her to the location. Even her sister had ignored her questions for nearly a week before responding cryptically, and warning her that the place might not be worth the trouble.

But Zuri was desperate.

Already three groups had passed through the level two portal and most of the others were close to the solution. The only benefit of their success was that it left the archway free to examine, whereas before she'd had to worry about being attacked.

Of the six parts of the problem, she'd solved the Ward portion right away, had a decent start on the Infernal, and was currently stuck on the Faez riddle. Using references she'd found in her personal library, she was looking for a tome called *Caudice Simul Magus.* The problem was no one had a copy. She'd inquired with some of the groups that would still talk to her, but they were tight-lipped about its existence. A confirmation that she was on the right path, if there was any.

A scouring of the city's bookstores had proved to be a waste. The only one that had given her any indication that the tome actually existed was Seppi's Rare Books and Teahouse, but the proprietor, a former warlord from the realm of Brodaria, wanted a lock of her hair for information only. A price that was too high in Zuri's mind. A few strands of hair wasn't too dangerous in the hands of another mage, but an entire lock, freely given, was a completely different story.

Thus the search for Grimoire & Gold.

Zuri strolled past pizza parlors and coffee shops, dodged around street vendors, and wondered if she'd somehow gotten confused by her sister's directions.

"It should be right here."

She stomped her foot for emphasis. Neither the ice cream shop or haberdashery looked like they were hiding a rare book depository in back. Zuri checked the address for the umpteenth time.

"Think, you impatient twit."

A woman in a pantsuit talking excitedly on her phone gave Zuri a funny look as she strode past.

Frustrated by the waste of an afternoon, Zuri stared into the distance, listening to the honks and revving engines on the busy streets, the cries of hot dog vendors, and the crackle of sparks from a burning sign a few doors up. Unfocused and uncaring, Zuri caught a strange quiver at the corner of her vision, but when she turned to look, the only thing she saw was the brick wall where the two shops connected.

"Strange."

She went back to staring into the distance, but this time with a purpose. Zuri knew that Look Away enchantments could keep people from noticing you in busy places, but could they put them on entire shops?

Eventually with her vision blurred, she caught the outlines of a narrow door on the brick wall. Zuri closed her eyes and took steps until she was standing before the location, ignoring the assholes who cursed at her for being in their way. Casting the revealing spell without sight wasn't terribly challenging except for the last part where she had to connect the fingers from both hands to make a figure eight.

The tingle of enchantment passing over her body was pleasing. Zuri's eyes shot open to see a strange shimmering door, barely wider than herself, on the brick wall. It looked like it was vibrating. No one else noticed it. The handle was warm to the touch despite the chilly air.

Once through, she was presented with descending stairs. The brick walls on either side were plastered with old band posters, public notifications, or random graffiti, some that went back decades. Down With the Cabal! JFK is a secret mage! Invictus lives! Zuri had the impression that this bookstore had been around before the other buildings were constructed.

At the bottom of the long stairs she found herself in a musty, dim place with high crooked shelves and glass cases tucked in crowded corners. It felt like she'd stumbled into the back of a bookstore rather than the front, since she saw no desk or welcome area. A hint of cigar smoke came from somewhere deeper.

"Hello?"

The shelves were filled with tomes in ancient languages, a quarter of which she'd never heard of. Zuri spotted a few titles that shocked her. *The Patience of Dying. The Assassin's Guide to Killing from Afar. Secrets of the Winter Fae.* Each were tomes she'd heard of, but never expected to find sitting on a shelf unguarded rather than in a protective case, which stayed Zuri's hand from pulling one out. She felt a trespasser.

"Is this Grimoire and Gold?"

She followed the smell of cigar smoke as the floor changed levels more than once. Nothing significant, but she found it strange to have to go up or down stairs that were only three steps. It felt like the entire store wasn't quite settled.

In a corner Zuri found a slim woman high on a ladder that rolled around the shelves, rearranging books as she puffed on a stunted cigar. She wore black, form-fitting clothes, including a dark green skirt. From Zuri's vantage, she could see the woman was missing a leg beneath her left knee, replaced with a silvery stump.

"Do you work here?"

The woman half-turned on the ladder. Zuri's breath caught in her throat as she saw the chalky gray skin, the high cheekbones, and one gray eye. A maetrie. City Fae. But human too.

"My apologies," she quickly followed up. "You're the owner."

"Call me Murder. What are you looking for?" asked the owner in a husky voice that sounded like she smoked a lot of cigars.

The woman's voice scrambled Zuri's thoughts, a side effect of her maetrie heritage. She wasn't the first maetrie that Zuri had encountered in her life, so she knew the best way to counter their aura was to hold a small amount of faez in her mind. The home of the maetrie, the Eternal City, was an older realm where magic was more free-flowing and malleable.

"I'm looking for a copy of *Caudice Simul Magus*. I'm under the impression that you might have a copy."

The odd smile was like a slash on her thin lips. Murder clucked her tongue.

"I'm sorry, did I say something wrong?" asked Zuri.

The owner extended her arm back the way Zuri had come.

"You'll find it past the desiccated dragon claw."

Zuri hesitated before speaking again. "I'm sorry. Is it okay that I look at it?"

By this time, Murder was back to fussing with the books on the shelves, pulling them out and putting them back in, sometimes in the exact same place.

Zuri found the dragon claw first. It'd come from a small one. The claw was as big as her head, but that would make it barely a youngling. The placard on the glass case noted the date of 1645, which didn't spark any historical events.

The deeper into the back of the bookstore Zuri got, the more she worried that she was being lured into a trap. Why had the owner smirked at her request and then sent her after the book without another word? Nothing made sense. Not that the maetrie, even half-breeds, were known for making their intentions clear. Zuri's parents had warned her years ago to stay away from the city Fae, that they couldn't be trusted, and that their deals were always barbed.

Zuri heard the throat clear before she saw the other person. Nestled into the corner of the shelves, they sat with a tome resting on their thighs. Zuri almost didn't recognize her fellow first year: pale hair that almost seemed ghost white and pulled back on the sides. Black pants and a striped green top.

"That top doesn't go with those shoes," said Zuri.

Iona glanced up, suspicion on her brow.

"I got some blood on the shirt they goes with."

"Is that *Caudice Simul Magus?*"

"It might be."

Zuri leaned against the shelves casually.

"I never see you at the portal. How did you know to look for that book?"

Iona leaned back and closed the tome with her finger holding her place.

"I only go when everyone else is asleep or elsewhere. As for the book, I overheard the Siren Sisters talking about it. You'd be surprised how comfortable some of the groups get when they think no one is listening."

"I wouldn't know."

"Why does Blake hate you?"

Zuri recoiled in surprise.

"I dared to refute his bullshit and exposed him for the psychopath he is."

"Yeah, I don't know what that means."

A heaviness overtook Zuri. How many times was she going to have to tell this tale? Which only made her feel guilty for the thought. Gemma had died. What was a little explanation in the face of the eternal void?

"He killed my best friend and then when I testified against him in court, he turned me into a pariah."

It was Iona's turn to be surprised.

"Wow. At least you earned his hate."

"Did he come after you?"

Iona shook her head while snorting softly.

"I foolishly thought that they would let me into their group because I know some stuff about advanced Kemetic magic. Scarlett had me believing I could find a place in Coterie. I'm under no illusion now."

"What happened?"

Iona gave a short explanation that had Zuri whistling in response. If even half the tale was true, and she didn't think the girl was lying, it made her even more intriguing than she'd thought before.

"You're lucky to have survived that."

"I'm lucky Blake didn't call my bluff. I probably couldn't have managed to create a sparkler after blowing all my faez into the mirror."

"For all his bluster, he's a coward. Nothing he hates more than being stood up to, or embarrassed. A mistake I made when I went against him."

"He killed your friend," said Iona, exasperated. "You had every right to seek justice."

"Justice. That word doesn't mean the same thing as you think it should in the circles I run."

"I run in those circles now."

"No you don't. No offense, Iona. But they'll never see you as one of them. Look at Head Patron Pythia. She was a member of Coterie for a year and they despise her because she came from nothing."

Iona stared straight at her.

"What do you think of me?"

The accusation in her voice stung.

"I don't know why you're here. Not the Halls, but Coterie. Again, no offense, but this isn't your world. Coterie is hard enough if you were born into it, but coming from a little town in Missouri with no formal prep or real mentorship? It's insane."

"Offense taken," said Iona flatly.

"I'm not judging," said Zuri. "I'm just stating facts."

"A convenient excuse to be an asshole." Iona sighed. "But at least you remembered where I came from."

A half-dozen quips formed on her tongue, but Zuri swallowed them. She'd already insulted the poor girl—assuming that was possible—and didn't want to antagonize her further. Besides, Zuri had few other options yet and this ignorant farm girl was her only option remaining.

"You know there's still time to ally," said Zuri.

"You'll excuse me if I have a problem trusting anyone in Coterie."

"What? You think I'd backstab you when I have no one else but myself? I'm as much an outsider as you are now."

"I doubt that."

Zuri held her hand against her forehead as anger brought heat to her chest. She tried not to let the emotion thread her voice, but it cracked as the first words came out.

"I stood up to Blake when no one else did, costing me everything. My life, my friends, my *future.* Despite everything I'd done before. Despite all my accomplishments. My sister is a hero of the Invasion and that meant nothing when it came to my word against Blake's. They didn't want to hurt *his* future. Mine was irrelevant."

Iona squeezed her knees against her chest, trapping the book as she studied Zuri.

"Did you know everyone was going to turn on you, or did you think they'd have your back?"

"I thought, well, I was…" Zuri exhaled as she struggled to find the right words. "I thought they would have my back. I thought they would take my side, but they didn't want to ruin his life. Instead they ruined mine."

"So you didn't do it because you thought it was the right thing, you did it because you thought you'd win."

"I was furious. Gemma was my best friend. I didn't think about any of that. Only what he'd done to her."

"That's fair." Iona shifted her mouth to the side and scrunched up her forehead. "What was the Invasion?"

"Seriously?"

"Seriously."

"That was the biggest news story in the world, or realms for that matter, five years ago."

"We didn't have a TV and had to steal the Internet from a neighbor when they were asleep. I'd never been out of my hometown until I came here. Hell, I'd barely been out of the farmhouse except for short trips to town for groceries or the post office."

"Seriously?"

"Seriously."

"Merlin's tits, I don't even know how to take that. The Invasion was when some stupid mages opened a portal to the Infernal realm, which caused an invasion of demons. My sister, Nandi, was one of the mages who stopped it."

"Your sister, the hero."

"Hasn't done me any favors." Zuri gestured towards the book. "How many of the six have you figured out?"

Iona let her knees relax, which allowed her to reexamine the book.

"One."

"Kemetic, right?"

She nodded, then asked, "What about you?"

"One. Wards. I'm close on two others, which is why I'm here for that book."

"My book," said Iona with a grin.

"So do you want to ally?"

The question made Iona squirm against the bookshelves.

"I don't trust when people ask me. I feel like they want something."

"I want to be your ally. I want us both to succeed. To survive and somewhere down the road of this shitshow, graduate."

"You don't respect me."

"I don't know you," said Zuri, catching a hardening of her gaze. It was going to take more than logic to sway her. It was going to take the truth. Even if it hurt. "Yes. I find your taste and upbringing appalling, and if circumstances were different, I would never have looked at you sideways."

Iona crossed her arms.

"But," said Zuri, holding a hand up. "I am not without room to grow. And you've shown yourself more than competent, despite having an unusual upbringing. And does it matter if we have anything in common? Or that we even really like each other? We could hold hands and sing hymns together if you'd like. But that's not going to help us against the other groups. Against Blake and Scarlett. Being stuck in our ways, well, my uptight and probably insular ways, won't get us to the second level. Right now, between us, we only have a third of the answers. If we don't get to work soon, we're going to fall further behind."

Iona tapped on the tome.

"Three answers, maybe. Need to confirm against the symbols of the portal, but I think it might be right."

"Three then." Zuri squinted. "Does that mean you'll ally?"

"A week ago, I would have said no. I've heard how much Blake hates you, but now that he's tried to kill me, I figure it's less of a negative than it was before."

"That's good logic."

"But that's not why I'm agreeing to ally."

"That's not? Why?"

"Because you remembered where I was from. It's not much, but it's something."

"Mississippi, right?" asked Zuri with her mouth hitched to the side.

Iona started to match her smile but then it faltered. She visibly shivered as her eyes darted around.

"Is something wrong?"

"We should go."

Zuri checked down the crooked path between the shelves.

"The owner?"

"No."

"Anything you care to tell me about?"

"Maybe later," she said, standing and shoving the tome back into the shelves.

The girl's sudden change in behavior had Zuri worried, but she wasn't about to back out due to a little strangeness. Zuri followed Iona out of the bookstore. When they stepped onto the sidewalk, an older woman walking by exclaimed as if they'd appeared out of thin air.

"Anything that you can tell me that will help us with whatever mysterious problem you're having?"

Iona turned her head, checking down the street.

"The fastest way you can get us out of here."

A vibration on Zuri's left wrist had her checking the warning bracelet she'd enchanted shortly after she'd come to the Obelisk.

"Huddle close."

Face-to-face with a small gap between them, Zuri put a Look Away spell over them both.

"It won't stop serious practitioners from finding us, but it'll at least give us some protection."

Iona didn't look pleased by the news, which told her the danger wasn't just an old boyfriend or a random person in the city that she'd pissed off.

"Taxi!"

Iona grabbed her hand and yanked her toward the street, nearly knocking over a group of college students in Penn State sweatshirts.

The yellow cab slowed and Iona threw herself in back, checking behind them as she yelled at the driver.

"Go, go."

The vehicle pulled gently into traffic while Iona was still staring out the back. Zuri couldn't see anything but the bracelet on her wrist was vibrating more intensely.

Once they were a block away, Iona relaxed into the backseat, exhaling with her eyes closed.

"Care to tell me?"

"No. Not now. Not in the City where he can hear. Give me some time. I have to, well, I have to decide how much I can tell you."

When Zuri had offered to ally with Iona she thought that the country girl would be taking the larger share of the risk, but after their weird escape from Grimoire & Gold, she thought she might have taken the larger share of the balance.

TWENTY-ONE

Iona wasn't sure how she felt about having an ally in Coterie. Then again, she'd never even had a friend, let alone someone she was supposed to trust with her life and share things with implicitly, which was why she hadn't told Zuri about Fenris yet. She didn't want to scare away the first person who had agreed to work with her.

The first week after the fateful meeting in Grimoire & Gold had been awkward. Iona nearly blasted Zuri when she came to her room, thinking it was one of the weird stalkery creatures that could sometimes be found in the main level. With most of the groups working on level two, it made their areas more dangerous, because there were fewer students to take care of the supernatural beings that slipped out of old hiding places.

The faez problem for the portal had proved more challenging than she'd first thought. Iona had taken the right notes from the tome, but they required calculation and arcane math. Thankfully, Zuri seemed to know a lot about the theoretical aspects of magic, but even still, it was going to require some experimentation.

Eventually Zuri decided that they would need a place for testing the solution. Somewhere that couldn't be compromised. They'd already heard about how Tristan had received a serious injury when someone had sabotaged his alchemy project by putting nyxworms in the nightshade solution. The left side of his chest had been turned to a gooey slime that required constant attention as not to overtake his entire body. They thought he'd eventually recover from the worst of the damage, but that part of his flesh would be permanently marred.

Iona knew the perfect place to set up an experiment, but it took some convincing with her ally. The mirror-mummy room was in an out-of-the-way location and she was certain that Blake and his group would never think to look there. Plus, when she'd destroyed the mirror, it'd eliminated the eldritch magics that had made the room into a dangerous trap. She knew this because she'd gone back a few days later to search for any other items like the thumb-sized onyx and found that the room was relatively normal, for the Obelisk anyway.

Cleaning out the old carpets, plaques, and other junk had proved more laborious than either of them thought possible. Iona wasn't unused to physical labor. Fenris required her to do all the maintenance and cleaning of the old farmhouse, which was considerable at times, given the age of the building. But Zuri had barely ever carried her own luggage, let alone heavy rolls of smelly carpet or waterlogged armoires. She downed a few elixirs the second day, but that only helped her complete the tasks. The aftermath on her muscles left Zuri unable to move until she found a potion to counteract the muscle soreness.

It took five days. Two to clean it out. Another two to destroy or hide the rest of the junk so no one figured out what they'd done, and the final day to acquire the equipment and move it to the room. Iona let Zuri go into the city to purchase the astral refractor and void pulse analyzer that would be required for their tests.

The testing portion took longer, but was infinitely more interesting to Iona. Between running the analyzer, when there were no samples to prepare, Zuri showed her the basics of arcana that she was lacking: the proper way to rotate shapes in her head, how to draw faez smoothly, finding a rhythm for longer spells, etc. As the gaps were filled in, Iona could see the deliberate obfuscation of Fenris' tutelage. The skills and spells she was learning would have given her ways to escape him that wouldn't have left a trail.

"I can't believe how much advanced magic you know, but the little things like how to curl spirit faez for divinations are completely foreign to you. We used to cast spells to find out who liked us in middle school."

"I thought using magic without a patron was dangerous. That you could get faez madness."

Zuri snorted as she sat on the throne-like chair they'd liberated from another section of the Obelisk. The mixers were running at high speed, forcing them to talk loudly over the noise.

"One, we were kids. And no amount of warning could keep us from using the forbidden magic." She made air quotes around the last part. "Two, it takes regular use of faez to warp your brain. The fact that we didn't know a lot of the bigger flashier spells was probably a good thing. We all used dumb little spells. The ones that tell you who likes you. Or who thinks you're cute. Or to fix your hair, or make your skin glow."

"Your skin already glows, Zuri. You look like a goddess when you're working over the refractor."

She put a hand under her chin.

"I have naturally good skin, but I also buy a lot of D'Agastine products. Creams. Exfoliators. The works. There's a reason Celesse is hundreds of years old but looks early thirties at best."

"She's hundreds of years old?" Iona frowned as she kicked her feet from atop the prep table. "I mean, I guess I should have known that, being the patron of Alchemists and all, but when I see her face plastered everywhere, I can't quite fathom it. The first time I saw her on the side of a building, I thought she was a model."

The conversation made her wonder how old Fenris was. He hadn't preserved himself like Celesse. Nor kept up with hygiene like the other Coterie students. He liked to wear the same clothes for days as he delved into his tomes, or brewed new potions, or whatever arcana he was working on in his private laboratory.

"How old can people get? Mages, that is."

Zuri looked up from picking at a fingernail that she'd chipped on the analyzer.

"Thousands? There really is no limit, I guess."

"Thousands?"

Iona's jaw swung open.

"No one knows for sure how old Invictus is, the founder of the Hundred Halls, but there are a lot of ancient paintings and stories that sound a lot like him. And he's never denied it. Some say he was the inspiration for the fictional Merlin, but I think they want to see him as a force for good in the old days."

"You don't?"

"Most of the old stories about magic are horrific. Having that much power, while probably going mad, and people out to kill you. It's a recipe for disaster."

"How can you tell if someone is going mad?"

Zuri hunched her forehead.

"Thinking of someone in particular?"

Iona kept swinging her feet and stared at the floor. She'd been holding back any information about her former captor, but after a few weeks of working with Zuri, she felt like she owed her an explanation.

"His name is Fenris."

"Is that the person you were worried about the day we met at Grimoire & Gold?"

"He was the one that taught me magic."

"He wasn't doing it for your benefit."

"No. He was working on a ritual. Piecing together spells from ancient books."

"Do you know why?"

"No. But sometimes he would disappear from the property for days. When he left, he'd be all twitchy and hard to be around, snapping at the slightest thing, but when he'd come back, he'd be in control of himself again."

"Do you know where he went or what he was doing?"

"The only thing I know is there were a lot of missing people posters at the grocery store in town. More than other cities in the middle of Missouri."

"Seven hells, he wasn't a vampire, was he?"

Iona sat straight.

"Those exist?"

"Not in the way the movies or books talk about them, but there are mages who've learned to feed on other humans to increase their power."

"I never saw fangs. Or any blood. He liked meat, but cooked. I trapped the rabbits that liked to eat in our garden. He loved those, fried and dipped in Amish mustard with sides of pickles. But otherwise, that sounds kind of right." She shook her head. "Not exactly, but like that?"

"What about those tattoos? Do they have to do with his ritual?"

Iona had already shown Zuri all the etchings on her body: the weird incomprehensible writing on her forearms, the jackal heads on her shoulders, the beast/heart along her spine.

"He told me they did. Each one served a purpose. But the only ones I understand are the jackal heads."

"A battery is a weird thing to build into someone. Unless he was worried that the spell he needed you to cast was too powerful for such a young mage."

"He said I had a really high Merlin score."

"Even if you do, when you're young, you don't know how to use it efficiently or effectively. He probably needed the power of an older mage."

"With the ignorance of a young one," said Iona, looking up.

"Fenris," said Zuri, as if she were tasting his name. "That's not common. Or modern. Is that why you were asking about age earlier?"

"Yeah. The more I learn, the older I think he is."

"Which means he's dangerous. More than Blake or any of those assholes. I can see why you don't like going into the city. But you can't hide in the Obelisk forever. They kick us out during the summer."

A cold fist wrapped around her heart.

"They do?"

"Yeah, sorry to be the bearer of bad news. But this isn't like the other Halls. They use the summer to reset things, prepare for the new class."

"I thought that if I passed my first year, I could stay during the summer. Stay out of his way. This changes everything."

"I'll help."

Iona shared a smile with Zuri, even as she didn't quite believe her. It was one thing to take on the dangers of the Obelisk, it was an entirely different thing to take on a powerful mage of possibly ancient origins.

The analyzer dinged.

They rushed to the machine. Zuri pored over the numbers, checking them against the chart they'd copied from *Caudice Simul Magus*.

"Seventeen point eight. Thirteen nine."

Zuri ran her fingers down the columns of numbers then leaned back and closed her eyes.

"What? What's wrong?" asked Iona, leaning over her shoulder.

Zuri turned and placed her hands on Iona's shoulders as her eyes widened.

"We got it. First and hardest step is done."

"Oh, thank Merlin. If I had to mix another lidocaine solution, I was going to scream."

"We're not done yet. But the next steps are much easier. We should be able to finish the last part and know the answer for the faez section of the Six-Fold Trial."

Zuri stretched her arms.

"We should call it. Especially given what day it is."

"What day is it?"

"Seriously?"

"It's Christmas, you dope."

"And? I mean, I know it's a holiday, I saw all the stuff at the grocery store in the winter, but is it important everywhere? I didn't know if it was just a local tradition."

"Oh bloody hell, Iona. You are a marvel of ignorance. Come now. Everyone else is out of the Obelisk for the holidays, let's go down and have ourselves a proper Christmas feast."

They each went back to their rooms and dressed for the occasion, meeting up in the massive dining hall when they were finished. Iona chose a pleated crimson skirt and a sleeveless cream top. Zuri was in a body-hugging gold dress that looked painted on, with her hair straightened and woven into pleats. She'd already put an order in with the kitchen staff, who had been kept on for the holidays despite the lack of students in attendance. The only ones they knew were in the Obelisk were some of the upperclassmen who were probably not even aware that it was the holidays as they were in the highest levels, and a few of the professors who generally stayed in the Obelisk to work on their private projects.

The meal was a whirlwind of tastes that Iona was little prepared for. They started with oysters Rockefeller served in a bed of ice with champagne mignonette, then were treated with foie gras canapés with truffle honey and edible golf leaf. An hour into their feast, a rich and creamy lobster bisque with a hint of cognac left Iona reeling.

The main course was roast goose, more than enough for an entire family, but they picked off the best parts themselves—dark, greasy, and dripping juice—while laughing and toasting with champagne. There were sides and sorbets between rounds. By the end, Iona could scarcely see straight, but Zuri showed her a spell that would allow her to gorge without feeling sick.

When Iona thought she couldn't eat another bite, dessert arrived. Macarons. Christmas pudding. Yule log decorated with meringue mushrooms and dusted with edible gold.

"I probably shouldn't have drank so much," said Iona, hearing her country accent thicken after too many glasses of wine as she leaned her head against the back of the chair. "But it tastes so damn good."

Zuri had her feet on the table with a glass of brandy nestled against her chest.

"There's a spell for that too."

"I don't want it to go away. I've never been drunk before. I feel at peace for once."

"We'll have to get our minds right before we return to our rooms."

"I know, I know. But let me revel in the illusion for a little bit longer."

Iona felt a glowing tranquility. As if she were finally set free of her bonds and was expanding at a comfortable pace. Happiness in the old farmhouse had been getting a spell right and not getting shocked, or Fenris gone for a few days leaving her to her duties without his overbearing presence, or the joy of catching a fat rabbit in the garden snare.

She didn't know this was possible. To be happy. To feel joy. She had a home, an ally, and was nearly halfway to solving the Six-Fold Problem.

It was like the world was playing a song written just for her. An ode to Iona. She grinned, laughter spilling out past her lips, uncontrolled. An attempt to stop it only made it worse, and soon it spread to Zuri, who had been staring with her head tilted until mirth burst from her lips. Then they were roaring, bent over, eyes wet and guts pounding.

Iona had no idea how long it lasted. She was dizzy and tingly, leaning on the edge of the table, having knocked over her glass sometime during the loss of control with little bubbles of laughter escaping randomly.

When silence finally fell, it was peppered with the heaving of breath and long sighs of relief. But it was quiet enough to hear a distant sob, traveling through the dining doors. Iona heard it first. Then Zuri sat up, forehead hunching with thought.

Wordlessly, they moved from the table, stalking to the grand hall beyond. The lower part of the Obelisk had been built like a cross between Notre Dame and a sorcerer's den, with leaping archways, grand statues, and unusual magical artifacts left in protected glass cases. The echoes made it hard to pinpoint the direction of the crying, until Zuri gestured to a darkened hallway.

They came upon a single figure, legs curled beneath them in an alcove beneath a bust of Malden Anterist. It was Justine Thornlock in what could only be described as a crimson sexy Santa's helper outfit, which looked exquisitely handmade.

When Justine looked up, Iona was struck by her big, tear-filled eyes—like a rabbit's. Her cheeks were ruddy against her pale skin, and Iona couldn't help but think of a rabbit in a snare, looking up in terror just before it was throttled for dinner.

"You shouldn't be here all alone without protections, Justine. You know better than that," said Zuri.

Justine sniffed and gulped, still trying to get ahold of her emotions. Her lips trembled, but she couldn't muster the words to speak.

"We should take her to the dining room."

Zuri checked around them, before nodding. The room was barely defensible with multiple exits and a balcony overlooking from the second floor, a perfect place to spell snipe someone, but thankfully none of their classmates were in the area. They half-led, half-carried Justine back to the feast and let her sit in a chair across from them while she settled down. At least three different times, Iona thought she'd gotten herself under control before the trembles and sobbing started again.

The idea that Justine was a defenseless rabbit in a snare wouldn't leave Iona's mind. Ready to be strangled, then gutted and served for dinner.

Am I a killer like the others?

Zuri had the same look. Like they'd found a wounded animal that wouldn't survive a return to the forest.

Something had broken the poor girl.

"Justine. You need to get your shit together," said Zuri angrily. "If someone comes back, they're going to know how messed up you are right now and they'll take a go at you sooner rather than later. This breakdown is like chum in the water. You should be with your group."

"I, I don't have a...group anymore."

"Merlin's tits," exclaimed Zuri, giving Iona a shake of her head.

This was worse than a little breakdown. It was one thing for her or Zuri to survive as a loner, but Justine? She might as well cut her own throat.

Iona knelt before Justine and captured her hands.

"What happened?"

"I screwed up. I couldn't do it."

Iona looked back to Zuri, who gave her a shrug.

"Do what?"

"A spell. It's not that I couldn't cast it, but I didn't want to do it. They were going to kill Limon. He'd left a gap in his room defenses. The spell would strangle him in his sleep, his blanket, he'd never know it was coming. I couldn't do it."

"Like right now?" asked Iona, confused by the timing and her dress.

"Yesterday. But my group kicked me out during dinner in the city. Said they'd had a vote before I arrived and told me I couldn't be trusted to have their backs."

"Why'd they want to kill Limon?" asked Iona.

"He insulted Declan. Someone overheard him saying that Declan had cheated his way into Coterie, so he said this was an insult that had to be repaid in kind."

"By killing him..."

"Yes, by killing him. He's probably dead already."

Zuri crossed her arms.

"Come on, Justine. You know this is the deal. Your father was legendary for how he killed the other students in horrific ways. He even took down some older classman, which nearly caused a class war in the Obelisk, but backed off when Malden asked him to."

"I hate my father. He's the worst person imaginable. He's a monster."

"Then quit."

"He'll cut me off, probably have me killed for embarrassing him. He said I only have one choice. To graduate from Coterie. No other options," said Justine, wiping tears off her cheek with her thumb.

Zuri stalked away with her hands on her head.

"Stay here. Drink some champagne," said Iona and followed her ally away from the table for a conference. "What are we going to do?"

"She's not our problem," said Zuri with arms crossed.

"Come on. If we don't do something, they'll kill her."

"Do something?" asked Zuri with pinched lips.

"Invite her to our group. We could use a third. You know that. She's not incompetent. Just..."

"Not Coterie material. Do you seriously want to have to watch her back because you know she's going to screw it up? You've seen her in class. She's nervous and twitchy, bad traits for a mage, worse for Coterie."

Iona checked back to Justine, who was sipping from the champagne glass using both hands as if her limbs no longer worked. She looked like a child. Or a rabbit. The idea of letting her go, injured and alone, felt like dragging the knife across her throat herself.

"Yeah, I do."

"Why?"

"Because if I don't, then I'll be like them. Like Blake."

The last part hit Zuri hard because she snapped upright, looking like she wanted to throw punches, but then the fever broke and she shook her head.

"I hate that you're right."

When they returned to Justine, she was looking like a doll that had been leaned into the chair with legs splayed and head lolling to the side.

"Justine. We have a proposal for you," said Iona. "We'd like you to join our group."

"Wait. What?"

"You're alone. It's just the two of us. A trio is much safer. Stronger. Like a tripod."

Justine burst out crying again, but before Iona could decide if they were happy or sad tears, she launched herself at her with arms wide in a massive quivering hug.

"Oh, thankyouthankyouthankyouthankyou..."

She repeated the gesture with Zuri, who appeared annoyed but allowed it to happen.

"You won't regret it. I'll be a great teammate. I swear. I just don't want to kill anybody."

"Yay," said Zuri without a trace of excitement. "We're a team."

TWENTY-TWO

The laboratory had been perfectly sized when it'd just been her and Iona, but three was too many. Justine kept bumping into them, standing in the way, or asking a million questions when they had equipment to tend.

"Go over there," said Zuri after the third hour, extending her arm to the corner like a parent admonishing their child.

"I'm sorry—"

"Stop saying sorry," said Zuri, gritting her teeth.

"Sorry..."

Justine hung her head and trudged to the indicated spot, climbing onto an extra stool and clasping her hands beneath her chin with doll-like innocence.

When Zuri turned, Iona was staring at her with lips curled to the floor. The look deserved the response: *well, you invited her.* But Zuri knew the truth, they needed a third member. Even if she wasn't excited that it was

Justine. After all, she'd tried to recruit her early in the semester, though that was back when she'd hoped that Justine was more like her father than the wet noodle that had showed up to their private laboratory.

That Iona was reminding her to be nice was a wake-up call. The girl had been the captive of an older—and possibly ancient—mage and still managed to retain a bit of her humanity. Or maybe that was the thing: Iona hadn't grown up in the cutthroat world of Coterie. Yet, she didn't seem intimidated by the hardness of the school. She'd survived on her own for the first half of the semester and had thus far proved a valuable ally.

Maybe working for that old warlock had taught her a thing or two about survival. Unlike Justine. Her father's teachings had slid off her back like rain off an enchanted umbrella.

"Do you have any siblings?" asked Zuri over her shoulder.

"Huh. Me? No. They had to visit a Russian witch to even conceive me.

"What about you, Iona?" asked Justine, her lips trying to smile but collapsing into sadness.

"Just me."

"How did you end up with Fenris?" asked Justine.

She'd been given the basics of Iona's past, but nothing more. Not that Zuri knew much beyond that.

"My parents were drug addicts. Starshine or something like that. They traded me to Fenris when I was four or five for a bunch of the stuff."

"Seven hells, Iona," said Zuri. "That's horrific."

"As horrible as it sounds, I think I was lucky that it happened. I don't remember much, but I remember trash piled up in the old house, rats giving birth beneath my bed, the smell of formaldehyde, always being hungry."

"Are they still alive?" asked Justine while her hands moved independent of the rest of her body, jerking as if she were sewing or pulling strings.

"No," said Iona with a shrug. "Fenris said they died a year later. Overdose. Probably for the better."

Zuri shared a glance with Justine. Neither of them could believe it. They'd each heard stories on the Internet about awful neglectful parents, but never expected to be confronted or by someone who survived that.

The heavy subject forced them into silence while they worked the machines, whirling and beeping, the occasional gurgle followed by a burst of sulfur.

"Anyone seen Orion in a while?" asked Iona.

"The less you see of him, the better," said Zuri while leaning over the void pulse analyzer.

"He's not that bad." When no one spoke, Iona followed up with, "Right?"

"The Dreadmarsh family is not to be messed with. They consorted with demons centuries ago to acquire their supernatural gifts and it made them odd. Dangerous."

Justine cleared her throat.

"Even my dad said to stay away from Orion. Or any Dreadmarsh for that matter."

"He doesn't seem that bad. Did he, like, kill someone at St. Jude's or something?" asked Iona.

"He was there for class but nothing else. He never attended dances, events, parent teacher meetings, anything," said Zuri.

"I heard when he wasn't at school that he worked as a mercenary in Krakatow or Brodarian, killing for hire," said Justine.

"Really? That sounds a little far-fetched," said Iona, checking to Zuri for confirmation.

"I heard rumors, and not just the shit you hear in middle school.

Even the parents talked about him in hushed tones. When he would be gone for a while, break or whatever, he usually returned with new scars or burns. One time, the teacher made him join our thunderball game because we were short a person. He broke Jakob's arm in three places when he ran into him, then stormed off the pitch. When he was back in the building, he screamed or something, and every piece of glass in the entire wing shattered. We never asked him to play again."

"Okay, okay," said Iona, holding her hands up. "I'll stay away. But my suite is near his and he's never caused me any problems."

"He probably doesn't see you as worth his time," said Zuri. "Sorry. It's just the way people like us think. Especially people like him or Blake."

"Zuri...that's pretty rude," said Justine.

"How can I take offense?" asked Iona, lifting a single shoulder. "I did grow up with pigs."

"Did you really?" asked Justine.

"No, she didn't," said Zuri with a sigh.

"Oh shit," said Iona, checking the clock they'd fixed to the wall where the mirror had been before. "Professor Petrov's class is in fifteen."

The professor was the resident expert on hexes and she'd hinted the subject would be related to the Six-Fold Problem.

"The analyzer is almost done. You two go on, I'll finish this, swing by my room, and meet you in class."

Iona grabbed her backpack, slung it over her shoulder, and followed Justine out of their private laboratory.

"Don't be late. You know how Petrov hates it," said Iona on the way out.

The solution in the analyzer came out in the red shift, which meant it was related to the fire element of faez. Another failure. But it crossed another possibility off the list. Maybe a few dozen more and they'd finally get the answer they were looking for.

Zuri renewed her wards before she left the room. Traveling alone in the Obelisk was never safe. Having a team to rely on had made things easier, and the rest of their class was on the second level, but she wasn't about to let her guard down.

Using a secret passage that went behind the kill rooms in Telchine's Circle brought her to the stairs that led back to the student living quarters. Early in the Obelisk's existence, there had been elevators, but they became such an easy way to kill other students that they were removed. The stairs were no joke either. Zuri released a mouse-construct made of cardboard, silver wire, and sculptor's putty to lead the way. It'd been enchanted with her "presence," which should trigger any traps specifically designed for her.

The Hawthorne suite hadn't been her first choice, but now that she'd been there for over a semester, it felt like a weird kind of home. Safe at least.

She passed the balcony that looked down to the first floor to the big room near the dining area, where Professor Horace Green was walking through with an unknown upperclassman at his side, chatting quietly. It was rare that the fourth and fifth years made appearances in the lower floors because of the difficulty of the upper levels. Zuri wondered what those higher spaces in the Obelisk were like. More danger, of course, but her sister had hinted that her experiences there were the ones that made her the mage she was today.

Zuri was busy thinking about what she needed to grab on her way to Professor Petrov's class when the charms on her wrist tingled with warning. A heavy footfall alerted her to the presence of another person.

Blake Lockwood.

As soon as she saw him stepping around the corner, muttering and gesturing, she knew it was an ambush.

Zuri burst towards her doorway, determined to throw herself through the door and into the safety of her suite. Her fingertips almost brushed the handle before she realized it would be a mistake. She didn't need a spell to know that they'd trapped her door.

The stairs were the next best escape route, but as she turned to flee that direction, Scarlett Calloway appeared, blocking her path.

"Going somewhere?"

Her arrogance was proof enough that they'd tampered with her door. They knew she was trapped. Zuri thought about fighting back until Jakob Wagner stepped through a wall. They had her on three sides. A perfect killing field. She'd never be able to defend against three separate attacks.

As the sharp tint of faez filled the air, Zuri did the only thing she could think of to escape.

Zuri threw herself off the balcony.

Landing knocked her dazed with blurry vision. She groaned at the sharp pain in her arm and entire left side at the point of impact. Broken bones for sure.

Rolling onto her side, which used muscles in her chest that squeezed those broken bones, Zuri dug her fist into the side pocket of her backpack, pulling out a vial of swirling green-brown liquid. The taste was bitter and metallic, but the moment it went down her throat, the pain went away and she felt a surge of energy, which was important because she didn't have much time.

Back on her feet, numb and a little lightheaded, Zuri ran for the stairs on the opposite side of the first floor.

"She's going the other way!" yelled Jakob from the balcony.

A hardwood chair exploded right behind her. One of Blake's spells, but it'd missed by a few feet.

Zuri knew she couldn't outrun them, and didn't know how many others were on the hunt. She ran until she was out of sight, then curled back around, heading through the kitchen area, which was technically off-limits, but what would she care if she were dead?

The white-coated staff looked up with dead eyes at her entrance, but said nothing as she hurried past chefs cutting vegetables for the evening meal.

The dining hall was empty except for a trio of attendants setting the tables with fresh cutlery. She limped past them and headed back to the original stairs that went past her room, hesitating on the bottom step. If she were wrong, and ran right into Scarlett, it was going to be a very quick end, but her arm was too injured for her to do any spellcasting.

Every step upward was like having a cavity drilled without an analgesic. Her ribs, her arm, they screamed mutely in pain. The emergency elixir was making it so she *could* move, but it didn't come without its price.

When she passed the second landing without spotting Scarlett, she thought she had a chance, but then she heard steps behind her as she hit the third.

"She's above me," cried Scarlett.

The ringing of footsteps followed Zuri upward. She needed a safe place. Other students or professors would be enough. A little light murder was condoned in Coterie as long as no one saw you do the deed.

Scarlett was a half-level behind when Zuri hit the fourth floor. The auditorium was only a short sprint away. She saw Blake running from the opposite direction, a snarl on his lips, trying to cut her off.

Zuri pushed past the pain and made the final sprint to Professor Petrov's class, throwing herself through the door. The professor had been pacing before the front row of the sparsely attended class; her teammates were two of only nine, and they immediately rose to their feet when she arrived.

"Miss Musa, glad you were finally able to make it," said Professor Petrov.

She was the embodiment of the stern teacher, with her brown hair pulled into a tight bun.

Blake, Scarlett, and Jakob came in through the opposite door, heaving with breath and angrily glaring at Zuri for her escape.

The professor took one look at them and then back to Zuri.

"Miss Musa, it appears that you require some medical attention. Your arm is at an unusual angle and you have blood on your lips."

Wetness came away on her fingertips as Zuri pulled them away. The reminder that she'd survived a thirty-foot fall wasn't lost on her.

"Justine, why don't you and your friend take Miss Musa to have that taken care of?"

As soon as she'd spoken, Blake and the other two started to back out of class, but Professor Petrov snapped her fingers.

"Mister Lockwood, I don't think I gave you or your friends permission to leave my class."

"I'm sorry, Professor, we didn't mean to join. We went to the wrong room. We'll be leaving now."

Professor Petrov slapped her hand on the desk, stopping him in his tracks.

"I don't think I gave you permission to leave, Blake. Come, sit down here. Front row, please. It seems you have a thing or two to learn about manners."

Then the professor turned her head and winked, which was their sign to leave.

Outside the classroom, Zuri almost collapsed, but her friends managed to prop her up.

"Where should we go?" asked Iona, clearly worried.

"Not the hospital," said Zuri, shaking her head.

It wasn't forbidden, but it was generally frowned upon to allow others outside of Coterie to see the kind of things that happened in their Hall. If too many students went to the hospital, eventually the medical professionals would figure out that something was amiss in Coterie.

"Can we go to your room?"

"It's trapped," said Zuri, gritting her teeth through the pain.

"Mine isn't ready for visitors," said Justine without prompting.

"I guess we'll head to mine," said Iona.

"Just enough to get me stable and not in pain. Then we can head to a private healer in the second ward that my family goes to."

"I'm sorry," said Iona as they helped her down the stairs gingerly. "We never should have left you alone. We won't make that mistake again."

Zuri agreed even though she knew it was likely they'd make a different, equally fatal mistake at one point, unless she took care of Blake Lockwood once and for all.

TWENTY-THREE

Twelve sets of black eyes stared at Justine from the two wyrmwood shelves she'd built onto the wall of her bedroom. She wasn't wearing a skirt, but she mimed a curtsey.

"Okay, ladies, which one of you would like to join me today? It's going to be a special, special day! You're going to help me with a secret, a special secret. One that can help me and my new friends. But we can't tell them how we found it. I like them, all well and good, but they don't know me like you do. Isn't that right?"

Justine looked from left to right and back again. Black eyes followed her. Waiting. Hoping. They all wanted to be her special friend.

"Come on, now. Don't be shy. I need a volunteer. Will it be you, Margret? Or how about you, Abagail?"

Twelve handmade dolls, six to a row, sat on the shelves with their legs hanging over. Not all—some of the dolls were smaller, so their little feet went right to the edge. A few of them like Jasmine were larger and they barely fit, so she had to keep them on the top row.

"You know I don't like picking," she said as her head rotated back and forth. "But I will if I have to. I promise you that, while it might be a little frightening, it will be equally, and more, exciting!"

Justine rocked on her heels, grinning at the dolls as her hands twitched. She never felt so alive as when she was alone with them. When she'd lived with her parents, she'd had to wait until they were on vacation to pull out her dolls, because her father didn't approve. He didn't understand how important they were. She was the Dollmaker, which was better than any mean magics he tried to instill in her.

"Enie, meanie, minie moe..."

She went through the choosing ceremony, landing on Abagail, but as soon as her finger touched the cloth doll, she knew it was the wrong choice.

"I won't make you do it, Abagail."

Her heart knew exactly which one she should choose, but her mind was afraid.

When she'd first started making the dolls, she crafted them out of cloth and plastic, held together with thread and glue. They wore pretty dresses and were like hugging a kitten when she squeezed them to her chest.

But none of those were going to work for what she needed to do next.

There were three dolls that had been made with hand carved and polished darkwood, titanium rods, and silk threads from *purpura domina aranea* spiders—dressed in clothes Justine had sewn herself. The rods had been cast by an alumnus of Metallum Nocturne as a favor that he thought was for her father, and the runes, meticulously etched into the substructure, were from a tome dating to the Middle Ages thatt had no known origin.

While three were of that make, only one made her heart flutter when she looked at it. It was the same as the other two in all ways except one: it had a tiny seed-heart that had been harvested from a nekyia tree.

Ludmilla.

The doll had straight black hair, cherub-like cheeks, and two different colored eyes: one coal-black and the other silver-grey. The glass eye hadn't been that color when she'd first installed it, but a week later, she'd found that it'd turned.

Justine carefully lifted Ludmilla from the top shelf and set her on the bed, then smoothed her black smock so it lay lady-like on her body. The doll was the largest of her collection, nearly two feet tall, and could sit up on her own.

Her heart fluttered in her chest as she locked gazes with Ludmilla.

"I'm not afraid. I'm really not. Not for me. Maybe we shouldn't jump into this all at once. We could start small if that's what you'd like."

The spell was full of jerky motions, barely any somatic components, but the mind-pictures were some of the more difficult she'd had to master as they helped connect the limbs of the doll to her own. The moment of connection was like a piece of ice getting shoved into her mind: shock then comfortable coolness.

With a twitch of her wrist, the doll jumped off the bed, landing with knees bent and then striding forward. The first part had taken months to learn, how to translate her own bodily movements into the doll.

Ludmilla strolled around the room, confidently marching in a way that made Justine jealous. Head up, chin lifted, making eye contact with the other dolls. Justine wished she could be like Ludmilla. Cool. Confident. A bit of an extrovert.

"That's good, Ludmilla. Thank you. I didn't realize I needed that as much as you did."

Justine bowed to the two-foot doll and Ludmilla returned the gesture.

"This next part might be a little scary," she said, realizing that she was probably more worried than Ludmilla.

First Justine broke the connection. She didn't want to confuse the poor doll with multiple command structures. That way lay madness. And she wasn't mad. No matter what her father had screamed at her before she left for the Halls. No matter that he'd torn his shirt and broken the door frame with a heavy punch.

This time she cast a proper spell. One with many difficult, tricksy words. Speaking had never been her strong suit. Not when others were around. They made her think about every syllable, every word, and how it flowed across her tongue. They made it impossible. She was better in the privacy of her own suite. It was one of the reasons she enjoyed the company of her dolls. They didn't judge her. Not like her classmates at St. Jude's or the other Coterie students. Even Zuri judged her, though Justine suspected there was a kind heart beneath that bristling exterior. The only one who hadn't was Iona, even though she frightened Justine. Not for her own safety. But for everyone else's. There was something feral in Iona like a wild beast loosed in a dark cage. Only Justine saw it, because she saw people's true selves. That warlock had changed Iona, twisted the wiring with those tattoos. That's how Justine knew. She saw the person they wanted to be, just as she knew in her heart who she wanted to be too.

Justine knew it would hurt. For her and for Ludmilla. But it was the only way she knew to get the answer to the Veil problem. If they couldn't get past the Six-Fold Problem, then they wouldn't pass, and she'd have to return home a failure. Her father wouldn't abide that. He'd made that clear—very, very clear.

And besides, except for all the killing, she liked Coterie. She got to spend her time working on her dolls without anyone telling her that she couldn't. She hadn't told any of the professors about her project, but she knew they would approve. Coterie was about pushing past limits, going places that magic wasn't supposed to go, and she was about to step over one of those lines.

As Justine came close to completing the spell, she realized she might have made a mistake. She was still standing and didn't know what would happen afterwards.

When it finished, she felt a sudden vertigo. Nothing terrible like the time her father took her through a portal to Ice Hold, when she fell on her knees and vomited on the nice carpet—he hadn't been happy about that—but it made her dizzy, so she closed her eyes.

Justine rocked on her feet.

She felt different. More purposeful.

Before she could tumble over, Justine opened her eyes. Only to find herself staring at her own midsection.

The body that she'd existed in for nearly the entirety of her life was rocking on its heels without her consciousness.

Justine intended to speak, but no words came out. She'd neglected to install a voice box or some other arcana into the doll, so she couldn't speak. But that was okay. Today's exercise wasn't about communication. She could add that capability later.

Using Ludmilla's doll body, Justine ambled around the bedroom stiffly. It was the same awkward gait that she'd had to learn when she first controlled a doll with the string-spell method. It would get better with time and practice. There was a spell for a higher level of control that she could perform, but she didn't need that one now and it was kind of dangerous because it involved a bit of her soul.

Comfortable that she'd made the connection, Justine pulled herself onto the bed, crawling to the pillows, where she made a throne. It was strange seeing her body at the end of the bed, blankly staring into space, but it wasn't like she'd ever felt comfortable in that meat suit. Justine rapped her knuckles against her wooden thigh, smiling at the hard, hollow sound.

Legs crossed with her hands resting on the knees in a lotus position, Justine closed her eyes and concentrated on Ludmilla's heart.

All dolls made for control had a heart. It was the center. The germ of its personality. A nekyia tree was a natural portal to the Veil—the place between the living and the dead. She'd been given the seed by an admirer of her father who'd tried to garner favor by buttering up to his daughter. Little did he know how fruitless an exercise that was.

But the seed had been a priceless gift.

And now it would help her find the answer in the Veil.

Justine had gotten the idea when Iona told her the story about the mummy-mirror. The preserved corpse had been left with a connection to the Veil. No one knew if it was linked to the actual soul that had once inhabited the body, but it didn't matter. Any old imprint of life could animate a corpse purposely made for that.

The nekyia seed wasn't linked to a specific soul imprint, but the tree's existence as a portal between the two realms had primed it with the essence of many, many souls. Alive and dead.

Justine/Ludmilla reached out to that other place. A realm that wasn't safe for the living. But as a doll, she could inhabit that space without the same fears. Not that it wasn't dangerous, but much less so.

When she opened her doll eyes, she saw a featureless plane covered in skeletal trees while swirling dark green mist hid the lower half of her little body. The ground was spongy. She spotted a burned glove not far from her left foot, but she hadn't come to investigate the old memories, but solve a troublesome problem.

The Veil portion of the Six-Fold Problem was part riddle and part spell. But it had to be cast inside the Veil, or so they thought. A trip that was dangerous for a living soul.

"Head, feet, heart, toes.

Sinew, song, treble, woes.

Living, dead, no one knows.

Curl the fist, anger your foes."

The incantation created black sparks in the air like negative energy. Justine performed the rest of the spell that they'd deciphered from the runes, her hard little doll hands moving with spastic grace.

This was the part she wasn't sure would work. Could she complete a spell using the doll body and not her own?

Justine imbued the incantation with faez, willing the riddle to give her the answer.

The shadowy sparks grew more frequent and thicker, connecting at points before disappearing into the ether. She worried that it hadn't worked before she realized that the miniature explosions of negative energy were forming a symbol. A rune. An answer.

She waited patiently as it formed before her eyes. It looked like the old draugr runes she'd learned in middle school.

The answer.

Justine memorized it and forced herself to draw it in midair to confirm, before the rune dissipated into the Veil air.

A mournful howl sent shivers down her spine.

She'd been discovered.

With the answer firmly in her head, Justine dismissed the connection to the Veil and returned to her suite.

She had a moment of confusion, forgetting that she was in Ludmilla's body, not her own.

But the joy of the answer had her leaping to her feet and doing summersaults around the cushy bed.

In the excitement of wanting to tell Iona and Zuri, she tried to leave the suite, but as her hand clanked over the door handle, she remembered she needed to return to her body first.

Cutting the connection was harder than she expected. Justine felt real for once. Perfectly placed in a body that she'd created herself.

When she returned to her meat suit, Justine fell to one knee. The separation had been harder on her mind than she'd expected.

But eventually the ache passed, and she gathered her things for a trip across the Obelisk.

She'd found the answer, and she had to tell her new friends!

TWENTY-FOUR

The last part of the Six-Fold Problem was the Hex. For Zuri, it made sense that this was the final part for them to solve. Hexes were offensive. An attack. They rarely had any purpose except to hurt others.

Which was why she'd never been a fan, even when Blake had been her boyfriend. She'd thought it was just the male's predilection to be edgy and slightly cruel. A proving ground. Boys will be boys and all that.

"This is number eighty-seven," said Justine, reading from a clipboard. "The bone-rattler."

They were no longer working in the mummy-mirror room. It was too small for what they had to do, and the equipment would only get destroyed. Instead, they'd set up shop in the open part of the level, near the fountain. Since they were the last group, no one else was around.

Not that they hadn't left up defenses because if Blake's group caught them unawares, it would be a seven-on-three battle. Each day before they began, Zuri set up her personal defense cubes. It was a pain in the ass, because she had to do it twice, once to set up at the fountain and again when she returned to her suite.

"Give me a moment," said Zuri as she studied the spell.

Most hexes were only a few words and gestures. They were meant to be used in battle, and a long, drawn-out ritual would only leave you exposed to the enemy's attacks.

"Okay, got it."

The language was an offshoot of Sumerian. Zuri stood thirty paces away from the sensor wall with her hands up, mentally reviewing the words before she spat them out.

The hex had no visible tell. When she completed the spell, the wall shook for a second before returning to stillness.

"Anything?" she asked Iona, who'd been sitting on a table they'd dragged from the room with her knees against her chest.

"Same as the rest."

Zuri put a hand to her forehead, massaging the tension with her forefinger and thumb. They'd been at this for days.

"What if we run out of hexes?" asked Iona.

"Unlikely. But I'm not sure this is the right method either." Zuri smiled at the mousy Justine. "If only we could solve it as elegantly as you solved the Veil problem."

Justine hid her grin with the clipboard, cheeks growing rosy as her eyes glittered with excitement.

"Someday you'll have to tell us how you did that," said Iona.

"I will," said Justine with a tight nod of her head.

Since she'd solved the Veil problem, Zuri had noticed a change in Justine. She seemed more confident, less prone to flinching at any random loud noise and engaged when they spoke to her.

"Ready for the next?" asked Justine.

Zuri leaned against the table stacked with tomes that they'd taken from the library. *A Hex to Remember. One Thousand Hexes to Impress Your Friends. Ancient Curses of Samaria.* They'd grabbed any book that they thought might have a spell they could use.

"No."

"I can take a turn if you're getting tired," said Iona.

"That's not it. Trial and error is taking too long. I shouldn't have suggested it."

Iona lifted her shoulders.

"It's not like I'm bringing anything to this one. Weirdly enough, Fenris wasn't into hexes."

Zuri gritted her teeth and exhaled sharply.

"This is on me. I should know better. It's not like I didn't study hexes, but I just never really liked using them. I always preferred to protect myself rather than hurt someone else. It just felt, you know, more elegant. Restrained. Hexes just feel messy and imposing. Gauche."

"The best defense is a good offense," said Justine.

The phrase sparked a memory in Zuri. Where had she heard that before?

"Problem?" asked Iona, but Zuri waved her off. She didn't want to interrupt her thoughts, so she paced around the tables while her friends watched her carefully as if she'd gone mad.

"Professor Kingsley said that to me last semester when I was asking her a question about le Fay's Paradox. Wait. No. She didn't say that exactly. What she said was, '*the best defense can't beat a good offense, but not for the reasons you think. They're opposite sides of the same coin.*'"

"I literally have no idea what that means," said Iona.

"Neither did I at the time. I was asking her about the math of her thesis. She said no one had ever tried to confirm it and that practice was better than theory, or something like that. By why opposite sides of the same coin? What is she…"

The answer hit like a sledgehammer. Zuri had never experienced a eureka moment. She'd thought the descriptions of them a little overdone, but now she understood. It was as if her entire body had been lit up with fireworks.

"That's it. Why didn't I see that before?"

"See what before?" asked Justine.

"The professor was giving me a hint and I completely missed it."

Zuri pulled out her phone and scrolled through her notes back from the beginning of the semester when she'd first encountered the Six-Fold Problem. She'd solved the Ward almost on sight.

"Two sides of the same coin. The Ward answer was a clue to the Hex. The protection spell was based on ancient Egyptian, derived from hieroglyphs found inside the hidden chambers in the Great Pyramid of Giza. Which means, the Hex needs to be the opposite of that. Seven hells, why didn't I see that before?"

There was a whole line of thinking that her mind raced after about the connection between hexes and wards, but she couldn't express it to her allies, nor did she want to interrupt her thoughts. Instead, Zuri gestured into the darkness and ran headlong into it without regard for her safety. She had to get to the Six-Fold Problem to test her theory.

After squeezing past the statue of Anubis and hurrying down the hieroglyph-covered hallway, Zuri stood across from the rune-covered archway. Six runes. Six problems.

"Are we doing it?" asked Iona when she arrived out of breath.

"I'm ready if you two are," said Zuri.

Three people. Six runes. They settled on each of them performing two of the answers. When they concluded their spells, the matching rune on the archway lit up with a strange purple-black glow. A faint hum filled the air. Each new rune increased the frequency until the hairs on Zuri's arms were standing at attention.

She saved the Hex for last. When she completed the rune, the entire circuitry around the archway lit up and the flat stone beneath it changed to swirling mist.

"We did it," sighed Zuri.

She'd been so worried that they'd never make it to the next level. Somehow dying to Blake would be preferable to letting him beat her at magical puzzles. But these weren't just puzzles. They were lessons. And now she knew something about the relationship between hexes and wards that had already begun to unlock ideas.

"Hands together?"

The archway was wide enough for three to squeeze through. Zuri was at the center. Portal travel was familiar, but her heart rate doubled at the approach. It wasn't the journey, but what was on the other side.

The moment they touched the swirling mist, they were thrown somewhere else. Travel was instantaneous and gut-wrenching.

Zuri came to on the other side with Iona already on her knees, while Justine seemed strangely unaffected.

"Why is that so terrible?" said Iona, but Zuri was barely paying attention because she couldn't believe her eyes.

The place that they'd come from had been a study in darkness with shadow-filled hallways and hidden alcoves while the air itself seemed to absorb any light. Sometimes it took conjuring two or three mage lights to equal the output of a single one.

This place was the opposite. Zuri held her arm up over her eyes because the glare was almost sunlike. High in the cathedral ceiling was a burning orb that shone across a wide space covered in sand and white buildings.

"Where are we?" asked Iona.

For a moment, a stab of fear made Zuri think that perhaps they'd gotten the runes wrong and sent themselves to another place entirely.

"It's the Obelisk still."

"This is bigger than the interior of the Obelisk," said Iona. "I know. I walked the outside perimeter. This is at least twice as big, or bigger."

Justine cleared her throat and spoke in an accurate imitation of Professor Ravenscroft, who'd given them their first lecture in Coterie.

"*The Obelisk is filled with secrets. More secrets than you could discover in a dozen lifetimes.*"

"That's pretty good, Justine," said Iona, smiling.

"This is like ancient Egypt, but different," said Zuri.

She walked onto the sands, feeling the silky crunch beneath her shoes.

"I hate the beach, the sand gets into everything," said Justine, still grinning.

"I've never been on the beach," said Iona, crouching down and running the sand through her hands. "It feels weird."

They walked towards the first building, its white walls adorned with hieroglyphs along the roofline. There were larger buildings further in, but Zuri didn't want to rush into danger, not when they understood little about the new location.

"Oh shit, it is them," came a voice from their right.

A dusty-looking Melanie with a headband and a shovel over her shoulder trotted into view. Her boyfriend, Marcus, appeared from behind.

"Hey, Zuri," said Melanie, waving. "Glad to see you finally made it. Was starting to worry about you."

"Me too."

She craned her neck in all directions.

"What is this place?" asked Iona.

Melanie and Marcus shared a glance, clearly not interested in answering questions from the newcomer. Since they'd been stuck on the Six-Fold Problem with none of the other groups around, Zuri had forgotten how much the rest of her class disliked the Missouri girl.

"Not trying to expose your hard-earned secrets, but what is everyone calling it?" asked Zuri.

"The Oasis."

"Seems big."

Melanie pulled the shovel off her shoulder and dug it into the sand.

"Bigger than you think."

"What about places to work?" asked Zuri.

"Lots of spots to claim, if you can claim them," said Melanie with a smirk.

Zuri was clued to the arrival of Blake and his group when Marcus cursed under his breath. From their left, the seven members of Blake's group appeared on a stone road that looked like it wove through the buildings.

"I told you it was them," said Jakob, which made Zuri want to check for sensors they'd left near the entrance. A concern for future exploration.

Blake was wearing a tan explorers outfit looking like he was leading an archeological dig.

"I thought I said anyone caught helping them would pay a price," said Blake, glaring at Melanie and Marcus.

"I'm not helping," said Melanie. "We just came to see who'd come through the portal."

"You gave them information."

"What this place is called is hardly secret-worthy."

Blake crossed his arms.

"I thought I was perfectly clear. Any help, no matter how small, would be punished."

Melanie rolled her eyes, then turned and disappeared the way they'd come.

"You have such a way with the ladies," said Zuri.

"It worked on you."

"Sometimes you have to cut something open to learn that it's rotten inside."

"You shut your dirty mouth, scab," said Jakob, stepping forward with his fingers working the beginnings of a spell.

Blake reached out and put his hand over Jakob's arms, pulling them down.

"Not here, Jakob."

"But—"

"I said. Not. Here."

A sudden awareness came over Jakob and he stepped back, shaking his head as if waking from a dream.

"Yeah, sorry, I forgot."

"Shut up, you dolt," said Blake under his breath, then turned back to them. "Good luck keeping up with us. We're almost to the third level."

Her former boyfriend walked back through his group, leading them around the tall white building where they quickly disappeared from sight.

"Well that wasn't ominous," said Iona. "Why was he so cautious about attacking us here?"

Zuri looked around but saw nothing obvious.

"Maybe this is a protected place. The professors didn't want the portal to be an easy place for an ambush or something."

"Where do we go now?" asked Justine.

"My sister told me there were great places to hole up on the second level because it has great ward anchors. We should try to find one."

"Did she tell you where to look?" asked Iona.

"I wish it worked like that, but things change in the Obelisk."

"Then let's find a new home," said Justine cheerily.

"Hold up," said Zuri. "We need to treat this place as hostile. I think we've gotten too complacent about our old setup. Reapply your wards."

They spent the next ten minutes casting protective spells, layering them until it felt like having invisible magical armor.

The direction they picked to explore was opposite of where Blake and his friends had gone. While it was certainly possible they'd hurried around to ambush them, Zuri wasn't so sure he was that decisive about action.

Not everything was covered in sand. Fitted white stone paths made travel easier. The buildings varied in size and shape: from longhouses to miniature pyramids. At the entrance to a cube-shaped house, burn scars outlined the doorway, which they thought was either a clever way to keep other curious first years away, or the result of a trap explosion.

Exploration took many hours, as it was slow going through unfamiliar territory. After reviewing the area, they decided on three different candidates for their Oasis home. The first was a longhouse that had a nest of stone scarabs inside which had taken a fair amount of firepower to clear out. The second was a pyramid, but after a brief review they decided that it held too many secrets to make it their base. In the end, they choose an old tomb that expanded into a big open space at the back where the traps were easy to unravel.

By the end of a long day, probably more like a day and a half, they'd made the old tomb their new home. It'd taken a few trips back to the first level for clothes and other living supplies, and they'd had to set up new wards and the protective cubes. Eventually they'd have to go into the city to purchase cots and other camping stuff, but for now they'd use the big comforters from their suites.

Zuri wasn't sure how the other two felt about their new abode, but for her, it was a major milestone. She'd heard the stories from her sister about the challenges of the Obelisk, and how they'd shaped her to be the mage she was today. Passing the Six-Fold Problem with an unorthodox group and with Blake and his sycophants always on the lookout to take her down felt like a big step. It certainly wasn't success.

She had nearly four and a half years more to survive, but after the rough start to her Coterie experience, making it to the Oasis and finding a good spot to hole up felt pretty damn good.

TWENTY-FIVE

The black wig made Iona's scalp itch. She'd never worn one before. Nor worn a costume. Or gone to a big party. Her friends—could she call them friends...allies for sure, but she wasn't sure if their connection would extend out of the Obelisk or would have happened if they hadn't a choice—wanted her to go.

Not that Iona was worried. They needed her as much as she needed them. The only thing that mattered was survival. Not a hypothetical timeline in which none of them would have given her a passing glance had she not joined Coterie.

Iona tugged on the black braided wig until it was properly placed, then pinned it so it wouldn't move. The lights around the mirror hummed and grew brighter for a second, then returned to its previously warm glow. The entire electrical system of the Tomb, as they'd come to call it, had been designed by Justine, who had tapped into the latent magic that seemed to run everywhere on the Oasis level.

The strange, mousy girl had been full of surprises since she'd joined the team. There seemed to be more lurking in the boxes she'd hauled up from her suite and never said word one about the contents of, but given her solving the Veil problem without input from either her or Zuri, they decided they could let her have her secrets.

"Does this look right?" she asked.

Zuri was adjusting a golden headdress with an ankh on her forehead. She'd already squeezed into a white dress that made her black skin glow from within.

"Smashing. Your Cleopatra is going to kill. Straight-up murder."

Iona hadn't been so sure about attending the Sanctuary Party. It seemed like a bad idea, imbibing drinks and letting their guard down, but Zuri had assured her that any shenanigans would be dealt with by the entire class. If Blake tried to kill one of them, the rest of the first years would annihilate him and his team.

But more importantly, she'd argued, they needed to talk with the other groups without creating an excuse for Blake to seek retribution. While they couldn't ally with any of the others, it would be possible to trade information, or strange reagents or items they'd discovered in the Obelisk.

Iona pulled the thumb-sized piece of onyx from her pouch. It wasn't just any gemstone. The fact that it'd come from the mummy after she'd destroyed it confirmed it was a heart-seed, which gave it more value than a normal stone. Zuri had suggested that it could either be turned into something she could use or traded for an item already made.

The clop-clop of heavy steps had Iona turning to find a jackal-headed figure holding a golden staff. When the mouth moved with the voice, Iona nearly fell over.

"How do I look?" asked Justine from beneath the jackal mask.

"Seven hells," said Zuri, shaking her head incredulously. "Like the ancient god Set come to life."

"Creepy and cool," said Iona.

Justine gave an ungod-like curtsey and they finished up their preparations, heading to the party on the white stone paths that everyone used to get around the Oasis. They headed for the center of the huge space, which had a small blue pond; the outer ring had been covered in open tents with elixir and smoke stations.

"Remember," said Zuri. "No trouble. We're here to find information and do some trading. Avoid Blake and his crew at all costs."

Most of their class was already in attendance, gyrating to the thumping beats that one of the Siren Sisters, Coral Thalassa, was playing on her DJ equipment. She had light blue body paint on beneath her white wrap. The headphones matched her skin tone. Word was that she did late-night sets in the second ward a few times a month.

Zuri had warned there were at least four other Cleopatras, but Iona didn't care if theirs were better. They'd come to make deals and acquire information, not win a costume contest.

But that didn't mean she didn't find herself nodding to the music. When they weren't working on the next ritual, Fenris would play the local stations on a cheap radio that tended to static. But that was simple music that grew repetitive the more she heard it. Beneath the artificial sun of the Oasis, Iona found the complex beats over unusual melodies were scrambling her thoughts, and she'd only taken one small hit from the jar of alchemical smoke in her fist.

Someone bumped into her purposely.

"Hey Brenna, you've got to check out the Mirage Bar. It's blowing my mind."

Iona turned to find a guy whose name she couldn't remember—Derek or Damian, something like that—in a golden guard outfit.

"Oh shit, Pig Girl. Sorry, I thought you were Brenna."

The name stung a little, but who was she kidding, these people would have never associated with her in a million years. The fact that she was here in their midst was a minor miracle. Not that she liked them. They were conceited, arrogant assholes, but it was like getting a private tour through a castle that held untold riches.

Iona went in search of the Mirage Bar, which she didn't find until she was almost upon it. She'd been clued in by the shimmering field across the pond and the other first years wandering away with colorful glasses in their fists. As she neared, the wooden bar came into view with Scarlett Calloway behind it. She was wearing an outfit that made her look like a cobra.

"I can't believe you'd stoop to serving other people."

"And I'm surprised you showed your face," said Scarlett.

"I wanted to see how the other half lived."

"It's the better, not other, and it's not half. We're the elite few. The best of the best. Which is why you shouldn't be in Coterie. You're mucking up the place with your piggy smells."

"If you're truly the best, why didn't your little trick work? I'll admit, you had me fooled. I thought you had a kernel of humanity in that empty shell, but I was wrong. You're Blake's little windup toy. What's it like being his minion?"

"You know it's not going to last. Eventually we'll catch you with your guard down and we'll no longer have to worry about the stench of bovine in the Obelisk."

"Your schtick is tiresome, Scarlett. Either make me a drink, or shut up."

Scarlett blinked heavily. Either she was surprised by the rude response, or the request for a drink.

"One Nile Nectar, coming right up."

Iona didn't bother watching Scarlett. She didn't care. When the redhead was finished, she handed over a glass of orangish-amber liquid that sparkled on top. It smelled sweet and tangy.

"Thanks," said Iona, lifting the glass and disappearing the other way.

She spotted Jakob Wagner in a pharaoh's outfit and headed straight for him.

"Scarlett made this for you."

"What?"

He was confused, but accepted the drink.

"Don't ask me, I'm just the delivery girl. Said it was a Nile Nectar."

Jakob sniffed the liquid.

"I like Nile Nectars."

"Have fun," said Iona, strolling back to the other side of the Oasis. Before she'd made it twenty feet, she heard an explosion of glass, followed by cursing in thick German.

"You fucking bitch, you broke the rules of Sanctuary Party. I'm going to kill you!"

He came marching towards her as the other first years in range gathered around like a noose. His lower lip was scorched as if he'd tried to drink scalding hot coffee.

"Don't blame me," said Iona, smirking. "Like I said, I was just the delivery girl. I didn't touch your drink, and Scarlett was the one who made it. If you have a problem, take it up with her. She's on your team, after all."

The other first years had initially looked sympathetic to his argument until her response. Then they were glaring at him as he began to cast a spell that looked to be a powerful hex.

Blake came running over in another pharaoh costume, but his was more grandiose than Jakob's.

"What did this bitch do?"

Jakob let his spell falter and pointed to his jaw, which was bright red from the alchemical burn.

"Does everyone see that?" Blake asked the group. "Because she tried to kill Jakob, which means she's ours."

"Nice try," said Iona. "Scarlett made that drink for me. It's not my fault that Jakob drank it."

Blake grabbed Jakob by the shoulder.

"Is that what happened?"

"How am I supposed to know?"

Blake's eyes darted to the other first years, gauging their willingness to allow retribution.

"It looks like Pig Girl didn't do anything. No harm, no foul. If she didn't do it, you can't go after her."

"Seriously?" asked Jakob, turning on him and pushing him away.

"Yeah, seriously. Now watch your fucking tone and settle the fuck down."

Jakob's rage quickly dissipated. He hung his head.

"That's right, keep your dog on a leash," said Iona.

The gathered crowd laughed, which turned Jakob's face beet red as he rushed away.

"The Sanctuary Party isn't forever, Pig Girl," said Blake. "One day we'll catch you digging in the mud, and that'll be it. We'll have ourselves a BBQ. A little sweet meat from the white trash."

She was furious, of course. But she couldn't show it. This was a battle of wills. If she backed down, it would only encourage him and cement his place at the top of the food chain.

A reminder to the group that it'd been Scarlett's intent to kill her might have swayed a few minds, maybe created an argument about whether or not Scarlett should be punished, but that would only make Iona look weak. Which she couldn't afford.

It was the same with Fenris. She knew he'd killed his other assistants. They'd disappointed him in one way or another. Or he just grew tired of them. He'd expected her to be self-sufficient and to feed and care for him while learning magic and providing a canvas for his tattoos. Not hers. The etchings in her skin were still a mystery.

But that wasn't her immediate concern.

Iona knew she shouldn't taunt him further, but he was so smug, so condescending that it felt like the right thing.

"Bring it, Worm. Because that's all you are to me, and don't act like you know why that's your name. I made you scurry away after you tried to kill me in the Mummy Room. I'm not afraid of you. But you clearly are of me."

It was Blake's turn for his cheeks to bloom crimson. His hands curled to fists at his side, but before he could say another word, he side-eyed the others watching him and forcibly relaxed.

"I'm watching you, Pig Girl."

The crowd, disappointed by the lack of fireworks, went in other directions, leaving her by herself until she decided it was officially over.

Chest full of adrenaline, Iona milled around the Oasis. Whenever she neared a group, they usually spotted her first and turned their backs.

"Good job, Pig Girl," she admonished herself, remembering Zuri's instruction not to cause waves at the party.

"You shouldn't poke the hornet's nest," said a deep voice from beneath a palm tree.

Iona spun around to find Orion Dreadmarsh in his street clothes. She'd never been so close. He was big, at least six foot five, probably more, and thick like a heavyweight wrestler, but without the bulging gut. She was pretty sure he could snap her neck without trying very hard.

"Oh, hi."

Orion stared at her like a bug under a glass. She could feel his intensity. It was like standing next to raging, invisible fire.

"I didn't expect you to join the party."

There was a brief moment when she thought he would answer, but then he turned his head as if he'd heard something and marched away.

"Well that was...something."

As Iona curled around the party looking for her friends, she saw miniature sandstorms whirling away on the dance floor. The other dancers were avoiding them. She wasn't sure who was controlling the sandstorms, but they gave the party an otherworldly feel, which would have been more enjoyable had she not tangled with Blake and his friends.

"What have I got myself into?"

Iona spotted the jackal-headed Set across the party, leaning against a palm tree. She was going to join Justine when she heard someone trying to get her attention.

"Iona."

Her first instinct was that it was a trap, but when she turned she found Melanie leaning around the corner of a white building covered in moving hieroglyphs.

"Hey, Melanie," said Iona, checking over her shoulder.

The girl seemed nervous and didn't know what to do with her hands.

"You really showed Blake and Jakob back there."

"Well, they're assholes. The worst thing you can do is believe their bullshit," said Iona, who had no idea if that were true but it sounded good and Melanie seemed to agree.

"I hate them so much. I feel like I can never relax, always looking over my shoulder."

Iona saw an opening but she didn't want to press too hard. She knew that Zuri had already tried to recruit them to no avail.

"The bigger the group, the easier it is to protect yourself," she said.

Melanie opened her mouth. Clearly she had something she wanted to say, but checked over her shoulder and sighed heavily.

"It would be, but you know, Marcus has a hard time trusting others."

"A team of five would be strong."

"I know." Melanie closed her eyes for a moment as if she were in pain. "I heard you found a heart-seed onyx from that mummy."

"I did."

"Is it for trade?"

"Possibly. What do you have in mind?"

"A telekinesis glove that's super useful for disarming all the traps that are around here. Or a shielding brooch, which would help in case of ambush."

"Yeah, those sound interesting. Let me see what else is on offer and let you know. I don't want to pull the trigger too fast."

"Totally understandable," said Melanie, biting her lower lip. "I'd do the same, but you know, if you have another offer, give me and Marcus a chance to up our bid."

Feeling a little jittery from the encounter with Blake and then Orion, Iona went straight for the dance floor. She'd never danced except by herself, so it was an odd experience gyrating to the music while others were doing the same. While no one came near her during the dance session, a few people made eye contact and gave her subtle nods, which was more interaction than she'd had with any of them since she'd arrived at Coterie.

They don't completely hate me, she decided.

Or maybe they liked what she'd done with Blake. To be fair, she was making herself a lightning rod, which was good for them. Not for her. She'd only ever had to deal with a bully once when a kid a few years older than her knocked the bags of groceries out of her hands, smashing at least two jars, and spilling the vegetables over the concrete.

She'd been so mad. Furious. Because Fenris knew every penny she spent and if she had to replace groceries, there could be punishment. Iona had done the first thing that came to mind, and swung the bag in her other hand against the bully's head. The cans of beans smashed him in the temple, knocking him down, but she didn't stop there and kicked him over and over until a parent came over and pulled her off. They'd never messed with her again, and she was glad because in the heat of the moment, she'd felt like she could have killed him.

When she grew tired of dancing, Iona grabbed another smoke from the bar and found a spot to sit.

"I thought I said not to cause a scene," said Zuri, who came up from behind and leaned against the same boulder.

"A raging bull will miss its target in its haste for revenge."

"Bullshit, Iona. I mean, you might not be wrong, but you didn't learn that in Missouri. You've already told me enough about your life that I know you never messed with any bulls."

"I saw a few on the way into town. Big balls. Big horns. No brains. A lot like Blake."

"Minus the big balls." Zuri sighed. "Well, it's not like they hate us any less. Anyway, Candi Thalassa heard about your heart-seed onyx. She made an offer for it. Pretty good one. A couple of trinkets and a danger-sense enchantment from their private library."

"Melanie made an offer too."

"Good. The more bidders the better."

"She might even be interested in teaming up. I think it's Marcus holding her back."

Zuri swirled a neon green drink around her glass while Iona looked on. She could never quite tell what the other girl was thinking. Was she parsing through the complexities of these elite students, or was she wondering if it'd been a mistake to ally with her?

"Would be nice."

"Do you think any of them are worth it?" asked Iona.

Zuri lifted a single shoulder.

"The heart-seed is pretty powerful. But you have to know how to use it. If you've got something in mind, you might want to hold onto it. On the other hand, Candi's offer is good and could get better."

"Not planning on doing anything with it today, but I'll keep them in mind. On a different note, I ran into Orion a little bit ago."

"Seriously?"

"I think he was just passing through the party. Told me I shouldn't taunt Blake and his friends."

"When Orion Dreadmarsh is the voice of reason, you might want to listen."

"I know, I know. But I figure they already want to kill us. Might as well get our shots in and show the others that they're not the badasses they think they are."

"I wish that was true. I really do, Iona." Zuri turned her head. "I'm going to go check on Justine. She was talking to herself a little bit ago, scaring off the new magics."

Iona saluted her ally and leaned back to inhale a bit more smoke from the alchemical jar. The turns her life had taken since she made the decision to escape Fenris were almost incomprehensible to her former self. She started to wonder where Fenris was, and if he truly was in the city as she suspected, but decided to save those thoughts for another moment. She was, possibly, maybe, having a good time.

TWENTY-SIX

The air, the streets, the cars—everything bothered Blake. It wasn't the city as he wanted it. It wasn't the city he deserved. It didn't feel *his*.

"Babe," said Scarlett while squeezing his hand. "What's going on? You barely said a word during dinner. Even the chef noticed. He's worried that you didn't have a good time or the food was bad."

"The food was fine."

"Fine? I had to trade some big favors to get that table at the last second. He's the top chef in the city. Maybe the world. Those mystdrakon steaks covered in gorgonzola pepper sauce were divine, but you left half of it on the plate. I don't know if they'll ever let us come back."

Blake yanked his hand away from Scarlett.

"I'm fine."

But he wasn't. He wasn't fine. He wasn't good. He wasn't anything. Everything felt off. Like up and down no longer mattered. It was that Pig

Girl bitch. She'd embarrassed him in front of the entire class. And if they saw weakness, then everything could come crumbling down.

"You don't look fine."

Blake spun on his girlfriend, putting his finger in her face.

"Don't you ever tell me how I feel. I'm fine. I just didn't feel like coming out tonight, but you had to try this stupid place because you're sick of the food in the Obelisk. It's not my fucking job to entertain you."

Scarlett recoiled, taking two steps back as a few passersby gave them side-eye.

"I think I'll find my own way back to the Obelisk."

"That's probably a good idea, *babe*."

Blake hated the way Pig Girl had scrambled his thoughts. Zuri was bad enough, but at least she was old magic. But Pig Girl? She wasn't even good enough to be dead magic. How the Halls could have let this backwater yokel from Mississippi into Coterie was beyond him. They had standards. She wouldn't even be allowed to be a server if it were up to him.

If he could have marched up to Head Patron Pythia right then, he would have given her a piece of his mind. Explained why it'd been a bad idea to let her in. She was like a piece of rotten meat in a pot of soup. No matter how small it was, the entire broth would taste wrong. The soup was ruined. That's what she was.

"Fucking bitch."

Blake started off, slamming his shoulder into a businessman, who started to turn around until he saw the glowing flames on his hands.

He marched down the street, daring people to get into his way. But fortunately, or unfortunately, they avoided him.

It wasn't until he was almost to the seventh ward that he realized where he was. The back edge of the first ward wasn't the same as the area around the Spire. Not that he was worried, but it didn't have the same exclusive feeling that he was used to. There was a couple wearing cheap

Hundred Halls hoodies across the street, eyeing him as if he were the one out of place.

As he spun around, getting his bearings, he felt a trickle of warning in the bracelet around his wrist. Nothing big, but enough to put his head on a swivel. Someone was watching him.

Blake reached into his coat pocket and rubbed his thumb over the enchanted piece of amber, filling it with faez to activate the wards. A tingle covered his entire body, which was both soothing and a little annoying. He hated being defensive.

"Whoever you are," he called out, "I know you're watching and I'm ready for you."

No one answered. Not that he expected them to. But the feeling of danger in his breastbone was front and center. Like a piece of food that refused to be swallowed.

"This city's a joke."

Blake spun on his heel to head back the way he'd come and find a proper taxi, or maybe a ghost taxi, when he came face-to-face with what he first thought was a homeless man by the matted hair and scraggly, grey-dusted beard. But then he saw the eyes. Void black. Barely any white around the edges. Could smell the power too. Never experienced that before. It was like watching a hurricane rush into the shore.

"Blake Lockwood."

That the old man knew his name sent alarm bells through his head, but he couldn't muster a movement. His hands were frozen against his side and his thoughts were scrambled. Blake knew he was in danger, but he couldn't do anything to stop it.

"How do you know my name?" he asked eventually, hating the way his voice cracked.

"I've been watching you and some of your fellow Coterie students." The old man's mouth turned into the semblance of a grin, but beneath the wiry hair looked like a cavern of teeth. "I think it's safe to release you. Don't worry. Nothing's going to happen to you except a nice conversation. Please, follow me."

Blake didn't get the impression that he was being given an option, and besides, he was a little curious. And terrified.

"No," he said, surprising himself. "Not unless you tell me what this is about."

The old man leaned in close enough that he could see the color of his hair was mostly dirt with specks of pale beneath. Blake spotted the specks of blood on his jaw. He smelled like the deep earth. Like iron and limestone.

"Pig Girl."

Hearing that name didn't surprise Blake, even if he didn't understand why.

As the old man turned and headed towards a doorway, not even bothering to look back, Blake steeled himself and followed.

It took two seconds for Blake to realize that the old man wasn't the owner of the building. A middle-aged man and woman were sitting on the couch with their throats cut, eyes staring vacantly. There was no blood on their necks, or clothes, and the knives were in their hands.

Drawn by the fresh kills, Blake approached the couch while the old man watched. The couple had strange, almost familiar runes on their arms. Burnt in. But not from the outside. It was as if the runes had climbed out of their skin to sear themselves into the flesh.

Blake's arm extended to brush the jawline of the woman. She wasn't pretty by any means, but something about the absence of a soul made her beautiful.

"Don't touch. It's not polite."

"I'm sorry," said Blake, facing the old man, feeling a bit of the spell wearing off. "What's your name?"

"Fenris."

Blake looked to the symbols burnt into the flesh and back to Fenris.

"Iona worked for you. I recognize those from her tattoos."

"Very good. You're not as stupid as I first thought," said Fenris.

In any other situation, he would have made him pay for an insult like that, but Blake knew when he was outclassed. He'd been invited into the monster's den, and hopefully, he wasn't on the menu.

"I've been watching you, Blake Lockwood. We share a desire."

"You want Iona. What did she do to you?"

The sour grin on Fenris' lips made Blake want to retch. It was like staring into a bloody, infected wound.

"She's my...property. I want her back."

This made Blake smile. He could understand property.

"You've come to the right person then. She doesn't belong in Coterie. She's been stinking up the Obelisk with her piggy blood. She doesn't even deserve to look at it, let alone be a member."

"She has more power in her little finger than you have in your entire body, but that's neither here nor there. She's mine and managed to get away. She had no right, after all I've given to her. She must be returned. I have plans."

Blake had a good idea that those plans were not going to end well for Iona, a fact that he couldn't help but enjoy.

"What do you need me to do?"

"I need in the Obelisk."

"I can't do that. We don't allow visitors."

Fenris stepped forward with his fingers extending like claws. The feeling of immobility returned to Blake's limbs.

"Then I have no need for you."

"Wait," said Blake, forcing his hands up. "I have an idea."

"Good. I like ideas. I would hate to think you're not as clever as

Iona."

This made Blake mad, but he did his best work when he was angry. Gemma had been a royal bitch until she'd pushed him too far and then he'd managed to take care of her and get rid of Zuri, who'd become too mouthy for her own good. Scarlett was a superior girlfriend in every way.

"I can get you in as kitchen staff. The badges they wear will get you past the entry wards. It'll take me a few days, but I can manage it."

"And then?"

A plan came to mind immediately. Getting Fenris through the portals would be easy since they'd already solved the puzzles. Then it would be a matter of setting up the perfect ambush. He was proud of himself. It would rid him of Iona and Zuri. The perfect plan. And he wouldn't even have to get his hands dirty, though everyone would know it was him. They'd see the result and fear him more. His hold over his fellow classmates would be complete.

"This is how we're going to do it..."

TWENTY-SEVEN

The meeting was at an all-night diner across the ring road in the fifth ward. It wasn't too far from the Obelisk, and also wasn't a place that Blake or his cronies would ever set foot in. Zuri wasn't even sure *she* wanted to be there. It smelled like grease and sadness. The only one who seemed to be enjoying herself was Iona, who was shoveling a forkful of pancakes into her mouth while humming to some inane song playing over a jukebox.

"Do you really have to make a scene with those?" asked Zuri as she stared at Iona with disgust.

Iona looked up with a mouthful of pancakes, eyebrows stretching upward.

"You're missing out," she said around the food.

Justine was on the opposite side, poking her plate as if it were a live snake.

"Are they really that good? They look so...plain."

Iona swallowed and leaned back.

"Come on, you two, they're pancakes. We're not eating cobra livers or some weird shit that they serve in the Obelisk. It's basically bread and sugar. The two best food groups. Well, and cheese."

Justine sighed and placed the smallest piece of pancake on her tongue and after eventually swallowing, her eyes lit up.

"Those are...good."

Zuri wasn't sure she trusted Justine, given her tendency towards strangeness.

"Come on, Zuri," said Iona with her mouth stretched into an odd grin. "Try some."

For the first time in months, Zuri was reminded of Iona's peasant background. While she wasn't a pig farmer like her fellow first years taunted her, she was equally as unknowable as Justine.

"I'd rather not. I doubt the chef has won any awards here."

Iona chuckled.

"They're not chefs, they're cooks."

Zuri pushed the plate away from her as Justine picked up speed, eating larger and larger bites, making noises of enjoyment.

The dinging of a bell announced newcomers to the nearly empty diner.

"Oh, thank Merlin," said Zuri with a sigh as Melanie and Marcus approached. She wanted to get out of the diner as quickly as possible.

"What is this place?" asked Marcus with his hands in his pockets.

"It was Iona's suggestion."

The pair joined them in the booth. The waitress appeared moments later with a pot of coffee.

Zuri eyed the pair as they settled into the booth. Melanie looked nervous while Marcus appeared ready to bolt at a moment's notice.

"How's progress?"

Melanie shared a glance with Marcus, who gave a half-assed shrug.

"We found the portal."

"Any luck?"

"Nothing yet, but we know Blake and his friends made it through a few weeks ago."

"Good," said Justine. "I hate looking over my shoulder all the time."

"I hate to say it, but Blake wants you bad," said Melanie.

"Which is why I didn't think we should meet, but Mel talked me into it. So don't drag this out. Let's get to the meat of it. I'd rather not be seen with the three of you if I can help it."

"Assuming they didn't follow you here, I think we'll be alright," said Zuri.

"Blake's group went into the third portal a couple of hours ago. We're good. For now, anyway," said Marcus. "So get on with it."

"I'll make it simple. There aren't any small groups anymore. Well, minus Orion, but he doesn't count. Everyone else has gotten big enough that they can afford to play offense and defense while researching the next problem. We're idiots if we don't group up."

"Why would we want to catch Blake's heat?" asked Marcus with his arm draped over the back of the booth.

"Because if he takes us out, then you know he'll come for you next. Better to team up now so that never happens. But I don't want to make this just about fear of that asshole—we have a lot to offer too."

Marcus stared back dead-eyed.

"Your pedigree is impeccable, Zuri, but these two? No offense, but Iona's from nowhere anyone cares about, and most of the class is convinced Justine is adopted."

"I'm sitting right here," said Iona, dropping her fork on the plate. The clatter turned a few heads in the diner.

"Hey," said Marcus. "I'm just laying it all out. I don't know anything about you or what you're made of. At this point, I think the only reason you're allied with Zuri is because she was desperate. Not a great position to negotiate from."

"I can vouch for her. And Justine too. We may not look like a normal Coterie team, but I assure you we know our shit."

"I don't know, I don't get it," said Marcus, clearly unmoved.

Melanie turned to him.

"Hun, shouldn't we consider it?"

He stretched as if he were about to get up.

"Marcus," said Zuri. "We need each other. You know it as much as I do. Blake's a sociopath. He won't stop after us."

"No, you need us. We're doing just fine with the two of us. Come on, Mel, this was a bad idea. It's only going to get us killed."

Iona stabbed the stack of pancakes so hard with her fork that it startled the few customers in the diner and froze Marcus before he could get up.

"Do you know what happens to the sheep when the wolves come into town?" she asked.

Startled and a little confused, Marcus answered, "What?" though Zuri was sure he was wondering what her point was more than wanting to know more about the topic. Zuri didn't understand it either, but she'd gotten him to sit back down, so she kept her mouth shut.

"If a sheep is alone, the wolves can surround them, tear them apart. It's an unholy mess. Sounds like hell too, the poor sheep screaming bloody murder until its throat gets ripped out. But if it sticks with the pack, then when the wolves try to grab one, the others kick out their hooves, smack the wolves in the nose, and eventually, if they fight back hard enough, the wolves move on to easier pastures. You might think that Blake is after us first, but eventually he's going to realize that it only makes sense for our two little groups to team up, and then he's going to realize that his best move it to take you out so that can never happen. I know you don't want to, but I don't think you have a choice. It's either group up and kick hard, or prepare for the screaming."

The silence was palpable. Marcus was no longer staring at the exit, but the floor, deep in thought.

"Anyone have room for pie?" asked the waitress when she intruded, not understanding their tension.

"Pecan?" asked Iona, smiling as if nothing was wrong.

"Coming right up."

After the waitress was gone, Marcus looked to Melanie and nodded.

"Yeah, we'll ally."

"That's great."

"We have some other errands to run, but we'll meet you at the Malden bust when we get back to the Obelisk. Can work out the details then."

After they left, there was a collective sigh at the table.

"Wow, Iona. That was great. I thought we'd lost them until you told that story. Do you really get a lot of wolves in Missouri?" asked Zuri.

"Wolves? Oh, hell no. Not even sure if there are any sheep near where I grew up either. Mostly cows and corn. That was all bullshit."

Justine snorted under her breath, hiding a grin behind her cupped hand, which made Zuri laugh too.

"Don't ever tell them that."

"Wasn't planning on it."

For the first time in a long while, Zuri was optimistic. Hopeful, even. With the five of them, they could really make progress in the Obelisk. While they were still outnumbered, Blake's seven to their five, it wasn't a complete mismatch, and Zuri was sure that they might be the better all-around team.

"Yeah, this might turn out all right," said Zuri, nodding.

Moments later, the waitress appeared with a healthy slice of pecan pie on a white plate. It wasn't the most uninteresting thing Zuri had seen in the diner. She looked to the waitress and said, "Can I get one of those too?"

TWENTY-EIGHT

Two weeks. It'd been two weeks since Justine had been in her suite. They'd been sleeping on the second level, working, working, working with their new allies. She sat across from Ludmilla on the bed. Crisscross applesauce. The doll's black smock was spread out around her perfect body like living shadow.

"I know, Luddy, I know. But we didn't have a choice. Blake and his mean friends would hurt us if we didn't."

Melanie was fine, even if she wasn't the strongest mage. But Marcus. He was always rolling his eyes and muttering under his breath as if he was indignant to be on the same team.

Justine didn't like the way that made her feel. When it'd just been the three of them, she'd been allowed to be herself. But with Marcus there, she didn't feel safe anymore.

"I can't reveal you. Not yet. They'd probably leave the team. I can see it in their eyes. I'm sorry, Luddy. I really am."

Ludmilla spoke to her in her head. Of course, Justine knew that the doll couldn't really talk, but it was just easier to hear hard truths that way.

"I know, I've been too busy to work on you. And I don't think we're ready for the next step. We need a second heart-seed. I know that's it, but we have to find the right one."

Justine tilted her head, listening to Luddy's complaints.

"You want to leave the room? I don't know, Luddy. I really don't. What if someone sees you? Hmmm...is that so? A good point. The Obelisk is filled with weird things. I heard Charlotte say that there's a sneaky black cat on the upper levels that no one can catch."

She giggled.

"That would be fun if they thought you were part of the game. Ludmilla the secret watcher of the Obelisk. Okay. I guess I should let you go. It'd be good for me too. We haven't practiced lately."

It was the fourth time she'd completed the ritual. The shift into Ludmilla's body was as jarring as it was the first time, but the hard enchanted wooden body didn't feel so unfamiliar. Not yet comfortable, but she didn't feel like a stranger.

The door wasn't hard to navigate this time, even if it did require leaning on her tippy-toes. When it clicked behind her, she didn't feel the normal dread she experienced whenever she left the safety of her suite.

At first, she walked down the center of the path between the statues, but remembered that she wasn't in her own body. That was back in the room. This was Ludmilla. And her. She didn't want to be seen. Yet. Maybe someday she would show her friends. She might have revealed the truth to Zuri and Iona when it was just the three of them, but Marcus worried her. Not like, backstabbing worry, but he didn't have the malleable mind the others had. He was stuck in his ways. A real shame too.

When Justine had come to Coterie and the Obelisk, she'd been afraid.

Real afraid. The kind of fear that woke her in the middle of the night screaming.

But despite the danger, the Obelisk had another thing she'd never experienced. Freedom. The freedom to push herself in directions she wanted to go. Not her father's.

She would have never had the freedom to bring Ludmilla and the other dolls to life if she'd been at home. Or stuck with her old group. It was a blessing that they'd kicked her out and that Zuri and Iona had found her crying in the great hall. Anyone else, and they might have ended her right there. It wasn't that they weren't hard people. If they weren't on her side, Justine would be very afraid of Zuri and Iona. Iona especially. Sometimes when Iona looked at her, she felt like a sheep about to be devoured by a wolf.

The student quarters were a maze of hallways and open spaces, leaving plenty of room between so it was harder to kill each other. Justine felt lucky that only two of their class had died so far. Poor Limon Walker and then some new magic Salena girl, who'd been reading in an open area when a gloomrend had snuck upon her unawares and put a claw into her belly.

Justine kept to the shadows. It was safer that way. She wasn't sure what her goal was, out and about in the main areas, but it felt like trespassing.

She paused beneath a painting of Malden Anterist defeating a horde of demons in an unknown place. The echo of distant voices had her creeping forward on wooden feet. Who else was in the student area? Marcus and Mel were out of the Obelisk, and Iona was with Zuri in her suite, working out a new protection scheme for whenever they reached the third level.

The other teams had all been on the second level, working on the solution to the problem. This time, it was a singular problem related to hexes, based on an old spell from ancient Damascus that had been written on an old goat hide.

If it weren't them, then who could it be? As she crept closer, she heard the whispers of two familiar voices. Jakob Wagner and Scarlett Calloway.

Justine's first urge was to hurry back to the safety of the suite. If those two were lurking about, then who knew if the others were in the area. While she was in the body of her doll, if they managed to capture Ludmilla they could trace the link back to her suite and use that to get her. The risk was real, but curiosity got the best of her, especially when she heard the word "tome" in their conversation.

It took her a little bit to realize they were above her, on a balcony near the place where Salena had died. As she grew closer, she could tell their voices were being scrambled by a protective ward. She could only hear every fifth word, and even those were fuzzy and static.

The privacy bubble extended beneath the balcony. She could see it when she turned her head. Justine had given Ludmilla enchanted eyes, but they weren't quite strong enough to see magical fields all on their own. She needed to get closer if she wanted to hear what they were saying, which made the choice of being in Ludmilla's body both a blessing and a curse.

The doll wouldn't trigger the normal sensing wards, since she wasn't a fleshy body, but her small stature was going to make it hard to reach the proper height to get past the privacy bubble.

Lucky for her, the architecture of the Obelisk on this level was filled with crenellations and alcoves as it was inspired partially by Notre Dame.

When she moved through the field, she felt none of the tingles she could have experienced on her flesh. But she still couldn't quite hear what they were saying.

Justine shoved her wooden hand into the gap between the alcove and the wall where the horse-head feature had slightly pulled away. Using it like a climber uses a fissure in a rock wall, she hauled herself upward until she was standing on the outcropping, but it was still too far away from the bubble. The muted voices sounded distant even though they were only a dozen feet away.

But climbing the last section would be hard. There was a wall fixture for a light, but nothing else.

Justine stood on her toes again, just like she had when she opened the door, only to have her wooden fingers click off the metal bar on the bottom of the fixture.

Maybe she should give up, she thought. The risk was too high. There was too great a chance to get caught.

But whatever they were discussing seemed important.

Justine wanted to show the group her value. Especially Melanie and Marcus.

Springing upward, Justine managed to snag the metal bar. She wasn't sure if she could have grabbed it in her human body. She was weak. Thin, spindly arms. Her father had called her a willow. And not in a nice way.

But Ludmilla was strong.

The body was built with arcana using the lost souls from the Veil to work it. In some ways it was better than her own body.

Teetering on the light fixture, she managed to stick her head through the privacy bubble.

"...don't like it. Neither does Blake. We shouldn't trust the Siren Sisters, no matter what they're offering."

The voice was Jakob's. It appeared she'd arrived in time for the juicy parts. Her foot slipped a little, but she caught it.

Scarlett spoke in a low voice. "Blake doesn't always think these things through. He's impulsive. You've seen that already with Pig Girl. He's obsessed with getting back at them. We need to get him focused on the task at hand. If we just keep progressing, eventually we'll never see them again, and they'll probably wash out of Coterie all on their own. Plus, we could use that spell. It seems it might be useful for the third portal."

"It might, but in exchange for the answer to the second? Seems like an uneven trade. In my home country, we have a saying that amounts to *only fools give up what they own for nothing.*"

"I agree," said Scarlett. "But we don't own the tome. It's right there in the library for anyone to find."

"We should get rid of it. Destroy it."

"Which would only clue everyone in our class to its importance, and it's not like they couldn't find a copy outside of the Obelisk. Remember, everyone else is watching us, looking for clues to passing the next trial. That's how the Siren Sisters figured out the Veil problem. Better to trade that information now while it still has value."

"I could get rid of it without anyone noticing. The *periculosum* section is a mess already. I can hide my tracks. Trust me, I can get rid of it."

Justine was so enraptured by the conversation she forgot where she was and her foot slipped off the metal casing, causing her to tip precipitously. She managed to grab the fixture to keep herself from falling but the hard wood on metal rang out like a gong.

"What was that?" asked Jakob.

Two sets of steps approached the edge of the balcony.

"I don't see anything," said Scarlett.

Justine could tell they were looking out over the empty space for intruders. If they bent over the edge and peered beneath, they would find her clutching the metal lighting fixture rod. She would have held her breath, but she didn't breathe. Or require oxygen. The power of the Veil kept her wooden body alive.

"I don't think it was anything. Maybe some gloomrends, or someone moving around. Either way, they couldn't have heard us through the privacy shield. Let's get out of here. We can discuss it further when we get back to the third level."

After they left, Justine leapt from her perch, landing hard, but with no injury. She hurried back to the suite and let herself back in. It was a little startling to find her human body leaning against the bed like a forgotten doll, but she quickly pushed it out of her head.

"I have a book to find."

TWENTY-NINE

No one believed it. Even as Zuri had the tome in her hand with the spell that seemed to fix the level two portal problem.

"I don't understand," said Justine. "Why don't you believe it?"

Zuri didn't have the heart to tell the sweet girl. Not even Iona believed that it was the gift she said it was.

"Because it seems too convenient, too easy," said Zuri.

Iona tapped the book in Zuri's hands.

"I trusted them in the mummy room and it nearly got me killed. This? It's probably a trap. Even if it looks right, it isn't."

"They couldn't have known I was listening."

"Come on, Justine. You know as well as any of us how easy it is to detect when someone else is around, especially if you're in their privacy bubble," said Zuri.

"But I wasn't in their bubble," Justine said emphatically. "I was back in my room."

"Then how did you hear them?"

Justine seemed to shrink inward on herself as she let out a little squeak.

"If you can't tell us, how can we believe you?"

"Please, will you trust me? I promise. They couldn't have known I was there."

Zuri looked to Iona, who gave a "what do you do" shrug.

"Mel? Marcus?"

"It's probably a trap," he said right away.

"I tend to agree," said Zuri, even as she wanted to trust her.

Justine was so earnest. The timid girl rarely stuck up for herself, or spoke any louder than a whisper unless absolutely necessary. That she was arguing with them despite their insistence felt meaningful to Zuri.

Justine clasped her hands together in prayer.

"Zuri, I swear..."

"Seven hells," said Zuri, exhaling. "We'll try it. But we're going to test it carefully first, and take every precaution under the sun. We have to assume this spell is trouble and act accordingly."

"Yay!" said Justine, clapping her hands in tiny motions.

Zuri pointed at the girl.

"But eventually you have to tell us what this secret is that you've clearly been keeping. We're a team. We need to trust each other."

"Okay," said Justine meekly.

The journey to the second level where the portal was located felt like a doomed procession. Zuri was certain that this was going to be a bust. She couldn't imagine that Scarlett of all people would have been that sloppy. Blake maybe. He was so sure of himself that he had blind spots for days, but the redhead? She'd shown herself to be cunning. Zuri didn't trust it.

The portal to the third level wasn't on a wall like the previous one. A dark pit surrounded by runes that glistened in the mage light made it look like an awake eye.

Iona crouched by the edge, peering into the darkness.

"Anyone else hear whistling wind?"

Marcus crossed his arms.

"Let's get this over with so we can get back to the real investigation," he said.

Justine watched meekly from the side, twirling a strand of her hair.

"Let me confirm this first. I want to make sure we didn't miss anything."

The spell was relatively simple. Unusually so, which added to Zuri's concern. But on the other hand, it was an elegant solution to the problem. The runes around the outside asked a simple question: what is the nature of a soul?

The spell didn't answer that question directly. What it did was take an etching of what magic thought of as the soul. It was like taking paper and charcoal to a tombstone to record the information. Much as it was thought that dying released the soul from the mortal coil only to have it pass through the Veil, sometimes pieces of it got stuck, or an imprint was left on the beings that lived there, becoming a facsimile of the original person.

The spell required a lot of subvocal grunting. Sometimes the older arcane writings weren't as elegant as one would have assumed. But Zuri had long ago gotten over her embarrassment at the oddness of spellcasting.

When it was finished, a strange sensation started in her stomach. Like a stomach ache, or when the body was getting ready to vomit, but hadn't quite moved to the violent stage. Everyone watched her with concern. Had they replaced the original spell with something awful?

"I—"

The word was cut off as her stomach muscles twisted into a knot, bending her at the waist. She didn't feel sick, or nauseous, but the convulsions continued.

"Do we need to stop this?" asked Iona.

Zuri shook her head. She wanted this to work. For the team's sake. For Justine's sake.

Then her stomach felt like a giant hand was squeezing it upward, pushing something both cold and hot towards her throat. It came out like a paper bird made from black crepe paper—not quite wings, not quite a creature.

Zuri grabbed it with her hands. Her stomach no longer hurt, but she felt empty. Touching it was like hearing an echo of herself in her head. Within the ephemeral element was the imprint of her soul, not the complete thing, but random moments in time. The memory of a time when she was seven years old came bubbling up—she'd gotten mad at her sister during breakfast and every bowl on the table exploded due to an unexpected surge of magic. It was then she knew that she would be a mage. The memory both scary—because her father had been furious—and joyous, because she knew then who she truly was.

She released the imprint into the pit.

As the elemental memory floated into the darkness, runes lit up around the edges. It was like dropping a glowing feather into a deep well. She watched until she couldn't see it anymore.

When it was gone, the runes remained lit.

"I think that's it," she said, stretching her abdomen.

"How do we pass through it?" asked Iona, and when everyone looked at her, she said, "Really?"

"Come on, everyone hold hands. We can do this together," said Zuri.

The five of them stood around the pit. It looked like they were jumping into a fathomless abyss.

"One, two, three..."

The fall was rapid, accelerating quickly and then they were somewhere else. As the vertigo passed, she opened her eyes to find they were in a twilight space. Unlike the last level, which had its own artificial sun, this place had a faint ever-present glow that seemed to come from nowhere and everywhere at once.

"Whoa," said Melanie, releasing her hand and walking towards the center of the huge space.

"Don't touch or do anything until we know what we're dealing with," said Zuri.

But she found herself quickly enthralled by what Melanie had sighted. They'd landed in a big space, not as large as the last level, which had been cavernous, but they couldn't see the far wall. At the center, or what appeared to be the center, was a black pyramid, and it was putting off that twilight glow.

"Mel, stop!" yelled Iona.

But it was too late. Melanie had stepped onto a line of runes which immediately lit up. The lights continued outward along a maze of runes like a marquee lighting up before a big concert. In the span of thirty seconds, the glow traveled around the main section of the room, then from the four corners, shot towards the center and briefly lit up the pyramid like a beacon before returning to gloom.

"That was beautiful, and scary. No one move from where we're at," said Zuri, holding her hands out.

"You were locked in," said Iona.

"But it didn't seem to affect you."

"Nope. But the important thing was that Justine was right," said Iona, smiling at the mousy girl.

"These runes are Kemetic," said Marcus, crouching by the area that Melanie had triggered. "The whole place looks like it's built on Kemetic circuits."

Zuri summoned a mage light to her fingertips and then released it, pushing it towards the pyramid, which was about a hundred meters away. The soft light floated over the ground, revealing more Kemetic circuits and black pools of water that didn't reflect. Long before it reached the black pyramid it winked out as if it were being suppressed.

"Should we explore?" asked Iona.

"Yeah. There's no sign of Blake's group and we'll need to find a defensive spot. Let's check things out, but we're going to do it systematically. No wandering off."

The warning proved right as they found there were frequent magical traps designed into the Kemetic circuits. These were an older, more advanced version of the Kemetic symbols they'd been learning in classes. The ancient Egyptian magic had always been a bit of a contradiction because it was equally or more powerful than some of the modern magics. Whatever secrets they'd uncovered to design the Kemetic system had been lost to time.

The group disabled what they could and avoided the rest. It was clear that this level would require them to increase their Kemetic knowledge, though Iona unsurprisingly knew more than the rest of them. A few times, she pointed to runes on the floor that matched her tattoos.

Zuri really wanted to check out the pyramid, but there were too many traps on the way. That was a mystery for another time, but they did manage to find a defensible building near the wall and outside of the circuits that could be their home base.

There was no sign of Blake's group, or where they'd made their home, but that wasn't surprising given the largeness of the space.

"Tomorrow we'll start moving our wards and equipment from the second level. No one comes here without at least two others. In fact, until we know the deal with Blake's group, we probably shouldn't come here with any less than the full team."

"Hey," said Iona, grinning. "Y'all know what this means?"

Zuri looked among the smiles and nods.

"Yep. We're passing our first year," said Zuri. "Which means we should celebrate. We've been working hard for months. I think it's time to take a day or two off. After we get set up here, but I think we've earned it. You especially, Justine."

The mousy girl beamed with pride as everyone patted her on the back.

Maybe things were looking up. It'd been a rough start to the year, but now she had a good team and they were making progress. Zuri was starting to feel good about her first year. It was going to be great.

THIRTY

The limousine could have fit a dozen, but it was only the five of them wearing their finest as they pulled away from the Obelisk. Melanie was laughing and pouring drinks while Iona sat in the corner, peering out of the darkened glass as the city streets passed in a blur, much like her life for the last year.

It was nearly unrecognizable from when she was trapped in the farmhouse with the warlock Fenris. Iona dug into the clutch purse Zuri had picked out for her, which matched her crimson silk dress, and found the hard little piece of petrified chrysalis that was one of the few things that she'd been given by her parents.

You'll become a beautiful butterfly.

They'd told her that when they'd sold her to Fenris. At the time she'd been confused about why any of it was happening, so it'd sounded nice. What little girl didn't want to become a beautiful butterfly?

Later, once she realized she was stuck with Fenris, she looked at the chrysalis in a new light. It was petrified. Stone. It wouldn't ever become anything, just like her. Stuck in the lair of an ancient warlock who had mad designs on her life, never to grow, never to change.

But look at her now.

She rubbed the rough edges, the smooth curved sections, and wondered if there was a spell that could bring forth a butterfly. It might be stone, but it could fly. Just like her.

The question now was where was Fenris? She sensed he was in the city somewhere. Waiting. Not patiently. He was not a patient man. If he was a man at all. He would come after her. It was only a matter of time.

"Iona!"

Zuri threw herself into the spot next to her, bumping into Iona with a grin plastered on her face.

"It's a party, remember?"

Iona shoved the petrified chrysalis into her purse before her friend could spy it.

"I was thinking about how much my life has changed in the last year. I don't recognize myself."

A hand touched her pale white hair, smoothing it past her ear.

"Except for your hair, I don't recognize you either. You clean up pretty good for a farm girl."

The black pantsuit with the deep-V jacket made Zuri look like a model and Iona told her as much.

"It helps having a fashion designer on call. Luxy is divine. I trust her with all my difficult decisions."

"Where are we going tonight?"

Zuri hooked her and leaned against as if they were old friends who'd known each other since childhood. Iona didn't know how to react except to smile back in a way that she hoped looked normal.

"Don't worry about it and just have fun," said Zuri, clearly sensing her unease.

"Are you worried about being seen with me in public?" asked Iona.

Zuri rolled her eyes dramatically and held a hand to her chest with mocking disdain.

"It was a struggle, but I've learned to suffer with the lower class. I should get a medal for it when all is said and done. Helping the lonely, the downtrodden—"

"The ready for you to be done blathering so you can hand me one of those drinks," Iona said.

It was still light when they left the Obelisk on that early March day. The limousine dropped them off at a private screening of the new Garbage Kings movie, which wasn't even out yet. Even Iona had heard of the world-famous band.

After leaving the theater, they had an exquisite prix fixe meal at La Petite Sorcière, where magic met the culinary arts. Iona ate things like condensed spirit breath, crisped hellbender skin, and honeyed blue tongues. The staff treated them like royalty. It was overwhelming.

On the way to a private karaoke club, Iona was sitting with Justine. The normally quiet girl had been chattering all night.

"I'm so glad we got to be on the same team and become friends," said Justine, leaning her head against her shoulder.

There was hardly any fabric in her dress, which had created a lot of looks at the restaurant.

"I'm glad too. I've never had friends before."

"What? Oh, that's right. Stupid asshole Fenris," said Justine, screwing up her face in exaggeration.

Not wanting to talk about her former captor, Iona switched the subject.

"How's that secret project that you never tell us anything about going?"

Justine blew out a breath, which flapped her lips in a very unladylike manner.

"I can't find the right heart-seed. Or a second one really. I know I'm close, but I just can't figure it out."

"You're really smart, Justine. I'm sure you'll figure it out."

"You really think so?" asked Justine, her voice rising to a higher pitch.

"I really think so. You figured out the Veil problem, you stole important information from Blake's group. And someday, you're going to tell us all about your secret project. I can't wait to be amazed."

"Yeah, not so sure about that. I'm weird. Like really weird."

"I grew up in a farmhouse in the middle of Missouri captive to a crazy-ass warlock and the rest of the class calls me Pig Girl. You're hardly the weird one here."

Justine took a long drink and then poked Iona in the arm.

"Did you ever trade that onyx?"

"Charlotte from the second years has the high bid now, but the Siren Sisters have upped their bid three times previously and have asked for an extension to figure out a new bid. It's crazy what they're offering. I'll be filthy rich and have a handful of cool trinkets to help protect me. I'm glad that Scarlett tried to kill me."

"I bet."

The way Justine spoke clued her interest, even though she'd never said anything.

"Would the onyx work for your secret project?"

"I mean, yes, but I don't have the kind of stuff to trade that they do. My father has put me on a strict budget because he doesn't think girls have a mind for money."

"Would it work well? Or it's just something that might kinda fit?"

"Oh no, it'd be perfect. I don't think I could find a better one."

"Then it's yours."

"What? No. You can't do that."

"Of course I can. It's mine to give. You've been the best teammate and friend possible."

"But you're giving up all that stuff."

"And making the team stronger."

"But you don't even *know* what my secret project is. It could be stupid."

"I trust you, Justine. With my life. If this project is important to you then it's important to me."

Justine looked like she was about to burst into tears. She buried her face in Iona's shoulder and hugged her almost violently.

"Thank you so much. I've never had friends like you, well, not in a long time."

Iona was saved from further tears and embarrassment when they arrived. Zuri had acquired a private karaoke room with a view of the city. Iona had never sung in front of others, but after a few more drinks and encouragement from her team—her friends—she managed to get on stage and fumble through an old song that she'd heard on the radio back in Missouri.

The rest of the group was more experienced with karaoke. To her surprise, both Justine and Marcus had wonderful voices. They sang a few duets to rapturous applause and then Justine disappeared to the bathroom while Melanie took the stage.

At first, Iona didn't think anything of Justine's long absence, but then the time grew more weighty and she couldn't help but stare at the sliding door expecting her friend at any moment.

"I think I need to check on Justine," she said, rising.

Before she reached the door, it slid open violently, startling Iona to fall back into her seat. She had a moment of concern until she saw Justine standing in the opening with a group of similarly aged students in plainer clothes.

"Hey! This is my friend Tim. We were paired up in the second round of the Trials. I invited them to join us for karaoke, if that's okay."

Zuri looked a little miffed, but she clearly didn't want to upset the evening and welcomed them in. Introductions went all around, though Iona wasn't sure she could remember half their names. A tall athletic guy with dimples who seemed kind of shy sat next to her. Scott or something like that. The drinks and confusion scrambled her thoughts.

Before long, Iona forgot about the nervousness. Dimples. That's how she thought of him as he made her feel interesting. He spent most of the time between their cheering asking questions.

The party took a weird twist when they realized the other group was from Arcanium. Coterie and Arcanium drinking and doing karaoke together. Who would have thought. But the reveal didn't seem to impact the festivities—in fact, Dimples seemed even more interested in Iona afterwards.

Near the end of karaoke, when it seemed like various members of the party were pairing up, Zuri pulled Iona outside their private room.

"I need to teach you a spell."

"What? Why?"

Zuri bunched up her lips.

"Come on. You two have been hanging all over each other. Your hand was in his lap just five minutes ago."

Iona blushed.

"You noticed?"

"Everyone noticed. But if you're planning on taking him back to the suite upstairs, you need this spell. It'll protect you from STDs and those nasty little spermies."

The heat in Iona's cheeks wouldn't subside. She didn't know how to tell Zuri, but then she recognized the look.

"Oh shit. You've never?"

"With who? It's not like I went to school or anything."

"Fenris?"

"No. Never showed any interest, thank Merlin."

"The spell will help with that too. Any first-time pains."

"Thanks, Zuri. Anything else I should know?"

Zuri chuckled.

"Have fun."

The party broke up as soon as they returned. Melanie and Marcus disappeared on their own. Justine had two guys hooked on her arms as they headed up to the suite, while Zuri was whispering in this girl's ear who had been sitting on her lap for the last three songs.

"Do you want…?"

Iona barely got the words out before Dimples was nodding enthusiastically. She led him upstairs, heart leaping around in her chest like a jackrabbit. She'd never been so nervous. Not even at the Trials, or her first day at Coterie. A million things were going through her mind as she brought him to her room in the suite.

"Can you give me a second? I have a spell," she said as she avoided his gaze.

"Me too."

They stepped away from each other. Iona pulled up the spell Zuri had sent her, and as she started casting, she couldn't help but hear the moans coming from next door in Justine's room.

"All done," she said, not knowing what to do with her hands. "Now what—"

He jammed his lips against hers and every thought and concern about how the night would unfold went out the window.

THIRTY-ONE

The trio of powerful lights dimmed with a high-pitched buzz, the furthest one going nearly dark before the bulb exploded, shattering glass over the stone floor. They'd set up about a hundred meters from the pyramid near a brass gyroscope that had been the focus of their attention for the last two days.

No buildings stood near their location, which gave them a clear line of sight to everything nearby, making it a safer spot for investigation than some of the others they'd found. The maze of Kemetic circuits went past the area with a single length connecting the gyroscope, which was why they'd decided to investigate. Occasionally they saw signs of the other group, but they were on the far side of the level and only their faint outlines were visible in the dim.

"Marcus?" asked Zuri.

"On it," he said, reaching into the storage box.

"We can't keep replacing them. Isn't there a spell we can use?" asked Melanie.

Zuri put a hand to her forehead. Progress on the third level had been painfully slow. Unlike the first two levels where the portal had been the majority of the problem, this one presented obstacles at every turn. She'd wondered why Blake hadn't bothered them since they'd arrived, but now that they'd had a few weeks of trap removal, she understood.

"If you can find one that doesn't interfere with the gyroscope."

The gyroscope was as tall as she was, made of brass and without a single rune or word on it to clue them to its purpose. But as they'd learned so far, everything on the third level mattered, and skipping things only led to disaster.

Iona came back from the edge. She was wearing denim overalls with a white tank top beneath. Melanie had given her trouble the first day she'd worn them, telling her that she was only going to encourage more name-calling, but then Iona had shown them all the pockets and places to hold reagents, magical cyphers, and other gear. Function not fashion had been her argument.

"I saw that shape again."

Everyone looked up from their tasks.

"At the pyramid?"

Iona nodded. Her pale white hair was pulled into a topknot that left wisps falling around her cheeks.

"It can't be Blake's group. They're only a little further than we are."

"Maybe it's a second year who hasn't made it to the fourth," said Justine.

"Doubtful. Though I guess it could be one who came back to use some magical facilities in the pyramid. Either way, we're not close enough to care. Let's get back to work," said Zuri.

She caught a look from Marcus. He bristled at her leadership, clearly wanting to be the one in charge. He was a good teammate, but didn't always want to listen and had to be convinced of every minor detail. It was exhausting, so when he only made his displeasure known with a glance, she was relieved.

After the lights were replaced, Zuri cast a new set of spells on the gyroscope, but the material seemed to repel her attempts at understanding it. She lasted another hour of testing before she gave up and sat on the boxes they'd brought.

"This is pointless. I'm clearly missing something. I hate puzzles I don't understand."

"Maybe it doesn't do anything," said Iona.

"That'd be rich. But I doubt it. Everything seems to have a purpose."

Melanie had been quiet for the last half hour, staring from the side with her forehead hunched. Technically, she was in charge of combing through the tomes for new spells to try, but she clearly was thinking about something, so Zuri let her cook.

When she approached the gyroscope, everyone looked up but no one said a word. Zuri could sense that Melanie was deep in thought.

She reached out and spun the gyroscope. A few quick tugs had it blurring into motion.

"Mel," began Marcus, but Zuri shushed him.

Melanie stared into the whirling rings, which could maintain their momentum for quite a while. Zuri was expecting her to cast a spell on the gyroscope while it was in motion, something they'd tried previously to no effect.

Instead, she drew lines on her arms with her fingernails, muttering an incantation. It was a minor ritual. Rituals were different from spells, which tended to be quick and to the point. The longer version of casting was more powerful, but required weaving together more complex phrases and gestures. Most rituals were meant to be performed in concert with others, but Melanie seemed to be handling it quite well on her own. Within a minute, her arms were glowing with golden light. Radiating to the point of making everyone squint.

Melanie looked like she was working herself up to something once the ritual was complete. She stared into the heart of the spinning gyroscope and before anyone could stop her, shoved her arms into the center.

The whirling brass discs should have ripped her arms off. Zuri leapt to her feet, thinking that Melanie had made a fatal mistake, but despite the logic of physics, her arms were still inside the gyroscope.

"How is…?" asked Iona, her words trailing off.

Melanie was moving her arms, suggesting she was manipulating something inside the gyroscope.

A pop and a hiss from nearby, a spot close to where Marcus was standing, and a plate slid out of the way, revealing a dark passage into the ground.

Melanie yanked her arms from the gyroscope, which rapidly spun down to stillness as the glow faded.

"I did it!"

"I don't know what you did, but that was incredible. How did you know that would work?" asked Zuri.

"It was something I read, I can't remember where, but it made me think that it might work."

Marcus was on his feet, peering into the darkness of the passage.

"Where does this go?"

"Only one way to find out," said Iona, grabbing her pack.

"Hold up," said Zuri. "Let's talk this out before we go sticking our noses in something we don't understand. The last thing we want is another repeat of those black pools."

Using a floating mage light, they explored the passage to find that it led to a doorway covered in Egyptian hieroglyphics that presented a riddle

Zuri was fairly certain she knew the answer to.

Zuri made the decision to explore the passage herself, along with Iona and Justine. Everyone grabbed extra gear in case they ran into problems. Melanie and Marcus would stay up top and communicate with them using enchanted comm stones.

"Everyone stand back, I'm going to trigger the hieroglyphs," she said.

The sandstone was rough under her fingertips. The answer had to do with the rising and falling of the Nile. It wasn't a particularly difficult riddle, not after years of competing in the Arcanix competition for St. Jude's, but the penalty for getting it wrong was much worse in the Obelisk.

To her relief, the door slid into the wall, revealing a diorama of a city on a stone pad in the center of the room. The three of them entered, spreading around the miniatures. The city was nothing like she'd expected, with raised roads that looked like their elevated trains, and the buildings were much taller than the ones known to have been built by the Egyptians.

"It looks like an Egyptian city if they'd become modern," said Zuri, leaning down and examining the tiny buildings.

"What do you think this room is for?" asked Justine. "It doesn't look like any of the others we've seen so far."

A building at the center of the diorama looked a lot like the Obelisk. As she crouched to examine it, she noticed Kemetic runes on the walls of the buildings. They weren't as easy to notice from a standing position.

"I found some runes," she told the others. "Which means this is probably another puzzle, except this one looks a little harder. Can you see the runes on the other side?"

Justine leaned on the stone table with a heavy backpack on. She'd been wearing it the last few weeks without ever explaining its purpose or what was inside.

"I can see a Ra-Khet and another I don't recognize that looks like a crook with a weird star thing."

"Weird star thing? Let me take a look."

Before she could circle the table, Iona pointed to the corner.

"I don't think we want to be here."

Waving her hand, Zuri made her mage lights glow brighter so she could see what Iona was indicating. Scrawled on the wall in what appeared to be blood or something that looked like blood was a phrase: Don't touch anything! Get out!

A pang of worry was quickly replaced with suspicion.

"That can't be real. They clean out the levels during the summer. They would have never left a message like that, so either it was made by the professors, or Blake's gang did it."

"I don't know," said Iona. "Looks kinda real to me."

A crackle came over the comm stone. Zuri lifted it to her ear.

"Everything okay in there?" asked Marcus through the stone.

"Found a diorama with runes, working out the riddle," she responded.

"Okay, 'cause it got darker out here."

That was weird.

"Are you sure?"

"Positive," he responded.

"Maybe we should leave until we figure that out," said Justine.

"Got to be a coincidence," said Zuri, then she spoke into the stone. "Keep an eye out, and let us know if anything changes. We'll keep on the runes."

"Roger that, but don't be long, it's getting darker and darker by the second."

The urge to leave was strong, but so was the desire to stay and figure out the riddle. She hadn't said it to the others, but she really wanted to get to the fourth level before Blake, because she knew how crazy it would make him. If she managed to get the group there before the end of the school year, he'd have to stew on it all summer.

"Are you sure?" asked Iona. "Something doesn't feel right. Even if Blake didn't write that message, it's a warning."

"I'd make a large bet that it was Blake, which means this room is important. He's trying to scare us off."

"What about the dark outside?"

"Coincidence."

"This isn't a race. Not anymore. We can take our time," said Iona. "Better safe than dead."

"Hey, the runes are glowing brighter," said Justine, who'd continued to examine the diorama.

True to her word, the entire miniature city was glowing intensely. Either they'd triggered something, or it had started once they'd entered the room. Her desire to figure out the riddle was quickly being overtaken by concern.

"Okay, maybe we can step outside with—"

The words fell dead in her mouth when the door slid shut with a grinding finality. She ran over to search for a lever or button, but found nothing.

"Seven hells."

"Oh, no. This isn't good," said Iona.

Zuri saw it immediately. Tiny holes had opened around the entire room, including the floor and ceiling. She feared that they would be inundated with scarabs of some dangerous kind, but in a way it was almost worse.

At a couple of points around the walls, spearheads started to extend out of the holes. This was followed by a crackle from the comm stone.

"What's going on? We heard the door close. It's nearly pitch-black out here. Not even the floodlights are working," said Marcus frantically.

"Yeah, we're definitely trapped and there are spears coming out of the wall. Can you answer the riddle on the door for us?"

"A moment..." They waited while the spears continued to poke out. There were a dozen so far, but given the holes, there could be hundreds waiting. "Nope. Nothing lit up. It's not working."

"That's okay. We probably have to figure it out from in here. I'm confident we can do it."

"I'm not excited about being out here," said Marcus.

"Stay in the tunnel, and put some wards up until we know what's going on. The darkness might be related, or it might not."

"Roger that."

"Ow, fuck," muttered Iona as she shook her hand. "They don't break easy."

"How many are there?" asked Zuri, trying to keep her voice calm so her fear wouldn't trigger the others.

"There are three on my side," said Justine, who looked near to tears.

Iona hurried to the other section, peering around buildings.

"Two here."

"Another four, which makes nine total. That's a lot of combinations, which means we can't just guess."

A clicking sound alerted them to a new set of spears exiting the walls. There weren't enough to be an issue yet, but things would get real hairy soon.

"Focus on the runes, we can't do anything about the spears," said Zuri.

"Let's see about that," said Iona, fingers articulating for a quick five elements spell.

A condensed blast of force hit the spear shaft, making the entire thing quiver, but not even coming close to breaking it. In the aftermath of her spell, they heard more clicking, and not only did new spears appear, but the ones that were out sped up.

"Oh shit. That's not good."

"It appears they react to magic. Which means we have to figure this out without it. Everyone describe their runes."

Iona and Justine started speaking at the same time in a hurried rush.

"Iona first," she said, cutting them off.

They went around the table while more spears joined their brethren. Two-thirds of the runes were known, while the final third were similar to others, but seemed to be an entirely new symbol.

Zuri was having to move back and forth on her side, which was getting more difficult with the spears getting in her way.

"Ideas?"

"The door had to do with the Nile flooding. Maybe this is similar? Or that was a clue," said Justine.

"Great. Yeah. The one with the wheat and daggers. That could be the tilling of the soil afterwards," said Zuri.

"Twenty-four," said Iona gravely.

"What?"

"Twenty-four spears."

"We can't do anything about them. Focus."

They continued their discussion of the runes while occasionally Iona spat out a new figure. The spears were increasing in both speed and number. Zuri could hear a clock ticking in her head.

"Come on, ideas, ideas."

"I don't know," said Iona. "These aren't the Kemetic runes I know. They're not like anything we know. Even the familiar ones are slightly off."

"Ask the others," said Justine as she had to shift out of the way of a spear.

The room was quickly looking like a torture device with spears crisscrossing at various heights and sections of the wall. At some point, they'd no longer be able to maneuver out of the way and they'd get skewered in slow motion. Not an end she was looking forward to.

"Marcus, got a moment?" she asked through the comm stone.

A crackle of static and then a whisper returned. She asked again, but there was no response. Not even the suggestion that the message had gone through.

"I think he turned it off," said Iona. "That's not good."

"Well, we can't help him from here. We have our own problem."

Justine snapped her fingers.

"What if this is like the Aggamor Problem?"

"Yeah, could be," said Zuri. "Good idea."

"I don't know that one," said Iona.

Zuri wanted to get mad at Iona for distracting her, but then she remembered that Iona hadn't gone to prep school.

"It's a famous problem about a small town that had celebrated the use of magic rather than fearing it as most did at the time. They used magic to grow crops, to keep their irrigation lines full, and things like that. But then they lost half their mages when an awful sickness came through the town. It wasn't just them, it killed people all over. But without the mages, they couldn't keep up with the crops and the fresh water, and their town collapsed and many died. The moral of the story is a warning about relying on magic when regular methods will work equally as good."

"I don't get it," said Iona, scrunching up her face.

"It's not an arcane problem. We were punished for the use of magic, which means it's a different kind of solution. Linguistic. Logical. Something that I haven't yet figured out but it's right at the tip of my brain."

"We'd better hurry," said Iona. "Pretty soon we're not going to be able to reach the runes."

Iona was right. Time was down to the quick. To reach the four runes on her side, Zuri was having to grab a spear that had crossed the room and throw herself over the others sliding beneath. There were fewer and fewer free spaces in the room and there were still runes that needed to be activated to solve the puzzle.

"Not magic, huh," said Iona, crouching down. "I almost hate to say this, but I think the runes have to do with farming. The door riddle was about the rise and fall of the Nile, which was what made that region so plentiful. They were the breadbasket of the world."

"That's it! Don't ever let anyone call you Pig Girl as an insult."

"I mean, farm girl would make more sense," said Iona offhandedly.

"Do we know an order? Is there a logical starting point?"

"Ouch!"

Justine was examining her side, where a spear edge had sliced through her clothes.

"Sorry, I was looking for the runes. I didn't see it."

"The first one. Anyone? I don't think it's on my side," said Zuri.

"Maybe it doesn't matter. We just have to get them in order," said Iona.

Zuri nodded.

"I think I have two in order over here. I'll try them and see if you're right."

The runes were warm to the touch. The first one lit up in a silvery glow, which gave her hope. Then the second one followed, which let her relax a tiny bit. She described the runes, which prompted Justine to squeal with excitement.

"I've got number three! It's a wheel with spokes."

They found the next two easily, leaving only four left. The end of the puzzle was in sight.

"I think I have five," said Iona, climbing over the spears which had formed a cage around her area. She managed to sneak a hand through to touch the rune which looked like a scythe. When it lit up, she cheered, but then Zuri saw the problem.

"Iona, get out of there!"

She tried scrambling back but a new spear had slipped in behind her, which trapped her in place. Iona could slide to the left or right a few feet, but that was it.

"I'm out. You'll have to finish without me."

"Iona," said Justine with fear in her voice. "There's a spear headed for your side."

"Then hurry."

Zuri found the six and seventh runes, but then she was blocked off from her other side of the sandstone table.

"I have no more runes over here," said Justine.

"I can't get to mine," said Zuri as a sense of hopelessness intruded. "I'm too big. Seven hells. We're done."

It happened so fast. She thought they had more time. The spears formed a cage around them, blocking them from reaching more runes or the exit.

"We were too slow. Fuck. I should have figured out that it had to do with farms earlier. I screwed us. I'm sorry," said Iona as she stared at the spear slowly moving toward her side. It was positioned to go right through her hip above the bone.

Zuri turned to check on Justine, but she had pulled something out of her backpack and set it on the ground. She was chanting softly in a language that Zuri didn't recognize.

"What is she doing?" asked Iona.

"I have no idea."

A forced exhale was followed by a cry from Iona as the spear tip pressed into her flesh and then slowly pierced her like a needle through fabric. She gritted her teeth as tears formed in her eyes.

"Behind you," she grunted.

Zuri shifted out of the way of the spear she hadn't seen coming, but it was her last axis of freedom. The next one that appeared would be the end of her.

Then she heard the scrabbling of tiny hands only to find a small humanoid a little over two feet tall and wearing a black smock climbing onto the diorama. Zuri thought it was alive at first until she saw the wooden arms sticking from the dress. A doll. How? Why?

"Merlin's balls," exclaimed Zuri.

But then she saw Justine with her eyes closed, wavering on two feet, and finally understood. The mousy girl had never explained what kind of magic she'd studied in prep school. Now she understood.

Their human bodies were too big to fit through the gaps, but Justine's doll was just the right size. She slipped across the table near the two final runes. The doll pointed its slender wooden arms at them in order.

"Describe them."

The doll shook her head and pointed to her throat.

"Of course you can't speak. I don't know. I guess we have a fifty-fifty shot. Pick one."

The doll stared back with dead, black eyes before reaching out to one of the runes.

"Not that one!" yelled Iona even as the spear was poking out the other side of her hip. Blood was gushing onto the table, covering a white stone building in crimson liquid.

"It's the other."

"Are you sure?" asked Zuri.

"I think so."

"Do as she says," said Zuri.

The doll had to maneuver over a couple of spears, but managed to duck down and press the eighth rune. It was so lifelike. When nothing bad happened and the others remained lit up, a kernel of hope formed in Zuri's chest.

"Hurry," said Iona.

A spear was closing the path that the doll had crossed. Zuri thought there wasn't enough time, but the wooden humanoid made an inspired leap through the gap, deft enough to impress a gymnast, and pressed the final rune.

Zuri wasn't sure it had worked until she realized there was no more clicking signaling the introduction of new spears. As she checked around them, she saw they'd stopped, even the one that had broken through Iona's hip.

"Now what?" asked Iona, breathing heavily.

It was a strange scene. The three of them trapped in a cage of spears, Iona stuck on one, and an unknown doll standing on the sandstone diorama staring back with no emotion.

A loud thunk sounded, followed by Iona's scream as the spears retracted back to the walls. In the matter of thirty seconds, there wasn't a single spear in the room. Then the center of the table opened up like a hatch, revealing an ornate scroll case.

Zuri ignored the prize and ran to Iona, who'd fallen onto the table, covered in blood. A cauterizing spell stopped the worst of the bleeding, which would give her time to retrieve their elixirs from outside.

"Is she okay?" asked Justine, appearing suddenly.

Zuri did a double take. The doll was lying limply on the table, the black smock spread out like shadow.

"I think so. I just hope Mel and Marcus are alive."

Justine hunched her forehead.

"Please don't tell them."

Zuri glanced to the doll and nodded.

"I won't."

"Same," said Iona.

"Let's get her outside."

After Justine grabbed the scroll case and put the doll back into the backpack, they helped Iona to the door, which opened automatically when they neared.

To their relief, Melanie and Marcus were crouched in the hallway looking like survivors of a horror movie.

"Everyone okay?"

"I think so," said Marcus. "What happened to Iona?"

"We'll tell you about it in a bit. Let's get her patched up first."

The lights had returned by the time they ascended from the passage. While Melanie retrieved the alchemical box, Marcus told them what had transpired.

"After it got real dark, we retreated to the door. When it wouldn't open, we put wards on the stairs, but it was like they wouldn't stick. Then it got real quiet. At one point, I thought I heard the scuff of footsteps. I was sure something was about to come down the stairs after us."

"Blake?"

"Not Blake. Whatever it was, it scared the ever-living shit out of me. I could feel its power, its hunger. Never experienced anything like that. Then the lights started coming back on and then it was gone. And you three appeared."

"It was close, but we managed to solve the puzzle. Thanks to Justine."

"Anything good? Or was it just another dumb trap to kill us?" asked Melanie as she bound Iona's side.

Justine pulled the case out, popped the top, and revealed the scroll. The parchment felt old. Not the normal enchanted paper that the professors liked to use. The spell was written in another kind of Kemetic language that was foreign to Zuri's eyes.

"What is it?" asked Marcus.

Everyone shook their heads. Everyone but Iona, who was staring at it with her jaw dropped.

"You know this?"

Iona nodded. Her blank look turned to a smile.

"It's a solution to the circuit problem. Maybe not the whole solution, but it might get us to the pyramid."

THIRTY-TWO

Somewhere on level three, a flash of arcane lit up the dome-like structure, crackling like lightning before fading to darkness. Fenris smirked from his perch on the pyramid. It was the little prince's group. They'd figured out the tomb shaft problem. It wouldn't be long before they could reach his hiding place.

Not that it mattered. The other group wasn't far behind. Iona. The little traitor would finally be in reach.

He'd planned on taking her right away. As soon as she'd reached the third level, but once he'd found the pyramid and understood what it was for, he knew that he'd have to bide his time. He was hungry, but he could wait. It would all be worth it. Iona returned to the fold, an answer for the hunger, and an opportunity to expand his reach.

The Obelisk was a vast treasure trove of secrets. Some Fenris suspected that even the owners of the structure didn't understand.

Fenris moved around the base of the pyramid to a section of shadow that would hide his observation. Iona's group had been disarming one of the black pools. Her friends had proved more cunning than he expected, more than the little prince's group. If Fenris were back in Missouri, he would have culled them already. Fat, juicy mages, plumped up on their own importance, blind to how the real world works.

If it weren't for the patrons and other beings in the city, he would have moved to Invictus long ago to hunt.

A rumble formed in his chest, like the distant echoes of thunder. Not strong enough to affect him yet. He'd gorged himself before entering the Obelisk, knowing that it might be some time before he got to feed again. Not that it had removed all the hunger, but a trip to the second level had proved most fortuitous when he'd stumbled upon an unaware student outside their room.

Fenris watched Iona from his hiding spot. She was talking with the girl with lustrous black skin. The little prince's old girlfriend. There was something that intrigued him about her. Not enough to spare her life, but he figured he'd learn more once he could unleash the hunger.

Iona glanced up, staring directly at the pyramid, which made Fenris shrink into the shadows. She was curious. Maybe concerned. He'd been careful not to trigger the runes in her flesh. That time would come later. But she clearly suspected something. It could be the pyramid itself. At the very least, its presence would muddle her thoughts. Make her believe that the ancient structure was the cause of her suspicions.

The hunger in his belly rippled through his form.

"Not yet," he whispered.

He could attack now, but he knew the odds were against him. Better to wait for them to step deeper into his trap where they couldn't escape. The Kemetic magics contained within the level were more cunning than the two groups understood, and their failure of imagination would be his boon.

"Once they get to the pyramid," he told himself, "I will unleash my trap and there'll be nothing they can do."

Then Iona and he had unfinished business. He'd kill the others and do with her as he wanted. Finally. She would be the one. Iona was the strongest candidate by far. A danger of course, one that he knew he was risking, but all the others had failed. Either their bodies were too weak, or their minds not strong enough to hold the cage of magic.

Not Iona.

He'd failed many times, and for many, many years before he'd realized the reason why. But the solution had taken years to ripen and now it was finally in his grasp.

Once he could complete the ritual that he'd been working towards for so many decades, he would be free of the hunger. Free to rejoin society. Then he'd show them a thing or two about power.

"Soon, little one. Then we can be reunited."

THIRTY-THREE

Justine didn't like Professor Horace Green. He was grumpy, prone to outbursts, and didn't appreciate how difficult it was to be a student in Coterie.

But he was filled with knowledge that she desperately needed. Which was why she'd been coming to every one of his lectures. She was one of the few who bothered. The other students thought he was a bore. A relic of an older time. The fact that he wasn't an alumnus of Coterie bothered some, but not Justine. To her it meant he had knowledge outside of the insular Hall.

The class contained three others, none from her year. The others were upperclassmen. Justine recognized one of them from prep school. Donal White. But he looked nothing like the preppy upbeat older classmate he'd been before. Now he wore dark clothes with long sleeves that hid his arms, had constant bags under his eyes, and twitched like a drug addict with the DTs. She'd tried to talk to him earlier in the year, but he'd stared right through her with glassy eyes. Whatever he'd experienced in the upper levels of the Obelisk had changed him.

"Does anyone know why the ancients were prone to sacrifice? And if you tell me that they were trying to please the gods, I'll strap you to this altar right here myself, and tear your heart out."

Professor Green was leaning against a stone altar that had been taken from the forests of Germania. The edges were worn down with time, so it didn't have the same shape as it had when it'd been first carved out of the earth. It'd been used for rituals during the Dark Ages. The stains of sacrifice could be seen in the bowl-like depression.

"They were mages using the sacrifices to fuel their own power," said Donal in a raspy voice.

"A correct, but simple answer. Does anyone have a more in-depth version?"

The urge to raise her hand was strong, but Justine hated being noticed. She always felt like people were judging when they looked at her. Her nose was too big, her skin too pale, and she wasn't anything like her father, the famous Justice Thornlock. More than once his friends had asked her if she were adopted.

"Justine. Are you going to squirm in your seat all day or let those thoughts out of that head of yours?"

She was thankful that it was a small class. If it had happened in one of the larger ones, she wasn't sure she would have been able to answer.

"Sacrificing someone to use their soul is like burning down a perfectly good power plant to stay warm instead of using the equipment itself to generate your power. While some used souls in this wasteful way, others were killing to figure out the secrets of magic. They would find fledgling mages with little idea of their own power, and bleed them on the altar while they forced them to use magic. It was like doctors doing experiments on live patients to understand how the body works."

"Very good, Miss Thornlock. Care to illuminate us on what you can do with a working soul still connected to its body?"

Though she was sitting on the opposite side of the lecture hall than the other students, she felt their glares. Donal's in particular.

"A soul is a collection of all our experiences, our energies, our magic. But trying to use the soul alone without the body is wasteful. We're more capable with a body of flesh and blood to direct our magics, rather than use it as a power source. Unless the body has been prepared in some way, shaped for a particular use, it's really wasteful to sacrifice someone for their soul. But I guess that's why they called them the Dark Ages."

Professor Green rapped his knuckles against the altar.

"You see, Donal, this is why you're behind the rest of your class."

The moody upperclassman grabbed his bag and stormed out of the auditorium, glaring at Justine the whole time, which only made her shrink.

"You shouldn't hide yourself, Justine. It's not your fault Donal is failing."

Failing. It was a nice way to say that he was either going to push himself past his limits and possibly die, or get kicked out if he didn't. Justine wondered if she'd become like him, a husk of her former self. Her father had lectured her time and time again about how the Obelisk was a forge for the soul, that it changed people in ways they never expected, that it'd changed him.

Justine wasn't so sure about that. The stories her father had told about his time in prep school proved he'd been a terror long before he joined Coterie. The Obelisk had only sharpened that cruelty.

She was so lost in her thoughts that she didn't realize the lecture was over. The others had left the room and Professor Green was cleaning up his scattered notes from the edge of the stone altar.

"What was it you wanted to ask me?"

"What?"

Justine swallowed.

The professor's deep brown skin crinkled at the corners of his eyes. Sometimes she thought he was from a different time entirely.

"I'm not blind, Miss Thornlock. Or deaf. There's very little you've learned in my classes. You know the material as well as any fourth or fifth year, which means you're not here to learn what the others are here to learn."

She grabbed her backpack and clutched it against her chest as a shield when she approached the altar.

"I wanted to ask about soul phylacteries," she said in a voice so quiet she was surprised that he'd heard.

The professor raised an eyebrow, which only made her feel like she'd done something wrong.

"You're full of surprises, Miss Thornlock. You realize that's very advanced, very dangerous magic." He jutted his chin at the empty auditorium. "I wouldn't even begin to teach the others anything about it."

"I've read some books..."

"Which ones?"

She cleared her throat.

"*The Malleable Soul*, *Eighteen Locks for the Empty Mind*, a *Feast for All Time*, and the *Puppeteer's Maleficent Manual*. There are others, but I thought—"

He chuckled.

"How you even found a few of those titles, let alone acquired them is interesting to say the least, but I guess you really *are* Justice Thornlock's daughter."

The comparison shocked her. No one had ever said anything like it. He had to be mistaken.

"Do you have a specific question?"

"I wanted to know how dangerous it is, and how much soul you can transfer to an inanimate object."

"That all depends on what you're trying to do. Some think you can hide part of your soul in a phylactery which will protect you from death should your body be destroyed, but that would only trap your soul in a place that you can have little effect. Sure, you might haunt the world around you as you slowly go mad, but it's not a life I would want to lead. Death would be preferable."

"What if the object isn't stationary?"

The professor made noises in the back of his throat as he regarded her.

"I suppose it would be less limiting, but the dangers to one's sanity remains. We're creatures of the flesh. To live otherwise would be painful."

To some, thought Justine.

"Thank you, Professor Green."

She started to turn away but he put a hand on her shoulder.

"Come by my office in an hour. I have a tome that you might be interested in. It's old and some of the material is out of date, but I think you're astute enough to figure out what to use and what to discard. I believe it would be helpful on this little personal quest of yours."

Justine beamed at the professor.

"Thank you!"

She started to lean forward to hug him, but caught herself.

"You might not want to thank me. This is dangerous, advanced magics, but you seem to be hell-bent on learning it, so I might as well give you the best resource you can't find on your own."

"I promise I'll be careful."

Professor Green leaned forward until his face was all she could see.

"If you go down this path, there might not be a way back. Be prepared, but most importantly, know yourself, or you might find yourself quite lost. Permanently."

THIRTY-FOUR

The black pool bubbled as Iona stepped near. The liquid smelled woody, rather than tar-like as she first would have thought, but the third level was full of surprises. She held out the staff and funneled faez through it, filling the air with unspent raw magic.

"I'm ready."

A shape formed at the center of the black pool, almost human-like with a head and arms and a torso.

Marcus and Melanie stepped to spots that formed a triangle around the pool, each with a staff. They'd been carved out of wyrmwood and enchanted for theatrical productions, but that's not what they were using them for. The staves helped them direct the faez outward without risking the inhabitants of the pool.

"I'm good," said Marcus, followed by a nod from Melanie.

"On the count of three. One. Two. Three."

As the oily black figure started to move towards her, they activated the spell that they'd placed on the cheap staves. Crackles of electricity burst from the air, forming a cage around the figure, which writhed in pain before collapsing back into the pool.

"All good," said Iona as she pulled back the staff.

The pool no longer boiled. A few small ripples were calming, but the surface would be glass smooth in a minute.

"Set a timer," said Zuri from nearby.

Every three hours they had to deal with the black pool, but now that they had a procedure, Iona didn't mind. As long as they paid attention, there'd be no danger.

"How's the circuit?" she asked upon approach.

A pair of round, brass-lined goggles made Zuri look like some kind of steampunk adventurer.

"Being a pain."

Zuri leaned down and coaxed pale blue light from the runes. It looked like she was pulling taffy from the floor, yanking and twisting. Iona knew that she was seeing something entirely different through the goggles, but it made her look like a mad scientist.

At a location fifty feet away, Justine was monitoring the reaction on the circuit with another pair of goggles.

With nothing to do, Iona stood back and took in the area. They were about a hundred feet from the pyramid. At this range, the twilight gave the structure a haunted feel as if it were being occluded like an eclipse.

Sparks erupted at a point off to her left, startling her, but she quickly relaxed. Their investigations sometimes caused them. Kemetic magic was powerful and hard to understand. She'd been learning from Fenris for years and she barely understood the things that were happening in the Obelisk. How the ancient Egyptians had figured out such powers was beyond her. It was almost as if they had modern knowledge of circuits and electricity, because some kinds of Kemetic magic operated as such.

The kind of Kemetic magics present on this level were made to work with large structures or grand spaces. Some researchers thought the outer shells of the pyramids had once been covered in runes, making them into enormous magical beacons. For what? No one knew.

There were similarities to the tattoos on her body, but they were from a narrower sect of Kemetic magic. One that seemed to be more preoccupied with maximizing personal power. But the underlining concepts were the same, which made her wonder what Fenris' intentions were.

"All done," said Zuri, pulling off her goggles, leaving lines around her face.

"Done, done?" asked Iona.

Zuri shifted her mouth to the side.

"I think so. Mel, Marcus, can you check the ward cubes on that side? Justine, could you get the others? I'd like to verify we're good before we try activating this again."

Again. For the fifteenth time, perhaps? But Iona felt like this might be the one. Or that they were close to it. What would happen once they triggered it? They had no idea, but they felt like it would be another major step towards reaching the fourth level.

Zuri stood near with her arms crossed. She'd been pensive all morning, even with their continued progress.

"He's not here. Blake took his group to the exit an hour ago."

"That doesn't mean he didn't leave a spy."

"Even if he's watching, he'll have no idea what you've been doing with the runes. Seven hells, I barely know."

"I only half understand what I'm doing, but each time we try I understand a little more." Zuri scuffed her shoe on the stone. "What do you think will happen when we activate it for real?"

Iona gestured towards the pyramid.

"Something over there. It couldn't be anything else, right?"

"I hope so. I just want to get away from him."

Him. Blake.

"Unless you're planning on killing him, or we get lucky and he trips himself up somewhere, I think we're going to have to deal with him for another four years."

Zuri glanced over. Her eyes were bloodshot and Iona didn't think it was from the goggles.

"How do you do it?"

"Do what?"

"Kill."

The accusation was like a sharp prick to her breastbone. Anger rose up in her throat, but she pushed it down.

"I've never killed anyone," said Iona.

"But you've killed rabbits and other animals."

"It's not the same. Or at least I don't think so."

"You'd kill Fenris."

"I doubt I could kill Fenris," said Iona. "I mean, I *want* to kill him, but he's an ancient warlock with power I can't even understand. Blake's just a spoiled sociopathic rich kid. You might very well get your chance someday."

"I know, that's what I worry about. I loved him. How could I kill him?"

"How could you have loved that?"

"He was sweet, funny, and made me feel good. I grew up on stories about Coterie and the Obelisk and how it changed people and made them great. I think I half thought that this experience would make us both better, but we never even got here. Not as a couple, anyway."

"Good thing. Or I'd probably already be worm food. Or Fenris would have gotten me somehow and who knows what would become of me."

"He's an asshole, you don't have to think about him while you're in here."

Iona smirked.

"You know, when he was away from the farmhouse for a few days, I would piss in his special elixirs. Not a lot, but enough to feel like I was getting back at him."

"Gross." Zuri turned her head. "We should get ready. The others are almost finished."

Iona was about to turn away when a stab of pain hit her right in the spine. The tattoos on her back felt hot. She felt feverish for a few seconds but then it passed and everything returned to normal.

"Are you okay?" asked Zuri, touching her arm. "You were bent over in pain."

Iona stared at the pyramid.

"It felt like...which it can't be. He can't be here. It's not possible."

"Fenris?"

"Yeah. It was the same as when I sensed him in the city. It always helped me know when he was about to return to the farmhouse. But this felt so...near."

"Maybe he's outside the Obelisk and you can feel that," said Zuri.

"Maybe..."

Iona pushed it out of her mind as she prepared for the next attempt. Her role in the activations was simple, but in some ways the most important. She flooded her tattoos with faez, and the energy charged within her body made the hairs on her arms stand up straight as if she were outside during a lightning storm.

"I'm ready," she told Zuri.

"Hold off until I give the signal."

The black girl knelt over the section she'd been working before. Zuri cracked her knuckles, then her neck, and took a deep breath.

The words that slipped from her lips were a form of Coptic. Instructions for the runes as she fed them raw faez. Iona watched closely, because if the circuit refused to start, she had to be ready to jump it with her reserve. It was like jump-starting a car with another battery.

A tickle at the back of her neck had Iona staring at the pyramid. Fenris? Or maybe it was something else. Something awakened by the circuit that she could detect with her tattoos. The thing that Mel and Marcus had sensed during the spear trap room.

Zuri jumped back, falling on her rear as the runes glowed blue. Iona surged forward to add her own faez, but the circuit was lighting up without her intervention. In a matter of seconds, the glow traveled along the paths, spreading out as the light hit new sections and reflected off the black pools. The luminance went around the outer areas, but then from four points, darted towards the pyramid, hitting the corners and exploding in radiance, which made her throw her forearm up to block her eyes.

The pyramid at the center of the level went from twilight to beacon, then the light blasted away like a corona, followed by a rumble in the ground as the structure began to move. The four sides peeled away like a flower, the one side shifting into the floor while the other three remained as walls, creating an altar ringed with twilight.

"Seven hells," muttered Zuri from beside her.

The five of them shared glances.

"Grab your stuff and keep on your guard. We have no idea what new dangers this revealed," said Zuri.

The warning made sense even as Iona resisted the urge to rush forward and see what kind of treasures lurked inside the pyramid. There were no more black pools, which made the approach feel less dangerous even though she knew the Obelisk was awash in hidden threats.

They reached it without incident. Justine looked jubilant, clutching the straps of her oversized backpack.

"We did it. We're ahead of the others. I can't believe it."

Iona couldn't help but smile. Poor Justine had more pressure on her to succeed than any of the others due to her famous father.

"Be careful," said Zuri, frowning.

The altar was made of glossy black stone. Not obsidian. Maybe marble, or something like it, smoothed and coated with a polish that made it otherworldly. A curved dagger waited in a catch, the hilt made of ivory and gold.

"Justine, wait," said Zuri, but it was too late.

The ebullient girl rushed onto the dais where the altar was located. She ran her hands over the smooth stone.

"It's okay, I recognize this from one of my books. It's a soul altar."

"A what?" asked Marcus.

"A soul altar. They would use them to understand how magic worked. I read about them but didn't think they were real."

Iona shared a glance with Zuri, who was equally confused. The mousy girl held a treasure trove of secrets.

"I'm not even going to ask why you're researching one of the more forbidden subjects of magic."

"It's only forbidden if you apply those techniques on unwilling subjects," said Justine with an unexpected verve to her voice.

She was glowing with excitement.

"The question now is what we do with the altar and the knife," said Melanie, examining one of the pyramid folds.

"Maybe we should take a break," said Marcus, pulling out a handkerchief and wiping the sweat from his forehead. "We've been at this for hours."

"I'm not tired," said Justine as she circled the altar, running her fingers over the smooth stone. She started babbling out facts about soul altars and the peoples that had used them. Most of it was gruesome stuff, which was strange coming from her.

Zuri on the other hand was deep in thought, chin cupped in her hand, staring at the overall area.

"I really thought it'd open up the entrance to the fourth level. This feels like another puzzle."

"Don't worry, Zuri. We'll find it. But we should be excited. This means we're officially ahead of Blake. We only have a month before the end of the semester. More than enough time to reach the fourth, and then we'll have it all to ourselves at the beginning of next year."

"I know—"

A third familiar stab at the base of her skull had Iona spinning on her heels just in time to see something dark rise up from behind Justine as she was examining the bowl depression in the front of the altar.

Iona's heart caught in her throat as she saw the haggard old man wrapped in overlapping, dirty robes. She'd forgotten how creepy he was, or maybe she'd never really known until she'd been outside the farmhouse and Missouri. Fenris wasn't tall, but he towered over Justine. The blade, which was no longer on the altar, rose high like a scythe about to cut down wheat.

A flash of the weapon had Justine spinning away, blood flying in a wide arc. The blade clattered to the ground as the mousy girl collapsed like a marionette with her strings cut, hands to throat, trying to hold back the flood of lifeblood.

She was on her knees, the crimson liquid bubbling through her fingers, rushing down her shirt.

Iona heard screaming before she realized it was her own voice. The others hadn't seen it because they were still paying attention to the pyramid.

Fenris.

The ancient warlock.

He was in the Obelisk. He was here and killed Justine, and now he was coming for her.

Then everything went dark.

THIRTY-FIVE

No!

The image of Justine falling over with her hands trying desperately to hold back the tide of blood was seared into her vision.

Zuri felt an ache she hadn't experienced since Gemma. The world turned upside down.

"No!"

This time the words came out, but they were weak with shock. Zuri had always considered herself good in an emergency, but she froze when Justine collapsed on the dais. It was too late. She was already dead.

Zuri recognized Fenris from Iona's description. He was worse than what she'd imagined. Somehow both tall and shriveled, powerful yet frail.

When the lights went out, the only thing she could think of was how she'd failed her friends. How she'd failed Justine.

Screams and cursing erupted from nearby.

A burst of pale blue light appeared near Marcus. The darkness was pushing in on the illumination, swallowing its attempt to reveal.

"Zuri!"

It was Iona. She was shaking her arm.

"What do we do?"

The unfolded pyramid was no longer in view. Darkness shrouded it.

"We have to get away from here."

"Yeah," she said, but it sounded like someone else had said it.

They scrambled away from the pyramid. Zuri's limbs were weak from shock. Part of her wanted to go back to check on Justine, even though she knew there was no way she could have survived that. And the presence of Fenris made rescue impossible, if even a quarter of Iona's stories were true.

"I'll lead," said Marcus, taking the front with the mage light hovering near his head.

Zuri thought about casting a second, but didn't want to slow them down. They needed to get away from the pyramid. From Fenris.

Guttural incantation sprung up from behind them. A deep, gravelly voice spoke in unfamiliar tongues.

Iona cursed.

"What?"

Iona scowled.

"He's here for me."

"He's here for all of us."

"He'll kill you all for sure, but that ritual. That's for me."

Zuri glanced backwards to see sparks exploding from the darkness, briefly illuminating the unfolded pyramid. There were no colors, only black and white, as if the ancient warlock's presence swallowed the life from the world.

As they neared the black pool that they'd disarmed a short while ago,

Zuri realized the circuit was no longer lit up. It'd gone dark. Dormant.

Marcus was circling the glossy black pool when she shouted.

"Get away from that!"

He half-turned, realization dawning on his brow as an appendage reached out and grabbed his leg. The next part happened in slow motion while she was frozen. Marcus screamed. The liquid in the pool was dangerously corrosive.

Zuri tried to reach him, but Marcus had gotten too far ahead. The thing in the pool yanked him over the edge. His body barely splashed upon impact as if the liquid was waiting for him. A scream and he was gone. The surface boiled for a few seconds before returning to smooth.

She knew he was dead when the mage light winked out.

Melanie screamed.

The two of them had been together since prep school. They'd been voted most likely to get married first.

Zuri fumbled for a mage light. Two appeared at once, which confused her until she saw Iona.

"Grab her," said Zuri, starting to feel her thoughts line up logically again.

Melanie was sobbing and holding her hand over her mouth. Iona yanked her away from the black pool when she started to stumble forward.

"He's gone. There's nothing we can do now."

"Follow me," said Zuri, determined to get them out of immediate danger.

She led them through the pathways with the assumption that all traps had been reactivated like the pool. When she came upon a runic trigger, she quickly disarmed it and kept them moving. This was something she could understand. Solving problems. And right now, they needed to survive, get back to the exit, and escape the third level. Then they could muster the professors to take it back from the ancient warlock.

When they reached the gyroscope, which was where they'd left a bunch of supplies, Zuri had them stop.

"What are we doing? We have to get out of here," sobbed Melanie, red eyes rimmed with grief.

"I'm so sorry, you two. I shouldn't have let Justine climb onto the altar, or Marcus get so close to the pool. This is all my fault."

In her head she said, *It's all happening again.*

It felt the same when Gemma died. She felt helpless, not at all the powerful mage that she knew she was destined to become. Did her sister ever feel doubt? Somehow, she didn't think so.

Get it together, Zuri. You can still get out alive.

She mustered herself, even as her hands were quivering.

"I can hear him chanting. What is he doing, Iona?"

The pale blonde girl's lips were pulled to a point. But not in fear. In anger. Iona looked ready to throw a punch.

"It's for me. He's here for me. Which means there's no way the portal back to the other levels is open. I know it. I can feel it in my bones."

"We have to try," said Zuri.

"I know," said Iona, meeting her gaze.

"Melanie, grab those potions. Iona, take the Miter. We'll get to the portal and then figure out what's next." She stopped. "First, while he's fucking with his ritual, we need to put on fresh wards. Be quick."

Zuri layered protective enchantments over her body. She wished she had more time for better wards, but some protection was better than none.

"Everyone good?"

Iona and Melanie nodded, which prompted Zuri to lift her chin. She could no longer hear chanting. The hunt had begun.

"Stay close, move quickly, and let your magic fly if something tries to stop us."

As they moved away with a plan, she was feeling more herself. The person who'd panicked near the pyramid seemed far away. There might be a dangerous, ancient warlock after them, but they were still three talented Coterie mages. They wouldn't go down without a fight.

THIRTY-SIX

Blake was giddy was excitement. This would finally be the day that bitch got her comeuppance. He paced before the portal with a barely contained grin.

"Blake, babe, what are we waiting for?" asked Scarlett, sitting on a ledge and chewing gum.

He hated when she had gum. It made her look like a stupid cow chewing grass, but he wasn't going to let her ruin his big day.

"Yeah," said Jakob, sitting across from Scarlett. "The others are probably headed into the city already. I'm really looking forward to getting my shine on."

"I said, we just have to wait a little longer and then we can go. It's going to be a glorious day."

Scarlett and Jakob shared a glance.

"Why? What are you planning? Is this why you've kept us away from the pyramid these last weeks, even though we know how the circuit works?" asked Scarlett.

Blake grinned.

"I want to see that bitch's face right before the end."

"Zuri? I mean, I'm all for getting rid of that hag, but how?"

As if her words were the signal, the pyramid at the center of the level exploded with light, dispelling the gloom and making them squint.

"Verdammt," muttered Jakob as he held his forearm up to block the light.

Blake bathed in it, because he knew what was coming next.

"Go investigate your prize, you dumb witch."

The anticipation was killing him. He stared into the distance, wishing he could see what was happening. Then he heard it. The long, drawn-out scream.

"What's going on?" asked Scarlett, rising to her feet and staring at the pyramid.

"The end of an era. Alright, I'm satisfied. Let's get out of here. I'll tell you all about it once we're in the city."

He hoped that Fenris would leave the Obelisk once he had his fill, but if not, Blake planned on telling the professors that Iona had let the ancient warlock in because of her past connection. He had no doubt their collective power could take care of one wrinkly old mage.

Before Blake reached the portal, the lights went out. Nothing to worry about. That was Zuri's problem. Not his.

Two mage lights bloomed into view. The pale blue illumination brought out Scarlett's freckles, which he hated.

"Come on, let's go celebrate."

Activating the portal was a few simple gestures and a trigger word. He'd done it a hundred times since they'd reached the third level. When he didn't feel the sudden dislocation and the stab of vertigo, he assumed he must have made the wrong gesture.

Then he realized his friends were still with him. There was no way they'd messed up the portal command too. A sickly feeling climbed from his belly into his throat.

"Blake? What's going on? Is this part of your trick?"

He cast the portal spell again. No luck.

"It should work."

Jakob was standing away from the portal, staring in the direction of the pyramid and coaxing more light into his orb, as the darkness was pushing against it.

"What the fuck is going on, Blake?"

"It should be fine. We made a deal."

Suddenly, Jakob was in his face.

"Made a deal? With who? One of the upperclassmen?"

That idea sounded blessedly preferable to the current one. Blake jutted his chest out, bumping Jakob backwards.

"No, and you'll watch your tone, or maybe I'll replace you."

The threat got Jakob to back off, but didn't reduce his anger.

"Blake, babe, what's happening? What did you do?"

"You have to promise not to tell anyone."

"Come on, babe..."

"Promise."

Scarlett kissed her fingers and touched her heart. When he looked at Jakob, he said, "Fine, whatever, I promise."

As quickly as he could because he wanted to figure out how to get out of there, Blake told them about his encounter with Fenris, and the deal he'd made.

"I can't believe you let him into the Obelisk."

"He wanted Iona. That's it. That's why she has all those damn tattoos. It's part of whatever he was preparing her for. Why wouldn't I make a deal? Get rid of her and maybe this guy is worth knowing later on?"

Blake wasn't telling them everything. How creepy he was. The dead people in the house that he'd been invited into. The way his thick black nails looked like claws. He hadn't slept for days after the meeting, but he knew it'd been the right choice.

To his utter shock, Jakob got right into his face, pushing him backwards.

"You fucking imbecile. You've killed us. You think some jacked-up warlock from ancient times cares about a little deal? What the hell, man? How can you be so stupid?"

"I warned you..."

"Why would I be afraid of you now? I always worried you were full of shit and now I know for real. If we get out of this, I'm telling everyone what a fool you are. I'm telling them exactly what you did so they know what kind of traitor you are to Coterie," said Jakob, then he stomped away, leaving Blake feeling empty inside.

"Scarlett?"

But she wasn't listening. She was applying wards and enchantments. A good idea. He followed her lead as Jakob stood at the edge of the light and peered into the darkness.

"We should move away from the portal," said Scarlett. "This Fenris of yours will probably come here, hoping to catch the others trying to leave. If there are any left."

"He's not mine."

"Whatever, Blake."

"I don't need attitude from you too, Scarlett."

"Now's not the time."

He opened his mouth to rebuke her but realized she was right. They needed to get away from the portal.

As he considered where to escape, he suddenly felt unsafe. Blake frantically looked around, but saw nothing, except Jakob still checking into the darkness.

He was about to tell Jakob to join them when he saw an interference at the edge of his light. Like two bubbles pressing against each other.

Blake almost opened his mouth to warn his friend, but then he remembered how Jakob had just disrespected him. Questioned his leadership and threatened to tell everyone how he'd let Fenris into the Obelisk.

"Blake? What are you looking at?"

Scarlett followed the line of his vision, but before she could piece it together, Blake shouted, knowing it was too late.

"Jakob, watch out!"

Blake had seen videos of orcas closing on prey, their massive rows of teeth clamping onto the seal or other creature before they could get away. The carnage had always thrilled him. That's how he saw himself. A predator. To be feared and worshipped.

The darkness shifted over Jakob like an orca, followed by screams and the sounds of bones breaking. Blake caught a flash of pale hair and the extension of a jaw too large to be a regular human's. He was thankful that the mage light had winked out the moment Fenris had hit him. It'd been bad enough the day in the apartment.

Blake ran. He didn't remember making the decision, but one moment he was staring at a severed arm lying a dozen feet from his location, and the next he was fleeing through the darkness, oblivious to the dangers of the Obelisk, certain that today would be his end.

THIRTY-SEVEN

She knew this day would come eventually. Fenris hadn't given her the tattoos as a gift. They were a brand, a mark of his ownership. While they'd had some utility over the years, the tattoos were mostly a mystery. A trap burned into her flesh with needles and magic.

"Where is he? Can you still feel him?" asked Zuri.

Melanie was sobbing nearby, even as she activated the warding cube. They'd retreated to a spot as far away from the pyramid as possible. A few large chunks of stone were the prominent feature of the area, but they'd proved long ago that they were dormant. Iona suspected that a larger structure had been destroyed in the past. She wondered why it'd never been fixed.

"Not close. He's on the level for sure, but not near the pyramid. He probably went straight for the portal."

"Why aren't we going there?" asked Melanie, barely holding back her tears.

"Because that's exactly where he would have expected us to go," said Zuri.

There was a moment right after Marcus had died that Iona had worried about Zuri too, but then she'd clamped down on her fears and took back ownership of the group. They would need her leadership if they were going to survive this.

"Then what? Are we just waiting for him to kill us?" asked Melanie.

Zuri looked to Iona.

"What can we do? You know him best. Does he have a weakness?"

Iona chewed on her lower lip.

"I wish I knew. If I had this Coterie training before, I might have been able to understand what he was all about, but back then I was just trying not to screw up."

"Iona, you have to give us something. Our lives are on the line."

"Right, right." Iona shook her head. "When he would leave the farmhouse for a few days, he would come back different. The way out, he was irritable and prone to outbursts, but then on return, he seemed calm and in control of himself. I never learned what he was doing, but more than once I overheard people in town talk about how cursed they were, and that there was another accident, or another group of missing people. I always sort of assumed it was Fenris."

Further conversation was cut short when Melanie let out a little scream and dropped her cube. The ward was pulsing with warning.

"Something's coming," said Zuri, facing the darkness.

"It's not Fenris," said Iona, joining her.

"I see something."

Iona leaned forward until she could see faint shapes heading in their direction. More than one.

"Mel, with us," said Zuri.

To her credit, Melanie wiped her eyes with the back of her hand and joined them.

"I don't want to die here," whispered Melanie.

Zuri didn't turn her head. "We're not. We're going to survive. But we've got to fight. *You've* got to fight."

The sniff was followed by a nod from Melanie. She put up her trembling hands.

The shapes ambled towards them without sound. Taller than a person and moving with purpose.

"Get ready," said Zuri.

She made quick motions, like wrapping up a stone, and sent it forward. Light bloomed into existence in a wave, flowing over the circuits and chunks of stone that made up the corner of the level.

Three figures approached. They were made of shadow, but Iona could make out their long snouts and the claws at the end of their long arms.

"Shadow warriors."

Iona had seen a spell in one of Fenris' tomes that would summon them to do his bidding.

"What do we do?" asked Zuri.

She'd only seen the spell in passing. A quick glance before Fenris might notice her peeking.

"They're not an extension of Fenris. He'll have given them an instruction, but that's all I've got."

Melanie grunted as she threw a force bolt at the lead shadow warrior. The dislocated air barely impacted the approaching figure.

"They're warded against minor spells," said Iona.

"Fine," said Zuri, snarling as she made big motions which ended with a wave of flame roiling towards the shadowy figures. The heat crisped the air and revealed jackal heads, but the lead figure broke the flame with a casual flick of his staff.

"Seven hells, that should have annihilated them," said Zuri.

"They're made of shadow, I think. We need to stop them another way."

Zuri lifted her arms like a conductor. "Do you two know the Chains of Acquiescence spell?"

"I think so," said Iona as Melanie nodded.

"With me."

Zuri started the spell and Iona followed her gestures, quickly catching up like a drummer who was initially behind on the beat. The three of them weaved the spell together, which summoned a huge set of ghostly chains, then Zuri pushed her arms forward and the restraints flew forward until they wrapped around the jackal-headed shadows.

"It's working!" said Melanie as she clapped her hands.

Zuri grunted. "Focus."

The three of them poured faez into the chains to squeeze the shadows and keep them from moving forward. Iona was tempted to use the reserve of faez she had in her battery, but didn't want to expend it just yet. She knew if they were going to escape Fenris, they'd need every tool available.

The shadows kept moving forward, tirelessly straining against the chains that threatened to break.

"More!"

Iona threw everything she had into the spell, hearing her own grunt as she squeezed the faez from her mind.

The jackal-headed shadows were mere feet from their location. Still moving forward incrementally.

A tight-lipped yell exited Zuri's lips. She was clearly throwing everything she had into the spell.

Then the chains collapsed around the jackals, annihilating the shadows and exploding into pale sparks which dissipated completely.

Iona almost fell over from the sudden lack of strain. She was breathing heavily and a migraine was forming at her temples. The spell had taken everything she had.

"Recover quickly, we're sure to see more from Fenris," said Iona.

Zuri chugged from a water bottle while she stared into the darkness.

"Can your battery help us?"

Iona took a long drink from her own bottle.

"It's charged and ready to go, but I don't want to use it unless it's a last resort."

"Right. Fenris. Would it work?"

She lifted her shoulders.

"There's someone coming, or someones," squeaked Melanie as she backed up.

It was from the direction of the portal. Shit. Probably Fenris. Or another one of his spells. But it was too soon. She'd barely recovered from the shadow warriors.

"Again, with me."

The three of them faced the darkness. Iona had always expected that she'd die young. None of Fenris' previous assistants had lasted but a few years. As far as she knew she'd survived the longest. But those precious few years were rapidly coming to an end.

"The moment they're in range, we hit them with a force wave," said Zuri.

As the shapes moved nearer, Iona squinted, but she couldn't make out the details.

"On the count of three," said Zuri. "One. Two. Three–"

THIRTY-EIGHT

Zuri summoned her magical reserves, determined to destroy whatever was coming after them. As the last number left her lips, she saw two figures streak into the light.

"Wait! It's us! Don't shoot."

Melanie's force wave narrowly missed Blake and Scarlett, brushing them sideways, but failing to injure them.

"Sorry," she whispered.

The pair jogged into the circle of light. The air was tense as no one spoke.

"Where's the rest of your team?" asked Zuri with arms crossed.

She couldn't believe that it was them. Why did it have to be Blake and Scarlett of all people?

"It was only us plus Jakob. The others left a while ago, but we got caught here when the portal closed. Do you know what's going on?" asked

Blake.

"Where's Jakob?" asked Melanie, looking past them.

"Something got him. None of our spells worked, so we ran," he said.

"What's going on?" asked Scarlett. "What's hunting us? We saw you near the pyramid and then the lights went out."

Zuri shared a glance with Iona. There was something off about their experience, but given the circumstances, she didn't think she could be picky about allies when their lives were on the line.

"You should tell them," said Zuri with a nod.

Blake and Scarlett looked to Iona. It was probably the first time Iona had been in their presence since they'd tried to get her killed in the mirror-mummy room.

"Before Coterie, I was the assistant to this ancient warlock named Fenris..."

Iona went on to explain the highlights of her experience and how she'd gotten her tattoos.

"And you let that bastard in the Obelisk," said Blake when she finished.

"No. I did no such thing. He got in on his own. I don't know how, but he's an expert in Kemetic magic. He may have found a weakness in the protections or something like that."

"Professor Sinclair isn't going to be happy when he hears about it," said Scarlett.

"If we're lucky enough to survive, I'll be happy to talk to him," said Zuri. "Let's focus on making it to that day. We've already had to fend off one powerful spell. There's sure to be more."

Blake and Scarlett shared a worried glance.

"What?" asked Zuri.

"We saw something when we were running here. Probably something from your Fenris."

"Did it look like a jackal warrior?" asked Iona.

"No," said Scarlett. "Much smaller. It was brief. Could have been my imagination."

"I wouldn't count on it," said Zuri.

"We have to get out of here somehow," said Blake. "We have to figure out how to break the portal open. Otherwise we're all gonna die here."

She didn't see it at first. He was good at hiding it. She'd seen it once before on the first day of the criminal trial, before his dozens of character witnesses took the stand, before they'd eviscerated her in the papers. Zuri had always wondered if he felt fear, but now she knew for certain. He was afraid. Deathly afraid.

Which told her that he knew more about the situation than he was letting on. Otherwise, he'd be acting his normal, cocky self about taking on Fenris. It was possible that Jakob's death had spooked him, but Zuri didn't think so.

"No," said Zuri. "We have to kill Fenris."

The incredulous looks she received were expected. Even Iona looked pessimistic. But she knew something they didn't. Something she'd learned during the decoding of the arcane circuits.

"We've barely survived that throwaway spell he sent after us," said Iona. "How are we going to deal with him directly?"

"We're not," said Zuri.

"We're not? Have you gone mad?" asked Blake.

"I must have been for ever dating you," said Zuri.

"Hey now, you—"

Scarlett put her hand on his arm.

"Hey babe, let's focus on not dying."

He let the air out of his chest.

"I will if she keeps her comments to herself," said Blake.

Zuri ran her fingers over her heart in an "X." "Promise."

"What's this plan?" asked Iona.

"We'll use the circuits against Fenris. There's more than enough power to take him down, but we have to get him to the right spot."

"That's stupid," said Blake.

"No, she's right," said Scarlett. "We almost got caught in a runic trap on the way here. When Fenris reactivated the circuits, he put all the energy back into the system. It's charged and ready to go. But how do we turn that against him? Clearly he understands this magic more than we do."

"He doesn't know everything," said Zuri. "The circuits all converge at the pyramid near the altar. I didn't realize it until Justine said, but it was a soul altar, which is extremely conductive to magic. We need to connect the altar to the circuit, lure Fenris back to it, and get him to touch it at the moment we close the circuit."

"How do we do that?" asked Scarlett.

"Le Fay's Paradox."

"What? That doesn't make any sense," said Blake.

Zuri ignored him and continued her explanation.

"The general idea behind le Fay's Paradox is that a good offense is better than a good defense, but why it works matters more. Magic wants to flow towards other magic. It's the raw stuff of creation. Putting up defenses only makes the attacks work better."

"Fenris is the biggest source of magic in the Obelisk right now. It'd be like putting up a big steel rod in a lightning storm," said Iona.

"Exactly."

Melanie started raising her hand and then let it drop. "How will you overcome the arcanix resistance?"

"That's where Iona comes in. She's a charged-up human battery. At the moment we connect the circuit, Iona can flood it with magic, which will overcome the resistance and get all the pent-up energy in this entire room to turn Fenris into human char."

No one spoke. She knew it was because they were coming to the realization that she was right. It was a way out. A solution to their horrible problem.

"Great," said Blake, sarcastically. "And how do we get this warlock, or whatever he is, into position without him killing us?"

"I can lure him to the altar," said Iona. "He needs me for whatever his sick ritual is, but that's going to leave me exposed."

"I can confuse him with illusions," said Scarlett.

There was a brief realization in Iona's face. Zuri caught it too. Scarlett had been the one behind the demonic pig illusions at the beginning of the year. Not that it mattered now when they were all likely going to die.

"I'll connect the altar to the circuit," said Zuri. "I'm pretty sure I'm the only one who can do it."

"I probably could," said Blake.

"I'm going to need you and Melanie to hit him with a Fae Fire Hex when he gets near Iona. At the same time if you can manage it. We need him to be as conductive as possible."

"That spell has a short range. How are we going to do that without getting killed?" asked Blake.

"You're not. We're all at risk here. If we don't work together then we'll be dead for sure. That's the other reason I need both of you to do it. If one of you gets attacked, the other has a chance of getting the spell off."

"I don't like this," said Blake, scowling.

"None of us do. And if we manage to survive, you can go back to hating me, but for now, let's act like it's old times."

She hoped the little pep talk might encourage more teamwork, but Blake turned away. On the other hand, Scarlett gave her a brisk nod.

"Any questions before we head to the pyramid? Everyone have their wards up?"

No one spoke, which meant they were ready.

"Let's do this."

Zuri grabbed her backpack by the strap and headed into the darkness, followed by her ex-boyfriend, his new girlfriend, and the only friends she had left in the world.

THIRTY-NINE

The journey to the pyramid was fraught with concern and the occasional trap they had to disarm, but no Fenris. Iona was barely paying attention, because she was so focused on her tattoos, expecting them to be their early warning system.

It almost made it worse to have no sensation of him. She knew Fenris was on the level. He wouldn't have left while his prize awaited.

But what was he doing? And would their plan work?

When they neared the unfolded pyramid, a strange, soft light like the sky during an eclipse bathed their approach. Colors were muted and it was hard to see past the dome of illumination, but there was definitely no Fenris.

No sign of Justine either, or her backpack, but blood smears led away and into the darkness, on an opposite trajectory than they'd come. Iona hoped that he hadn't eaten her body. She deserved that much. The poor girl had worked so hard to overcome her fears and was starting to grow out of the shadow of her famous father.

Iona shared glances with her teammates, but she didn't want to disrespect Justine's memory by talking about it in front of Blake and Scarlett.

"Want me to take the dais?"

"No, I want everyone to watch my back while I hook up the circuit to the altar," said Zuri.

The odd light made her skin lustrous and shiny. Her eyes reflected the pyramid and her intensity as if she were going to will them all to success.

"Let's not wait too long."

Zuri got right to work, using paint markers to continue the circuit of Kemetic runes towards the altar. Iona silently cheered her to go faster, but she knew that if even one symbol was drawn incorrectly it would screw up the whole plan, so she kept her mouth shut.

An incessant tapping from Blake's foot had her glaring at him, but he gave it right back. Iona didn't trust him, but she hoped that the circumstances made him an ally. If not, they were all screwed.

After twenty long, excruciating minutes, Zuri announced that the conduit was complete. Iona took her position near the altar, carefully stepping over the old blood that remained from Justine's brutal death.

Another twenty minutes later and she was still at the altar, waiting for signs of Fenris.

"What do we do if he doesn't come? Maybe he senses a trap," suggested Blake, hiding behind a stone block.

"He's not afraid of us," said Iona.

"Then why isn't he here?" asked Blake.

"I don't know."

She gave it another few minutes before cupping her hands around her mouth.

"Come after me, you bastard!"

After the long quiet, her voice boomed into the vast twilight space. It echoed off the ceiling, then fell flat, leaving her feeling exposed.

"You're a fraud! A two-bit warlock with a fetish for flesh! We're not afraid of you! *I'm* not afraid!"

It sounded good, even though it wasn't true. Of course she was afraid. She'd been afraid the entire time she'd lived with him in the farmhouse, but she'd channeled that feeling into action. A plan to get away, or die trying.

Thinking about all that she'd done to escape him and make a life of her own, only to have him show up and threaten to take that all away, made her angry. Not the surface pain that came with minor inconveniences of normal life, but real gut-twisting rage. Fury even. She'd gotten into the Halls, then into Coterie, and survived long enough to garner allies. Maybe friends, too. And now he was going to erase all her work. Remove all meaning to her short, pain-filled life.

"You're nothing but a monster, Fenris! Locked in your little farmhouse in the middle of Missouri, away from the world, away from society, because you know how much they would despise you. How much they would hate you! You're not like them, no matter how you try to remake yourself. And you know it."

The words were not only directed at Fenris, but herself, which was why she knew she'd get an answer. She was rewarded moments later.

"They don't love you either, Iona Storm. You're an outsider. A freak. Even before I rescued you, I knew you were a special one. You have no idea how special you are."

The voice came from nowhere and everywhere at once. Her allies crouched behind their hiding places, heads searching for the source. Zuri caught her attention and motioned for her to keep him talking.

"Why am I special, Fenris?" she shouted into the void.

The second reply came not as an amplified voice, but rather one spoken softly in her ear like an old friend. It reminded Iona of the quiet mornings when she would make them breakfast and he would talk tenderly about the nuances of the project he was working on. It was usually over her head, but she enjoyed being let in on the secret. Sometimes she would forget that she was trapped there.

"Because you're a monster like me," he said in that quiet intimate tone. "You know what it's like to be rejected by the very people who should love you. You know what it's like to feel their scorn, their hate. To push you away until you can become the only thing left for you."

The answer that had climbed into her throat was left unsaid when the tattoos on her back quivered with excitement. Joy even. She felt a strange reverberation like the growling of a great beast, except it was coming from her chest.

"See, Iona. You feel it. You know it. I'm not going to hurt you. No more than you were going to hurt yourself. I'm not the person you have to fear. It's the others. Look how they've treated you. Even your so-called allies only allowed you into their circle once they had no other choice. They don't love you like I do, Iona. I should have told you what I was planning for you long ago. You deserved that much as my best pupil."

"I wasn't a student, I was a slave."

"Look what you've achieved because of my teaching. If I hadn't come along and rescued you from your deadbeat parents, you'd be dead by now. I'm your family now. I'm all you have. Join with me and we'll rule the Obelisk from within. Harvesting these rich boys and girls, taking from them what they've taken from the world without earning it. Imagine how easy it would be. You and I would become gods here."

Time stood still. She existed in a bubble of light while the others were barely moving. They could neither see nor hear her. Or rather, they were seeing something else, a different conversation, perhaps, while she was having the real one.

"You're not my family. You're a monster."

In a spot thirty feet beyond the pyramid, not far from her friends, stood the warlock Fenris. He'd changed since she'd seen him last. Maybe it was the time away from the farmhouse, or his workshop, which he worked in for days at a time without shower or sleeping, that improved him. Or the fact that he'd just killed two students and their energy had revitalized him.

When he would come back from his "trips," he would always be in a better mood, he'd look more hale and hearty, and the wrinkles in his face would be smoothed away until he almost looked middle-aged rather than the hunched-over warlock he did when he was in the depths of his work.

But it was more than that.

Fenris looked like an entirely different person as if the one she'd been seeing in the farmhouse had been an illusion. His pale hair was brushed until it had a sheen, the robes he wore were black and trimmed with gold runes, and blood covered his jaw and bare chest.

"I'm both."

That's when it hit her. The paleness of his hair matched her own. She'd seen pictures of her parents. Her father had coal-black hair and her mother's was dirty blonde.

"You understand now."

"No," she said.

"It was the only way. Your mother was very sweet. I was sad upon her passing."

"I hate you."

"You only hate what you don't understand. I'm here now, Iona. Think of all you can learn from me. If you think Coterie will be your savior, your teacher, think again. Think how easily they cast aside their own students in the name of competition. I would raise you up. I would make you a goddess."

The part that hurt the most was that she wanted it. She wanted the power, the ability to control her own destiny. It's why she'd escaped him in the first place.

Coterie of Mages hadn't been the panacea that she'd hoped. She'd leapt from one boiling pot right into the next.

"I don't want to be like you."

"Too late. I know you have the urges. I know you have those thoughts, because I have them too."

"I'm not a monster."

She wished the denial had sounded more earnest than it had. The words had felt empty and ashen.

"We don't have long now we must deal with your friends. I offer you this: a chance to set your own path. Join with me and we'll end this farce. Then I can show you real power. The Obelisk is a treasure trove of secrets they don't understand. But I do. This place isn't what they say it is. It's much more than that."

She hated herself for considering it. Iona glanced to her friends, who were staring forward as if nothing was wrong. That Fenris could give her great power was not a lie, that much she knew. And the Obelisk, well, she'd seen for herself that it hid much.

With Fenris at her side, slaughtering the others would be as simple as strangling a rabbit. She'd done that many times. Dozens. Hundreds. What was one more slightly bigger rabbit? Or four of them?

She knew she had that capacity. The visions of death and murder that haunted her mind, they were hard to ignore. Would they only get more difficult to disregard with age? Would it be better to accept her true self now and be done with the backstabbing battles that plagued Coterie of Mages?

They'd never accepted her. Zuri had been forced to take her as an ally when no one else would.

A bottomless hunger filled her gut, bringing visions of gorging on bloody meals. The feast would be horrific—and glorious. She hated and loved it.

As she looked to the black girl crouched behind the stone block, oblivious to the danger, Iona remembered why Zuri had no allies in the first place. Because she'd stood up for her friend when Blake had killed her, even when it had ruined her own prospects and made her into a pariah.

Zuri was trying desperately not to be a monster.

"No. I will not join you. I will not turn on my friends. I will not become a monster."

Fenris stared back with a flat, merciless stare.

"Oh yes you will. No matter what happens here, I guarantee that you will become a monster. It's your destiny."

"You can't—"

The weird bubble that they'd been existing in popped, which made the air and sound and her adrenaline rush in. Iona intended to shout *He's here!* but she couldn't move her mouth, nor her limbs.

The ancient warlock surged toward the pyramid. Inexplicably, they hadn't seen him yet. She was shouting in her mind for them to react, to defend themselves, or spring the trap.

Fenris crept towards Zuri, oblivious to the danger. There was nothing she could do. She was trapped. They were going to die. Everything was going to happen exactly as he'd said it would.

She would become a monster.

FORTY

The fact that nothing was happening worried Zuri more than any warning signs. She watched as Iona stared into the darkness expecting an answer, but none came.

Zuri thought that Fenris would have attacked by now. He was cunning and powerful, but she couldn't imagine that he would let them taunt him without repercussions.

Scarlett seemed equally confused, craning her neck in all directions, even giving Zuri the double shoulder shrug as if to say she didn't understand either.

The other two, Blake and Melanie, were in their positions, crouched and ready to spring the trap. Everything was as it should be, but nothing felt right.

The longer the silence went on, the more Zuri was convinced that something was wrong, but she couldn't figure out what to do about it.

Zuri gestured to Scarlett since she seemed to be the only one who had equal concerns.

The red-haired mage made quick gestures, the final one looking like she was sweeping away dust from the air. Nothing. She repeated the gestures facing a new direction.

While Scarlett cast her spells, Zuri considered pulling them away from the pyramid. Nothing felt right. Fenris should have shown himself by now and the fact that he hadn't proved to her that it was a trap.

She was about to explain her thoughts when the air nearby shimmered like a mirage.

A pale-haired Fenris appeared not ten feet from her location.

"He's here!" shouted Scarlett.

Fenris reached for Zuri with long claws before she could react. He moved in a blur. There was no time to defend herself.

A blast of force slammed into Zuri, tumbling her backwards until she rolled into a stone block. Melanie had knocked her out of the way with a force bolt.

Crackling eldritch sorcery filled the air around Fenris. Scarlett's spell held him for a few seconds until he sliced his hand through the air, ending the restraint.

As Zuri summoned her own magic, she yelled at Blake, who was standing with his arms at his side, mouth open and eyes blank in horror.

"Do something!"

The ancient warlock took one look at them and moved with great speed. Zuri flinched, expecting to find herself at the end of his claws, but when she opened her eyes, she saw Melanie hoisted above him wrapped in shadowy chains that drained the life from her body. In a matter of seconds she went from healthy nineteen-year-old to an empty husk, which he tossed aside to shatter into dust.

It took a moment to realize that despite Iona being held in suspension and Melanie's death, Fenris was standing near the unfolded pyramid, right where the circuit connected. Their plan had a chance to succeed.

"Keep him in place," she yelled to Scarlett and Blake.

The redhead made big swirling motions with her hands, and an angry dust devil flew forward, capturing Fenris in battering winds. They kept him off-balance and not moving.

Zuri knelt by the circuit, placed her hands against the runes, and shunted every bit of faez she could into it. The glow flickered like an engine sputtering to get going, but after a few false starts, the runes turned dull grey. It wasn't enough.

She slammed her hand against the ground. They needed Iona, but she was caught in some field that was keeping her immobile. Zuri would have gone after her friend herself, but Fenris was in the way.

"Blake, help her! We need Iona or we're fucked!"

He broke from his stillness as Scarlett was wresting with the spell, trying to keep Fenris from escaping the swirling winds, and took two steps towards the pyramid where Iona was locked down.

"Oh thank Merlin," muttered Zuri as she drew on her faez, causing thorny vines to grow out of the stone and wrap around Fenris' calves.

The moment the spell had Fenris, she felt his power. It was like trying to rope a hurricane.

"Blake, hurry!"

Her ex-boyfriend was moving too slow. Every step he took was interrupted by a glance to Fenris to make sure he hadn't freed himself. They didn't have much time. Fenris was too strong.

For a moment, she thought Blake was going to make it. That he would overcome his concerns and free Iona, but then Fenris slammed against his restraints, nearly escaping the vines and wind, and Blake stumbled backwards and then inexplicably fled into the darkness.

That's it. We're dead.

The thought came unbidden. She knew it was true. They couldn't hold Fenris much longer and there was no one to free Iona.

She was going to die.

Zuri always knew it was a possibility, but she'd assumed she'd always find a way to survive, just as she always found a way to win the Arcanix contest, or solve any problem. It felt like destiny.

After all, her sister was the famous Nandi Musa, savior of the Invasion. Surely her younger sister could defeat one ancient warlock?

When Fenris shattered their spells, it knocked Zuri on her rear. The blowback was like getting punched in the throat. She couldn't breathe or see straight, and before she could recover, Zuri was being held by a ghostly black fist.

To her left, Scarlett was lying on the ground unconscious and face down, legs and arms splayed awkwardly.

They were done, and there was no one left to save them. Blake had fled like the coward he was. His retreat was proof of what she'd always known, and unfortunately, she had to learn this truth at the expense of her life.

Fenris ascended to the altar like an emperor to be crowned.

Iona was held in stasis, except for her eyes which begged for mercy. He lifted her up and set her on the altar as simply as if he were moving a piece of paper.

The ancient warlock coaxed power from the air, which wrapped around Iona and caused her tattoos to emit crimson light as he chanted in ancient Egyptian. The words were only vaguely familiar as he spoke in a dialect that sounded as close to the lost original as could be.

At first, Zuri thought that Iona was going to be sacrificed on the altar, but then the warlock leaned back his head as his jaw extended. He looked almost reptilian.

More was happening beneath his robes, lumpy unnatural movements, suggesting further transformation. Zuri was thankful she could not see it.

Then something happened that Zuri had no words for. It was as if a second soul was lifting from Fenris. The shimmering shape was even more reptilian, but also humanoid. This apparition was shifting towards the immobile Iona.

Zuri knew in her gut that when this ritual was complete, whatever had been in Fenris would be in Iona, and it would be hungry. She wasn't sure how she knew, but she knew for certain that her destiny was to be devoured by Iona Storm.

It was the fate that Scarlett and eventually Blake, whenever they caught him, would endure.

There was nothing she could do to stop it.

The reptilian shape was almost finished shifting onto Iona. The transfer was nearly complete.

Zuri prepared herself for the end. She hoped it would be quick.

A hint of movement near the base of the altar transfixed Zuri. At first she thought something had been knocked off, or fallen away from Fenris. She squinted to see what it was. It was too small to be human, too large to be a cat.

Then Fenris screamed.

The reason for his yell was unclear until Zuri saw a short humanoid in a dirty black smock holding the sacrificial blade, slamming the weapon into his legs like a serial killer unleashed.

Her eyes deceived her until she realized what she was looking at. It was Justine's puppet.

This made no sense, because she knew her friend was dead. Justine couldn't have survived the deep slice to the neck.

There was no time to debate the miracle when the bonds that held Zuri collapsed, freeing her from the stasis.

Iona was released too. She fell on the altar awkwardly, but the two of them were moving in concert as if they'd planned it the entire time.

Fenris kicked away the puppet, sending it sliding across the stone like a discarded rag, but it was too late. They were free.

Before the ancient warlock could turn around, Iona grabbed him around the shoulders right as Zuri slapped her hand against the runes, energizing them with her remaining reserve of faez.

But the real thrust came from Iona, who unloaded the stored magic in her tattoos right into Fenris' chest. The two circuits connected and the energy contained in the entire Kemetic relay blasted through Fenris, sending him off the altar in a high arc like an animal that had gotten too close to a high voltage power line. He landed in a heap, bloody and torn, looking like charred meat.

Zuri climbed to her feet, preparing to finish him, when the hunk of flesh that was Fenris scrambled away at great speed from the unfolded pyramid.

FORTY-ONE

The pain. The horror. *The indignity*!

Only one eye worked, the other had been burned to the root. Fenris smelled his own flesh. It smelled like the raccoon that had gotten caught in the power lines near the farmhouse.

Each forward motion, each touch of the stone against his knees and hands was excruciating. Worse was the realization that he was dying.

He needed healing. But he feared those bitches would come after him. How could they have done that to him? How could Iona have hurt him? She didn't know the power he was going to bestow on her.

A cubby between two buildings provided a place to hide. To heal. Fenris summoned his ancient powers, but the sorcery wouldn't come. Keeping his charred body from collapsing from its own injured weight was sucking what little reserves were left.

The great hunger in his belly woke. He'd already infuriated it with the ritual.

"Please," he begged. "Save me."

Fenris stared at his cracked and bloody hand. It looked like a piece of pork that had cooked too long on the grill.

A few sparkles of golden light appeared above the deepest wounds before falling silent.

No!

"I've kept you safe, given you a home all these centuries. You owe me. I am your savior. You would have died without me," rasped Fenris.

The hunger rattled his body. Shook it like an earthquake. How could this be the end? How could she do that to him? His own daughter. She was the best of them. The one that could have succeeded him.

"I should have picked one of the others," he lamented as the hunger tore his body apart.

A fissure in his chest like a crack in the earth opened up. He screamed but no voice came. Fenris writhed on the ground as the being inside of him forced its way out. A long claw sliced through the outer casing of his stomach, then a second, and then the entire fist, a scaly but bloody reptilian hand, pulled itself from his guts.

Fenris watched as the ancient Ammit, an almost fetal creature with hands and claws too big for its small body, crawled out of his midsection. It splashed onto the stone, no bigger than a small dog, and as the light faded from Fenris' eyes, Ammit crawled into the darkness.

FORTY-TWO

Zuri rushed straight to Iona, who had fallen onto the stone looking like she'd been thrown down a mountain in a barrel. But she was alive. Zuri held her up.

"Are you okay?"

"I felt it. I felt it entering me."

"What?"

"The monster inside Fenris. You have to finish him. You have to finish it."

"I'm not going to leave you."

Iona grabbed her by the jaw painfully.

"You have to. Now."

Zuri left Iona on the altar and followed the trail of blood. The traps and black pools appeared dormant.

The route disappeared, leaving Zuri unsure of what to do, so she climbed onto a nearby building hoping to spot Fenris. When she didn't see anything, she leapt to the next roof.

Quiet as a mouse, she crept to the edge. A sob followed by a wheeze had her wondering if she'd found the ancient warlock.

Then she saw him.

Not Fenris.

But Blake.

He was crouched behind a stone wall, quivering in fear with his eyes closed and mumbling to himself.

And he didn't know she was there.

Despite the horrors and the battles, Zuri was certain she could kill him. He was unaware and completely defenseless because she knew all the wards he'd applied, so she could easily circumvent them.

A body bind. Then a simple black vine would wrap around his neck and choke away his life, one thorny squeeze at a time.

She had no doubt that she could do it. He deserved it, after all, for what he'd done to Gemma. For what he'd tried to do to her and Iona. It would only be fair. Karma. What comes around goes around.

Zuri summoned the faez to her mind as she worked the silent gestures. Once he was immobilized, then she could make all the noise she wanted.

As she completed the final gestures, Zuri let the spell falter. Uncast.

We're all monsters in the dark.

Those words had never been truer.

Her sister had warned her. The Obelisk changed people. Warped them in unexpected ways.

But she didn't want that to be her. She didn't want to kill him. That would only make her like Blake.

And what would keep her from killing another? And another?

After all, survival necessitated many things. Horrible things.

One more time, Zuri tried to convince herself to do it. To end Blake's life, which she knew would save her many troubles ahead, but she couldn't do it. She couldn't be like him even though she knew it would cause her trouble in the future.

Zuri returned to the hunt for Fenris. She found where she'd lost the trail. A streak of blood clued her to his direction.

A few minutes later, she found the mound of burned and discarded flesh. It looked like someone had taken a bucket of parts and dumped them on the ground. The only thing that confirmed that it was him was that his face, except for a few deep burns and a missing eye, was mostly intact.

Zuri sighed.

The nightmare was over.

She made her way back to the unfolded pyramid to find Scarlett and Iona sitting on the dais together.

They rose when they spotted her.

"Is he…?"

"Dead."

"Are you sure?"

"Fenris looked like he'd been cut in half."

"Was there anything else?" asked Iona with unexpected worry.

"Not that I saw. Was a bloody mess, though. Unloading the whole Kemetic circuit really did a number on him."

Iona sat back down, nodding.

"Have you seen Blake?" asked Scarlett.

The way she stared suggested that she already knew the answer, but Zuri lied and shook her head.

"He's a coward and a sociopath, Scarlett. You could do much better than him."

"He is what he is."

"Thanks for not running away," said Zuri.

"Trust me, I wanted to, but I figured better to die quickly in battle rather than being hunted down in the dark."

Scarlett rose and glanced around the carnage. There was blood everywhere.

"I don't know how you did it, but I'm glad you did. I should go. I'm sure the portal is free now. Maybe I'll find Blake on the way out."

The redhead trudged away from the unfolded pyramid, leaving them alone.

"Are we going to talk about what happened?" asked Iona.

Zuri raised an eyebrow.

"Justine?"

"Her puppet, you mean."

"Yeah, I'm not so sure."

As if summoned by their conversation, the diminutive puppet in a black smock came ambling into the light. The wooden hands were covered in blood.

The puppet motioned for them to follow. Zuri shared a glance with Iona before going after the wooden construct.

They didn't have to go far before they found Justine's body. A great pool of blood surrounded the face-down girl. Small, bloody footprints led away from the scene towards the pyramid.

"Is that you in there?" asked Zuri, gesturing towards the body.

The puppet nodded.

"Seven hells."

"Can you go back?" asked Iona.

The puppet shook her head.

"What do you want to do now?" asked Zuri.

The puppet walked between them and put its hands out. She wanted them to hold her hands and walk with her as if she were a toddler.

Iona gave her a shrug, before grasping one hand. Zuri took the other.

It was surprisingly warm.

"Let's get out of here. I really, really want a shower right now."

"Do they make a shower for the soul?" asked Iona.

"I wish."

Zuri left for the portal with Iona and the puppet.

FORTY-THREE

The pack full of alchemy supplies weighed on Zuri's shoulders, but they had to get their things out of the Obelisk before the semester was over. No students were allowed to stay over the summer.

"Did anyone see the mortar?" she asked.

The clacking of wooden feet on stone announced the puppet's arrival. The smock had been replaced with clothes more fitting for Justine: a cream blouse and black capris. The doll's hair was pulled into a functional ponytail. The puppet almost looked like a diminutive girl if she squinted. Justine held up the ceramic cup they used for crushing and mixing reagents.

"Thanks, Justine."

The puppet gave her a wry smile, which Zuri still wasn't used to. The facial expressions were very evocative of her friend while being completely at odds with what she expected. Zuri still wasn't entirely sure that it was really Justine's soul in the puppet, but there was no way to prove otherwise and she'd saved them from Fenris, so there was that.

Justine made hand motions, which took a few tries to interpret.

"Yes, we'll take the scope with us too."

Justine rocked her fist, which was the ASL version of "yes," followed by "thank you."

"This is going to be a lot easier when we get you a voice box," said Zuri.

Another smile, and Justine disappeared into the back for more supplies.

Iona appeared from below with an armful of tomes. She set them in the cart they'd been using to move their gear back and forth from the portal.

"This is the last one," said Iona as she glanced around wistfully.

"Don't tell me you're going to miss this place."

Iona snorted.

"Not a chance."

"Are you still going back to Missouri?" asked Zuri.

The question flattened her lips.

"I need to. There are some questions I still have about Fenris and my parents and it's the only place I can find them. I figure I can stay the summer at the farmhouse and hopefully come back with answers before next year."

"Are you sure you don't want us to come?"

"Bringing a living puppet to the middle of Missouri would make a scene that I'd rather avoid. And besides, she needs your help with the voice box, because I'm not learning sign language on top of all the other reading we have to do this summer."

"A shame. I was really hoping to see the pigs."

Iona started to answer until she realized it was a joke.

"It would bore you, Zuri. There's not much to do. The only bright spot is that it's beautiful. After nine months in the city or the Obelisk, I'm looking forward to hearing the rustle of the trees."

"Well, if anything changes, you know where we'll be at. My parents were generous with my summer lodging stipend for finishing my first year. There's a spare room for you."

"You should have told them about Fenris, maybe they would have given you a bonus," said Iona.

"Please don't take this the wrong way, but I didn't tell them about you. They wouldn't understand."

"Wouldn't understand what?" asked Iona.

Zuri put a hand over her heart.

"What I was forced to learn this year. That your upbringing, or lack thereof, doesn't indicate the kind of person you are. I should have known that from Blake, but it appears that lesson takes more than one hammer upside the head to get through my thick skull."

"If anyone could prove that upbringing isn't everything, it's Blake," smirked Iona.

"Well, look at me," said Zuri, laughing. "Friends with a farm girl and a puppet. I'm lucky they don't disown me."

The three of them hauled the last of the gear to the portal. Once they reached the lower level, Justine climbed into the cart and went deathly still. As far as the rest of their class knew, Justine had been killed a few weeks ago, along with Jakob, Melanie, and Marcus. It was assumed there'd been an all-out battle between the two groups, though no one would give details. Neither their group nor Blake's wanted to admit that a dangerous warlock had been on the third level.

After storing their gear in Zuri's suite, they called for the porters to take their luggage outside the Obelisk. A hired driver was waiting for Iona at the entrance. They shared hugs and then Iona climbed into the back of the vehicle before pulling away into traffic.

"I just don't know if we'll see her again."

The puppet made the gesture for "no."

"You don't think so? She came to Coterie to get away from Fenris, but now that he's dead, why stay? It's not like we've been welcoming to her."

The puppet reached out and took Zuri's hand. Then she pulled out a pen and wrote on the palm.

Zuri read it out loud.

"Iona needs family." She sighed. "You might be right. For the record, I *do* hope she comes back."

Justine nodded.

"Come on," said Zuri. "Let's get to the apartment. We've got a lot of work to do setting up the wards and protections."

Their driver gave Zuri a strange look when she carried the puppet into the back of the vehicle. It was just something she was going to have to get used to.

As they pulled away, Zuri pressed her face against the tinted windows, watching the towering obsidian Obelisk recede into the distance, then disappear completely when they turned towards the third ward.

Zuri had been full of hopes and fears when she first arrived at the beginning of the school year. Now she understood the danger and secrets the Obelisk entailed. It wasn't just the traps and puzzles, or the unwanted attention of your classmates, but the lure of having no obvious consequences for your actions. Everyone's worst enemy in the Obelisk was themselves.

Zuri settled into the seat enjoying the sensation of movement. Everyone had told her that the Obelisk would change her—and it had—but just not in the way everyone thought it would.

She'd resisted the worst of the urges contained in the dark and come away with two friends, albeit not the friends she'd expected to find, but ones she trusted more than the rest of her classmates. The darkness of the Obelisk contained monsters, but none of them were her.

Zuri rapped her knuckles on the window and spoke quietly to herself. "You can do this. You don't have to be a monster."

FORTY-FOUR

The journey back to Missouri took longer than Iona remembered, mostly because she'd been awake the entire time. She'd taken a bus rather than the flight that Zuri had offered to pay for, because she'd never been on a plane or navigated a confusing airport. Besides, she wanted the time to think and to see the countryside that she'd missed while she'd slept on the way to the City of Sorcery.

Zuri had paid for a luxury bus trip with a private booth, a table, fold-out bed, and a curtain so she didn't have to deal with the rest of the passengers. Iona hadn't thought much of it at the time, but now that she was almost home, she appreciated the comfortable space in which she could consider all that had happened and how much she had changed.

The battle with Fenris still lingered in her mind. He'd had complete and total control of her at the altar. There'd been nothing she could do to stop him and only Justine's unexpected return had saved them.

There were two parts that still bothered her. The first was the awful presence during the ritual that had tried to enter her body. Is that why Fenris disappeared sometimes for days and came back different than when he left? Before the Halls existed, older mages had to pledge themselves to supernatural beings or risk faez madness. What had Fenris pledged himself to that had given him such powers? And had he been trying to transfer that creature to her? There was little in her readings that explained how magic had worked before the Halls' existence, probably because those techniques were either lost to time, or jealously guarded by their practitioners.

The second part that bothered her was that Fenris was her father. Or claimed to be. She didn't want to believe it was true. She thought she'd hated him before for what he'd done to her, but that revelation had changed the meaning of everything that had happened.

And did that make her a monster? One of the last things he'd said to her still reverberated in her head.

I guarantee that you will become a monster. It's your destiny.

Had he been lying to her so she would agree to join him? Or was there something he hadn't told her that informed her future?

Before she'd left Missouri, Iona had been convinced that her fate was to die at his hands in some obscure ritual, but maybe that's not what he'd wanted. Maybe he was being truthful in that he could offer her great power. It was something she'd secretly desired, but not at the expense of her friends.

It was one of the reasons she'd wanted to come back to Missouri alone. Iona hadn't told her friends about what had really happened when Fenris had her in the ritual. She didn't want to frighten them, and besides, she barely understood it. Which was why she hoped to find answers in the old farmhouse.

The luxury bus dropped her off in town, which was a few miles from the farmhouse, a trip she'd taken many times. Iona headed straight for Huddle's Grocery to grab some supplies before she made the final journey.

The cheap sandwiches in plastic containers no longer looked edible after a year eating from the private kitchen in the Obelisk, so she found the "expensive" deli section and bought supplies for a few meals until she could return later and fill up the refrigerator.

The checkout attendant, Doloras, didn't recognize her after nine months away. Then again, Iona barely recognized herself in designer black slacks, a long-sleeve aquamarine blouse, and dark sunglasses with a stylish daypack on her back.

It felt strange walking down the long gravel road to the farmhouse in pumps, but at least she knew spells to make the journey easier. It was a far cry from the frenzied escape nine months ago in oversized work boots during a heavy thunderstorm.

Iona wanted to scream when she turned the corner to the old farmhouse to find a burnt ruin instead. The fire looked recent based on the growth of the burnt grass around the cellar stones.

Had it been burnt by the townsfolk who saw an opportunity during Fenris' absence? Or had it happened after he died, a fail-safe to keep his ancient secrets safe?

Iona kicked a charred board, then crouched on her heels and put her face in her hands.

There weren't enough curse words in the world to illuminate her agony and frustration.

Once the worst of her pain went away, Iona tried wading into the destroyed building in hopes of finding answers, but it was mostly char and crumbled stone.

"Seven hells!"

She followed up the scream with a force bolt that slammed into the corner of the study, exploding the remaining timbers and sending up a plume of dust that made her choke. She stumbled away from the destruction and collapsed onto the grass, letting the anger fill her with unrepentant rage.

"Why?" she asked.

But no answer came.

Besides the truths she'd expected in the farmhouse, she'd also hoped to claim the arcane treasures that Fenris had built up over the centuries. The tomes, the trinkets, even his personal notes were outrageously valuable to her. Somewhere in the destroyed house was a book that could tell her how to translate the tattoos on her arms.

No longer.

Iona stared at the burnt farmhouse for a while longer until she realized that it would get dark in a few hours and she didn't want to be out in the middle of the countryside without a place to stay. Not that she was afraid. The year in Coterie had taught her how to defend herself, but she really didn't like the idea of sleeping outside near the ruins of her former home.

There was another place she could stay. Assuming it still stood. She hadn't been past it in many years.

It was down another long gravel road. She was thankful no one passed her on the way. She knew a few other families lived down the road.

Iona reached her childhood home as the sky turned a faint orange. The dappled specks of fading sunlight painted the trees.

The old house was a forgotten ruin covered in vines and fallen tree branches. The entry was choked with grass and Iona spotted a deer trotting away as she arrived.

Iona fought her way through the foliage. The front door was rotting, so she easily kicked it down, revealing a water-stained beige carpet. The place stunk like animals. Raccoons and other critters probably made their home in the old house.

She barely remembered the layout, but knew which room had been hers when she was a young child. Lines on the doorframe marked her height, which was barely at her waist now.

Old toys and a rotted bed filled the small room. Iona gave it a long glance before searching the rest of the house.

She found her parents' bedroom through the next door. An old picture frame sat on the side table, showing the happy family of three sitting on the back patio for her third birthday. Everyone was smiling.

Iona could barely remember those days. They seemed like a dream that she'd had once, not a real thing that had happened.

"Why did you abandon me to him?" she asked the smiling couple in the picture.

But she knew the truth, even if he hadn't said it. If she were his daughter, then he'd likely ensorcelled them to hand her over. Iona wondered if this was a thing he'd frequently done, and if he'd been the one to hook them on the drugs that had eventually claimed their lives. They looked like normal, happy people in the picture, not the apparitions of addiction they'd been in later years.

When she couldn't stay in the old house any longer, Iona rushed outside and in a fit of anger, blasted the building with forceful spells. The structure collapsed immediately as the rot in the walls combined with her sorcery ensured its demise.

She felt no relief at the destruction.

The walk back to the old farmhouse was filled with shame and anger. When she reached her former home it was nearly dark. A hovering mage light cast the destruction in faint blue.

Iona had nearly decided to return to town for a room at one of its dingy motels when she saw the reflection in the fallen, burnt timbers. She waded into the pile to find an ornate box made of darkwood and covered in pearl with Kemetic writings that she hadn't seen before.

When she lifted the box, she revealed a stack of mostly burnt papers. Iona was going to ignore them until she remembered that there were spells that would be able to uncover the lost writings.

She shoved the box into her pack and the burnt papers into the plastic bag from the grocery store, before heading back into town.

The next morning, she called Zuri and charted a ride back to the City of Sorcery. The bus ride took much longer than the way out, finally depositing her in the third ward.

Zuri and Justine were waiting for her when she arrived, but didn't ask the questions that she knew they wanted to ask. Those discussions would come later.

After Iona settled into her room, she asked Zuri about a spell that would help her read the burnt papers. Zuri sent her the spell over her phone and closed the door behind her.

Iona stared at the writings on her phone, deciding if it was worth knowing, or if she should just toss them in the bin and forget about Fenris forever.

But curiosity got the best of her.

Most of the papers were too ruined for the spell, but she managed to coax a few sections to give up their secrets. The majority were letters to private collectors, asking about the availability of their tomes, or copies of certain sections contained within. It was all rather boring stuff. She was about to give up on the whole exercise when she came upon a letter with an entirely different tone. As soon as she started reading it, she was no longer tired.

"...trip through Romania has been exhilarating. I spoke with the purveyor of flesh as you suggested and it was quite illuminating. I can see why you spoke highly of him. I'm much improved by the visit.

"Despite the joys of travel, I find myself missing our regular discussions. There are few in this life worth knowing, and even if we did not have our deep unbreakable bonds, I would count you as one of those blessed few. Sometime soon, I shall return to the Americas and meet this new prodigy of yours. I hope for your sake she's as capable as you say.

"That is all for now. The next time we speak, I hope that it shall be in person.

Your favorite daughter,

Ilyana Storm."

§ § §

This ends the first book of the Cotere of Mages series. Stayed tuned for the second book:

RUTHLESS

Special Thanks

Forty books! Yes, you heard that right. Monstrous, which is the first book of the Coterie of Mages series, is the fortieth book of the Hundred Halls Universe. That's a lot of books. It's also a lot of help along the way. A long series like this doesn't happen without readers and an excellent support team. I can't express how much I appreciate all the help I've recieved over the years in getting this massive world of books out to the public.

First and foremost, my wife and first reader, Rachel Carpenter deserves a lot of credit over the years keeping me on the right path with this series. At times, some of my ideas have strayed too far from what makes a good Hundred Halls novel and she's nudged me back to where I'm supposed to be. I must also thank my team who help make each novel as best as it can be: Sasha Almazan & Gene Mollica from GS Covers, Tamara Blain from A Closer Look Editing, the beta reader team (Tina Rak, Lana Turner, Phyllis Simpson, and Melanie Coupland), as well as my writing group that we affectionately call the Murder Cabin (Andrea Stewart, Anthea Lawson/Sharp, Annie Bellet, Megan O'Keefe, Marina J. Lostetter, Jamie Thornton, and Tina Gower). Additionally, the Vanguard plays defense for little errors that sneak through the cracks, and for this book, I have Tony Lavely, Jane Peatling, Paige Grimmer, Roe Adams, Jeremiah Vaille, Inger L. Ticker, Debbie Davis, Phyllis Simpson, and Brian Busby to thank.

ABOUT THE AUTHOR

Thomas K. Carpenter resides in Colorado with his wife Rachel. When he's not busy writing his next book, he's hiking, skiing, and getting beat by his wife at cards. He keeps a regular blog at www.thomaskcarpenter.com and you can follow him on Bluesky @thomaskcarpenter.bsky.social. If you want to learn when his next novel will be hitting the shelves and get free stories and occasional other goodies, please sign up for his mailing list by going to: https://thomaskcarpenter.com/sendy/subscription?f=1Lnd7j2n0ZXtOzPUaaV7892afuK-38926t4ZDTPrWw3bnlViLZdE7R5fE35C8922xbGounE. Your email address will never be shared and you can unsubscribe at any time.

www.ingramcontent.com/pod-product-compliance
Lightning Source LLC
Chambersburg PA
CBHW030421310726
48979CB00009B/1560/J

* 9 7 8 1 9 5 8 4 9 8 2 8 6 *